A MOMENT OF IMPROPRIETY

Jake ground his mouth gently into hers, and she returned his embrace, clinging to him, enjoying the slow, gentle movement of his hands over her body. His lips had left her mouth and chased into the hollow of her neck, one moment voracious, the next soft and gentle, tingling like raindrops along her skin. Her back hollowed as she leaned against him, her breasts craving the solid caress of his hand, although a part of her knew it was wrong.

It was that part that spoke up, louder and louder, until she heard it dimly through the mist of pleasure. As if slapped hard across the face, Charlotte suddenly realized what all this kissing and hugging led to.

She shrank back against the wall of the cave, shocked at herself. Jake looked at her, his face flushed, and there was something hard and bright and dangerous in his eyes. "Don't you touch me!"

Jake stared at her for a long moment, then smiled wickedly. "I see you're back to your old self." He stepped back. "I was going to tell you, when I was so rudely interrupted by your . . . enthusiasm in seeing me still alive, that we can go now. I'll get the horses. He turned and walked away.

Other *Leisure* books by Annie McKnight:
SUPERSTITIONS

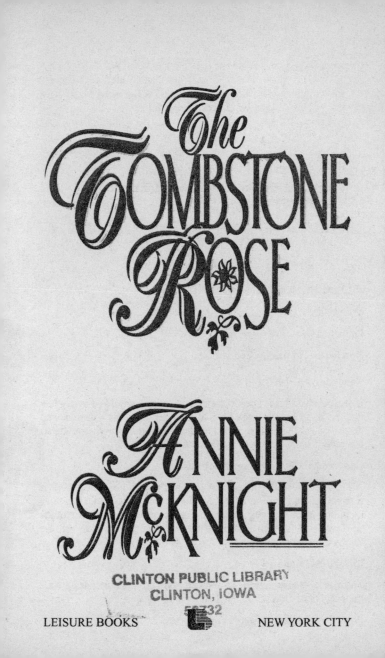

The TOMBSTONE ROSE

ANNIE McKNIGHT

LEISURE BOOKS   NEW YORK CITY

To Kim, Carol and Vicki
The Girls of Summer

A LEISURE BOOK®

May 2000

Published by

Dorchester Publishing Co., Inc.
276 Fifth Avenue
New York, NY 10001

ISBN 0-8439-4681-4

ACKNOWLEDGMENTS

Thanks to Harrison Mattson, for generously sharing with me his expertise on mining and mining rights. Any mistakes in this area are solely the fault of the author. Thanks also to Brooke Borneman, Rob Cohen, Don D'Auria, and the members of the Tucson Writers Group: Dolores Affainer, Dave Eff, Karen Hancock, Donna Lepley, Jim Lewis, Wendy Marcus, Vicki Thompson, Don Valdez, and Wanda Wright. Finally, special thanks to my parents and husband, who—as always—offered me their unwavering support.

In the course of my research, I read several books with conflicting accounts of the infamous gunfight at the O.K. Corral, among them: *The Earps Talk*, by Alford E. Turner; *And Die in the West*, by Paula Mitchell Marks; *The Earp Brothers of Tombstone*, by Frank Waters; *Wyatt Earp: Frontier Marshal*, by Stuart Lake; and *I Married Wyatt Earp*, by Glenn Boyer.

—Annie McKnight

Part One

1881

Chapter One

The town of Tombstone lay scattered across the olive, dun, and white alkali tapestry of high desert called Goose Flats. Surrounded by torturously compressed limestone hills that concealed untold wealth in silver, Tombstone made up part of the sprawling San Pedro River Valley, ringed by mountains and long blue vistas on all sides. To the southwest lay the Huachuca Mountains, sparkling in the dry spring air, their uppermost peaks lightly dusted with a mantilla of snow. Beyond them sloped the broad alluvial plain and rich grama grass that eventually furred the lower flanks of Mexico's *Sierra de Ojos* from whence Jake Cottrell had taken leave two days ago. As the frigid morning warmed under the new sun, Jake pulled up on a knoll just short of Tombstone and let his horse rest.

Not that the Grulla needed it. With all the clean-bred horses of his Seep Springs Ranch to choose from, when it came to hard use Jake invariably rode the little Spanish horse. The steel-blue dun was tough and well-suited to this terrain—no question about that, with his hardy hooves and a hide to match—but the reason he wore so well had a simpler explanation: The Grulla didn't push himself. He would stop when he was tired, whether Jake deemed it a good time to rest or not.

But now, with the snow-laden air blowing off the mountains fresh in his nostrils, the Grulla fidgeted to be off. He shook his head, his thick black forelock almost touching his nose, and let out a ringing neigh, telling the world it was great to be alive.

11

"Hold on," soothed Jake in the quiet voice he always reserved for his horses. He squinted against the sun, trying to make out where the auction would be. From this perspective, the town looked unprepossessing and forlorn; board and batten structures weathered gray by the blistering sun and intermittent snows, poor adobe shacks, a few two-story brick buildings on Allen street, and a straggle of drab canvas tents, crowded onto muddy lots. The town reminded Jake of a gangly, uncouth adolescent growing erratically to adulthood.

A transient prospector named Ed Schieffelin had seen the promise in the barren hills when he'd ridden through them with the Fort Huachuca cavalry in 1877. Because Apaches still made depradations in the area, one of the army scouts had advised Schieffelin that all he'd find would be his tombstone. He found considerably more: two rich ore bodies, the Lucky Cuss and the Tough Nut, that had made him rich overnight. The camp town had gone through several names and locations: Watervale, Hog-em, Gouge-eye, Goose Flats. But the name Tombstone was the one that had stuck.

The grass stirred restively as a breeze played lightly across the hill. Jake spotted a cluster of corrals on the northeast side of town, hidden from the road. He only hoped that what he heard was true and he hadn't ridden all this way for nothing. He had not seen his father-in-law in a year, and he wanted to spend more time with him before returning to his own ranch.

The Grulla trumpeted again, his body shaking with the effort. Jake touched the horse with his heels, and the horse bounded forward. Jake let him have his head for a few moments before pulling him down to a walk. As fresh as he was, the little mount would still have to be plenty tougher in the next few hours.

Jake recognized Alejandro's fighting bull immediately. The massive black animal had been hidden from public view by a lean-to, so that the curious would have to walk all the way around the makeshift corrals to see him clearly. Jake figured Alejandro's herd was long gone, sheltered in some out-of-the-way canyon until they could be fattened, slaughtered, and sold by the men who had rustled them. But greed had gotten the better of the rustlers. The bull was a rare and potentially expensive commodity, and they had held on to it.

Jake skirted the town by keeping to the hills, ground-tying his horse in the lee of the hill closest to the corrals. No one was about, for it was early in a town that reveled until the wee hours.

He could retrieve the animal and be out of town with no one the wiser. All he had to do was persuade one ton of mean bull, with centuries of fearlessness bred into it, into going with him. But Jake had thought it all out ahead of time, and with Tom McLaury's help, he was reasonably sure he could do it.

Tom showed up a half hour later with the cow and some help. Introductions were made: Fred Meeker from the Lazy R, Dwight Purdy, and a man whose oddly shaped birthmark had earned him his name: Strawberry. Jake cleared his throat and addressed the men. The object, he explained, was to get the bull to follow the cow to Jake's ranch not far from here. From there, he himself would drive the bull with a herd to the Valdez *rancho* in Mexico. Whether they could hold him was open for debate; it would take all of their combined skill to keep the bull from a cow in heat.

"I'll pay you now." He handed the prepared envelopes around the circle. "Okay, boys, let's go."

Jake mounted, shook out his rope, and threw it. It settled around the bull's horns.

One, two, three more ropes zinged through the morning air, all settling over the bull's horns and neck.

13

Jake rode forward and slapped at the bull over the fence with his lariat. "Come on, get out of there!"

The animal bolted forward into a swinging trot, the rope tightened, and at that moment Jake realized that he had underestimated the animal's strength. The next instant Jake and his horse skidded across the expanse of rocks and yucca plants between the bull and McLaury's milk cow. Out of the corner of his eye Jake could see the others fared no better. Even the big roan couldn't hold his ground, but slid forward through the fountain of dust, the bull pulling him as easily as a horse might pull a child's sled.

Jake saw Tom's mouth drop open as the bull charged him. "Tom! Ride for it!" Jake shouted, reining on the Grulla and leaning back in the saddle. McLaury wheeled his horse and started off at a brisk trot, pulling the reluctant cow after him.

After much scrambling, Jake's horse finally gained purchase and sat back on its hindquarters. This, combined with Jake's own weight and that of the other three horses and riders, slowed the bull but didn't stop him.

Then disaster struck. The bull suddenly zagged to the right, pulling Dwight's rope sideways across Strawberry's path, cutting into his horse's chest. The horse reared in a panic and collided with Jake's in a terrible fleshy thud, and Jake's leg was momentarily crushed against the other horse's sweating side, Dwight's rope pulling them together like a bundle of mesquite. The Grulla stumbled to one knee with a grunt. Jake fell forward and the saddle horn slammed into his crotch. Everything went out of him at once and he felt weak as a baby. Dwight, trying his best to stay mounted, sawed frantically at the rope with his Bowie knife. A horse squealed and he heard another thud of colliding flesh. Somebody yelled.

Through eyes misted over with maddening pain, Jake saw the bull, all four ropes trailing behind him, mount the cow. Fred's horse ran past him, empty stirrups flapping. Strawberry's horse was bucking and sunfishing and the man was hanging on for dear life. Tom had dropped the cow's rope and was sitting on his horse at a discreet distance.

Dwight stood up, unhurt, and walked to his horse. The roan shivered, snorted, and backed away. Fred Meeker got to his feet and slapped his hat against his thigh, looking for his bay.

Suddenly Jake and Tom were laughing to beat the band, even though the laughing hurt. He winced as the pain in his crotch subsided to a dull ache, watched the two animals couple and wondered if he'd ever again be able to do likewise. "Well, Tom, looks like you're going to have a fighting bull."

"Yeah," Tom muttered ruefully. "If I get a heifer I'm sure not going to try and milk her. What are you going to do now?"

Jake looked toward town. Unbelievably, no one had come out to see what the commotion was about.

"You aren't going to get that bull as far as your ranch, let alone to the *Rio Plata,*" Tom said. "The only way you'll ever get him all the way to the Mexican border is if you run a whole herd with him. One milk cow won't do it."

"I'll get a herd, then," Jake said.

As Jake considered what to do next, the hired hands, well-paid for their bruises, rode off one by one. Fred Meeker was the last to go. He looked at the bull and shook his head. "First time I ever couldn't hold a beef," he said sadly.

Tom and Jake had no trouble herding the bull back into the corral, having had the foresight to put the cow in first, but in a comedy of errors, they could not get her out again. The bull stood between the cow and her rightful owner, pawing the ground and blowing fiercely. Tom decided he was no bullfighter, and said he'd come back for her later.

"I'll buy them both at the auction," Jake said.

"Fine couple of rustlers we are," Tom said as he reined

his horse around toward home. "Come to steal one beef and end up givin' the other away."

Jake had plenty of time to kill. He kept clear of the saloons, choosing instead to eat a big breakfast at Nellie Cashman's Russ House. He was feeling better now, although his strength had been sapped by the blow to his private parts.

As he emerged onto the boardwalk, Jake saw the crowd at the end of Fourth Street. He started in that direction, still angry at himself for having to pay good money for that bull.

He moved to the edge of the crowd, the raw wind bringing tears to his eyes. Only marginally interested in the horses being led before the auctioneer, Jake let his gaze wander. He was the only one who heard the little shout—a woman's voice—that came from down the street.

A young woman was flattened up against the wall of the Can Can Restaurant, her slender figure twisted in disgust. Two unsavory types, obviously stinking drunk, were harassing her.

At the moment Jake started running in their direction, the auctioneer announced that he had a special treat for the people of Tombstone.

The girl's hand whipped out and punched one of the men, and her bonnet fell off. Jake saw the tumble of dark red hair fall down her back, just as he heard the first bid for Alejandro's bull.

Two more running steps and Jake was in range. His fist crashed into the first drunk's face, dropping him in his tracks. The other one reached for his gun belt. Jake's pistol barrel came out and down to hit the man's head with a dull thud.

The auctioneer's voice drifted across the street. "Now, come on, folks. This is a fine Spanish bull. Why, you could make a fortune if you sold him in Mexico."

16

"And just how would we get him down there?" shouted a heckler. The crowd laughed.

Jake turned his attention back to the drunks. "You want more, you just ask," he said.

The two men, disoriented and bleeding, got up and started to walk unsteadily away. One of them glared balefully at the young woman, clamping his fingers to his shoulder as if he had been stabbed. Certainly her punch hadn't done that much damage.

The girl leaned back against the wall, breathing hard. Something needle-sharp glinted in her fingers: a hat pin, about four inches long and tipped with blood. Just looking at it caused a shiver to run down Jake's spine. "Are you all right?"

Her slim body straightened, and she seemed to compose herself. "I'm fine, thank you," she said in a refined English accent.

"Well, good." Jake glanced toward the auction just in time to see the hammer fall.

"Sold, to Wyatt Earp. And how you get him home is your problem!" The crowd cheered.

The girl started to tuck up her tresses, reinserting the hat pin into her bonnet. Something about the unhurried effort made Jake angry.

He let his frustration pour out in a vindictive tirade. "What are you doing walking around Tombstone by yourself? Don't you know how dangerous it is?"

She looked at him, obviously puzzled by his anger. Her hair spilled back-down.

"Where do you think you are? A lady's picnic?"

She raised her chin. "It's really none of your business where I think I am," she replied coolly.

For a moment, Jake was speechless. Not his business? When he'd lost his chance at his father-in-law's bull? He had ridden seventy miles for nothing. "Thanks to you, I missed out on a very important transaction!" He motioned to the crowd.

"No one asked you to rescue me."

"No one—? Of all the ungrateful . . ." He trailed off, unable to continue. Not only had she caused him a great deal of trouble, but she didn't have the sense to see that he had saved her from humiliation and worse at the hands of two pawing drunks.

The girl clapped her bonnet back on her head. It looked incongruous on top of the cascades of her fallen hair that glistened in the sun like hand-rubbed mahogany shot through with deep, velvety red. For a moment Jake found himself staring at the thick locks; he had always appreciated natural beauty. When she turned to walk away, his anger asserted itself. He grabbed her wrist, amazed at its frailty, like the bones of a bird.

She spun around at his touch. "Are you like them?" she challenged, glancing in the direction in which the drunks had disappeared.

He stared at her incredulously but did not let go of her wrist.

She stared right back, her brown eyes the color of clear creek water. Something lurked just below the surface like sharp stones, coldly defiant. Looking at her was to be thrown into the cold stream of her eyes, drenched by her icy disdain.

She certainly was a self-possessed little bundle. Jake found himself admiring her unflappability. And she'd had the guts to use that hat pin, where a squeamish woman wouldn't.

"No, I'm not like them," he heard himself saying. "I'm sorry. Maybe I shouldn't have interfered." He couldn't stop looking at her. There was something about her features— the white oval face, the pointed chin, her striking dark brows and large eyes. She reminded him a little of Ana— perhaps it was the proud lift to her chin or her delicate high cheekbones. Certainly there the resemblance ended, because Ana had been Mexican. . . .

His mind closed down like a fist on the desolation Ana's memory caused, and his hand involuntarily tightened on her wrist. "Next time," he said too roughly, "you can fight them off yourself."

"May I go now?" She glanced at the white-knuckled hand prisoning her wrist.

Jake let go as if her touch burned him, then bowed mockingly. "Be my guest."

She turned and walked up the street, the heels of her kid shoes rapping smartly on the boardwalk.

Jake tracked Wyatt Earp down at the Oriental Saloon. Earp smiled guardedly as he shook Jake's hand. "Heard you were down in Mexico. Seen any rustlers on the way up here?"

"Just Tom McLaury."

"Hell, he hasn't been rustling cattle. Too busy stuffing ballot boxes." Wyatt's expression turned hard. Although good-looking, the tall midwesterner had an austere, almost puritanical air about him. He was, Jake reflected, too driven in his ambitions to have a sense of humor.

"I see you bought that Spanish bull," Jake said. "What do you want him for?"

Wyatt shrugged. "No special reason. Just looked to me like he might turn out to be valuable."

"I'd like to buy him from you."

Wyatt set his drink down on the bar. His smile grew wider, and this time it reached his eyes. "You still have that sorrel horse?"

"I don't race him anymore."

"You ran him down in Mexico in September, I heard."

"He's still fit, but I'm going to retire him. I'm planning on making him my foundation sire."

"Why don't you race him one more time? Dick Naylor

19

against Old Scratch. If you win, you get the bull. If I win, I get your stallion. We can run 'em at the Watervale track next Saturday."

"I can't run that horse anymore. I'm just asking to buy the bull outright."

Wyatt's eyes were bright blue and as hard as cut glass. "I don't think so. I aim to take up bullfighting."

Jake laughed shortly. "You don't care much for living, then, do you?"

"Jake, I heard that bull came from the *Rio Plata,* so I know you want it bad. I've been trying to get you to race me for a year now. Here's my chance." Earp tried to sound jovial.

Jake stared out the window at the horses hitched to the rail. "I'll race you," he said slowly. "If I lose, I give you your pick of the colts from Old Scratch's first season at stud. You lose, I'll buy the bull from you at a reasonable price."

Wyatt clapped Jake on the back. "How about that? I finally get to see that wonder horse of yours run. It's worth it for that."

"I'm not racing Old Scratch."

Wyatt glared at him. "You trying to pull in a ringer? Which horse you want to race?"

Jake motioned to the window where the little mustang stood, hip shot, his chin resting on the hitching rail as if it were the only thing holding him up. "Him."

"Who?"

"That Grulla there."

Wyatt followed Jake's gaze and laughed. "You serious? That little runt couldn't beat a thoroughbred."

"He can if they run more than one race."

"What do you mean? My horse can run a mile! The more distance he covers, the better."

Jake continued as if he didn't hear him. "We can run them in the quarter mile. That's three heats."

"What if one of us doesn't win a heat?" Wyatt was obviously afraid Jake's Grulla couldn't even qualify at the Watervale track. "I don't want to race my horse for nothing."

"We could do it this way. Make it a match race, just my pony and your thoroughbred. Best two out of three."

Wyatt may have sensed a trap, but his pride got the better of him. "You're on," he said. They shook on it.

As Jake rode home toward Seep Springs, he wondered if he had done the right thing. Dick Naylor was fast and would like the distance; he was sure to win the first sprint. But Jake also knew that the Grulla had more than one sprint in him. Most likely, the thoroughbred did not.

Anger surged through him. He should have found a way to steal the bull back. Or challenged the man who tried to sell what didn't belong to him. But he had missed his chance, thanks to a girl barely out of the school room who probably could have defended herself without any help from him.

Abruptly, he found himself seeing her in his mind's eye; those eyes that made him feel as if he had been dipped in the Arctic Ocean.

I should have let her handle those drunks herself, he thought. *Those poor souls wouldn't have known what hit them.*

Chapter Two

Charlotte entered the little adobe house on Fremont Street she shared with Maria and Roberto. She closed the door and leaned against it, her legs suddenly weak from the rush of adrenaline. Maria was right. She should never have gone out by herself in Tombstone.

At least she'd had that hat pin. Those drunks hadn't expected that. But she had risked enraging them further, and two men against a woman—even a woman with a hat pin—wasn't an even fight. Lucky that cowboy had come along when he had.

But her rescuer had been almost as unsettling as her attackers. She could still see his penetrating gray eyes under even, dark brows; eyes that seemed to divine her innermost feelings. It was a wonder the man had tried to help her at all. For a moment, she'd thought he was going to break her wrist.

I didn't ask him to help me, she thought angrily. It wasn't her fault he'd lost his chance at some silly transaction!

The stove had gone out again. Shivering, Charlotte walked into the cold room and relit it. She had never seen her rescuer before, but she was sure he was a cowboy. His clothes, the deep tan from hours in the saddle, and the fact that he was unfashionably clean-shaven—all gave him away. He was nothing like the Earp brothers, with their starched shirts, neatly combed hair, and flowing mustaches.

Opening the door to the room she shared with Maria, Charlotte walked to the shrine atop the dresser. Her sister's wedding picture was propped against the mirror and draped with the rosary Mary had carried all the way from Lancashire when the two sisters had immigrated from England years before. Charlotte lit the candles surrounding the shrine, then knelt before the dresser to pray. As she stared at her sister's image, a familiar pain squeezed her stomach like a fist.

That night—the worst of her life—had started out glittering with promise. She remembered the excitement she'd felt as she followed Mary through the Tucson streets, bombarded by the sights, sounds, and smells of the night—the Chinamen in pigtails and long silk coats, the wood and water vendors, the foul-smelling cowboys and the dandified gamblers, the lighted saloons—so different from the sleepy town they knew by day. Everything had happened so quickly. One moment she and her sister were marooned with their staid and humorless cousin and his wife in Tucson; the next, they were about to embark on a glorious adventure. And it had all been precipitated by a terrible argument between Mary and her sister-in-law, Katherine, who had taken them in when Mary's husband died a few years before. This time the argument concerned the prominent doctor, Edward Chesser, whose trysts with Mary were quickly becoming an embarrassment to the family.

Mary had flown from the house, declaring she would never darken Katherine's doorway again. She and Edward would marry, she said, and they would take Charlotte to live in San Francisco, as he'd promised.

But when the two sisters reached Dr. Chesser's house, his manservant refused to admit them entrance. Even now, Charlotte recalled the entire night in vivid detail.

"I must talk to Edward!" Mary insisted, pushing past the doctor's servant.

Charlotte moved to follow, but the manservant blocked her path. Over his shoulder she saw Mary reach the open doorway of the bedroom. From inside, a man shouted, "What in Sam Hill?"

Mary reeled backwards, clutching at her breast. A red-faced bearded man burst through the doorway, a coverlet tied ridiculously around his waist. He stumbled on the trailing material, his weight catching Mary a blow on the shoulder. She fell, but the man retained his balance. Charlotte recognized him from the few times he had visited their house: Edward Chesser, Mary's future husband and their salvation. "What are you doing here?" he shouted.

Mary lay on the floor, trying to get her breath. Chesser

23

knelt beside her. His expression changed to horror and he grabbed her shoulders. "Good God!"

Charlotte heard a scream. A woman, dark and beautiful, stood in the doorway of the bedroom, her face a mask of horror. Chesser bent down and pressed his ear to Mary's breast.

He's a doctor, *Charlotte thought.* Everything will be all right—

"Is she all right?" the other woman demanded. She clutched her robe about her, her raven-black hair entwining about her neck like coiling snakes. The area around her painted mouth was white, her nostrils pinched.

Charlotte had seen her before, just once, when she and her sister passed by Maiden Lane on one of their rare outings. This was a soiled dove; but a wealthy, important one. Her name was Dulccinata Estevez.

"Madre de Dios!" Dulcinata cried. "Is she dead?"

"Shut up!" Chesser began moving Mary's arms in and out from her body, as roughly as if they were pump handles. He paused, listening to her heart again.

Was Mary really dead? *Fear raced through Charlotte, but she could not get past Chesser's servant.*

"Do something!" Dulcinata's voice sounded harsh.

For answer, Chesser disappeared into his bedroom. Dulcinata followed, and though Charlotte could not see them, she could hear their voices. "What are you going to do?" Dulcinata asked.

Edward Chesser didn't answer.

"What are you going to do?" The woman repeated, her voice colored by rising hysteria. Chesser emerged, wearing a black coat, his shirttail hanging outside his trousers. "There's nothing I can do," he replied. "It's angina. Her heart's given out."

"You can't mean that!" Dulcinata cried. "Are we just supposed to stand here and watch her die?"

"You can do whatever you wish. I'm going."

"What do you mean, you're going? You're not going to

leave me like this! You expect me to take care of it? This is all your doing!"

Charlotte watched in speechless horror as Chesser walked to stand over her sister, his face etched with regret. Not grief, not panic, not anger. Simply regret, as if Mary were no more than a bird that had fallen to the sidewalk! He leaned down once more and checked her pulse, then folded Mary's hands across her chest, where they lay like lilies.

Her sister was dead, and the man responsible for it was coming her way. She felt herself being dragged backwards, out of Chesser's path.

The surgeon walked past them, adjusting his cravat. His face was smooth, his eyes expressionless. Her fear, her horror, turned to hatred.

"You murdered my sister!"

Chesser turned just as she launched at him, clawing at his face. He clamped his hands on her wrists and shoved her back.

That was when the manservant grabbed her from behind. He lifted her off her feet, kicking and screaming. Chesser wiped the blood from his cheek, stared at her for a moment, and then walked out into the street.

Now, at the shrine to her sister's memory, Charlotte stared at the dauguerreotype of Mary and her husband Tom, who had died in a mining accident in Crowned King. If Tom Connor had lived, Mary might never have met Edward Chesser, and that terrible night would never have happened. And Charlotte would never have ended up in Tombstone. . . .

It had been Katherine Connor who was responsible for Charlotte's current placement. Unwilling or unable to handle Charlotte in the wake of Mary's death, Katherine had decided to send the child to Emma Lake, a friend of hers who ran a boarding house in Tombstone. Emma was a no-nonsense type of woman who would know best how to deal with the girl's stubborn silences and occasional angry outbursts.

Charlotte had been packing for the trip when Dulcinata Estevez was shown to her room.

"Who let you in here?" Charlotte had demanded.

"I came to make amends."

Charlotte's hands flew to her ears. "Get out of here! Leave me alone!"

The proud Spanish courtesan seemed unaffected by her outburst. Spying Charlotte's reticule on the dresser, Dulcinata glided across the room, producing a slip of paper. Carefully, she placed the paper in the purse and drew the strings tight. "Katherine has told me you want to be an actress. This is the address of a friend of mine in Tombstone. She runs a theater."

"Get out!"

"This lady can help you," Dulcinata said and, without another word, left the house.

The next day Charlotte had left for Tombstone. She was just fifteen.

Now, at eighteen, Charlotte crossed herself as she stood up from the shrine. Her sister had always wanted her to be an actress. They had talked about it, dreamed about it, so often. Mary had always been a dreamer, and she had convinced Charlotte that before long, the whole world would fall at her feet. They had spent hours planning and dreaming of Charlotte's advent on the stages of London, New York, and San Francisco. And Charlotte had believed it, utterly. She *would* become a successful actress—first in Tombstone, and later, in San Francisco. And when she was rich and powerful enough, she would find Edward Chesser and destroy him, as he had destroyed her sister.

The first step toward her goal was to make sure she

never forgot Mary, not for one day. The shrine helped her to remember.

Charlotte removed her coat and hung it in the armoire. Although she didn't feel like singing, she knew she must practice. The most important quality in an actress was discipline. Maria and her brother had gone to visit friends in Charleston, so she had the house to herself. Now would be the ideal time.

She checked the windows to make sure they were closed, then stood in the center of the room, hands clasped in front of her, and started one of the new songs she'd just memorized.

She sang for half an hour before the wind picked up, rattling the windows. Maria's dog, chained to the porch, began to howl. The noise was so great that Charlotte couldn't hear her own voice, so she gave up. She wished Ruff would stop that infernal howling; it frayed her nerves. Sometimes it seemed that Ruff did it just to annoy her; every time she opened her mouth to sing, he would shriek like a banshee. She crossed to the window, thinking that she might be able to reprimand him from there, but the border collie must have gone around the corner of the house and was hidden from view. Wind blasted dirt against the glass. The sky was clear, but the sun brought no warmth. She was about to close the curtains when she spotted her rescuer from earlier that day. He rode down the center of the street, sitting easily on a blue-gray horse with a long black mane and tail.

As he came even with her window, something made him glance her way. Although he couldn't have seen her, Charlotte ducked quickly and didn't raise her head until she was sure he had passed. Why had she reacted that way? She couldn't make any sense of it, nor of the hammer blows of her heart against her rib cage.

She pictured the scene before the Can Can again. The

cowboy's lean muscled forearm flashing up and then down as he buffaloed one of the drunks, the hard line of his jaw, his dark hair—was it black? or dark brown? She couldn't remember—and his angry gray eyes, glinting like pewter. He'd looked for that one moment as if he couldn't stand the sight of her. She rubbed the bruise on her wrist. Imagine, a common cowboy treating her like that! Rescuer or not, he had no right to manhandle her that way.

Well, she doubted she'd see him again. He was just another example of the riffraff that plagued this town, the kind the Earp brothers were sworn to clean out. And they'd do it, too, as sure as roses had thorns. They'd have done it sooner, if their hands hadn't been tied by so-called lawmen like Sheriff Johnny Behan. Why, if the Earps had a free rein, the criminal element in Tombstone would have scuttled out of this town like insects from an overturned log.

Unbidden, Morgan Earp intruded into her thoughts. She had only seen him from a distance, but she liked him best of all the brothers. There was a glint of humor in his eyes that his siblings didn't have. He looked . . . approachable. And once, when Charlotte was walking with Maria on Allen Street, they had spotted Morgan leaning against the hitching post outside the telegraph office. Charlotte was certain he had winked at her. It wasn't a leering wink, either. More of an appreciative one.

She forced her mind away from the last time she'd seen him, jumping down from the guard's seat on the stagecoach and striding for the Wells Fargo office, that big Winchester lying in the crook of his arm as if it were part of him. . . .

A rumble of wheels broke her reverie. She looked out the window and saw Roberto's spring wagon. Maria hopped down and struggled to carry a large roll of black-and-white striped canvas to the door, dragging it through the dust. Without a backward look, her brother clucked to his team and drove off.

Charlotte helped Maria carry it in. Depositing it on the

floor, Maria sank onto the purple horsehair davenport and closed her eyes. "*Madre de Dios!* That thing is heavy."

Maria was much shorter than Charlotte, but there was a great deal of strength in her tiny hourglass figure.

Charlotte glanced at the canvas on the floor. "What is this?"

Maria kicked the roll with her toe. "Good money, that's what. It's an awning for Sloan's store. Or it will be, as soon as I can sew it."

"Where'd Roberto go?"

Maria rubbed her hands. "*Cabron!* He went gambling."

"I thought we were going out to the Westphalia tonight."

"We're going nowhere. He told me to stay home and sew tonight. Can you believe it? So he can—" she kicked the canvas to emphasize each word "—throw our hard—earned—money—away!"

Charlotte's heart sank. She had been hoping to see Delia Delight, the Westphalia's featured singer.

"At least I got him to take us to the races on Saturday."

"Really?"

"Maybe if we're lucky, the Earps will be there. Wyatt runs his horse there sometimes."

Charlotte said nothing. Wyatt was not the Earp she was thinking about.

Chapter Three

More than five hundred people turned out for the match race between Wyatt Earp's thoroughbred and Jake Cottrell's cow pony. Buggies and wagons of every description lined the strip of dirt known as the Watervale Track. Men

laid bets while women sat in the wagons under parasols or
occupied picnic blankets spread out on the grass. The bab-
ble of voices even rose above the clank and squeal of the
stamp mill operating on the hill overlooking Watervale.

Two cottonwood trees marked the finish line, where
Charlotte and Maria stood with the other spectators. A
shiver of anticipation ran through Charlotte as she peered
through the crowd, trying to spot the Earp party.

Maria, who had her hands full holding an excited Ruff,
nudged her. "There he is!"

Charlotte followed her gaze. Wyatt Earp rode through the
crowd astride a massive chestnut horse, its neck bowed as it
pranced under a tight rein. The hairs of its coat caught and
reflected the sun like hundreds of tiny straight pins. Earp
wore a boiled white shirt, tan breeches, and brimmed cap,
his long legs bent to fit the stirrups of the eastern saddle.

The rest of the Earp party kept pace with long, ground-
eating strides. Charlotte's heart lurched as she recognized
Morgan, one lock of dark blond hair falling over his forehead as he held the horse's bridle. As they passed by, Morgan glanced in her direction. He paused and let the forward
motion of the horse pull the bit out of his hand.

Charlotte blushed, feeling the heat of his gaze. He
touched his forelock in salute and pivoted, taking a couple
of extra long strides to catch up with Wyatt.

"Did you see the way he looked at you?" Maria asked.
"He's smitten."

"I couldn't care less," Charlotte said, but every extremity tingled with pleasure.

"You don't have to pretend with me," Maria replied
smugly. "You'd fall over in a dead faint if Morgan Earp
said hello to you."

"A fat lot you know! You're always prattling on about
how wonderful men are, but I haven't met one of them
who didn't think women were just slaves to do their bidding! Roberto's left us here to go off drinking and bet-

ting with his friends, as if he's ashamed of us, and—"
She stopped as she saw another rider come through the
crowd. "Why that's—"

"Who?" Maria asked impatiently, trying to see around
the crowd.

"That's the man I told you about, the one who was so
rude to me the other day. Certainly he's not serious about
racing Wyatt on that."

The man beside her snorted. "Look at that pony. Really
thinks he's something."

The little mouse-colored horse arched its neck and
pranced daintily, as if it enjoyed being the center of attention. Charlotte compared this shaggy cow pony to the magnificent race horse Wyatt rode, and she felt sorry for him.
This Jake Cottrell, however, seemed unconcerned by the
impression he made. He rode bareback, so at one with the
horse's movements that Charlotte was reminded of a cen-
taur of myth. He, too, glanced in her direction. Her pulse
quickened as his gaze touched her briefly, then moved on.

The arrogant so-and-so! He had forgotten her already,
had he?

"That is the man who saved you?" Maria asked.

"He didn't save me," Charlotte said through gritted
teeth. "I'm perfectly capable of taking care of myself."

"He is *muy guapo*. Very handsome."

Charlotte was surprised at the vituperative tone in her
own voice. "He's nothing but a low-down cowboy. It
wouldn't surprise me if he runs with the Galeyville
crowd." Galeyville was a rustler hangout in the Chiricahua
Mountains southeast of Tombstone.

"I hope not. I like the way he looks," Maria said sadly.

"How can you say that? You of all people should know
what a lawless place this is. There is no room in a decent
community for people like that." The man had to be a
rustler. He certainly didn't look as if he made an honest living; not with that poor excuse for a horse he was riding.

31

Almost all the so-called small ranchers were rustlers. Maria had told her all about it. They rustled cattle up from Mexico, and they didn't want anyone poking around their ranches to catch them in the act. That was why many had joined forces with the Townlot Company—a corrupt outfit that sold lots twice over to unsuspecting newcomers—in a conspiracy to keep the Earps from cleaning up the town. Virgil Earp had been defeated in his bid for marshal because each cowboy had voted two or three times, even letting their horses vote. Not only that, but Wyatt had been tricked out of becoming under-sheriff. Earlier this year, in exchange for Wyatt's dropping out of contention for the sheriff's job, a little weasel named Johnny Behan had promised Wyatt the position of under-sheriff. Wyatt would then have had a free hand with the criminal element and done the dangerous police work, leaving the glory to paper-pushing Behan. The lawman who had tamed Dodge City couldn't care less about the official title; he just wanted to serve the community. Then in a blatant double-cross, Behan gave Harry Woods the job instead.

The riders were at the starting line now. What a strange-looking pair they made: Wyatt cut a dashing figure on his thoroughbred, and Jake Cottrell was leaning forward slightly, grasping his pony's mane along with the reins, his knees drawn up to clasp the animal's ribs.

The starter fired the gun. The horses ran up the straight track toward them, the chestnut outdistancing the pony easily.

When they flashed past the finish line, Wyatt's horse was three lengths ahead. Well, it served Jake Cottrell right for ignoring her.

"Miss?"

Charlotte turned at the male voice in her ear and nearly bumped into Morgan Earp.

The race was forgotten. Charlotte's heart gave a little jump, then settled into its own mad gallop. He was so close that his shirtsleeve touched her arm. His face filled her vision: the strong jaw, an Earp trademark, and the large, sensitive eyes that nonetheless contained an eagle-sharpness, as if he'd spent a lifetime squinting through a rifle sight. His mustache couldn't conceal the hint of humor that curled the sides of his mouth. Morgan's features were softer than his brother Wyatt's; more youthful.

Charlotte felt a peculiar heaviness in the vicinity of her stomach, just below her pounding heart. Her mouth went dry and she had the sudden urge to run. She tried to arrange her features into an answering smile, but her face felt like rubber. Although Charlotte had practiced her expressions often, her training deserted her now. She was afraid to speak, afraid to do anything at all except stare at him, like a rabbit caught in a hawk's shadow.

"Miss?" Morgan Earp repeated. "Or is it ma'am? Did you drop this?" He held up a dust-stained handkerchief.

Charlotte looked at it dumbly. "I don't believe I—"

"Yes, you did," Maria said quickly. "It was in your sleeve." Charlotte colored as she realized what Maria was trying to do. She snatched at the unfamiliar handkerchief. "Yes, it is mine," she said shortly.

Morgan grinned. "Now that we've met, maybe you ladies would like to join us at our wagon. We have a great view of the whole track, and it isn't so dusty up there."

As they made their way through the crowd, Charlotte could hardly believe that Morgan Earp had sought out her company. Maria had trouble holding Ruff, who had seen a few other dogs in the crowd and wanted to fight every one of them, so their progress was slow. Charlotte didn't mind; she gloried in Morgan's firm touch on her elbow as he guided her through the press.

Morgan introduced Charlotte and Maria to the Earps, their wives, and daughters. Only Wyatt was missing—he was still cooling his horse down. Charlotte had heard the rumor that Wyatt Earp had a common-law wife named Mattie. There was indeed a Mattie in the Earp party, a plain

33

woman with a perpetually hurt expression in her eyes. She couldn't possibly be married to a vital man like Wyatt. Charlotte glanced at Maria, who looked quite pleased with herself. Apparently Maria didn't believe it either. And she noticed Morgan didn't introduce Mattie as Wyatt's wife; he just said "Mattie Blaylock."

It was Allie Earp, Virgil Earp's wife, who made the strongest impression. The diminutive black-haired woman glared openly at Charlotte and Maria.

After the introductions, Charlotte curtsied. "I'm pleased to meet you."

Allie ignored Charlotte and addressed Morgan. "She's barely out of the school room, Morg. You've got the morals of a rabbit."

"You just shut up, Allie," Morgan said, taking Charlotte's hand in his.

Allie turned to her husband for support. "Virg—"

"Morgan's a grown man. Leave him be." Virgil Earp's tone brooked no argument.

Charlotte felt embarrassed by this exchange, and wondered what Allie didn't like about her. Just that she was young and pretty? Well, jealousy cropped up in the most unusual places. Still, the excitement of being with the Earps—and Morgan in particular—more than made up for it. Her world had been brought down to the warmth of Morgan's fingers clasping her own. What was it about this man that made her heart quake in her chest like a frightened bird? Was this the way Mary had felt about Edward Chesser?

"You ladies can sit up on the wagon. You'll see better," Morgan said. He released Charlotte's hand and helped Maria up onto the buckboard seat. When it was her turn, his hands spanned her waist. A thrill bolted through Charlotte as he lifted her up, his fingers burrowing through the heavy layers of clothing. His grip was strong and firm. She had no doubt he could hold her up like this forever, and half wished he would. He deposited her on the seat, then jumped up beside her. Everywhere their skin and clothing touched she felt a delicious heat. The molded muscles of his shoulder and arm through his crisp white shirt, the hard line of his thigh pressed against hers.

She glanced sideways at him through her lashes, and hoped he wouldn't catch her looking. But he did, and his eyes seemed to drink her in. "You sure are pretty."

She looked away, her face tingling with embarrassment. Tiny flashes of excitement danced in her blood, igniting every nerve ending, and her legs quaked under her skirts.

She tried to concentrate on the conversation around her, but the rushing in her ears was so loud it was difficult to hear what the Earps were saying. What was happening to her? She was completely in the grip of this feeling, something she had never experienced before.

Love! That's what it was. Maria was right after all. Love had swept her up in its powerful tide, and she was helpless to fight it.

"Am I really that ugly?" Morgan asked.

"What?"

"You won't look at me."

Charlotte knew she should be polite, but her neck felt as if it were set on rusty hinges. Would he be able to see into her soul and know how much she loved him? What if he laughed at her?

Morgan cupped her chin and gently turned her face to him. "That's better."

As they waited for the next heat to begin, Morgan made small talk. He asked Charlotte about her family, and told her a little about the Earps. A shiver of pleasure ran through her as the realization came home to her. Here she was, sitting with the famous Earps, privy to their conversation. If only her sister could see her now!

She savored everything; Morgan's close proximity that made her as sheltered and safe as if she were in the lee

35

side of a mountain, the way his fingers interlocked with her own. When he leaned past her to secure the reins, his shoulder momentarily pressed against her face, smelling of sun-warmed skin and tobacco. After he wrapped the reins around the brake he drew back, his chin making a little detour to rest against her neck. She felt his mustache brush against her nape, tickling like warm rain. Knowing she shouldn't let him take such liberties, Charlotte stiffened.

Morgan drew back and sat upright again. "Imagine," he said softly. "Me sitting here with a girl like you."

Charlotte heard Allie Earp mutter something under her breath, and Virgil slid his gaze sideways, his expression stern. "Morg, she's only a kid."

"I know, I know. I'm just bein' friendly." Morgan squeezed her hand again.

I'm not a kid! Charlotte thought indignantly. *I'm eighteen years old!* Why didn't they like her? Because she was young? Couldn't they see how much Morgan cared for her? Hadn't he called her pretty? Surely they would understand; surely even they had been in love once—

Morgan rose abruptly to his feet. "What the hell's Doc doing?"

Charlotte followed his gaze to the commotion on the track.

Wyatt Earp's horse had won the first sprint, but Jake knew the chestnut was tired. If he had been riding Wyatt's horse, he would have taken a tight hold on him at the end, winning by a shorter distance but saving more of the horse. Jake guessed it had been Wyatt's strategy to whip the Grulla so completely in the first heat that Jake would be intimidated. But the Grulla was just getting warmed up. The stamina that had carried Jake over hundreds of miles of rough country in all kinds of weather was just now beginning to show. Jake let his cow pony wind down slowly, picking his own pace. They pulled up at the top of the stretch, just as Wyatt turned back toward him, his horse lathered and blowing. Was it Jake's imagination, or did the chestnut look sore in his front legs? Both white-stockinged forelegs ended in pink hoofs, much softer and more injury-prone than the Grulla's dark ones.

Ten minutes later, John Clum, the mayor of Tombstone called for riders up. Jake swung aboard the Grulla and rode up the track, letting him loosen up again, stretching his muscles in a rolling lope.

As they lined up at the starting post, Jake glanced at Wyatt. The man looked worried. It was all he could do to keep his horse from turning inside out. Tom McLaury held the chestnut's bridle; Doc Holliday, Wyatt Earp's friend, held the Grulla's, as he had done for the first heat. At the sound of the gun they would let go and the race would be on.

Doc rubbed the Grulla's ear. The dentist was as light as a scarecrow, and already drunk. Lucky he was holding a placid pony like the Grulla, instead of Wyatt's firebrand. Doc's cheeks were like hard apples in his square, sepulchral face and Jake imagined he could hear the rattle of phlegm in his chest. Holliday was dying of consumption. "Heard that bull Wyatt has came from south of the border. Your father-in-law's a Mex, ain't he?" Doc asked.

"That's right."

"I hear tell she was one sweet little senorita. What was she like?"

Jake forgot where he was. He only knew that someone had insulted his dead wife. Fury hurtled through the corridors of his being, filling every nerve, sinew, and muscle with savage, deadly power. Body tensed like a coiled spring, Jake grasped his pony's mane, crouching as he prepared to leap.

"Rider! Get off your horse now and you forfeit the race," cautioned John Clum. The words broke through Jake's rage. Doc was trying to bait him, throw his concentration,

Annie McKnight

make him lose—and he would lose Ana's father's bull in
the bargain. Jake clamped down on his feelings with an
iron will, just as the gunshot shattered the air. Wyatt's
chestnut bounded forward. The Grulla made a little jump
but came up short, his hindquarters swinging around in an
arc. Wracked by a coughing fit, Doc clung to the Grulla's
bridle. Doc staggered, pulling Jake's horse toward the
arroyo lining the race course. The chestnut was several
lengths ahead and running all out.

Jake kicked out savagely, knocking Doc to the ground.
The Grulla leaped on to the track.

Charlotte saw everything from her seat on the buckboard.

"Dammit, he's drunk again!" Morgan shouted. "What a
damn fool stunt to pull! Now Wyatt'll probably have to forfeit the race!"

Charlotte clutched Morgan's arm. "Surely Wyatt could
beat him without Doc doing such a thing."

"You see that, Virge?" Allie snapped. "If he's dishon-
est enough to fix a race, he could have been in on that
stage robbery."

"He had nothing to do with it."

"Doc's got the whole bunch of you wrapped around his
little finger. One of these days he'll make you big trouble."

"Look! He's catching him!" shouted Maria.

The little cow pony ran like a jackrabbit. With each
jump, he cut into the chestnut's lead. Jake Cottrell was one
with the horse, his lean body low over its straining neck,
hands following the pony's mouth with each dip of his
head. Suddenly Charlotte found herself pulling for him.

"Come on, Wyatt! Use the whip!" shouted Morgan.

"Look at that little horse go!" cried Maria. "He's going
to win it!"

With a monumental effort, Jake Cottrell's horse poked
his head out in front. When the horses swept past the finish
line, pandemonium broke loose.

"Like David and Goliath, *no*?" Maria's eyes sparkled. Obviously, she had forgotten where she was. Although she worshiped the Earps even more than Charlotte did, Maria seemed to forget that she had finally been given entry into their inner circle.

When Doc arrived, Morgan shouted, "What the hell did you think you were doing?"

Doc grinned. "Had to have something to hang on to. You know how I am when I get to coughing."

Morgan spat. "You always got some excuse for draggin' our brother down in the dirt. Sometimes I don't know why we put up with you."

Wyatt Earp led his horse to them. The animal's face was spattered with dried mud and sweat.

Morgan said, "I guess that Cayuse of Jake's has some sand. Don't worry though, you'll beat him next time. I want you to meet—"

"I don't have time to meet another one of your conquests," Wyatt said shortly. "Doc, I want to know why you did that."

"I just had a coughing fit."

"Better explain it to Cottrell," Morgan said.

Charlotte followed his gaze. Jake Cottrell strode toward them, angry eyes glittering in a face like granite.

Wyatt Earp called out, "That little pony of yours is tougher than I thought. But we'll beat you next time."

"There's not going to be a next time."

"What do you mean?"

"I want satisfaction." As Jake said the words, his eyes caught Charlotte's. She stared back at him as coolly as she could. He recognized her now, but she could tell he didn't like what he saw. Why did everyone disapprove of her? What had she done to anybody? Then Morgan's hand came around her shoulder, and she sank gratefully into the firm warmth of his body. *Morgan* liked her. That was all that mattered.

"You'll get satisfaction in the next race," Jake told Wyatt. "Everyone saw what Doc did. My horse is too fagged out from trying to catch you to run another race."

"What did I do?" shouted Doc belligerently. "I didn't do a thing!"

Jake stared at Doc with undisguised loathing. "You tried to pull my horse down."

"You calling me a liar?" Doc's hand went to his gun. "Heel yourself then, and we'll see who's the liar."

Jake wiped his face with a grimy hand and turned to Wyatt, ignoring Doc completely. "I'll take that bull now. Name your price."

"You owe Doc an answer."

"I'm not interested in fighting."

Morgan's hand tightened on Charlotte's shoulder. He spat on the ground in disgust.

Doc waved his pistol right under Jake Cottrell's nose. "You a coward, Cottrell? I'm telling you I'll fight you now, if you've got any guts to get yourself a gun. You insulted my honor."

"Your honor isn't worth a fight."

"Sir, you are a coward."

Surely the man couldn't take an insult like that! But Jake only reached down and started plucking grass tops out of his pants. He didn't look at Doc when he spoke. "Seems to me you could find someone better with a gun to help you out of this world. That *is* what you're looking for, isn't it?"

Doc's face turned brick-red.

Jake looked at Doc and added, "Seeing how you're stinking drunk, I might have a chance. But after what you said about my wife, I don't feel like doing you the favor."

Wracked by another coughing fit, Doc pulled out a blood-streaked handkerchief and brayed into it, dragging up air in ragged gasps. "I'm calling you out," he rasped between coughing spasms.

"Doc, you're wasting your breath. He won't fight." Morgan's voice dripped with contempt.

Watching this exchange, Charlotte felt sick with embarrassment. Why didn't the man defend himself? He had ridden a tremendous race, and she respected him for it, but what was the matter with him now? Morgan would never turn from a fight!

"Some other time, Doc," Wyatt said.

Doc would have answered, but he was taken by another spasm of coughing. "Yeah," he said quickly, and stumbled around the wagon. Charlotte heard him retching.

"He'd kill you if he were well," Morgan muttered.

"You gonna race, Cottrell, or is that pony of yours so delicate he can't get over one bad start?"

Jake glanced at the chestnut, whose head hung dispiritedly. "I'd think you'd want to spare your horse."

"You decided the way we'd run it. You said that pony had stamina. Don't you believe it anymore?"

Jake paused for a moment, and Charlotte could see that he was weighing the consequences in his mind. "All right. But we rest the horses first."

Wyatt loosened the cinch on his horse. "That suits me."

Jake shot a glance at Charlotte, a mixture of amusement and contempt, bowed briefly, then turned and walked away without a backward look.

Morgan kept his arm around Charlotte but he seemed to forget her as the Earps talked about the stage robbery. Doc wandered off. Maria, who had been trying to catch Wyatt's eye and was so far unsuccessful, finally decided to take Ruff for a walk to see if she could find Roberto.

Marsh Williams and Luke Short, two friends of the Earps, joined the party. They talked about the weeks the posse spent on the trail trying to track down the stagecoach robbers. Charlotte found her mind wandering. It was enough that she was at Morgan's side, but she wished he'd pay a little attention to her. The stagecoach robbery was old news and patently boring.

"You sure Doc didn't have anything to do with it?" Marsh asked. "He was seen riding hell for leather back to Tombstone right after the robbery."

Charlotte knew the names of the robbers almost as well as she knew the Hail Mary. People had been talking about them for weeks. Leonard, Crane, and Head.

Marsh added: "You know as well as I do, Wyatt, Doc *is* a friend of Leonard's."

"He's my friend, too," Wyatt Earp said curtly.

Morgan shifted on the seat. His fingers rested lightly against her breast. Was it accidental? Should she protest? Charlotte was paralyzed, too frightened to move lest she make it worse.

Morgan's hand dropped to Charlotte's elbow and she breathed a sigh of relief. It *had* been an accident.

"Marsh is right about one thing—it makes us all look bad. We'll have to go out again, and not come back until we've got them." Wyatt turned to Virgil. "You think they're still in the San Jose Mountains?"

"Could be. But we've been wasting our days riding all over hell and gone after every outlaw in the county. Maybe that's how I lost the election."

"Maybe it's time we started putting a few feet to the fire," Wyatt said. "We can start with Ike Clanton."

"Ike Clanton? He's too stupid to know anything!" Morgan snorted. Charlotte knew all about Ike Clanton. He and his brother Billy were two of the worst rustlers; them and the McLaury brothers.

"Ike might not have been in on the robbery, but he sure as hell knows something. Might even help us if the price is right," Marsh Williams said.

"Ike!" Morgan snorted. "Help us?"

Wyatt rubbed his chin. "Marsh has got a point. I could offer him the reward money. Always was a greedy son of a bitch. What do you say, Marsh? You're Wells Fargo's representative. Think they'd come through?"

"I'm sure they would, if we explained it right."

Morgan shook his head, obviously thinking the idea was foolish. His fingers gently kneaded Charlotte's arm. She couldn't help shivering with delight, and it took a real act of will to sidle away from him. Morgan let his hands fall to his knees. Charlotte felt strangely disappointed.

Suddenly, Wyatt Earp stared at Charlotte, as if seeing her for the first time. "What's she doing here?"

"I tried to introduce you," Morgan replied.

"I don't want strangers around when we're talking strategy," Wyatt said coldly. "Get her out of here."

"But Wyatt—"

"Now."

Morgan looked at Charlotte apologetically. "Sorry, you're gonna have to leave." He jumped down from the wagon and lifted her up to set her on the ground. The adoration in his eyes was plain.

"Morgan?" Wyatt said sharply.

Morgan didn't look away from her. "In a minute." He spoke to Charlotte. "I'll see you sometime. Soon."

"He'll see you all right," Luke Short said, laughing.

"Shut up," Morgan said. "She's a nice girl."

"Be a good girl and run along!" someone else shouted.

Ears burning, Charlotte walked down toward the racecourse, head held high. The other men were making fun of her. Well, most men were crude. But Morgan had defended her. He was a perfect gentleman. She quickly blotted out the insults, and held on to Morgan's words as a keepsake. *I'll see you sometime. Soon.*

Charlotte found Maria near the finish line.

"Why aren't you with Morgan?"

43

"Wyatt thought I shouldn't be there when they were planning what to do about the stage robbers. But Morgan wants to see me sometime."

They hugged each other, both certain in their own minds that a love match had been made.

Charlotte had misgivings, though. "But what about the theater? I'm going to be a famous actress. I can't get married."

"You are a foolish one," Maria said. "Isn't your idol Lillie Langtry married? You can do both." Maria added, "I hope the little horse wins."

"I thought you loved Wyatt."

Maria shrugged. "That has nothing to do with it. I like the little horse. He has a great heart."

Charlotte had to agree, even though she colored when she remembered how Jake Cottrell had looked at her. She wasn't exactly sure what he had been thinking, but she knew it was demeaning. *I'll pull for the horse,* she rationalized. Not the rider.

When the gun fired, the Grulla took off like a jackrabbit. The thoroughbred tried gamely, but about halfway up the track the Grulla was way ahead. The dun horse ran easily, his short stride matching the thoroughbred's two for one.

Jake was almost to the finish line when Charlotte caught sight of something black in the infield. A cat?

Ruff saw it too. Maria, who had relaxed her grip on his leash, didn't notice until it was too late. Ruff jerked the lead out of her hands and bolted onto the track, right into the path of the running horse. The cow pony made a gigantic leap, twisted sideways in midair, and cleared Ruff by inches.

A gasp rose from the crowd. Jake's horse landed, and for a moment Charlotte thought he would be all right. But his front foot must have hit the ground wrong. In horror, Charlotte watched as the pony cartwheeled in the air. Time stretched unbearably as the Grulla's hindquarters lifted up on a dense pillow of dust before crashing down on Jake Cottrell's body.

Chapter Four

Jake slipped in and out of consciousness. His pain was a beacon, pulsing brightly in the darkness. Agony radiated from his core, a crushing, splintering pain that blotted out awareness of anything else.

He knew his leg was broken, although he could not remember how or why. The few times he was able to think at all, his brain didn't seem to work the way it used to. He was disoriented, unable to concentrate on anything. He realized his thinking was impaired, but it did not seem to matter so much when compared to the pure essence of his agony.

Once he felt sunlight stripe his body, and thought he was at the *Rio Plata*. He imagined he heard the tinny sound of bracelets banging together. If he opened his eyes he would see bright blue shutters against white walls, and the beautiful Mexican daughter of his host would sing softly as she wrung out a washcloth to cover his eyes with coolness. But something told him he was wrong, that the elusive moment was beyond him, locked forever behind a door in his memory.

He drifted again.

Later. Jake opened his eyes and saw delicate sprigged wallpaper and a china nightstand near the bed. It took him a moment to realize that his nurse was his old friend Emma Lake, not Ana. *Ana's dead,* he thought, and the familiar bleakness settled into his heart, robbing him of energy.

"Take this. It'll make you feel better." Emma spooned some vile liquid into his mouth. There was something he wanted to know, but it kept eluding him like a balloon floating just out of reach. It was a long time before he realized what it was. "My horse," he said through cracked lips.

"That little Grulla of yours? Sprained a fetlock. I been hosin' him down regular. Any other horse would've broke his leg, but that pony's got ankles as solid as oak trees."

"How long have I been here?"

"Two days. Doc Goodfellow says you have a concussion and a broken leg."

Good-bye, he said—or thought he did. He had spun down into delirium.

Jake was home again, back in Georgia. He had just buried his mother and father. They'd died within a year of each other, unable to cope with the bitter aftermath of the war. The Union army had destroyed the land, leaving it a blackened wasteland. What they had not destroyed, the carpetbaggers had taken; every inch of ground, every blooded horse and hound, every stick of antique furniture. They'd squabbled over the spoils like a pack of dogs.

George and Luke, Jake's older brothers, had fought for the Confederacy, but now they had gone their separate ways—George trailing cattle up through Texas, and Luke heading for California. Jake was too young, though. His father had wanted him to finish college and become a lawyer. Perhaps, if his parents were still living, he would have done just that. But standing over their graves, he realized that this was not his home anymore. He would go west too. Maybe he could find his brothers.

Somewhere, in the real world, he felt that Emma was giving him soup. She tipped the cup against his lips, then let his head rest against the pillow. His leg hurt like hell. He hoped a broken leg wouldn't delay his journey west; he couldn't bear to stay in this land of blighted dreams another minute. "I'm sorry," he muttered. "I've got to go." In his dream, he threw a rose on his mother's grave.

Jake had been twenty-one when he'd joined his first cattle drive up from Texas. The west was a big country; he never had found his brothers.

After trailing cattle for a few years, Jake had decided to stake out some ground of his own and raise quarter horses. He'd needed money to start such a venture, so he took a job as deputy sheriff in New Mexico. It was a lucrative position because he could keep ten percent of the taxes he collected, ten percent of about twenty thousand dollars a year. It had been good, but then six years ago Jake had trailed some horse thieves south of Animas into Mexico. He'd caught up with them near the Sierra de Ojos, south of the Arizona border. They'd shot him and left him for dead.

He'd awakened to the cool hands and sweet voice of Ana Valdez.

Pain bolted up his body. Jake was instantly awake, the bone-deep ache spreading through him. *I must have moved my leg,* he thought. Emma stood over him, glaring, a bottle of Mrs. Winslow's Soothing Syrup in her hand. "You oughta warn a body. Made me spill some."

He remembered everything: trying to retrieve the bull, racing Wyatt, the fall.

"You had some visitors this morning."

"Visitors." Damn, but he felt muzzy.

"Two young ladies. One of 'em used to board with me. They brought you some flan." Emma spooned some cough syrup into his mouth. "Maria—she's the Meskin—said it was her dog ran out in front of you like that. Says to tell you she's real sorry."

"Not important," he mumbled. He shouldn't have run that third heat. That was his fault.

"It was Maria that made the flan. Other one's useless as a chimney on a chicken coop."

He wished she wouldn't talk. It hurt his head to listen.

47

Emma shook her head. "Girl wants to be an actress. I reckon she's pretty enough. What do you think? Should I talk to Bob Euell, see if he'll set up an audition for her? Me, I don't hold with theaters at all, but the Westphalia's an honest one—as honest as a theater can be. The others are just glorified bordellos. What do you think, Jake?"

"Could you please . . ." He tried again. "So tired."

"She'll try it anyway, so I might as well see she gets a chance at a good place. Can't talk a lick of sense into her. Say, what's all this about a bull? You been talkin' in your sleep again. You have a bull somewhere? Want me to make sure he's all right?"

Pain, in a red mist, descended. Jake tried to form the words but couldn't. He wanted to tell her that the black bull had some of the finest blood in Mexico running through his veins, that he was to be the foundation sire of a great dynasty of fighting bulls. He wanted to say that he and Ana had bought the animal for his father-in-law as a gift, only a few weeks before she'd been stricken with typhoid while accompanying him to Nogales on a horse-buying trip. He wanted to say that the sight of her on that day, when she proudly brought her father down to the corrals and showed him her gift, was his last joyful memory of her.

But he said nothing, and slept.

Chapter Five

When Charlotte Tate arrived in Tombstone two and a half years before, she hadn't been prepared for Emma Lake.

On her first full day at the Silver Dollar Boarding House, she'd searched Emma out, wanting to know where the bathtub was kept. She rounded the corner of the house in time to see Emma break a chicken's neck with one deft twist. Seeing Emma kill a chicken was bad enough—Tom Connor had always taken care of that chore unobserved—but what scandalized Charlotte more was the fact that the woman wore pants. Men's pants. Charlotte jumped back as if she'd been bitten.

"What are you starin' at?" Emma asked, nonchalantly wiping her bloody hands on her trousers.

Charlotte blushed.

"You're not the type that gets megrims and vapors, are you? If that's the case, you better not come around here in the morning."

Charlotte fled to the house. That evening, when Emma brought out the chicken dinner, Charlotte picked at her food.

Emma sniffed, "There's some people around here think a chicken dinner drops out of a Heaven fully cooked." The boardinghouse guests, mostly old pensioners who gobbled up anything Emma set before them, only turned their heads to stare at Charlotte with disapproval.

Her days at the Silver Dollar seemed interminable. Everywhere Charlotte turned there were old men, coughing and shuffling and mumbling. They would sit out on the veranda, talking about past exploits, reeking of hair tonic and medicine and sour breath. A favorite theme among them was the decline of morality from generation to generation, and their uniform conviction that the young people of today were not a patch on the young people of their day. As one old alcoholic would say between swigs from a silver flask, "You can't put an old head on young shoulders."

"As if I'd want his ugly old fizzog sitting on my neck!" Charlotte would answer to her new friend Maria, who laughed until her sides ached.

Maria had been hired by Emma to sew curtains for the

boardinghouse. Charlotte was immediately drawn to the sunny-natured Mexican-Irish girl. Maria lived with her brother Roberto on Fremont Street, taking in sewing while Roberto guarded freight wagons for one of the mining companies. She was always asking Charlotte to move in with them, but that would take money, a commodity that was hard to come by for a young female person in Tombstone.

As Charlotte helped Maria hang the curtains, she would be treated to hilarious stories about goings-on in town. Charlotte hung on Maria's every word, starved for gossip about the brawling silver camp and its denizens. Maria was her only link to that glittering world. The raw excitement of Tombstone stopped at the door of the Silver Dollar Boarding House; she might as well live on an island.

Charlotte and Maria became inseparable. Often they would walk into town together on errands—the only time Emma would let Charlotte set foot in Tombstone proper. It was Maria who showed her the theaters in town, all grouped around the same corner of Fourth and Fremont Street. Maria also pointed out Wyatt Earp, the handsome lawman who used to guard the Wells Fargo stage. "That one," Maria prophesied solemnly, "will make his name here. He has that look."

"What look?" asked Charlotte.

"His eye is like an eagle's," Maria said mysteriously. Maria loved to flaunt her superior knowledge about human nature and what she called "the way people bend."

She did, however, share with Charlotte the more common knowledge about the Earp brothers. Wyatt Earp and his friend Bat Masterson had cleaned up Dodge City, and now they had come here to do the same thing. Wyatt's brother, Virgil, had been appointed acting city marshal after Marshal White was shot to death by the king of the rustlers, Curly Bill Brocious. His brother Morgan guarded the Wells Fargo stage. Maria went on and on about how handsome the Earps were, particularly Wyatt. Charlotte, who naturally gravitated toward success, didn't value looks anywhere near as much as she valued the power that seemed to emanate from Earp and his siblings. Many times she had seen both men and women respectfully make way for Wyatt as he walked the busy streets of Tombstone. Charlotte yearned for that kind of power, to command respect by her presence alone. Someday, she would. If she could ever get out of the Silver Dollar Boarding House, that was. She certainly wouldn't command must respect living with a passel of doddering old folks.

Charlotte bided her time and saved her money so she could move out of Emma's boardinghouse. While she waited, she practiced her acting in secret and became Maria's willing student in the ways of the heart. It would be no time at all, she knew, before she turned eighteen, and then she would finally be able to get out from under Emma Lake's thumb.

And so it was that shortly after Charlotte's eighteenth birthday, two things happened almost simultaneoulsy: she moved into the little house on Fremont Street with Maria and her brother Roberto, and she fell head over heels in love with Morgan Earp.

Chapter Six

Tombstone rollicked out of March and into April, as blustery and unsettled as the wind that swept across the bony lap of Goose Flats.

The silver town shouldered its way toward notoriety; crude, ambitious, and raw, for all its surface sophistication.

51

Annie McKnight

Already Tombstone was a financial center, its influence felt all the way to the New York stock exchange. The milling towns of Charleston, Fairbank, and Contention basked in Tombstone's reflected glow like planets around the sun. Gourmet restaurants served fare like poached salmon and *pinion a poulet aux champignons*, where not two years before the proprietor might have served beans and biscuits from a drafty tent. The hotels vied with one another in elegance and ostentation: crystal chandeliers, rosewood furniture and gold fixtures in every room. Fine imported wines and liquors graced the long mahogany bar of the Crystal Saloon. Tombstone was a town of contrasts, where sallow-faced miners in slouch hats and brogans walked the same broad streets as gamblers dressed by the finest San Francisco tailors. The silver camp had all the trappings of wealth and civilization. But only time would tell if it had the strength of character to survive.

It was an exciting time for Maria and Charlotte. They were on the periphery of the many forces that shaped Tombstone, and knew nothing of the underlying reasons for them. They only knew that the Earps were heroes, and they clutched to that with the ferocity of the young and romantic.

As Charlotte and Maria returned from Emma Lake's boardinghouse after dropping off the flan for Jake, they saw a gathering of horses and men on the corner of Fifth and Allen.

"What's going on?" Charlotte asked.

"I bet they're getting up a posse to go after Leonard, Crane, and Head again."

They inched closer, lingering at the edge of the gathering. The air was taut with excitement as the men mounted up. Charlotte spotted Doc Holliday step onto a bald-faced roan. He wore a gray derby and frock coat, his whiplike body brimming with nerve. It was hard to believe he was the same staggering drunk from the Watervale racecourse.

Morgan Earp untied his horse. "Hey, Doc, you look like you're dressed for one of them fancy hunt balls, not a posse," he called out jocularly.

"I aim for those boys to know who they're shooting at."

"I'll shoot Leonard for you, so you don't have to feel you're turnin' on a friend," Morgan offered.

The three Earps were mounted now, their horses dancing in place. Charlotte thought she recognized Bat Masterson, but wasn't sure. A little way off, another smaller group was preparing to mount, among them, Sheriff Johnny Behan.

Wyatt Earp spurred his horse over to the smaller group.

Johnny Behan's voice drifted toward them. "You go south," he said, his chest puffed out with his own importance. "And Billy, Harry and I'll head over Mesilla way. We'll meet up in San Simon in two weeks' time."

Wyatt Earp didn't answer. He touched his horse's side and the animal sidled closer to Johnny and the woman beside him, a slender, dark-eyed beauty.

Her voice floated past the crowd. "Be careful, Wyatt."

He leaned down and pushed a strand of hair from her face. Impulsively, the woman leaned up and kissed him on the mouth. Wyatt glancèd past her and his eyes held Johnny Behan's. Even from where Charlotte was standing, she could see he was enjoying Behan's discomfort.

"What'd you do that for?" Behan shouted.

"Shut up, Johnny," the young woman said. "You don't own me."

Behan looked as if he would shoot the other man right there. Earp sat still, one hand on his gun. The tension in the air was palpable. Finally, the sheriff turned back to his horse and busied himself with the cinch. "Let's go," he said shortly.

"You've always had the courage of your convictions, Johnny," Wyatt said. He wheeled his horse and returned to his own party.

"Who's that woman?" Charlotte asked Maria.

Her friend glared at the dark beauty. "I think she's Johnny's wife."

The posse started off. Morgan spotted Charlotte and Maria and grinned at them, raising his hat as he spurred his horse into a trot to catch the rest of the group. Suddenly, he spun his horse around and galloped back up the street toward the crowd, still looking in Charlotte's direction.

"What's he doing?" cried Maria.

With a loud whoop, Morgan stood up on the saddle and waved his hat as he galloped by. He sat back down, pulled his mount up, whirled him toward the posse and took off again, all the time screaming at the top of his lungs. As Charlotte watched, he swapped ends to face backwards, sitting on the horse's rump. The horse nearly collided with the retreating posse, but Morgan just grinned. Charlotte could swear he watched her until the dust obscured them and they were too far away to be seen.

"Look at that lout," muttered Emma Lake, who had come to stand beside them. "No more sense'n a headless rooster."

"I think he's quite clever," Charlotte replied.

After all, he had done it for her benefit.

For days, people talked of nothing but the posse. But within a week another big mine was discovered and the lawmen became old news.

At the Silver Dollar Boardinghouse, Jake Cottrell had finally begun to shake the effects of his concussion. Emma Lake still dosed him with Mrs. Winslow's Soothing Syrup, though, which did little for his pain but left him drowsy. Through the hazy edges of consciousness, he heard things; sounds and voices drifting in and out of his dreams.

He was aware of the sounds that gored the wind-ravaged air: the banging of hammers as new buildings went up, the heavy rumble of freight and ore wagons pulled by long mule teams, harnesses jingling and whips cracking. After the quiet of the ranch, the noises were oppressive to Jake's ears; the clanking of the stamp mills, the mining machinery squealing and grinding day and night, the shift whistles, honky-tonk piano, and gunfire erupting nightly from somewhere down on Allen Street.

Jake had never spent much time in Tombstone. He had divided his days between his own ranch and the *Rio Plata*, only coming into town for supplies. For the first time he was getting a picture of the boomtown, mostly from the talk that swirled around him at the dinner table, or funneled up through the window when the pensioners sat and talked on the veranda below. He spent a lot of his waking hours listening to them play poker. In the West, gambling was considered an honorable profession on a par with medicine and law, although Jake himself had little use for it. He balked at spending too much energy on something as inherently unproductive as gambling; not when there was wood to cut and horses to break. Jake thought there was a lot of wasted energy in a town like Tombstone, and it left a bad taste in his mouth. He certainly wasn't cut out for city life. By his fifth day at the Silver Dollar, he chafed at the bit to get back to Seep Springs.

The wind had finally died down, leaving a bright, chilly morning. Now that his head was clear, Jake was impatient for his body to catch up. His bed was near the window, where he could look out in the direction of his ranch at the foot of the Whetstone Mountains. This morning the desire to be out in the crisp air was greater than ever. Adrenaline rushed through his limbs like molten lava. He could smell the earth smells—the tardy beginning of spring—and feel the coolness of the morning shadows, see the undulating hills of golden grass shivering in the breeze. He longed for the feel of a good horse under him. It would be a busy time on the ranch, and yet here he lay, useless.

Damn the leg; it was shattered. Emma, who had known

him long and well, refused to take him back to Seep Springs. "You need rest for that leg to set right, Jake. You'll get it here." She refused to argue about it, and although he thought he might be able to get out of bed, he wouldn't be able to get much farther. Hitching up a team by himself was impossible, and he sure as hell couldn't ride a horse. He was stuck.

Feminine voices came from downstairs. Jake didn't think they belonged to any of the regular boarders. Without preamble, Emma flung the door open. "Jake, you got visitors."

Charlotte was more than happy to accompany Maria on her mission of mercy. She knew all about the principle of noblesse oblige, and decided this visit would make excellent practice for the day she became rich and famous. After all, it was Maria's dog that had caused all the trouble. The horrifying scene still haunted her dreams; the gallant pony going down in a cloud of dust, the way the cowboy lay prone on the track. The least they could do was try to cheer him up a little. She had followed Maria's lead and prepared a dessert for him. Doubtless the poor man would be grateful.

She wasn't prepared for the change in Jake Cottrell. Black stubble covered the lower part of his face and lank hair spilled over the bandage around his forehead. His face seemed gray under his tan. The room smelled bad, too; a sour, sickly smell.

He grinned with effort. "Ladies. Forgive me for not rising." His gaze lingered on Charlotte. She knew he recognized her, but it was difficult to tell what he was thinking. She handed him the trifle, grimacing as she caught a whiff of him. "This is for you," she said, stepping away quickly. "We're sorry Maria's dog caused your fall."

He turned his attention to the muddy-looking mixture. "You made this? What is it? Some kind of pudding?"

Charlotte's face flamed. "It's a trifle."

"There's no need to be modest."

Was the man being deliberately obtuse? "That's what it's called. A trifle."

Jake lifted the dish and scrutinized it. "You mean the English *dessert*? Isn't it supposed to be layered?"

The conversation was not going the way Charlotte had expected. She had come here to give him comfort and kindness, and how did he reward her? With ridicule. "If it offends you so much you can give it back."

Maria touched Charlotte's arm. "Charlotte, remember what we are here for."

"Jake's the one oughta apologize," Emma broke in. "It was nice of you girls to think of him."

"I'm sorry. Charlotte, is it? You will accept my apology?" Jake bowed from the waist up, and Charlotte saw a brief flicker of pain in his eyes.

"It must hurt bad, that leg," Maria said shyly.

A bell rang somewhere in the house. "That'll be Mr. Sweeney, wanting his medicine. You girls don't stay too long, you'll tire him out. And you, Jake, be polite." With that, Emma left.

"I wanted you to win," Maria said. "I thought your horse was very courageous."

Jake's gaze turned to Charlotte. "And how about you? Did you want me to win, too?"

She flushed. Why did he look at her that way? As if he could see right through to her soul, and didn't like what he saw. "I couldn't care less if you won," she blurted out. "I'm sorry Maria's dog got in your way, and I'm sorry your horse was hurt, but I'm not going to pretend that I wanted you to win."

Maria turned to her. "But you said—"

"I know what I said," Charlotte snapped. "I was pulling for the horse, not Mr. Cottrell. I always root for the underdog."

Jake shifted in bed, and his face went another shade of gray. "How commendable."

"A lot of people say Wyatt should have forfeited the race," Maria offered. "That was a dirty trick Doc pulled."

"It was my fault. I shouldn't have raced the last heat. I let pride get the better of me."

"Pride," Charlotte muttered under her breath. If he'd had any pride at all he would have stood up to Doc.

"You say something?" Jake asked.

"It wasn't important."

He grinned, his pewter eyes taking her measure. "Don't let me intimidate you."

Intimidate her? This—this coward? "If you must know, I thought you should have stood up to Doc." She glared at him, daring him to argue with her.

"You think I should have fought him then and there?"

"That's what I think."

"I'm not a gunfighter."

"He called you out! How could you just turn tail and—" Charlotte stopped, suddenly horrified. How had it ended up like this? She had come to comfort him, and here she was, giving him the worst insult a man could take.

To her surprise, he didn't seem the least bit perturbed. "You aren't going to take it back, now, are you? You have a right to your opinion."

He was treating it as if it were a big joke. She'd show him. "I thought you should know what people are saying."

"People?"

"Morgan Earp, for one."

"Morgan Earp! Now there's a man whose opinion I cherish."

"He's worth ten of you."

"Charlotte!" Maria touched her arm again.

"When it comes to dealing faro, I don't doubt it."

"If he had been insulted the way you were, you can bet he would stand up for himself."

Jake's face was unreadable. "No doubt."

58

"I'm sorry if I offended you, but I believe in telling the truth," Charlotte added stiffly.

"You've been a great comfort in that capacity."

That remark hit home. Charlotte realized he had been playing with her, trying to get her angry. Well, he had succeeded, but she wouldn't give him any more satisfaction. "I'm sure your leg must pain you, so perhaps we should take our leave."

"Thank you for this." He held up the trifle.

This, indeed! Charlotte tried to think of something else to say, something charming, to prove that she was a lady, but Jake had turned his attention to Maria and spoke in Spanish. It sounded as if he were thanking her for the flan.

Flattered that he could speak her first language, Maria answered in kind. The two of them carried on a long conversation in Spanish, effectively shutting Charlotte out. Fuming, she realized that they were flirting with each other. It annoyed Charlotte that Maria could be taken in by such a person—it was almost as if her friend were siding with Jake against her. "Can we go now?"

Jake grinned. "You sure can't stand to be anything less than the main attraction."

"Maria, I want to go *now*."

"We'll see you tomorrow," Maria said to the crippled man.

"I'm looking forward to it. But you don't have to bring your duenna."

After his visitors left, Jake lay back in the bed. His whole body ached. Maybe he wasn't ready to leave the Silver Dollar after all.

He shouldn't have teased the red-haired one so much, but she was so easy to rile. Emma had mentioned her more than a few times. So far, Charlotte Tate had fulfilled his expectations.

It had been obvious from the moment she walked into the room that she was playing a part: the compassionate lady ministering to the less fortunate. Jake didn't flatter himself into thinking she was genuinely concerned about him. But Maria, there was a real lady. Her kindness was genuine. He looked forward to seeing her again, if only because she reminded him of his wife.

Later that day Tom McLaury came by to see him. He was furious over a run-in with the Earps out at his ranch near the Swisshelm Mountains. Apparently the Earp posse had decided to go east instead of south, harassing neighbors as they went. "Damn Yankee bastards," Tom fumed. "Think they can run roughshod over the entire county. The Earps aren't the law in Cochise County. Johnny is."

There was no doubt that Johnny Behan had the upper hand for the moment—at least as far as the law was concerned. Whoever held the sheriff's office controlled the gambling interests and the real power in Tombstone. But even though Johnny had the sheriff's office, Wyatt seemed bent on making a conquest of his own: Johnny Behan's common-law wife, Sadie Marcus. It was one way to get even, but Wyatt Earp hadn't stopped there.

Because Johnny was sheriff, Wyatt could not openly go against him; it would cost him too much politically. He needed a foil, an antagonist against whom he could pit his courage and strength. To Jake's way of thinking, Wyatt had found his antagonist ready-made: the cowboys.

The small ranchers—cowboys—were convenient scapegoats for any crime in Tombstone's city limits. Wyatt Earp went about subduing them single-handedly; running them out of town, pulling them in to be fined for any misconduct, no matter how petty. As a former deputy marshal, he had the spirit, if not the letter of the law behind him. The citizens of Tombstone wanted a protector. They were grateful for Wyatt Earp's efficient justice. And they might be grateful enough next time to support him for sheriff.

And so in that uneasy spring of 1881, tensions escalated

between two groups that often found themselves seated at the same card game or riding on the same posse. There was no real reason for the animosity between the cowboys and the Earps, but insults and braggadocio prevailed, accumulating one on top of the other until any common ground receded into the past.

When Tombstone's tempest in a teapot was about to boil over, Jake was afraid that the cowboys would lose, and lose badly. Since he numbered among them several good friends, he hoped there would never be a showdown.

Chapter Seven

Charlotte stood on the wooden stage, feeling suddenly very small and alone.

"What are you going to sing?" Bob Euell asked. The owner of the Westphalia sat alone in the tiny theater, his feet propped up on the chair in front of him.

" 'Jeannie with the Light Brown Hair.' "

"Jamie, you know that one." Euell nodded to the piano player sitting at the upright below the stage. "Any time you're ready."

Charlotte's heart hammered against her rib cage and her throat constricted. When she opened her mouth, nothing came out. Jamie played a couple of chords, then stopped.

"Well?" Bob Euell smiled encouragingly.

Jamie said, "Don't worry, I'll follow you." Gaunt and fair, he had slim, delicate fingers and blue shadows under his eyes, but his presence was somehow comforting.

Charlotte's mouth felt like a dry lake, and her knees were shaking uncontrollably. *Get a hold of yourself!* she thought grimly. She knew that if she failed here, she would never get another chance. At least not in this town.

She straightened her shoulders and nodded to Jamie. "I dream—" Her first two notes came out in a squeak. She swallowed and sang the rest of the phrase. Her voice sounded tiny and strange in her thudding ears, but eventually her heart slowed down and she stopped trembling.

By the second stanza, Charlotte began to enjoy herself. Her voice became stronger, and it had just the right amount of tremolo, like Delia Delight's.

At the end, she curtsied prettily.

Bob Euell stood up. "You can start tomorrow," he said.

Charlotte arrived at six on the dot the following evening. A fat woman in a pink tulle dress fluttered toward her. "You must be the new girl." She led the way through a clutter of scenery flats backstage. The Westphalia shared the outside door with a neighboring restaurant, and the cooking odors were oppressive in the stifling heat of the closed space. For a moment, Charlotte thought she might be sick.

The woman scowled at Charlotte. "You're awful thin." She reached into a closet and produced a lilac-colored dress. "Try this."

Charlotte stared at the dress. The bodice was sleeveless and scoop-necked. There seemed to be far too little material to cover her legs. This was nothing like the classic Grecian style dress Delia Delight wore.

"You'll need these, too." The woman handed Charlotte a floppy cloth cap, a pair of pale blue opaque tights, and black lace-up boots.

Charlotte tried to put her best face on it. "Where do I change?"

"Right here's fine."

"Suppose someone should come by?" she asked.

"Honey, you don't have nothing that anyone here hasn't seen before." The woman saw Charlotte's horrified expression and her own face softened. "You can use the closet, if you're so finicky."

Charlotte sidled past her, feeling the urge to cry. This was not what she had expected at all!

After struggling into the tights and dress, Charlotte managed to pull the decolletage up a little by hitching the dress up higher on her waist, but that pulled the skirt up almost to her knees. It made her feel naked underneath. The tights and pointed boots made her legs look shorter and plumper, like two bluish worms. She tucked her hair into the snood and emerged from the closet, suppressing the urge to cover her legs with her arms.

The woman stared at her critically, then jerked Charlotte's bodice down a little. "That's better." She produced a paint pot and drew a line down Charlotte's cleavage with brown greasepaint, then dusted the top of each breast with white powder. "You'll sell plenty of drinks with that."

"Drinks?"

"Come one. I want Jamie to see you."

Embarrassed, Charlotte followed. She was in show business now, and would have to get used to this kind of thing. But how could she expect to move an audience to tears with her songs when she was dressed like a tart?

Jamie's face lit up when he saw Charlotte. "You look nice. Mrs. McCurdy, Bob wants this one to work the floor before the show. She's a good looker and we think she can sell a lot of whiskey."

Puzzled, Charlotte broke in, "When do I sing?"

"Sing?" Jamie stared at her. "If somebody asks you between acts, I suppose you could sing something. Just serve the drinks, and if someone asks for a song, tell them they're going to have to buy another drink." He dismissed her with a wink, then turned to Mrs. McCurdy. "Oh, and Mrs. McCurdy, take her hair out of that cap and leave it out. It's too pretty to hide."

As Charlotte learned how to make change and serve

drinks, she tried to keep the panic from closing around her throat. What had they hired her for? She had been tricked! She wasn't going to be allowed near the stage.

Her mind raced as she went through the motions. One part of her wanted to run out the back door and never come back. But an inner voice counseled her to wait. She mustn't alienate one of the few theater owners in town. Perhaps they were testing her in some way. Could Delia Delight have started as a waitress?

"Very good, sweetie. You learn fast," Mrs. McCurdy said, as Charlotte juggled two glasses and a whiskey bottle and set them down on a table. She patted Charlotte on the cheek. "But could you look a little happier? You want the men to like you, don't you?"

At midnight, the show was over. The suspension wire acts, the serio comics, the comedians, skit actors, specialty stars and singers had finished their acts, and the chairs were cleared from the floor.

Charlotte, who had always left the theater after the last performance, was surprised to see that the patrons weren't leaving. They gathered along one wall, as if waiting for something.

It wasn't long in coming. Jamie returned to his piano and struck up a wild, rollicking polka. Suddenly, Charlotte was grasped roughly from behind by a cowboy with whiskey breath and whirled into a blundering dance. She struggled to get away, but he held her fast.

At the end of the song, she managed to wriggle out of his grasp and ran toward the back of the stage, trying to get there before any other man decided to waylay her.

Mrs. McCurdy caught her arm. "Hold on, honey, there's another two hours of dancing ahead of you."

Stunned, Charlotte stared at her. "Dancing?"

"That's part of the job."

The frustration of the night finally caught up with her. "I've had enough. I'm going home."

"If you do, you won't be coming back. A man pays two bits to dance with you. That's where we make the most money."

"Mr. Euell hired me as a singer."

"He hired you as a percentage girl—a pretty waiter. You get men to dance with you and buy you drinks." At Charlotte's expression, Mrs. McCurdy's face softened. "I know it's hard at first, but pretty soon you'll·be kicking up your heels and enjoying yourself to beat the band."

Too shocked to argue, Charlotte allowed herself to be ushered back toward the dance floor. Men lined up to dance with her, and she was carted about the floor like a grain sack on wheels.

By the end of the night the small of her back ached and her feet were in agony. She was no closer to her dream of becoming a famous actress. In fact, the gulf between reality and her dream seemed to have deepened into an uncrossable chasm. Charlotte saw no way to go from being a singing waitress to the idol of millions. And so ended Charlotte's first night in the theater.

The following evening, Roberto and Maria walked Charlotte back to the Westphalia.

"Are you sure you won't give it another try?" asked Maria.

Charlotte's lips tightened with the stubborn resolve Maria had so often seen in their months together. "I shan't go through that again."

"Then we'll wait for you." Maria leaned against the stuccoed adobe building, and Roberto—who very rarely talked—squatted soundlessly beside the hitching post.

Charlotte walked into the theater. The door to the restaurant squeaked and Charlotte saw a chef's assistant carrying a large pail of potato peelings. He went through to the outside screen door and dumped the peelings into the alley. Charlotte caught him as he was coming back.

"Have you seen Mr. Euell?" she asked.

He shook his head. "Mrs. McCurdy and Maisie are in there." He nodded to the backstage area. Maisie was an old cockney woman who acted in the skits.

Charlotte threaded her way backstage. Muffled voices came from the small room. ". . . and fix the tassels on Charlotte's costume."

"That one won't be back."

"Now, Maisie, you're prejudging that girl."

"There's some in this world that thinks they're better than the rest, and that's one of them. You mark my words, she won't be back again. She's a quitter."

Charlotte's face flamed. A quitter?

Mrs. McCurdy said sadly, "Mr. James is right fond of her. Has this crazy notion that the girl might make an actress someday. I guess we'll see if she's got the right mettle or not."

"She won't," Maisie prophesied darkly. "You'll see. She'll be in here with that simpering look on her face, tellin' us she's just not cut out for the waitressing life."

Blood pounding in her ears, Charlotte leaned against the partition. Emotions bombarded her: rage at Maisie's cruel and accurate assessment of her, exhilaration at Mrs. McCurdy's words—Jamie thought she'd be an actress—and a curious void, because she knew she would have to stick with it. She would have to brave the rude remarks and roaming hands and hard, back-breaking work.

Charlotte took a deep breath and swept into the room as if she were a queen and Maisie and Mrs. McCurdy were her loyal subjects. She smiled at the two older women. "I thought I'd come by and see if there was anything I could do to help," she said with exaggerated sweetness.

She was rewarded by the sight of Maisie's mouth dropping open wide enough to catch flies.

* * *

Once she decided to stay at the theater, Charlotte proved herself to be a quick learner, and soon became skilled at talking men into buying her drinks. She didn't coax men to drink so much as she dared them. Charlotte made it clear she wasn't like most of the other song-and-dance girls, who offered entertainments of a more private nature after hours. An excellent listener, she gave men a feeling of self-importance. When one asked her if she'd like a drink, too, Charlotte's innocent eyes would light up with childlike delight. "Well, I've always fancied the taste of champagne."

At ten dollars a bottle, champagne was the most lucrative sale at the Westphalia. Charlotte always tried for that first. In fact, she was so successful in getting men to buy her champagne, that the other percentage girls soon became jealous. But because she hated the taste of alcohol, Charlotte would dash the offending liquid into a handy spittoon when the patron wasn't looking.

The bartender would slip her a check called a "bit" for every drink she sold. When the night was over she cashed in the bits, including those for her own drinks.

Charlotte was surprised at how much money she had by the end of the week. She had stashed the bills and coins in a reticule and stuffed it behind Mary's shrine. On Friday, she opened the bag and saw that she had almost eighty dollars. Some of it was from money that patrons had handed her on the quiet, bills she hadn't even bothered to look at. It all added up to a lot of money, more than two months' rent.

Maybe it would be awhile before she realized her dream of becoming an actress, but at least she had money. In the meantime, she would watch and learn, and study Delia Delight's every move.

A few hours each day, Jake sat outside on the porch. He was starting to master the crutches Emma had given him, although he tired easily.

One day Emma led the Grulla out and walked him around the dirt yard. "Looks pretty good, don't he?"

"Why, Emma, you're a miracle worker. He doesn't favor that leg at all."

Emma put the horse up and came to sit down beside Jake. "I've been thinking." She wiped her hands on her apron. "Every time Maria and Charlotte come here, they go take a look at my horses. I haven't been able to ride much of late, and I don't hold with keeping an animal that doesn't earn his keep." Her gaze slid to Jake and she asked slyly, "Why don't you give those girls some riding lessons?"

"Riding lessons?"

"Sure. You could sit right here and tell 'em what to do. My horses would get some use, and you'd have somethin' to keep you busy. How about it?"

Jake rubbed his chin. "I might, if you tell me what you really want."

"I told you—"

"Emma, when you do something, there's a reason behind it."

"All right." She sighed. "I don't much like what's going on with Charlotte and that theater. I've been hearing that she's getting a big head, thinkin' she's the best little trick in shoe leather."

"What's that have to do with horses?"

"You know my philosophy, Jake. A good horse brings out the best in a man. Or woman, for that matter. I like the idea of her riding out in the fresh air. Might give her some perspective, make her see there's more things in life than having a passel of men sniffin' around looking for what they can get. Now, Jake, I know you like that Meskin girl. It wouldn't be any hardship on you to show them girls a few of the basics. You ain't doing nothing else."

Jake glanced at Emma. She was an unlikely Good Samaritan, but he knew her well. As much as Emma complained about Charlotte's vanity and selfishness, it was obvious she genuinely cared about the girl. Well, he had no objection. He'd be leaving pretty soon anyway. A few easy rides beforehand couldn't hurt, and might help. "Fine with me."

"I feel responsible for her, Jake. Katherine Connor sent her here to me, and so far I haven't taken very good care of her. I got her into that theater, but I can't help thinking I shouldn't have done it. It's not a natural life."

Charlotte bought a French-waisted riding habit at one of the finer stores with some of her savings. It was hunter green with black braiding down the front.

When the girls arrived at the Silver Dollar Boardinghouse the morning of their first riding lesson, Emma's horses had already been brought out and tethered to the cottonwood tree at the edge of the yard. Jake stood near the tree, leaning heavily on one crutch and resting an arm over the neck of a little bay horse.

It was a beautiful morning for riding. A breeze lifted the leaves of the cottonwood tree, shuffling them like cards, so that half their surfaces glistened silver. Charlotte noticed Jake had shaved off his beard but left the mustache. His eyes registered her new habit and expensive riding crop with amusement. She lifted her chin and stared back at him.

"They're beautiful!" Maria breathed. "Which one is mine?"

"The bay."

Maria ran up to the stocky little horse and stroked its neck.

Jake helped Maria up into the sidesaddle. He gathered the reins and handed them to her. "You tug on the reins to stop him."

"What's his name?" asked Maria, patting the shining neck.

"Cricket." Jake untethered the other horse and nodded to

Charlotte, who stood back at a discreet distance. The horse raised its tail. Manure pelted the ground.

Charlotte lifted her skirts and stepped daintily around the offensive pile. She reached for the stirrup.

"Let me help you."

Charlotte thought of how the cowboy had looped his arm around Maria's waist. "I can do it myself."

"All right."

Charlotte put her foot in the stirrup and tried to haul herself up by the lower fork of the split pommel. The sorrel horse sidled away, causing Charlotte to hop in pursuit. She tried to remove her foot from the stirrup, but it had lodged there. She tugged back on the rein. The horse started to circle, jerking Charlotte around with it.

"You sure you don't want any help?"

"I can manage," Charlotte grunted. She fastened her hands tighter around the pommel and pulled with all her strength, ending up stomach down across the saddle.

She kicked one leg out and over, ending up astride as the horse started walking toward the corrals. Remembering what Jake had shown Maria, she pulled back on the reins, still seated precariously. The beast flung its head up and down and started to circle again.

Charlotte fought with her skirts, awkwardly clamping her leg over the forked pommel. At last she was seated properly, but by this time her horse was headed for the ditch at the edge of the property. She tried to shorten the reins but they slipped out of her hands. The sorrel stopped as suddenly as it had started, its neck dropping off in front of her as it started to graze.

Jake's laughter cut the air.

She managed to sit upright again, but the reins had dropped down over the sorrel's neck, out of reach. And so she sat, like a shipwrecked sailor, unable to go anywhere. Jake laughed so hard he dropped his crutch.

Fuming, Charlotte sat straighter in the saddle and lifted

70

her chin imperiously. "Perhaps when you have enjoyed your joke, you might do what you promised and teach me how to ride?"

Jake retrieved his crutches and hopped toward her, still laughing. He made a big show of lifting the horse's head up and handing Charlotte the reins. "You pull back like this," he said.

"I know what you do," Charlotte snapped.

"All right. Then let's get on with it." Wincing, Jake managed to hop back to the tree and lean against it.

Maria's bay, Charlotte noticed, behaved itself beautifully. Charlotte tried to emulate Maria, hauling back on the reins, but the horse apparently knew she wasn't boss. The animal tossed its head, trying to get to the grass. It was just like this man to give her the outlaw, and then laugh at her when she couldn't handle him.

"Jake, are you all right?" Maria asked. Charlotte followed her gaze.

Jake leaned against the tree, his eyes closed. When he opened them they were as dark as storm clouds against the stark whiteness of his face. He tried to smile. The place where his beard had been took on a blue cast in the sunlight. "I'm okay." He caught Charlotte's glance and added, "Don't you want to know your horse's name?"

"I suppose."

"Poco. That means *little* in Spanish."

The rest of the lesson was uneventful. Jake had them walk the horses in a cleared space of dirt in front of the cottonwood tree. It wasn't boring, exactly, but Charlotte thought she had grasped the mechanics of sitting on a horse at a walk. She wanted to gallop.

When she asked Jake when they would gallop, he replied, "When you can get on without making an idiot of yourself." Charlotte knew she should be grateful that he was willing to teach her at all, but the favoritism he showed Maria was beginning to rankle. He made such a big fuss over every little thing she did. "That's fine, Maria." "You're really catching on, Maria." "Maria, make sure you keep his head up or he'll try to eat." Jake virtually ignored Charlotte, who was doing at least as well. There was nothing to riding, once you got on. You just sat there and let your horse follow the one in front of you. So what? But it wouldn't hurt if Jake paid a little attention to her. Complimented her just once. She knew she looked elegant in her new riding habit. Why, any other man would be falling all over her.

At last Jake said, "That's enough for today. I don't want you to get saddle sore."

Charlotte blushed. The man had no tact. He didn't know how to talk to a real lady; that was plain.

Jake helped Maria down, his expression gentle. "That was very good for a first ride," he told her.

"It was wonderful!" Maria replied. She hugged the bay's neck, looking like a child on Christmas morning.

Jake swung his crutches out and pulled himself over to Charlotte. He leaned on one crutch and reached out his right hand.

Charlotte hesitated, then kicked her leg free from the pommel and slid toward him. Despite the fact that he could only use one arm, he lifted her as if she were a feather. Although the material of her habit was thick, she could feel his firm grip on her waist and the way his body momentarily sheltered her own. The sensation was similar to the time Morgan helped her down from the Earp wagon. But it wasn't the same. This was a cowboy, not the man she loved. Charlotte stiffened.

Jake dropped his arm but remained where he was, so close that she felt the urge to step back. His expression was impossible to read. Heart thumping, she hid her embarrassment by sweeping past him as if he were a servant. "Thank you, Jake."

"My pleasure."

* * *

After Charlotte's rather inauspicious beginning, she took to riding quickly. Jake was surprised at her persistence. She tried hard, concentrating on every little thing he told her. The girl was a born horsewoman. Maria, however, lagged far behind Charlotte after the first couple of days. She would rather talk than pay attention to what she was doing. This turnabout bothered Jake. He had pegged Maria as the one who would see things through, not Charlotte.

For Charlotte, the riding lessons became all-important. A fine lady must also be a fine horsewoman, and Charlotte turned her considerable energy to attaining that goal. But soon she discovered that there was more to riding than mere mastery. There was the joy of being outdoors every morning after the claustrophobic gloom of the Westphalia. She loved the power of Poco's muscles as he stretched in a trot or canter, loved the feeling of freedom it gave her. She could hardly wait to get to Emma Lake's every morning and start her lessons.

One morning, Charlotte walked into the parlor after dressing for her ride. Maria, still wearing her morning gown, sat before her black and silver sewing machine.

"Why aren't you dressed yet?"

"I'm not going today." Maria licked the twisted end of her thread and aimed it at the eye of the needle. "Thaddeus is coming by to get these curtains and I don't want to disappoint him."

"Thaddeus?"

"Thaddeus Marquart," Maria said patiently. "You met him the other day when we looked around his store."

Charlotte searched her memory. She remembered a man with thinning blond hair. "He's got that new store on Allen?"

Maria nodded. "I promised Thad I'd have them by noon." There was something proprietary in the way she'd said his name.

"I can't go alone."

"Roberto will walk you over."

"What will I tell Jake?"

Maria shrugged. "I've been thinking about it, and I don't know if I want to spend all my days riding. I'm not that good a rider, anyway. You're much better." She positioned the curtain and ran up a seam. "I thought I might help Thad mornings, at the store. There's so much to do."

As Roberto and Charlotte walked up Third Street, Charlotte mused that Maria was certainly running true to form. After seeing the way Wyatt Earp carried on with Sadie Marcus on the street the day the posse left town, she had expected Maria to transfer her affections to another man. But Charlotte had thought that man would be Jake.

Well, there was no accounting for taste. Personally, Charlotte thought that Jake was much better looking than the shopkeeper. Not for herself, of course. But another girl could do a lot worse.

When she arrived at Emma's, Charlotte was surprised to see Jake mounted on his grulla. He leaned his arms on the pommel and watched her. "Where's Maria?"

"She's busy."

After Roberto had assisted Charlotte into the saddle, Jake wheeled his horse around and rode toward the Charleston Road without looking back. Charlotte touched Poco and trotted to catch up. "Where are we going?"

"I thought we'd ride out toward the river."

"But what about my lesson?"

"It's time you started riding around the country a little bit, and I can't think of a better day than this one."

"Are you sure your leg is all right?"

"I have to start sometime."

They rode in silence. Charlotte found herself staring at Jake every once in awhile. She wondered if he had guessed why Maria hadn't come. Did he even care? It was hard to tell. In all this time he had dutifully given them riding lessons, listened to Maria's constant babbling, and yet Charlotte knew little more about him than she had when they first met. He never talked about himself, and if Maria asked him any personal questions, the cowboy always steered the conversation to something else.

Charlotte realized suddenly that she was in the company of a man she knew nothing about. "Maria couldn't come because she's sewing curtains for Mr. Marquart," she ventured.

Jake looked surprised at her attempt at conversation.

"I—I imagine she rather likes him," Charlotte added.

Jake grinned. "Oh, does she now?"

So Maria hadn't meant anything to him at all. "Don't you care?"

"Is he a good man?"

Charlotte slapped her crop against her boot. "I suppose."

"Then I'm happy for Maria."

"But I thought you and Maria—"

Jake looked at her again and she blushed. "Yes?"

"Never mind," Charlotte muttered.

Jake rode a little while longer, then asked unexpectedly, "Would you approve if Maria and I were more than friends?"

"I hardly think it's my place to judge."

"You're right about that."

Stung, Charlotte replied sharply, "I don't know why she likes you, anyway. You're not a patch on Wyatt Earp."

Jake grinned again. "I guess not. Too bad the Earp brothers don't stay in one place very long."

"What do you mean?"

"They're always charging out on some posse or other. It must be hard for the Earp women to keep the homefires burning."

Charlotte blushed. His insinuation was plain—he considered her one of the Earp women. Although in another man's mouth the statement might be flattering, clearly Jake Cottrell meant it as an insult.

"The Earps are doing their job! You certainly wouldn't risk your life on any posse."

"I wouldn't get very far with this leg." Jake reined his horse over to the side of the road as a mule team lumbered past. He swiveled in his saddle and stared at Charlotte. "Don't you wish Morgan would pay as much attention to you as he does those stage robbers?"

"You don't know anything. He—we happen to have a very special relationship." When Jake didn't reply, Charlotte shifted uncomfortably. It was obvious he didn't believe her. "I imagine you'll change your mind when Morgan and I marry."

"You've got a pretty good imagination if you think you'll come first with one of the Earps."

"What's that supposed to mean?"

"I've seen Morgan in action. His brothers come first. If he does marry you, prepare to be as unhappy as Mattie Blaylock."

Charlotte shivered as she thought of the plain woman with the hurt eyes—and Wyatt's obvious attraction to the beautiful Sadie Marcus. "Morgan isn't Wyatt," she said defiantly. "Besides, I'd want any husband of mine to stand up for what's right. He's only doing his duty."

"There are a few who think the Earps aren't on that posse for altruistic reasons."

"What do you mean?"

"You've heard the rumor that Doc Holliday was one of the stage robbers. It might be that the Earps want to get to those boys before they can be brought in to testify."

"Just what are you implying? That they'd shoot them down in cold blood just to protect Doc?"

Jake shrugged. "It's a theory."

"Well, I don't believe it. You just hate Doc because he tried to get you to fight and you wouldn't. While you sit on your hands, the Earps are risking their lives. When they bring Leonard, Crane, and Head in, you'll be laughing on the other side of your face!"

"Maybe so." Jake's tone was noncommittal. "Why don't we change the subject? I'm getting tired of the Earps." He turned off the main road and followed a horse path that wound around the Tombstone Hills. Because they rode single file, it was difficult to converse. No use trying to argue with him anyway, Charlotte thought. What would a cowboy know about honor, duty, or love? She decided to concentrate on the scenery. The topaz grasses rose almost to the horses' bellies, rustling in the breeze. Catclaw acacia, sleeved in harmless looking ruffles of dull green, tugged at her riding habit with hidden claws. Ahead of them, across the valley, Charlotte could see the Whetstone Mountains.

"Is that where your ranch is?" she asked.

"Yes."

"Emma said colts are being born there right now. I think they're so lovely, with those long legs and big eyes."

"You and Maria will have to come out and see them sometime."

Charlotte smoothed Poco's copper-penny neck, thinking how much she had grown to like the horses. She couldn't imagine how Maria could give up riding. "I don't think Maria will come. Not now that she's set her cap for Thaddeus Marquart."

"Then it'll have to be just you and me."

"I don't know . . ."

Jake twisted back to look at her. "You'll be perfectly safe. You're not my type at all."

Although Jake wasn't her type, either, Charlotte was insulted. Half the men in Tombstone were wild about her—including the wealthiest men from San Francisco and New York. But this cowboy found her wanting?

She decided then and there that she would make him want her. It shouldn't be too difficult; her experience at the Westphalia had shown her that. Men were easily led. She would make him desire her, and when he did, she would—

Well, she'd think about that later.

When Charlotte showed up the following day, Jake was sitting on the porch.

"I thought we were going riding."

"You go on ahead. My leg hurts today. Poco's saddled and ready in the corral."

Charlotte rode out a little way toward the river, but came back quickly. It just wasn't much fun without Jake as company. She had planned to flirt with him, and the fact that he'd stayed home took the wind out of her sails.

"How do you like my new hat?" Charlotte asked on the next occasion, tilting her head to show Jake her best side. She knew she made a fetching picture, the gray derby perched rakishly on her head.

"Very nice."

"Oh, Jake. You can think of something more flattering to say than that, can't you?" She glanced sideways at him under her thicket of lashes. No man at the Westphalia could resist her when she looked at him that way.

"You keep moving your head from side to side like that, you'll lose your balance and fall off that horse."

Charlotte didn't give up.

"Don't you find me the least bit attractive?" she asked one day as they watered their horses at the river.

"That's a silly question. Of course you're attractive."

"Could you, well, you know . . ."

"What?"

"Well," Charlotte said carefully, "half the men at the Westphalia are in love with me, and I just thought . . ."

"You thought?"

What was the matter with him? Was he really that dull-witted? Surely he knew what she was getting at. No gentleman would sit by and let her carry the brunt of such a delicate conversation! Angered now, she forgot to be coquettish. "If a man like Morgan Earp can fall in love with me, then surely a common cowpuncher like you should—" Her hand flew to her mouth. She couldn't very well order him to love her!

"Charlotte, are you asking me if I could fall in love with you?" He looked at her sharply. "What about Morgan Earp?" Her expression must have reinforced some hidden expectation, because when he spoke again his voice held firm conviction. "No, I couldn't love you. But I wouldn't let it concern you. You don't want me anyway."

If Jake seemed impervious to Charlotte's charms, the men at the Westphalia adored her. More than once Jamie mentioned how pleased Bob Euell was, implying that her patience would be rewarded. Charlotte construed that to mean that one of these days—perhaps the next time the show was revamped—Euell would put her on the stage. Jamie even asked Delia Delight to look out for her. At first, Delia was jealous of Charlotte's popularity, but Charlotte made it clear that she idolized the singer and wished to emulate her.

Flattered, Delia had decided to become Charlotte's mentor. She would be moving to Globe to live with her sister soon anyway. It might be interesting to groom a successor of her own choosing. The girl did have talent. So Delia gave Charlotte singing and acting lessons, and taught her all sorts of stage business.

Charlotte learned other things, too. Her ability to stay quiet and listen helped her when the other percentage girls were talking. Many of the waitresses supplemented their income by working in the cribs on Sixth Street, and they gossiped about their customers. Charlotte learned all about the prominent men of Tombstone; their weaknesses and their darkest secrets. One respectable banker with a wife and three children was particularly fond of Baby Dinkins, a pock-faced waitress who took him to her crib and beat him with a buggy whip. Charlotte thought this information might come in handy. On another occasion, a Cornish miner named Trevieghan admitted to Charlotte that he had let his partner fall down a mine shaft when he could have saved him. Weeks later Trevieghan's mine yielded up a lode of silver that made him a rich man overnight. If he remembered what he'd told Charlotte while he was in his cups, he didn't show it. Charlotte stored all this information in her head and waited for a time when she needed a favor.

She knew that a lowly percentage girl was still no match for a man like Edward Chesser. Revenge would have to wait. As long as nothing happened to the surgeon in the meantime, Charlotte could be patient. Delia's expression said it best: "Revenge is a dish best served cold."

Charlotte spent her mornings riding with Jake and her evenings in the nether world of the Westphalia. Although Jake's refusal to rise to the bait was frustrating, she found herself respecting him more. Instead of flirting, he talked to her the same way he talked to Emma Lake. He asked her questions about what she observed in town, and always listened carefully to her answers, as if her opinions mattered. It was a new experience for Charlotte, and she discovered that being taken seriously could be quite pleasant. Sooner or later his defenses would come down and she would captivate him with her beauty and charm. Until then, she could relax in his company and enjoy their rides.

They visited a horse ranch just over the bridge to Charleston. The sight of the foals' tiny bodies on stilt-like legs, their soft, innocent eyes and the way their tails flicked back and forth as they nursed, tugged at Charlotte's heart. She found herself smiling unguardedly at their playful antics, and caught Jake looking at her a few times, obviously pleased by her reaction. Embarrassed, Charlotte said, "Jake, stop grinning like that. You act as if you fathered those colts yourself!" She blushed and Jake laughed out loud.

"I like you, Charlotte. I really do."

"Really?" She used her best coquettish voice.

"Not like that."

"You certainly know how to make a girl feel ugly," Charlotte said, pouting.

"Nothing could make *you* feel ugly. Has Morgan come back from that wild-goose chase he's on yet?"

A cloud seemed to cover the sun. She missed Morgan so much. "No. He's still gone."

"Well, I expect they'll be back soon. Then you won't need me anymore." And he wheeled his horse and started riding toward the road.

They talked about a number of things: her early life in England, her dreams about San Francisco, the mares and colts and Jake's hopes for the Seep Springs Ranch. She knew he had been married before and his wife had died, but he never mentioned her. Charlotte instinctively shied from asking him questions about his wife, although she was intrigued by the thought of Jake as a married man. She realized that she had misjudged him. He wasn't one of the Galeyville crowd. She couldn't quite figure him out, but she knew he was honest.

For the first time in her life, Charlotte got to know a man as a human being. Not a convenience like Roberto and the men at the Westphalia, or an enemy like Edward Chesser, or even a hero like Morgan Earp—but a person. Never one to analyze her feelings, Charlotte did nothing with the information.

81

One morning in mid-May Jake told her that his leg was strong enough to return to Seep Springs. The next day, he was gone.

When Emma told her Jake had left for the ranch, Charlotte was stunned. She literally didn't know what to do with herself. Emma showed her how to saddle Poco, and she went for a ride, but it wasn't the same. Charlotte felt a curious void—and a small lump of anger. She couldn't help feeling that she had been abandoned again.

At the theater that night, Charlotte was snappish with her customers. Jamie took her aside.

"Charlotte, I know you miss Delia, but you can't act that way around the customers."

"Delia?"

"You didn't know? She took off with a miner name of Hurley this morning. He struck it rich and sold his mine for seventy thousand dollars. The star attraction of the Westphalia is gone."

Chapter Eight

Charlotte went to the theater before the show the following day. She found Jamie practicing the piano.

"What are you going to do tonight with Delia gone?"

"It's nice of you to worry about the show, Charlotte, but things will work out all right."

Charlotte took a deep breath. "Delia's been giving me singing lessons."

Jamie swiveled on the piano stool to face her. "You're

not expecting me to put you on stage, are you?" He looked sad. "Charlotte, Belinda will be singing tonight."

Charlotte's heart lurched in her chest. Belinda was Bob Euell's wife. She had just returned from a stint with a theatrical company in St. Louis last week. Charlotte stared at him, unable to say anything.

Jamie stood up and took her hands in his own. "I know you'd like to get a chance to sing on the stage, and maybe sometime in the future we'll give it a try. But right now, I'm afraid it's impossible. Bob wants to keep you on the floor. You're making him a lot of money—more than he ever dreamed was possible.

"It's you, Charlotte. You're special. We can't afford to move you to the stage. Men want to pay to sit with you, to have you to themselves. We wouldn't get anywhere near as many patrons if they had to . . . share you with others. Don't you see?"

Charlotte's voice shook. "I see, all right. You never intended to put me on stage, did you?"

"You were hired as a pretty waiter."

"All those times you told me what a draw I was, all the times you said I'd be rewarded . . ." She couldn't continue.

Jamie drew back and busied himself with the sheet music on the piano. "I'm sorry, Charlotte, but Mr. Euell wants you to stay on the floor."

"And he wants his horse-faced wife onstage!"

Jamie's voice hardened. "I'd watch what I say, if I were you. The decision's been made, and you can't do anything to change it."

The thought of sitting next to one more smelly lecher in that claustrophobic room was unbearable. "I quit, then," she said. She turned and stalked for the door.

For Charlotte, the week stretched interminably. With Maria in tow, she had gone to two other legitimate theaters in town: the Empire and the Turnverein. The owner of the Turnverein had explained that Bob Euell supplied liquor to every theater in town. Nobody would touch her.

But as it turned out, there was one theater Euell had overlooked.

On the way home from a fruitless audience with the owner of the Empire, Charlotte saw an unfamiliar buggy standing outside their house. It was a fine black buggy, obviously very expensive. A man dressed in a Prince Albert stood at the horse's head, feeding it sugar.

The man noticed Maria and Charlotte when they were several yards away and turned to greet them. Charlotte's heart skipped a beat before she realized that the man was not Edward Chesser. He had the same beard, the same broad nose, but his expression was openly curious and devoid of recognition.

He left the horse and walked over to her. "You must be Charlotte Tate," he said, bowing over her hand. "You are as beautiful as they say."

Maria gave him a dirty look and said to Charlotte, "I'll go feed Ruff."

The man removed his bowler and flattened his thinning hair with the heel of his hand. "My name is Jerome Pike. I have some business to discuss with you, something that I hope will be mutually enriching to both of us." As he saw Charlotte's wary look he added quickly, "I have a theater." He smiled in a self-deprecatory way. "It's a small concern, newly on the Tombstone scene."

Charlotte waited for him to say more, a tactic she had learned from her time spent at the Westphalia. People always revealed more about themselves when confronted by silence. They rushed to fill the void.

Jerome Pike licked his lips. "I confess I am quite thirsty. Perhaps we could discuss my proposition out of the sun." He stuck one finger in his stand-up collar, trying to keep it from choking him. Sweat trickled down his face. Charlotte wondered how the man could wear that hot black coat on a warm spring day in Arizona. She led him into the house and drew him some water.

He scanned the room and chose to sit on the plum-colored sofa. "What a lovely room," he said.

Charlotte smiled. She had made many improvements since starting work at the Westphalia. Lace curtains replaced sacking at the windows, and a tufted chair matched the davenport. Dried flower arrangements and lace doilies covered every possible surface. She had even managed to purchase an oriental carpet from a restaurant that had gone out of business. Charlotte sat on the chair now, tucking her feet under the hem of her white lawn walking dress. "You have a theater," she prompted.

"Yes." Pike leaned forward, elbows denting knees as soft and plump as feather pillows, and inched his fingers around the brim of his hat. "Permit me to be blunt. I have heard of your recent troubles, and that has encouraged me to approach you. I know that a person of your unquestionable dominance as a, er, femme fatale, would normally never be interested in a such a small theater, but . . ." he paused delicately. "I have heard you are an actress." He opened his arms wide. "I am offering you a chance to act."

Maria entered through the back door.

Charlotte stared at the man. Cigar ash dusted his shirtfront. She didn't like his personal habits, but what did that have to do with a job? Here was her chance to appear onstage, and show the Westphalia up at the same time. "What would I be doing?" she asked softly.

"Anything you wish. We would mount the production around you."

Maria asked, "What production?"

The man ignored her and spoke to Charlotte. "We have a fine musical director. He has just come down from Prescott."

"How would I be paid?"

"Twice what you received at the Westphalia. Plus commission."

"Commission?"

"We would, ah, expect you to mingle with the, er, customers between acts."

"You mean get them to buy drinks."

"I believe that was your primary task at the Westphalia."

"Where is this theater?" Maria asked.

Jerome Pike addressed Charlotte. "I have a card."

Charlotte glanced at it. "El Dorado Theater and Amusement Hall. Jerome Pike, proprietor."

Maria grabbed the card away from Charlotte. "Let me see that." She looked at it briefly and then glared at Pike. "It's on Sixth Street. Charlotte, you can't possibly take this man up on his offer!" That was among the cribs!

Charlotte silenced Maria with a look. "Is this a legitimate theater, Mr. Pike?"

Jerome Pike said gravely, "You have my word on it, Miss Tate."

Charlotte stood and held out her hand. "I'll have to think about it."

"Charlotte!" Maria cried. "You can't go on that side of town! That's the—"

"I know what it is."

"The Hutchinsons—you must have heard of them, they are legitimate theater people—are planning to build a theater on the corner," offered Mr. Pike. "The area is the coming thing. The er . . . frail denizens of Sixth Street won't be there for long. Sixth and Allen will be the new theater district, mark my words."

"I'll think about it," Charlotte said.

Jerome Pike walked to the door. He coughed politely. "I have to have an answer by the end of this week."

"You shall."

"Excellent. And may I say, Miss Tate, you are every

bit as gracious as you are beautiful." He bowed out the door.

"You can't be serious!" Maria said as soon as the door closed.

"I'm perfectly serious." Charlotte walked into the bedroom and put the card on the dresser.

"That man is out to take advantage of you."

She whirled on Maria. "What's it to you, anyway? You're the one who flaunts convention, not me."

"There's a fine line between having a good time and getting in over your head. I know where that line is."

"I am an actress, and I am going to act," Charlotte said, her voice hard. "No one else is beating down my door." She sat on the bed. "I'll show them. Jamie, Bob Euell, Belinda, all of them. I'll make the El Dorado the biggest name in Tombstone. You'll see."

"I hope for your sake you are right," Maria said darkly.

Charlotte snapped, "Be quiet. You're not going to spoil this for me."

Maria threw up her hands. "You are very stubborn, Charlotte. One of these days your stubborn nature will get you in trouble."

"Or make me rich." Charlotte hugged a pillow to her chest, and thought about the production the El Dorado would mount around her.

Just one short week later, Charlotte finally realized her dream of singing onstage before an audience.

It was not the wonderful experience she had expected. Her voice could barely be heard above the buzzing crowd of gamblers and cowboys who packed the El Dorado Theater and Amusement Hall.

At first she didn't notice; she was too frightened to notice anything but the dryness of her mouth and an overwhelming urge to swallow. She had learned so much from

Delia, but everything flew out of her head the moment she set foot on the boards. Locking her knees had no effect on the trembling of her legs; she felt as if her whole body shuddered from the cold. Her heart surged through her chest like a locomotive, and her throat closed when Krenz played the introduction to her first song—just as it had when she'd auditioned for Bob Euell.

Clenching her jaw to keep her teeth from chattering, Charlotte tried to ignore the need to swallow in the middle of each word. The more she thought about it, the more swallowing became imperative.

In a small corner of her brain, a voice cried in despair, *What have I done*? She had put herself in this position. Volunteered. She could just as easily stop now, walk behind the canvas backdrop, and never come back. Give up. No one would care.

No one but herself. All the practice, the boasting, the firm conviction that she would make it, all would come to nothing if she didn't stand up and face these people here and now. Charlotte squared her shoulders, lifted her chin, and tried to concentrate on what Delia had taught her. The audience wasn't watching; she didn't have to worry about them. She might as well be singing to her wall in the little house on Fremont Street.

That knowledge angered her, freeing the lock on her throat. By the end of the second number, she had loosened up and her arms came away from her sides. By the third song Charlotte played to the gallery like a veteran. Hardly anyone seemed to notice.

One person did, though. Jerome Pike stood at the back of the theater, arms folded across his massive girth. His sharp eyes caught everything. The girl's abject terror when she'd first appeared onstage, turning to white-faced determination as she worked at quelling her stage fright, to triumph as she conquered it. He admired that. She had sand.

He squashed his cigar into a cuspidor at his feet and

88

sighed. He admired sand, but it was not a bankable commodity.

He had ways to offset that particular personality problem. He just hoped he didn't have to break her spirit completely.

Chapter Nine

A hot wind rattled the rafters of the adobe theater on Sixth and Toughnut. As Charlotte and Roberto walked up the broad dirt avenue, dust puffed up from their feet.

In the west, the sun swam above the Mustang Mountains like a poached egg, surrounded by a scrim of white. It had been so hot lately that Charlotte's clothes seemed to wilt the moment she put them on, fresh from the bath she insisted on having every day. The bottom of her skirts were grimy and tinged green from the manure-stained ground. Her flesh crawled with perspiration under the stays of her yellowing corset; the French coutil had yellowed despite the fact that she soaked it in bluing every night. It was this awful dust, mixed with perspiration, that ground in the discolor. Her whole body felt slick in this heat. Sometimes she caught whiffs from the underarms of her dresses, a stale odor underlying the lilac water she had sprinkled all over her upper body.

Today had been particularly bad: hot and still with barely enough air to breathe, until just before sunset when the dust had kicked up, powdering her white lawn dress with a fine brown coating. Her lips were dry and cracked, and she could taste grit between her teeth.

How could she have forgotten the desert heat? It blasted the town like a furnace, leaving everyone dispirited and tired all the time. She had given up her rides on Poco. The mornings were too hot to ride, and besides, Emma never lost a chance to express her disapproval of Charlotte's move to the El Dorado. It was better to avoid those unpleasant scenes altogether.

She was so intent on picking her way around the horse apples in the road that she didn't hear the riders. Roberto nudged her, and she looked up just as the Earp posse rode up and dismounted before the marshal's office.

Charlotte froze. All the waiting, the dreaming, the hoping, came down to this moment! Morgan was back at last! Hastily, she snatched the lace-edged handkerchief tucked in her sleeve, wet it with spittle, and wiped her face. Heart pounding in her chest, she stood on the opposite corner to watch. Roberto hunkered down a short distance away, her silent shadow.

The Earps' horses were streaked with dried sweat and dust. They looked as if they had each dropped a hundred pounds. For once, Wyatt, Morgan, and Virgil didn't look crisp and clean. Weariness evident in every bone, the bedraggled party stepped down from their mounts and tied them to the hitching post. They walked like sailors just getting used to land. How drawn and tired Morgan looked! Charlotte felt a pang of motherly instinct for the man she loved.

A couple of other riders pulled up, obscuring Morgan from view. All the posse had come in by now.

Where were the bad men? Charlotte had pictured them often enough; they would be sullen and slumped in defeat, hands manacled before them. She saw no one of that description. Briefly, she remembered what Jake said about the Earps wanting Leonard, Crane, and Head dead rather than alive. Had they killed the robbers after all?

The mayor of Tombstone walked out to meet them, shaking hands with Virgil Earp. "Johnny came in two weeks ago. Hope you had better luck."

"We were too late. Two of 'em got killed over near Hachita. Hazlett brothers shot 'em. No sign of the other one."

John Clum removed his derby and passed a hand over his balding pate. "Well, there's more pressing problems, I guess. Ben Sippy ran off with the tax money."

Wyatt Earp whistled. "You don't say."

"Virge, we'd like to name you acting marshal, if you want the job. I wouldn't blame you if you turned it down, seeing how this town treated you in the election."

Stolid, walrus-mustached Virgil Earp didn't hesitate. "I'll take it, and be glad of it."

Morgan leaned against a porch post and dusted his hat against his leg. His face was grimy, almost black, a contrast to the bright blue eyes that scanned the street. His fine reddish gold mustache was dulled by a coat of dust. He spotted Charlotte, straightened, and grinned. For a moment it looked as if he might come over and talk to her, but then Doc Holliday clapped Morgan on the back and started talking to him. A few moments later, the Earp party filed into the marshal's office.

Roberto touched Charlotte's arm hesitantly. "You'll be late."

Reluctantly, Charlotte followed him. There would be plenty of time for a reunion later. Morgan was first and foremost a lawman. She imagined that Morgan had more important things on his mind right now than matters of the heart.

"You see that little pigeon across the street?" Doc asked Morgan as they sprawled wearily in the chairs of the marshal's office. "She sure noticed you."

"I could feel the heat from where I was standing," Wyatt said.

"Girls are always making sheep's eyes at Morg." Marsh Williams shoved Morgan's hat down over his eyes. "He's just so darned pretty."

"You boys are just jealous." Morgan had seen the girl, too; he never missed a pretty one. She looked familiar.

"I'm going to the bathhouse," Wyatt announced. "You comin', Virge?"

"In a minute."

Morgan got up to follow his brother. Suddenly, it came to him where he'd seen her: the race. He had gone out of his way to meet her. What was her name? Charlotte something.

He stretched his arms and popped his knuckles. *I just might look her up.*

Even if she weren't willing, he could think of worse ways to spend an evening than cadging a few squeezes and kisses from a looker like that. But as he started out of the marshal's office, he collided with Virgil's wife, Allie. She was one female he wanted no truck with.

"Where you goin', Morg?"

"I thought I'd go get a bath."

"And then what?" She didn't wait for an answer. "Before you go traipsing off to the first faro parlor you come to, you ought to know your wife's here."

"Lou?"

"You got another wife I don't know about? She's been here two weeks."

"Well, I'll be."

"You be sure to come straight home, Morg!" Allie called after him.

Morgan needed no persuasion from Allie. The idea of seeing Lou again excited him. Maybe she was well again. She had traveled all the way from California, and an invalid wouldn't stand the trip.

As he walked to the bathhouse, Morgan pictured Louisa Houston on their wedding day, in the full flower of her Scandinavian beauty. He always had admired blond women.

He didn't give Charlotte another thought.

* * *

"Thank you, Roberto," Charlotte said. Roberto nodded and melted into the shadows.

Excitement coursed through her veins. Morgan was back! She started to shake, partially from adrenaline and partially from the nerves that overtook her every night. But the immediate problem—appearing onstage—overtook her elation.

The evening sun had turned into a bloodshot eye. Pausing at the theater entrance, she felt the tautness in her stomach, like a tiny wire deep inside, tugging. Soon, she knew, the familiar urge to vomit would overcome her, and she would go under the pepper tree near the side door and be sick as unobtrusively as possible. It happened every night without fail; a kind of purging. After that, she could go onstage with only a mild nervousness. She took out her handkerchief and stepped through the herringbone pattern of pepper-tree leaves.

A hand whipped out and closed over her mouth, mashing her lips flat. Her scream was muffled as another hand wrenched her shoulder backward, dragging her off her feet. A body fell on top of her, as unyielding and heavy as a tree stump. The hand on her shoulder transferred to her breast, squeezing it so hard she nearly passed out. She kicked out blindly, hearing a muffled curse as her boot connected. The smell of him assaulted her nostrils—like rancid meat and chicken soup. She flailed underneath him, coughing on the dust and the sweat-stench of his palm.

"You said you'd share!" shouted another voice near her ear. Her heart was quaking so hard she thought it would burst.

"You wouldn't like her. Stringy as a jackrabbit haunch."

"Then let me have her. It don't matter what she looks like."

"Just a minute." Thick fingers fumbled up between her legs and jerked at the waistband of her drawers. One hand slithered down her hip, kneading and jabbing her flesh, searching for something. Revulsion filled her mouth like a briny tide, galvanizing her. She twisted and squirmed, kicking every chance she could.

"Hold her, will you?" her captor grunted. Charlotte bit the hand clamped over her mouth.

He howled and jerked away, then one huge paw swiped out and clouted her across the face. Blood, warm and sticky, ran down from her nostrils. Her ears rang and tears filled her eyes.

"You scrawny whore! That'll teach you to bite me!"

"Hurry up! Someone's coming," the other man whispered.

"You there! Get away from her!"

The man on top of her scrambled to his feet. She heard their gasps as they pelted away.

"Let's get you inside." It was Jerome Pike's voice. He led her to the rear entrance of the El Dorado, and took her into his office. After wiping her face with a handkerchief, he handed her some brandy. "Drink this."

She grimaced, but drank it down.

"This is insufferable!" Pike exclaimed. "That a young lady should be accosted on the street in plain view! The scum!" He walked to the window and squared his shoulders. "This distasteful incident has made me see that you are my responsibility, one I must not shirk."

Charlotte, still numb from the attack, stared at him. What was he talking about?

Jerome Pike paused, his expression regretful. "To be honest, my dear, I've had my doubts about keeping you on. I was going to tell you tonight."

Charlotte couldn't believe her ears. "Doubts?"

He patted her on the shoulder. "Never mind. I can see that now is, ah, not the time for such a conversation. You're quite shaken up. You don't have to worry. You'll always have a place here, whether I keep you on the stage or not. My, my, you've got a split lip." He dabbed at her mouth.

"I don't understand. What are you talking about?"

"Well, my dear, you've been somewhat of a, well, shall we say a disappointment? Not that you haven't worked hard! But the customers have been complaining. They want to see a girl with a little, er, meat on her bones."

Charlotte stared at him. The words of her attackers still rang in her ears. Stringy as a jackrabbit haunch. *Scrawny whore*.

"Now you run along home. You don't have to perform tonight, not after what happened to you. We'll, ah, talk about any changes we should make later this week."

Charlotte rose stiffly to her feet. "I'm going to perform, unless you have an objection."

"No objection," Pike replied quickly. "Maybe it would be good for you. Take your mind off . . . well, you know."

Gathering her skirts, Charlotte walked to the office door, head held high. But her body still trembled, and she couldn't help feeling filthy.

When she was gone, Jerome Pike sat back in his chair, laced his hands over his stomach and smiled. It had been well worth the money he paid those two ruffians, just to put a few doubts into Charlotte Tate's pretty head.

A loud snap, and the needle of the American sewing machine splintered.

Maria straightened and sighed, her gaze falling on the stiff canvas awning cascading down from the sewing machine onto the carpet. Her shoulders ached. "If I have to thread one more needle, I'll be cross-eyed for life."

Charlotte, wearing a brown grenadine dress patterned with cream-colored polka dots, emerged from their room. A crush of black dresses lay like wilted roses over one arm.

"What are you doing?"

"Getting rid of these!" Charlotte announced, throwing her mourning dresses on the horsehair sofa.

"It's about time. The closet is so full of your new clothing I can't find space for my own. . . ." She trailed off as she noticed that Charlotte was still standing over the black dresses, her posture a study in dejection.

"It's Mary, isn't it? She died in June?"

Charlotte turned slowly. Maria was shocked at what she saw. How could she not have noticed the delicate blue shadows under her friend's eyes? And Charlotte—always unfashionably slender—looked even thinner. She must have seen the pity in Maria's eyes, because her chin came up and she smiled bravely.

"Three years ago today," she said.

Impulsively, Maria hugged her friend. "I'm so sorry."

For a moment, Charlotte returned her hug with a ferocity that surprised her, then shrank away. "It's all right," she said with a forced brightness. "I miss her, but it's getting easier all the time." She adjusted the sleeve of her overjacket. "Mary would be so proud of me. I made it to the stage, just as I promised her I would. I did it for her." She paused, as if there was something wrong with what she had said, then added fiercely, "And for me."

It was true. She wanted to be an actress more than anything. More, even, than marrying Morgan Earp.

She closed her eyes, but could not blot out the image of Mary, first at their little mining shack up in the Bradshaw mountains, and later in the garden at the Connor house, spinning stories of how famous Charlotte would become. And how rich they would be. Sometimes Mary had punctuated her stories with sips from a slender blue bottle, to "calm her nerves." As time went by, the intervals between sips became shorter. Edward Chesser had introduced her to the laudanum early on in their courtship; not long before her death Mary went through a bottle every other day.

It hadn't seemed important. A lot of women took laudanum.

Charlotte recalled how they would go into town to see the train come in, how they'd watch the ladies disembark in their satins, silks, and other finery. "Someday, you and I will be far better off than them," Mary would tell her. "You will be the toast of America and Europe. You will be a more famous beauty than Lily Langtree."

Mary and her daydreams, Charlotte thought sadly. The night Mary died—during the argument just before they'd gone to Chesser's house—Katherine had called her foolish, gullible. She'd told Mary to get her head out of the clouds and that she was doing Charlotte no great service, making her think she could rise above her station.

And when Mary had told her she was marrying Edward Chesser and the three of them would be going off to start a new life in San Francisco, Katherine had laughed. "Everyone knows about Edward Chesser. He's nothing but a dissolute old rogue, and a famous one at that! You'll be back! And I'll have to take you in again."

But she was wrong about that. Mary had never made it back. Her heart, already overburdened by the laudanum, had given out and she had died of shame and shock on the floor of Edward Chesser's home. She had died, Charlotte thought, of a broken heart.

Much later, when Charlotte returned from the resale shop, she found herself standing before the full-length mirror attached to the door of the armoire.

Where were Mary's dreams now? Harsh reality stared back at Charlotte from the wavy old mirror, and for the first time in her life she was unable to take refuge in the web of airy fantasies Mary had spun for her.

Pike had promised her lots more money than the Westphalia paid, but so far she hadn't seen a cent, except for the tips she made on the floor. Those hadn't been all that good; most of the men at the El Dorado didn't spend money, unless the girl was willing to go into a back room with them. The only bright spot of the week was the night Doc Holliday came in. Just being in the presence of Morgan's friend had cheered her up. Doc had a lot of charisma when sober and could be a real charmer. That night he had been chivalrous and witty, and made Charlotte feel pretty again. He had even given her a new name: the Tombstone Rose.

The Tombstone Rose. She didn't feel like a rose today. Staring at the mirror, Charlotte wondered if Maria was right. Was she even thinner than before?

Fortunately, Jerome Pike hadn't said anything more about taking her off the stage, but he let her know in a number of ways how displeased he was with her. "You're looking haggard, my dear. Is anything wrong? . . . We'll have to get out the paint pot, put some color on those sharp cheekbones. You aren't a beauty, not in the accepted sense." His bumbling good nature had flown, replaced by sharp speculation. "It's that pointed chin. Makes you look a bit like a witch, my dear . . . I must confess I don't see what all the furor was about. You certainly don't draw the crowds here." Her acting was bad, her voice even worse. He often wondered aloud what had ever possessed him to lure her to the El Dorado.

Charlotte leaned forward, staring at the mirror. She tried to be objective, even critical. Try as she would, she could discern no difference in her looks. A little tired around the eyes, maybe, but that was all.

"If only you could sing. An audience will sometimes forgive a paucity of looks if the voice is fine enough."

Charlotte's mind closed down on Pike's words. What a load of rubbish! Hadn't Delia herself said she was a talented singer? Why couldn't she believe her own ears, her own eyes? The men at the Westphalia had fallen over each other for her company.

Except that didn't happen anymore. The men at the El Dorado didn't pay any attention to her performance. Except to whistle and shout at her and make obscene propositions.

Was that really what life was like for a woman in

Tombstone? Was a woman really only worth her looks, as Pike told her several times a day? He had made other insinuations, couched though they were in fatherly advice. Insinuations that there were certain types of women who seemed to attract violence to their persons. Perhaps it was a lack of modesty—or worse, something deep in their souls, a thing so black and evil that they themselves did not know it. Something unspeakably dirty . . .

Charlotte shuddered. Men had not attacked her just once, but—counting that minor tussle outside the Can Can—three times. Could she really carry with her something so horrible that men could see it?

Nonsense! She would not believe such a thing! Pike was only trying to throw her, for some twisted purpose of his own. Perhaps that was the way he kept performers under his thumb; she'd seen him do it to other people. Charlotte felt some of her old resolve returning. She would show Pike. She would draw the crowds in; she would prove that she was star material.

But the girl who stared back at her from the mirror looked lackluster and tentative, and frankly, just a bit plain.

Chapter Ten

Sixto Acevedo, the foreman of the Seep Springs outfit, was surprised when Jake Cottrell decided to accompany him into Tombstone on a routine trip for supplies, but Jake wanted to visit Emma and pay her for the time he stayed with her.

Over ham, eggs, and biscuits, Emma caught Jake up on

the happenings in Tombstone. They were almost through breakfast when he asked as casually as he could, "How's Charlotte?"

Emma's mouth hardened into a stubborn line. "Haven't seen her much since she moved to the El Dorado."

"The El Dorado?"

"One of those so-called amusement halls on Sixth Street. You know the kind. Most of the amusement goes on in the back rooms. She's performing on the stage there."

"You think she's all right?"

"She can take care of herself, if anyone can. But you walk through a pigsty often enough, you're bound to get a little muck on you."

"She hired on as an actress?"

"Yes, but I wouldn't put it past that Pike feller to change the rules in the middle of the game."

"*Jerome* Pike?" Jake asked sharply.

"He's the owner of the El Dorado. You know him?"

"Not personally." Troubled, Jake sipped his coffee. He had heard about Jerome Pike. The man had been run out of California for procuring.

Jake glanced at the horses eating breakfast in the corral. Despite Emma's protestations to the contrary, he knew she was worried. Setting his napkin down on his plate, he leveled his gaze on her. "Can I borrow your horses this morning?"

"Charlotte!" Maria called. "Jake's here!"

"Jake?" What was Jake doing in town? Charlotte glanced in the dresser mirror, hastily straightening the Valenciennes lace collar on her white muslin dress.

Lifting her skirts, she ran to the front door and stopped, taking a deep breath. She waited, hoping her heart would slow down a little, but impatience got the better of her. She opened the door.

Jake sat astride the bay horse Cricket and held Poco,

saddled and waiting. Swinging down from his mount, Jake stood between the two horses, a grin warming his face. "Hello, Charlotte."

Charlotte didn't think. Her response was swift, visceral. She hurtled into his arms, almost knocking him off his feet. Jake's arm folded around her back and he hugged her hard, crushing her to the solid wall of his chest. For an instant Charlotte felt a relief so deep that tears formed in her eyes. At that moment she didn't care about anything— what Jake thought of her, how her greeting might appear to passersby, her apparent lack of dignity. Heartsore and lonely beyond words, Charlotte succumbed to the comfort his arms gave her.

The moment passed too quickly. Jake took hold of her wrists and gently pushed her away, his gaze searching. "What have I done to warrant a greeting like this?"

His words broke the spell. Charlotte stared at him, suddenly horrified by her impulsive action. How could she have done such a thing? One did not hug a man in public. She had just made a complete fool of herself.

Jake's expression was gentle. "It's good to see you, Charlotte."

Mortified, Charlotte didn't trust herself to speak. The tears that had started in her eyes slithered unshed into her throat.

"Do you want to go for a ride?"

She nodded.

"I hope you're not expecting to ride in that." He motioned to her dress.

"No, of course not." She whirled and ran for the house.

As Jake made small talk with Maria, he found his mind wandering. Charlotte's exuberant greeting had completely thrown him off balance.

He felt the urge to clasp her in his arms again, fill the emptiness that burrowed like a phantom wind into his chest. His senses reeled with the memory of her closeness, the smell of her—lemon water and Pears soap. The crisp-ness of her dress, even in this wilting heat, the pressure of her taut breasts straining against the thin muslin material of her bodice. He was surprised by the emotion that coursed through him, filling his throat. Why had she done this to him?

When Charlotte emerged from the house in her riding habit, her manner had changed again. She looked self-pos-sessed, unapproachable. He boosted her into the saddle. Charlotte gathered her skirts daintily, bestowing on him a charming but distant smile.

So, he thought. She's in control of herself again.

As they rode out toward the river, they talked about inci-dental things, occasionally lapsing into long, uncomfort-able silences. It was almost as if her one show of emotion had changed things between them irrevocably, in a way Jake didn't understand. Her actions confused him utterly. One minute she was hurling herself into his arms, truly glad to see him, and the next, she had retreated to a place he could not reach.

It was not his imagination. She had changed. The change in her was subtle; if he didn't know her so well he wouldn't have noticed. For one thing, she didn't flirt with him any-more. Although he had always steeled himself against her flirtations, stubbornly refusing to become one of her ardent admirers, he found himself missing that playfulness now.

They followed a horse path to a bend in the San Pedro River that concealed the bustling towns from view. It was quiet here, the cottonwood trees rustling above them, their glossy heart-shaped leaves green in their summer fullness. The river ran more swiftly than usual from the spring snow melt in the mountains.

Jake assisted Charlotte down from the saddle, and they crossed the bank of the river to a cushion of bright green grass that grew in the shade of the mesquite, ash, and cottonwoods. Charlotte stared at the water, avoiding Jake's eyes. Was she still embarrassed about hugging him?

"I've missed our rides," Jake ventured.

"Me, too."

"About this morning—"

She looked him straight in the eye. Her voice was like ice. "I wouldn't entertain any notions, if I were you. I was just greeting an old friend."

The ground rules were clear. She chose to cover her embarrassment by turning on him. This was the Charlotte he remembered, the one who had no qualms about trampling other people's feelings. How could he have forgotten? "Emma says you've gone over to the El Dorado."

Charlotte nodded.

"Why didn't you stay at the Westphalia?"

"They wouldn't put me on the stage."

Jake debated whether to say anything, and decided he might as well be honest. "I wouldn't trust this fellow Pike."

"It's none of your business what I do," she said stiffly.

Jake grinned. A sore spot. "He's got a nasty reputation."

"For your information, Jerome Pike saved my life last week."

"Did he?"

"Yes. He drove off two men who"—she blushed—"attacked me in an alley."

"You seem to have a proclivity for getting into trouble of that nature."

Anger boiled up in Charlotte. Was it her fault that the men in this territory were little better than animals? "I'm getting rather tired of it, as a matter of fact. The men around here think that women are theirs for the taking."

"Pike's the worst of the lot."

"He saved me."

"Maybe he saved you for something worse."

"What are you saying?"

"He's a mac. You do know what a *maquereau* is, don't you?"

"Of course I do!" Charlotte knew that Pike pimped for some of his percentage girls, but she couldn't see the difference between the El Dorado and the Westphalia in that regard. There were always women of that sort around theaters, but it had nothing to do with the performers. She told Jake so.

"How old are you, Charlotte?"

"I'll be nineteen in August." What did age have to do with it?

"You're such an innocent."

"I am not! I know what's what! Emma put you up to this, didn't she? She's still trying to tell me what to do, treating me as if I were . . . as if I were a puppet on a string! Well, I'm old enough to make my own decisions. I don't need you and I don't need Emma, so just leave me alone!"

Suddenly, Jake was angry. Didn't she understand that there were bigger issues than independence? She made a fine show of talking about soiled doves but he doubted she understood the hard reality of their existence. Here she stood on the brink of a wretched life, eager to throw herself off into oblivion. The frontier was always cruelest to those who lacked respect for its treachery. He wanted to slap some sense into her. "Do you have any idea what you're getting into?"

"I can take care of myself! And if you don't like it, you can take a flying leap into that stream!" She stood up and strode toward her horse. Poco, sensing her anger, shied away, and Charlotte misjudged her step, toppling into the water.

She started to stand, but the swift current knocked her to her knees. Jake waded out and held out his hand. She grabbed it, eyes flashing her defiance. Leaning on his hand, Charlotte stepped unsteadily toward him, then froze.

"What's the matter?"

"My foot's stuck."

Jake waded closer and reached down into the water to pry the rock away. But as the rock tore loose, Charlotte lost her balance and she started to totter. Jake grabbed her before she fell, hoisted her into his arms and deposited her on the grass.

She sat there, looking bedraggled and helpless—and incredibly beautiful. Did she know what a picture she made? He had the impression that Charlotte thought of men as little more than chained bears—not too bright and dangerous only when unshackled. Her childish notion of chivalry was not likely to protect her from people like Jerome Pike.

Charlotte sorted out her sodden skirts and wiped the moisture from her face with the heel of her hand. Her hair had come free and fell in cinnamon-dark ribbons around her bodice. Looking at her, anger whirled up inside Jake like a vortex.

She rose to her feet and smiled at him, her own annoyance forgotten. "Thank—"

Jake grabbed her shoulders roughly and bent her face up to his, kissing her hard.

Caught off guard, Charlotte forgot to struggle—forgot everything, in fact, as a bolt of shocked pleasure shot up through her body. Sensations bombarded her, dizzying in their intensity: the feel of his lips—initially hard, resistant, but increasingly pliant. His hands transferred to her wrists, gripping them firmly, sending currents of excitement into every part of her being. She shouldn't allow this. It was wrong, all wrong, but Charlotte found herself wanting the kiss to continue, craving the feel of his lips against hers, reveling in the way he molded himself against her breasts, eliciting pinpoints of warm, sensual pleasure. His broad chest seemed to expand like an eagle's unfurling wings, encompassing her in such a feeling of safety, of belonging, that she wanted to merge with him and keep him close to her forever. She could feel his beating heart against her own, meeting with a kinetic force she could hardly fathom. And the smell of him—so clean—of horses and leather and fresh grass. It was all so different from the men at the El Dorado. Emotion welled up inside her, and once again she was a lonely, frightened child living in a foreign land, turning to the one source of comfort she knew.

Abruptly, Jake pulled away. Charlotte's lips tingled with the ghost of his kiss, craving more. She opened her eyes.

But Jake's expression did not mirror her emotions. His eyes were dark with anger. The warm feeling of being secure, loved, fled in an instant, leaving only adrenaline that flooded every extremity. Charlotte quivered like a bow that had finally let the arrow fly.

Jake cupped her head with his hand and leaned again to kiss her. Hurt and confused, Charlotte struck out. She slapped his face hard.

Jake drew back and touched his cheek. "I'm sorry," he said. "I must have lost my head."

Charlotte's voice had difficulty gaining purchase. "I want to go home now."

"All right." Jake stood up and helped her to her feet. He caught up Poco and held him while Charlotte placed her foot in the stirrup. She could feel the warmth of Jake's body near her, and when he hoisted her into the saddle she shivered, suddenly wanting the hard stamp of his lips on hers again. But the spell had been broken, and she could resist him now.

How could she have let him kiss her like that? It was so confusing. She loved Morgan, not Jake.

Jake mounted and wordlessly turned his horse for home. They rode back in silence. By the time they got back, the fierce June sun had dried Charlotte's habit completely.

* * *

At the Silver Dollar, Jake poured water from the nightstand onto his hands and scrubbed his face. He could still feel the imprint of Charlotte's lips on his, and the desire like a banked fire in the depths of his body.

He couldn't get the morning out of his mind, as much as he wanted to. He'd meant to shock her with that kiss to show her what she could expect if she continued to work for Pike. He thought that if she realized she was getting in over her head, she would run for Emma's apron strings. But it hadn't worked out that way. Jake had always thought she would be cold as ice, her lips carved out of porcelain, but they were warm and alive.

He wondered if Morgan Earp had kissed her yet. Well, Earp was welcome to her. She was one nasty piece of baggage, and he was glad he'd seen her again to remind himself just how unpleasant she could be.

She was out of his system now.

Chapter Eleven

Jerome Pike was at his most solicitous as he led his special guest to the best table in the house.

Aaron Fielding was an imposing man whose more salient features—a massive girth and an impressive pair of muttonchop whiskers—were overshadowed by a deformity sustained in a train accident years before. One eye was half an inch lower than the other, protruding from a mashed cheekbone that made Pike think of flesh-colored papier-mâché.

Jerome Pike cleared his throat. "She's a bit of a novice at singing, but I am sure you'll find her delightful."

Fielding dismissed the proprietor of the El Dorado with a look. He was well aware of Jerome Pike's nervousness, but he did nothing to set the man's mind at ease.

Pike babbled on, his voice grating to the ears. "I, ah, am sure that should you find her, ah, suitable, we could come to a quick agreement . . ." He trailed off, regarding Aaron with simultaneous fright and fascination, as a rodent might look at a King Cobra. That was all right. After admiring the King Cobra's hypnotic stare in person on one of his trips to the Mysterious East, Aaron Fielding took Pike's fearful look as a sign of respect. Jerome gulped and added, "No doubt you will, er, want a certain amount of privacy to make your decision." He bowed and backed away.

Fielding stretched his legs. It had been a long journey down from San Francisco, but Pike had assured him that this girl was everything he could possibly want. Since he had some business to attend to in Tucson later this month, Fielding had agreed to come early and take a look at this Charlotte Tate.

He doubted she would be suitable. Pike said this girl was English born, that she had red hair and fair skin. But he'd seen countless redheaded "English" girls throughout the west, and most of them were prostitutes, their hair dyed a ridiculous carrot orange. Did people really think him such a fool that he couldn't tell a virgin from a whore? Just because he had money to spend and wanted something specific, people thought they could palm anything off on him. Girls who were no more English than he was. Fakes.

Still, on paper, this girl was perfect. He cautioned himself not to be too hopeful.

Aaron Fielding had long ago come to the conclusion that a well-bred young lady might not look eagerly upon his affections at first. A busy man, he did not have the time nor the inclination for courtship. He needed a wife now; one who would be able to handle a great deal of entertaining—both public and private. He needed a nice, clean, well-mannered girl, and if she was a little bit afraid of him . . . well, all the better. Frightened women learned better; it was a matter of survival. Despite himself, he felt a stirring. If she really was the jewel Pike had claimed. . . .

If so, he would pay, and pay well. He was aware that women recoiled from him; even the fake virgins who tried to snare his fortune couldn't suppress their initial horror. But he was a great believer in training. Love was desirable, but not necessary.

He settled back in his chair and waited for the show, hoping that at last he had found the right one.

All evening, Jerome Pike hovered anxiously near Fielding's table, trying to divine the man's expression. It was impossible. He found himself staring at that hideous eye, which made him think of a sofa button that had popped off its spring.

Charlotte Tate's clear, light soprano barely cut the noise in the hall. Her face was framed by a curtain of wavy tresses, out of which large doe eyes projected a heady mixture of dignity, childlike innocence, and sensuality. Surely, Fielding must recognize how special she was.

From the moment he saw her at the Westphalia, Jerome decided that Aaron Fielding must meet her. He had provided several girls for the railroad executive in San Francisco, but none of them fit Fielding's specific tastes the way Charlotte did. The man was obsessed with finding a woman who reminded him of his first wife and Jerome knew that if he could find that woman, he would retire a rich man.

Some people didn't have a very good opinion of the service Jerome offered. Some called him a procurer. But he liked to think of himself as a matchmaker.

This girl had proven hard to crack. Most girls Jerome dealt with were gently reared, naive young women who had fallen on hard times. They had little or no self-esteem. It was a simple thing to assist them into utter dependency. But Charlotte Tate was made of sterner stuff.

At last, however, it seemed he might be getting results. Since her experience with the two ruffians a week ago, she seemed a little less sure of herself. Or did he imagine the flicker of self-doubt in those beautiful brown eyes?

He glanced at his favorite client again. Perhaps he'd made a mistake trying to soften her up. Aaron Fielding often said he admired spirit in a woman. As a highly paid executive of the SP Railroad—once a protégé of Collis P. Huntington himself—the man was surely capable of controlling one stubborn little girl.

Still, Charlotte Tate made Pike nervous. Sometimes he caught her looking at him. He had the funny feeling she was absorbing everything about him, recording his every word in a tiny ledger somewhere in her mind for future reference. She hardly ever talked, but he could almost hear her listening.

He decided he really didn't like her at all. If Aaron Fielding could take her off his hands and reimburse him generously for his trouble, it would make him a very happy man.

Chapter Twelve

Wind chased down from the Dragoons, trailing hot dry fingers through the grasses like licks of flame. The wind rattled the sabers of burnt-looking yucca and sent whorls of alkalai dust up from the honeycomb wagon trails leading into Tombstone. The land was yellow, brown, and gray.

Grama grass stopped at the edge of town; brittle, heat-curled combs nodding on long stems.

The wind died. A haze settled over the town, hanging in the air for hours. Goose Flats lay still and dead under the fierce Arizona sky, like the mangy pelt of some long-dead, randy-smelling animal.

It was Wednesday, June twenty-second, and still early when Charlotte reached the Westphalia Theater. The two-story adobe building had recently been repainted dark red.

Charlotte checked her reflection in the side window before walking around to the front of the theater. She looked, but did not feel, crisp and clean in her bleached muslin day dress trimmed at the elbows and neck with Mechlin lace.

Glancing around, she was relieved to see few people on the street. Although it was early afternoon, nocturnal Tombstone was just waking up. Jamie was here, though. His buckskin gelding stood at the hitching rail, shivering off a persistent fly from its withers.

Charlotte caught a movement across the side alley. Could someone be watching her? Did that person know how she had swallowed her pride, how the battle still raged inside her, so that she was almost unable to take the last couple of steps up to the theater that had once been her second home?

Charlotte tried to tell herself she wasn't crawling to Jamie. She had to give him a chance to reconsider his position, especially since Belinda Euell's reviews had been other than laudatory. He might need her now.

Nonsense. Who was she fooling? She wanted to get out of the El Dorado, wanted to get away from that smarmy confidence man Jerome Pike. She didn't care how much money he wanted to pay her. Besides, she hadn't seen a cent of it yet—and doubted she ever would.

Jake Cottrell had proved to be a false friend, but he was right about one thing. The El Dorado was no place for a lady. Not that Emma or Jake could convince her to do any-thing she didn't want to do. It was her own decision, pure and simple. She was simply tired of Jerome Pike's cruel slights, tired of the low sort of people who patronized the El Dorado, tired of feeling bad about herself. She'd rather work the tables at the Westphalia than sing onstage at the El Dorado, and that was that.

Taking a deep breath, Charlotte opened the door, and almost collided with Jamie.

"Charlotte. What an unexpected pleasure."

"Hello, Jamie." Charlotte opened her mouth to say more, then closed it again. How did she admit she had made a mistake and still save face?

"Do you want something?"

"I, uh . . ."

Jamie's eyes were kind. "What is it, Charlotte?"

"I thought you might have reconsidered your position," Charlotte blurted out.

"My position?"

"About putting me on the stage."

Jamie's expression turned sad. "I'm sorry, no. Maybe in the future, but I can't promise anything."

"Oh."

"I'm sorry, Charlotte." Jamie mounted, checked his horse's forward motion and leaned down. "But you're wel-come to come back in your old capacity."

Charlotte wanted to say yes, but pride choked her.

Jamie shrugged. "I guess that's that. It was nice seeing you, though." He wheeled his horse and started up the mid-dle of the street.

"Jamie!" Charlotte ran toward him, her kid boots send-ing up little puffs of dust.

Jamie's back stiffened. He stopped his horse at the junc-ture of Allen and Fourth streets, swiveling around in the saddle and resting one hand on the dorsal stripe of the buckskin's rump. "I'm sorry, Charlotte, but you're making this very hard for me. I'd like to put you onstage, I really would, but Belinda Euell's already jealous of you."

"Then I'll work the tables."

"In that case . . ." Jamie trailed off as his gaze fastened on something up the street. "What are they doing?"

Two men stood outside the Arcade Saloon just beyond Fifth Street. A liquor keg had been dragged out on the boardwalk. One man leaned over the keg, a cigar stuck in his mouth, and stuck a wooden stick into the top.

"What are those two fools doing? Don't they know liquor and fire don't mix?"

Charlotte dismissed the men with a look. "You'll hire me, then?"

Jamie stood in his stirrups. "Hey! You don't want to—"

A sudden *whump* rocked the air, a rush of sound. Jamie's horse clattered sideways, nearly unseating him.

Charlotte watched as a flower of flame—bright orange—climbed an invisible rope in an instant, igniting the awning that Maria had sewn only a month ago.

In moments, the front of the Arcade was aflame.

"Fire!" shouted Jamie. He spurred his horse forward, heading toward the conflagration. The horse jumped and twisted, balking, so Jamie jumped off and let the animal run. It dashed past Charlotte, eyes wild.

The fire spread in an instant, leaping from roof to roof, stitching down the sides and consuming the board and batten structures in voracious bites. Confusion reigned. People were milling, horses were screaming in fear, and the great trampling crowd was stained blue by smoke. Charlotte stood rooted to the spot, stunned, a morbid fascination taking hold of her as scarves of flame wound around a timber not three feet away, bright against the black skeleton of wood.

"Don't just stand there! Help me!" yelled a woman near the Maison Doree, as the porch roof caved in under a rain of sparks. Charlotte stared at the woman, who was tangled in a blanket as she tried to dunk it in the horse trough. Her face was grimy and strands of hair fell down into her face, but Charlotte recognized her. Nellie Cashman. "Get over here, girl, and take that end!" she shouted. Above them, crackling in the heat, fire flapped along the awning. A whole section of scorched striped canvas lurched, then spilled into the street. Charlotte jumped, but Nellie grasped her arm firmly and pulled her to the trough. Between them they soaked the blanket and twisted it, then Nellie Cashman socked at the flames like a bull whacker. She paused to shout at Charlotte. "Get that tarp, there. Soak it!" Next to Charlotte stood a wagon, piled high with someone's possessions, covered by the tarp in question.

"But it belongs to someone."

"You darn fool! The town's going up! They won't need that tarp now!"

Charlotte hauled the heavy canvas down and dragged it through the dust, choking on the acrid smoke. She piled it into the trough, then tried to pull it out. It took all her strength to remove the canvas, and then the wet material was too heavy to wield.

Charlotte dropped the tarp. The whole block was aflame now. There was no point trying to do anything about it.

"What are you doing?" shouted Nellie Cashman.

Charlotte suddenly remembered her own house on Fremont Street. Surely the fire couldn't have gone that far! She backed up through the milling crowd.

"Come back here!" Nellie's voice, angry.

Someone thrust a bucket in Charlotte's hands. The water slopped over, soaking her dress. She held it, stunned.

"Pass it on, you fool!" shouted the man who had handed it to her. Charlotte looked around and saw that she had become part of a line. A bucket brigade. Hastily, she shoved the bucket into the arms of the next person.

She didn't know how long she handed pails of water down the line, but it finally got through to her that she simply could not lift one more. She broke from the line and hurried down Fourth toward Fremont, dodging through the agitated crowd. The smoke stung her eyes and her lungs quaked for breath.

As she reached the corner, Charlotte started to pray. The fire couldn't have gone that far! But the flames seemed to keep pace with her, jumping from roof to roof and turning the air into a roaring furnace.

She paused at the corner, unable to face what she knew would be true. But it wasn't. The adobe shack was still standing! Charlotte started to run toward it.

A runner of flame leaped onto the tar-paper shack next to the adobe and consumed it in a matter of moments, flaps of glistening black rooftop curling in the tremendous heat. As Charlotte watched, the flames jumped the small distance between the tar-paper roof and her little house.

Hiking her skirts, she ran faster. Maria emerged from the house, a handkerchief clapped to her mouth with one hand, the other jerking at her small collie's collar. Ruff twisted and fought, yapping, and Maria stumbled and fell on the uneven ground. The collie bolted back into the house, instinctively heading for what he perceived to be its safe haven.

Maria tried to stand up, and sat down immediately.

Charlotte rushed to her. "What's wrong?"

"I think . . . I twisted my ankle." Maria stared into the darkness of the house. "Charlotte, you've got to get him!"

Charlotte wet a handkerchief in the trough near the gate and ran into the house. The smoke wasn't too thick, just a gauzy gray haze, but Charlotte could see that part of the ceiling was smoldering, glowing red in the darkness where the mud and straw had caught fire.

"Ruff!" she called. Her vocal chords felt rusty from disuse, and when she took another breath, her throat burned.

"Ruff! Come here, boy! Ruff!" Where was the silly beast? Didn't he know he was in danger?

The smoke was getting thicker. Charlotte inched her way toward the kitchen, passing the open door to her room. She glanced toward the dressing table. Her money was there, and Mary's picture. She changed course, heading for that room. It would only take a minute, and the smoke wasn't that bad yet.

Suddenly, she heard a whimper, and saw Ruff cowering in the corner of the kitchen. With a loud crunch, part of the ceiling caved in, sending a shower of sparks. Charlotte cried out as a spark branded her skin. The flames were twisting through the batting that lined the roof now, glittering malevolently. More of the roof looked as if it might fall in.

Glancing back at the bedroom, Charlotte could barely see the dressing table through the smoke. But she saw the armoire. It was partially open, and the rich colors of her dresses glimmered within—the garnet that she loved so much, the teal dress trimmed with jetted Spanish lace—

The dog whimpered again. Eyes smarting, Charlotte could barely see his huddled shape. She didn't have time for anything else. Scooping him up into her arms and nearly bent double with her burden, she bolted for the doorway. Every muscle ached, and her corset cut into her waist like a knife. The dog didn't struggle; he seemed to know she was helping him, but he was heavy.

Her lungs were on fire. She tried to breathe but the incredible heat snatched at her breath, clawed at her throat. At first she couldn't believe that she was inhaling but nothing was coming in. Plunging toward the light where the front door must be, Charlotte tried again to suck in air. Her vision blurred, even as Roberto's face loomed and his arms came around her.

Chapter Thirteen

Charlotte threw another brick onto the growing pile. Stained with soot from head to toe, she realized she must look a sight, if the appearance of the other women she'd seen was any judge. Shooting pains ran across her back, despite the fact that she had long ago discarded her corset, and her arms felt as if they had been pulled from their sockets. Her hair had fallen down from its neat coil; she had lost the pins one by one as she'd worked through the heat of the day. Charlotte straightened up and massaged her back with one hand, inhaling the bitter odor of char and scanning what was left of the business district.

Tombstone lay in blackened ruins about them. Here and there a scorched adobe wall rose up from the maze of burned litter and mounds of broken glass. One such wall belonged to the Westphalia a block over, its new coat of paint catching the last rays of sun like old blood. The rest of the building was gone. The evening wind lifted ash and sent it through the air, tiny specks flying into Charlotte's eyes and clogging her nostrils. Her throat was so sore she could barely speak.

The town looked like a flattened anthill. People crawled over the blighted landscape, tearing down walls and clearing away debris before nightfall, so that they could put up tents to shelter them against the coming storm. Thunderheads skimmed above the Huachucas, heavy with impending rain. Dark blue-gray, they boiled against the sky, lined with hot white light. At the sight of the building cumulus

117

clouds, Roberto's face fell. Charlotte knew he was thinking the monsoon season might come a month early—
which would have a disastrous effect on the rebuilding of
Tombstone.

Charlotte had been working for hours with Roberto. He,
knocking down the last remaining adobe wall to their little
house; she sorting the adobe bricks they could keep. Maria,
her ankle swollen, sat at the edge of the lot holding Ruff by
the leash Charlotte had given her. She pieced together
scrounged tarps for a makeshift tent.

A wagon lumbered by, trace chains jangling. Ruff
started up his infernal barking again.

"Will you shut that dog up?" Charlotte's voice was
barely a croak. "I'm beginning to wish I hadn't saved
him."

"I know you don't mean that," Maria said, gently
stroking the collie. "You risked your life for him."

Thunder rumbled ominously.

Roberto looked at the sky. "We've got to hurry." He
spoke with diffidence, but Charlotte understood his
urgency.

By dark, Roberto and Charlotte had raised the tent and
the four of them crawled in, exhausted.

The skies opened and a torrent of rain lashed the tent.
More tired than hungry, Charlotte curled up in a ball and
fell asleep immediately. Her hand still clutched the twisted
frame that had held the daguerreotype of Mary and Tom.

Dawn chased the storm away, leaving a fresh wash of
peach sky. A few plum-red high clouds streaked above the
Dragoon Mountains. The cumulus clouds were long gone.

Charlotte awoke before the others, disoriented by her surroundings. Then it all came back to her in a staggering
wave that crashed into her heart, leaving her breathless.

She was penniless. Her savings, her possessions had
been lost to the fire. All she had to her name was her torn,

scorched dress, the shreds of once-snowy Mechlin lace hanging at her elbows like black weeds. The dress, her shoes, her undergarments, and the blackened oval frame still clamped in her fingers: they were the sum total of eighteen years on this earth.

Charlotte sat up, every muscle protesting. She had slept in a cramped position on the hard ground. Twisting her neck to look out the tent flap, she winced at the agony that shot like an arrow through her shoulder.

The smell. It clung to everything, sharpened by the rain. The stink of doused fire made Charlotte want to choke. Maria and Roberto clung together in sleep like drowned rats. Ruff lay curled up beside them.

Charlotte couldn't help feeling a proprietary pride at the sight of him. She was his rescuer. There were few enough reasons to feel good this morning.

Aware of her scrutiny, the collie raised his head. Charlotte reached out to stroke him. Licking his chops nervously, he trembled and shrank from her touch, ears flattened along the back of his head, his eyes wide with fear.

The unfairness of the collie's reaction galled her. "If it had been up to me, we'd be eating grilled dog today," she told him sourly. He licked his chops again and watched her warily.

The thought of food turned her stomach, but the emptiness gnawed at her. She crawled out through the tent flap and stood up, swaying for a moment.

The devastation assailed her senses. Fremont Street was a morass of mud and ash, churned up by countless hooves and wagon wheels. The skeletal remains of charred wood and adobe contrasted with the dull white tents that billowed in the morning wind. Rows upon rows of them, like an army camp. Some people were already up, clearing rubble and cooking breakfasts over open fires. The smell of beans and side bacon filled her nostrils, clawing at her insides.

Charlotte couldn't stand to look at the town anymore. Instead, she stared out at the mountains, their toothy ridges pink in the dawn light. The desert stretched out to them like a nubby green-brown blanket, vast and inhospitable. The town that had seemed impregnable looked tiny and insignificant next to the enormity of that wasteland. How could anyone think he could conquer such wild environs? What optimistic fool would try to build a city in a desert? The audacious bravado of Tombstone, the Moet champagne and fancy foods seemed ridiculous now; the town's manic jollity rang false and pointless on this empty morning.

Had she, too, been fooling herself? She had followed a dream—her sister's dream—counting her triumphs on an invisible abacus. She had traded Mary's unrealistic fantasies for hard work. Her progress had been slower than she had expected. But there had been progress. She had made a fair amount of money. She had made it to the stage. Jamie had been about to rehire her. And then—in one sweep of fire—she had lost everything.

The red wall of the Westphalia reared against the aquamarine sky. There would be no help from that quarter.

Tears sprang to her eyes and a sob rose in her throat, but she stopped it. Lifting her chin defiantly, Charlotte glared at the ruins around her. Maybe her ambitions were foolish ones, but they were the only ones she had. The dream had tarnished—her nights as a pretty waiter at the Westphalia and the El Dorado had taught her that—but she had learned that that dream was within reach.

Charlotte looked toward the southwest side of town, where a huddle of buildings stood untouched by the flames. The El Dorado might still be standing. It wasn't her first choice, or even her third, but if she had to stay there, so be it.

She had to have clean clothing. Around Pike, she had

learned, it was always best *to hold* the advantage. Or at least parity.

Charlotte steeled herself, then started walking toward Emma Lake's boardinghouse.

Chapter Fourteen

The gingham dress was about three sizes too big, but Charlotte was able to cinch in the waist with a piece of ribbon. There was nothing to be done about the length, though. The hem hung two inches above the tops of her boots. Maria looked much better in Emma's calico.

This morning Roberto had gone out with a large crew to cut wood in the Huachucas for rebuilding the town. The ring of hammers sounded day and night. The stink of char had almost been replaced by the fresh smell of wooden planks and sawdust. In the Mexican quarter the men made money by mixing, molding, and firing adobe bricks. Roberto, Maria, and Charlotte could not afford to pay the inflated prices, so they had to make their own adobe, curing it for days in the hot sun. It was a painstaking process; mixing the adobe mud to a soupy consistency, pouring it into the ladderlike wooden molds, removing the molds to let the bricks stand free, and waiting days for the bricks to dry enough to stand them on edge. And then waiting again before stacking them against the one remaining wall of their house.

Charlotte scanned the cluttered camp. There was hardly any room to walk. The mixing pit took up the front of the lot; an ugly brown pudding of dirt, water, and straw.

Maria's *hornilla,* where she cooked their food, was supposed to be protected from the wind by the old house's wall, but it hadn't helped much. The tent at the back corner of the lot offered the only shade, but the heavy canvas trapped and magnified the heat. Charlotte could stand only a few minutes at a time in the tent before the heat drove her outside, where at least a breeze lifted her hair off her neck or cooled the sweat on her brow.

To make matters worse, Ruff's constant yapping played in maddening counterpoint to the sounds of the town rebuilding.

Maria squatted near the little fire, turning the skinned rabbit Roberto had shot for them. They would be eating their dinner early this afternoon; after a week's dry weather, the thunderheads were back, tops glistening white against the dark blue sky. The cloud's bottoms were dark.

Charlotte held a shard of mirror up and stared at herself critically. Without a hat, her skin had been at the mercy of the Arizona sun. The first day she had turned beet-red, and her face had peeled to a painful raw pink. But a week outdoors had wrought a big change. Now her skin was a uniform dull brown, murky against the dark red of her hair and brown eyes.

"Did you hear the commotion last night?" Maria asked, turning the stick.

Charlotte glanced her way, her stomach recoiling at the sight of their dinner. They'd had a constant diet of rabbit and beef jerky for a week now, and she was heartily sick of it.

"Remedios told me there were lot jumpers squatting on the business lots down on Allen. Vigilantes rode over in the middle of the night and pulled their tents over." Maria sighed. "I wish Thad would come back. Buddy Martin is looking after his lot, but it's not the same. He wouldn't defend it the way Thad would. I hope there won't be any trouble."

"I'm sure there won't be," Charlotte replied, squeezing a lemon onto her face and rubbing the stinging juice into her cheeks and across her nose. She had paid a day's wages for this lemon; fruit was rare in this town now. But she had to bleach her skin somehow. Her face was her livelihood.

"I heard that people have been trying to drive the legitimate owners off their lots. Anyone can claim they're there illegally."

"I'm sure Virgil Earp won't allow that."

"Sometimes you're so naive, Charlotte. He wouldn't be able to stop it. The records burned in the fire."

The enormity of Maria's words sank in. Charlotte motioned to the adobe bricks stacked diagonally against the one standing wall. "You mean all of this work might be for nothing?"

"People have been staying up at night and guarding their lots. It's the only way. Roberto's staying up tonight with the rifle. Maybe he can do it for a night or so, but sooner or later we'll have to relieve him."

"I'm sure no one will be out in the storm," Charlotte said. "They can't be that crazy."

"If they want this lot badly enough, they will."

The thought sobered Charlotte. She was so sick of the sticky heat, the dust, and the mosquitoes. The fierce sun smothered her like a hot cloth, and she was usually drenched with sweat from head to foot. Her shoes pinched, her back ached from bending over the mixing pit, and her hands were blistered from wielding the rake and shovel. Worse, tonight there would be rain again. The tent leaked. If they had to go through all this for nothing . . . it wasn't fair! "I wish we'd taken Emma up on her offer," she grumbled.

"We can't," Maria said patiently. "You know why."

123

They'd had this discussion a number of times already. Maria had turned down Emma's offer to put them up at the Silver Dollar until the house was built. They had to stay on the lot to make sure no one stole the adobe bricks. And if Maria were right about the claim jumpers, she would probably have to stay up all night, too.

Already Charlotte was doing double shifts; working all day helping Roberto and Maria make the adobe bricks, and then going to the El Dorado and working until one in the morning. She was dog-tired. The thought of mixing one more batch of adobe made her ill.

"You could stay with Emma, though. There's no reason why you shouldn't. After all, you're the only one bringing in any money right now."

Charlotte was tempted. But she looked at her friend, who looked as weary and disheveled as she herself felt, and knew that she couldn't do it. How would she ever be able to hold her head up in public if she deserted them? "That's all right, I'll stay."

After gnawing on the scrawny rabbit, Charlotte walked to the El Dorado.

The evening dragged by. Charlotte was too tired even be nervous. She was grateful she didn't have to go outside to be sick, because during her performance the storm struck. The rain came down in sheets, pounding the ground and drumming on the windows. She could barely be heard above the din the raindrops made on the roof.

Charlotte changed hastily after the show. She wanted to catch someone headed toward Fremont Street, but all the customers had gone by the time she emerged from the dressing room. She stood on the boardwalk of the theater, staring with dismay at the rain. If anything, it had increased in ferocity. Water churned down the street, turning it into the canal. She knew Roberto wouldn't be coming for her; Maria had made it clear that he would be guarding their lot.

The rain pelted down like silver bullets in the glow of the gaslights. Lightning veined the sky, momentarily illuminating the street. The brothels on Sixth Street had been spared by the fire and their amber lights gleamed mellowly behind the curtain of rain. Charlotte could hear piano music and see horses huddled around the hitching posts, fetlock-deep in water. But the street itself was deserted.

Shivering, Charlotte stared down at the water. Her boots would be soaked. That might not have been a consideration a week ago, when she had three pair. But now . . .

"You aren't entertaining the idea of walking home?"

Charlotte knew Jerome Pike was at her elbow. "Where else can I go?" But the thought of slogging through the rain and mud to a leaking, mildewed tent didn't appeal to her at all.

"You can stay here until the rain stops."

"Maria will be worried about me."

"Nonsense. No one is out tonight. We're in the middle of a flood, Charlotte." His hand squeezed her arm as he turned her slightly. She tried not to flinch at his touch. "Look over there. That branch must be as big around as a telegraph pole." He motioned to the junction of Sixth and Tough Nut streets, where the water shuttled a tree branch down toward the arroyo. "The water's rising every minute. You might not make it home."

There was some truth to that; Charlotte could see it with her own eyes.

"From what you told me, your friend is a sensible person. She would want you to wait out this storm."

"I guess I could stay until the rain lets up."

"That's being a sensible girl." He took her elbow and guided her back into the theater and over to a side door off the office that Charlotte had never noticed before. They emerged into a tiny courtyard and followed the uneven paving under a covered arbor to a small, separate house. Shivering in the rain, her dress plastered to her body, Charlotte followed Pike with alacrity. "Is this your house, too?" she asked, as they entered the parlor. "This is where you and your wife stay?"

"These are our private quarters."

Charlotte stared around her. Floridly Victorian, the room pressed in on her, making her feel claustrophobic. The wallpaper and overstuffed furniture were the same deep burgundy, vying for attention with an oriental carpet, fringed silk lampshades, a collection of fans in a glass case, bric-a-brac on every possible surface. Paintings and tintypes cluttered the walls; leering stone statues of dogs guarded the fireplace. Overwhelmed, Charlotte sat down on the couch, unable to look at anything in this dark, busy room for long. But with the rain coming down outside, it was undeniably cozy—certainly an improvement on Roberto's tent.

"Beezie is on a business trip to the coast," Pike explained. "You can stay as long as you wish."

Charlotte had only met Pike's wife once. Tall and gaunt, the woman looked as if she would be more at home running a prison than a theater.

"Thank you," Charlotte said, "but as soon as the rain stops I had better get home."

He poured two brandies and handed her one. Although she didn't care for liquor, she sipped it. She might as well be polite, since he had let her stay here.

The brandy burned going down. They talked for awhile, mostly about her act. Pike asked her periodically if she didn't like the brandy, and she dutifully sipped more. The rain continued. After awhile, Charlotte realized her glass was empty. Pike replenished it. She didn't object; the brandy went down smoother now. She felt warm and tingly. The rushing sound of the rain contrasted with the security she felt.

Pike leaned forward sympathetically when she told him about her sister's death, and how she wanted to become a great actress someday. How she had wanted to go to San Francisco, but how she thought her career might begin just as well in Tombstone. Her eyelids sagged, and she felt herself drifting off occasionally.

When Pike suggested she sleep a little—after all, the rain hadn't abated at all—Charlotte didn't protest. He led her to a bedroom. Beezie's guest bedroom, he said.

The bed's coverlet had been turned down. Two fluffy pillows rested against the tall, ornately carved headboard. Charlotte noted the ceramic nightstand on the dresser and a matching chamber pot near the bed. Imagine, a chamber pot! On the lot, Charlotte had to go behind the adobe wall, squatting nervously and hoping that no one came by and spotted her.

"I'll have Lila draw you a bath," Jerome said.

"Lila?"

"Beezie's maid. She has a room just off the parlor. She'll look after your needs. I will be in my apartments if you want me."

Charlotte almost protested. She knew Maria would be worried. But Pike was right; the storm still raged, and one look out the window told her that traversing this flood would be impossible.

A bath! She had only strip-washed in the past week, and felt gritty and filthy. What could it hurt for her to stay for the bath? Surely Maria couldn't blame her for that.

Deliciously sleepy, Charlotte crawled between the covers and waited for Lila.

Sunlight streamed through the lace curtains. Charlotte awoke slowly, unwilling to let go of the dream. Morgan, holding her in his arms and kissing her gently . . .

It was no use. Morgan drifted into misty fragments, replaced by pink sunlight under her eyelids.

She stretched luxuriously, enjoying the soft crispness of the feather pillows against her neck. If it weren't for the tiny throbbing at her temple, she'd feel perfect. And then she remembered that she would be waking up in Roberto's tent, but for Jerome Pike's kindness.

Still drowsy, Charlotte slipped out of bed and looked out the window, which was shielded by a decorative design of wrought iron. The sky above was its usual bright blue, the sun glinting off standing puddles in the hard bis-cuit-colored ground of the courtyard. Giant sunflowers steamed in the heat. It must be mid-morning. Maria would be worried.

A knock came on the door, and then Lila entered. "Did you have a good sleep, Miss?"

"Yes, thank you. But I'd better get home."

"But you want your breakfast, first, don't you?" She brought in a silver tray bearing an egg in a china egg cup, toast, a matching crystal butter dish, jam jar, and salt cellar. Charlotte couldn't very well refuse, could she? Lila had gone to so much trouble. Besides, if she went home now she would be breakfasting on hard tack or beef jerky.

"Just crawl right back in bed and I can set the tray on top." Lila unfolded the linen napkin and tucked it around Charlotte's waist. "I'll go draw your bath."

"Bath?"

"Don't you remember? You wanted one last night, but by the time the water was heated you were fast asleep."

After breakfast and a bath—it had to be getting on noon!—Lila returned with a blue frock over her arm.

"Mr. Pike wanted you to try this dress on. I'll wash your other dress."

"But I can't accept this. I've got to go home."

"Jerome says it's a gift. He doesn't want you walking around dressed like you were. It's bad for business."

She laid the frock and a new corset on the bed, and withdrew. Charlotte dressed quickly and checked herself in the mirror. The dress was striped changeable silk. Its midnight-blue color made a striking contrast with her dark red hair, making her skin appear lighter. Poor Maria! She had the one calico dress from Emma, and it was stiff with splattered mud from mixing adobe—

Abruptly, Charlotte realized that she would be going back home within the hour. Her heart sank. She wouldn't dream of wearing this dress back to that muddy little lot.

She would have to catch Lila before the maid washed her old dress. Pleasantly aware of the stiff rustle of her skirts, Charlotte walked briskly to the door and put her hand on the glass knob. It would be such a shame to—

The knob didn't move. It was frozen. Locked.

Stunned, Charlotte pulled her hand back. Lila must have locked her in by mistake. She knocked on the door and called, waited a few moments and knocked again, louder and longer.

"Lila! I'm locked in! Lila!"

They had forgotten her! She ran to the window and tried to lift the sash. It wouldn't budge. She rapped on the window, but the courtyard was deserted. Charlotte sat down on the bed. Her head started to ache in earnest.

She heard footsteps in the hallway. Running to the door, she pounded her fist against it. "Lila! Lila!"

The footsteps paused for just a beat, then continued.

It finally sank in. Pike had locked her in here! Heart thumping, she returned to the bed, stepping on the ruffle of the blue dress. It ripped a little, but she hardly noticed. Her throat felt dry and she wanted to cry.

Her mind ran around in circles. Why would he keep her here against her will? What could he possibly want of her?

Unbidden, Jake's words came back to her. "He's a mac."
A maquereau.

A pimp. What else had he said? She wracked her brain
to remember. *"He saved you for something worse."*

In her mind's eye she saw the prostitutes who ranged
nightly through the El Dorado, looking for customers. Her
throat closed.

No. Impossible! But sitting there huddled in her newly
acquired finery, Charlotte could think of no other explanation.

Chapter Fifteen

Maria huddled atop the salvaged adobe piled in the wagon,
shivering under the tarp. Roberto had dozed off again, his
twelve-gauge shotgun tipped down so that the muzzle
brushed the wagon's boards.

By the chill in the air, Maria guessed it must be early
morning. The rain had stopped hours ago. Where was
Charlotte? The treacherous flood had turned into a puddle
a child could wade through. She should have made it
across town by now.

Worried, Maria glanced at Roberto. She had promised to
guard the wagon and alert him if there were trouble. So far,
not a soul had stirred anywhere on the street, and she
doubted anyone would come out tonight after such a
storm. Torn between her loyalty to Roberto and her fear for
Charlotte, Maria waited. At last she dozed.

"You Maria Lujan?" Startled, Maria jumped. A boy on a
mule looked at her curiously.

She nodded, suddenly frightened. The boy handed her a note.

Relief vied with anger as Maria scanned Jerome Pike's letter. While she and Roberto huddled in the wagon like dogs, Charlotte was safe at the El Dorado, sleeping in the guest room! Furthermore, she would stay at the El Dorado until the house was rebuilt.

After the first quick spark of anger, Maria realized that in the back of her mind she had been waiting for Charlotte to desert them. If she was surprised, it was only that Charlotte had not left them sooner.

Panic scattered Charlotte's thoughts like birds taking flight at a rifle shot. She closed her eyes, clamped her hands around the mattress on either side of her, and marshaled her thoughts with an iron will. She must keep her wits together, for they were the only thing she had.

Maria would be looking for her. That was some consolation. Charlotte tried to follow this idea to its logical conclusion. Maria would come to the theater. Pike would give Maria some cock-and-bull story about how she had left after the show last night. Maria would probably believe him. What would she do then? Go to the sheriff?

Perhaps they would believe she had been carried off in the flood. They might search the arroyos near here, and then give up. Maria would make a fuss, but who cared about the feelings of a half-breed Mexican woman? Panic rose in Charlotte's throat again. This horrid headache! She knew it was from the brandy, the brandy that Pike had used to help lay this trap.

Her mind caught at another scrap of hope. People expected to see her on the stage. Her disappearance would be noticed.

Then she thought of the patrons of the El Dorado. They certainly wouldn't care. And Charlotte had a feeling that

131

unless her disappearance were discovered today or tonight, she would be long gone. Pike wouldn't keep her here forever. He obviously had plans . . .

Unable to sit still any longer, Charlotte tried the window again. It was nailed shut and sealed with old paint. The wrought-iron bars with their graceful curlicues were not merely decorative, but had a more malign purpose. She suspected that she had not been the first person to know Jerome Pike's hospitality.

That afternoon, Jerome Pike met the stage from Tucson. Aaron Fielding looked visibly shaken at the sight of the leveled boomtown. "Don't worry," Jerome said as he piled the bags in his wagon. "The El Dorado was spared. With my wife out of town, you'll have the run of the place. It can be a sort of . . . honeymoon retreat." He flicked a glance at the man's mashed profile, and couldn't help wondering how the high-and-mighty Charlotte Tate would feel with her husband-to-be.

When they reached the theater, Lila let them in through the side gate into the courtyard. Pike ushered his guest into the drawing room and set down the bags. "I suppose you'll want to see your, ah, bride right away."

"Perhaps your woman could draw me a bath first," Fielding drawled, removing his alpaca coat and loosening his collar. "This heat is remarkable. It amazes me how anyone can live in the desert."

"Lila, go and prepare Mr. Fielding's bath." Pike poured himself a drink. "Brandy?"

"Please."

"That storm was most fortuitous," Pike said, feeling expansive. "Truthfully, I had despaired of finding a way to get you two, er, lovebirds, together. I hope you did not have to cut your business short in Tucson? No? Excellent. Everything's working according to Hoyle, then." He paused, drumming his fingers nervously on the side table.

"I feel it is my duty to warn you. Miss Tate is a headstrong young woman. She may not consider herself . . . ready for such a big step as matrimony."

"You mean she'll put up a fight."

Pike reddened.

"I'm well aware of my effect on women, Mr. Pike."

Pike swished the amber liquid in his glass, staring at it with feigned fascination. "I'm sure that when a young lady gets to know your, ah, inner self—"

Fielding's glass hit the marble-topped side table with a loud crack. "I've changed my mind. I'd like to see her now."

Chapter Sixteen

Aaron Fielding had never planned to fall in love. One of a handful of prominent lawyers in San Francisco, Aaron had caught the eye of Collis P. Huntington of the Southern Pacific Railroad, rising quickly in the company hierarchy until he had become one of Huntington's few confidants. Power was an opiate to Fielding; the only thing he lived for. He hadn't needed love—until he met Ellen Childress.

Ellen had seemed exquisitely fragile, but Aaron had soon learned of the tensile strength beneath her gentle manner. The first time he saw her, she'd sang the title role in the San Francisco Opera's production of "Lucia di Lammermoor." Her voice shimmered, possessed of an unearthly and sometimes searing beauty.

Aaron could hardly believe his good fortune when the English soprano returned his ardor. At thirty-seven years old, Aaron Fielding had discovered what it was like to be in love. He'd had everything: wealth, power, and the woman he adored. And soon, he'd thought to have a son to carry on the Fielding name.

The ensuing tragedy wasn't unusual; it had been enacted by thousands of families in thousands of cities and towns across the country. Ellen died in childbirth. Her infant son lived only eight hours more. In the space of a few hours, he lost everything he cared about—except wealth.

Bitter and driven, he'd once again immersed himself in his work. This time the widower's grief was genuine. As a man the SP could trust, he'd been groomed for the political arena.

He might have lived a productive life as a senator from California, had tragedy not struck again. On a campaign trip from Los Angeles to Sacramento, the train on which he was riding crashed into a freighter coming from the other direction. A hundred and twenty people were killed. Fielding had lost the sight in one eye as a result of the accident, his face crushed into a corrugated shingle. But even in his terrible pain, he'd heard the cries of a baby in the dust and smoke, and managed to extricate a child unharmed from the wreckage. Later that day, the infant's mother came to the hospital to thank him.

He never forgot the look in her eyes. She had brought the infant along, meaning to let him hold her—but when he'd reached for the child, she'd pulled it away, her eyes bright with loathing.

That look had crawled through him and over him for the last ten years. The SP kept him on as legal counsel but, with his disfigurement, the door to the senatorial seat was closed forever.

He believed that of all the people he had known, Ellen alone would not have turned from him.

In Charlotte, Aaron saw the same fresh beauty, the same delicate white skin and dark hair. He heard it in her voice, a voice that had promise. Perhaps, that voice could be trained for opera. She would sing the arias he loved for him alone, as Ellen had done.

His hands shook as he pushed the key into the lock of the bedroom. Pike had warned him that she would fight, and he was ready. He knew the girl would love the life he could give her, once she became accustomed to it. He would show her love and beauty, if only they could cross together the obstacle of his deformity.

His pulse quickened, anticipation running like an electric current through his body. He would teach the nightingale to sing.

At the sound of the key grating in the lock, Charlotte whirled from the window. She had been trying to pry it open with a nail she had pulled out of the wall. The painting that hung from the nail lay on the bed.

Her heart fluttered against her rib cage, and she was aware of the pulse in her throat. Breathing deeply, Charlotte squared her shoulders and planted her feet firmly as she faced the door, concealing the blunt nail in her hand.

The door opened.

Surprise and dismay crashed into her full force. She had been expecting Lila, whom she could have overpowered, or Pike—an enemy she knew. But this man was more than six feet tall, broad-shouldered, and heavy-chested.

Shock followed as her eyes registered the man's deformed face, and despite herself she shrank back.

The man stopped just inside the door, aghast. "Your skin! You look like a red Indian!"

His words galvanized Charlotte. She swallowed her revulsion and swept toward him, her head held imperiously high. "What are you doing here? Who are you? Where's Pike?" She couldn't take her eyes off the man's ruined face.

The man ignored her questions. "What happened to your skin?"

"Where's Pike?" Charlotte demanded, her voice brisk to conceal the shaking of her body.

"Pike? I think he's at the theater."

"What about the maid?"

The man reached out a hand to touch her skin. "You've been in the sun without a hat."

His words made little sense to Charlotte. With morbid fascination, she watched his fingers come closer, and felt the gentle scrape of them across her cheek. She refused to flinch, sensing that any show of weakness would encourage more familiarity. Instead, she grasped her skirts and pushed past him, heading for the door.

Seeing her intention, he reached the door before her, deceptively quick for all his bulk. He turned his key in the lock and leaned against the heavy wood. "I can't let you do that."

"I want to see Jerome Pike at once."

The man shook his head. He smiled sadly, an element of pity in his expression. That, more than anything, jarred Charlotte. Cold fingers of fear wrapped around her vitals. "What do you want?"

The man gazed at her in wonderment. "That accent can't be faked. You *are* English."

"Give me that key." Charlotte reached for it, but he held it away, then pocketed it.

"You really are what Pike said you were."

"Let me out of here."

"If you knew how often I've been deceived . . . Charlotte. What a beautiful name."

Charlotte felt rage mount in her blood, igniting sparks of energy throughout her limbs, like a field of lava looping through each muscle until her fingers clenched, white-knuckled—and when she was ready she drove the nail into his chest with a quick, fluid motion.

His reaction was immediate and crushing. His hand came down on her neck and he spun her into his chest, yanking her head back. The nail dropped harmlessly to the floor. His heavy clothing had protected him.

"Let me go!" She twisted against his arms, choking on her revulsion at the coarse touch of his coat and the smell that emanated from him, an avid, wild odor of unleashed desire that rode on his sweat.

"Pike told me I'd have trouble with you," he grunted, restraining her with little effort. "But nothing worth having comes easily. You're a fighter, like Ellen. She was tough, strong. She looked so frail, yet her voice was powerful enough to fill the opera hall—"

"You're insane!"

His other arm came across her shoulder blades like a steel bar, locking her in a bearlike embrace. Charlotte squirmed, but the man was too strong. He pressed against her length, and through the thickness of his clothing she felt him grinding his stomach against her. She tried to pull away, but he pressed closer, insistent.

The hand on her neck was as big as a ham, clutching the slender column of her throat with ease. His nails bit into her shoulder as the fingers of his other hand came around and pried up her chin. "Look at me. Am I really that horrible?"

The lock on her throat was so great that Charlotte could only manage a harsh whisper. "You are hideous!"

He slapped her. The blow clacked her jaw together and her teeth came down on her tongue. Blood spurted into her mouth, warm and metallic. Before she knew it she had been yanked off her feet and rudely pushed onto the bed. The next thing she knew, he had pinned her under his weight, lowering his flat ruined face toward hers until it blotted out her vision. "My wife," he muttered, and his voice trembled with ardor. She didn't hear the rest of what he said, because she had begun to scream.

She shut her eyes and tried to move her face away but his wet lips crawled over her mouth in a snail-like blur, and the coldness inside her became an ache. When she realized it was futile to fight, Charlotte instinctively withdrew inside herself, pushing her mind as far away as the limits of his embrace would allow, until the child in her had crawled huddling into a dim space where his lips could not follow. Distantly she felt his hands jerk her arms above her head, one heavy paw clamping down on her wrists, heard the painting slide to the floor with a clatter, felt the bed list as he shifted his weight slightly away from her and his other hand drilled under the welter of skirts. Dimly she felt the heat of his body as she struggled, felt the stale breath on her face and the probing of his tongue between her lips, heard his endearments, his apologies, even as rude hands shoved her drawers down. And then his fingers pried her legs apart, just as those men had done the night she had been accosted on the street. The night Jerome Pike had come to her rescue.

But there was no one to save her now.

Chapter Seventeen

Jake Cottrell turned his back on the bronc tied to the post in the center of the corral and spoke in low conversational tones to George Dobbs, the horse buyer from Fort Huachuca. As they talked, the dark bay stopped leaning back against the rope. One ear came forward and then the other. He extended his neck toward Jake, shied, then leaned forward again. Jake was aware that the bronc had quieted down, but did not acknowledge it. "When this bay's broke I'll have twelve for you."

"Wish you had more. We're short right now. With things the way they are in San Carlos, we're going to need every trained horse we can get." He was referring to the fact that more Apaches had left the San Carlos reservation, headed for Mexico.

"I've got some other horses you can look at," Jake said. The bronc stood directly behind him now, as close as the rope would allow, and blew warm breath on Jake's neck. Jake moved slightly and the bronc jerked back.

"Say, that colt just might take a bite out of your hide."

Jake grinned. He knew his training methods were unorthodox, but effective. You could depend a lot more on a horse whose obedience wasn't based on fear. The bronc approached again, this time sniffing Jake's shoulder and then resting his muzzle there, blowing out through his nostrils. Jake turned his head slightly toward the horse's head but didn't look him in the eye. He blew out of his own nostrils and breathed in again, slowly inhaling and exhaling with the horse's rhythm. It was an Indian trick, imitating the way horses greeted one another.

"I don't have time to stand here and watch you kiss a horse. You going to let me see those broncs?"

"All right." Jake led George to another corral fashioned of bundled mesquite logs.

George Dobbs couldn't conceal his disappointment. "You know I can't buy *them*."

"Too bad, they're good horses." But Jake knew the cavalry brought only blacks, browns, and bays. This was partly because they wanted a uniform look to the regiment, but also for a practical reason. Bays and blacks were more durable in this hot country; their skin was black and tough. Cavalry horses carried McClellan saddles heavily laden with feed bags, outdoor canteens, carbines, and other equipment, and the extra weight could create chafing and saddle sores. But other horses—particularly liver chestnuts and duns—had black skin also. Jake surmised that appearance must be more important to the army than durability.

He pointed to a horse the color of a tanned deer hide. "That buckskin can go all day."

"You know I can't take buckskins," George said with real regret. "I guess that's it. I'll want those horses at the beginning of the month."

"You'll have them." Jake followed George Dobbs to his horse. "Have you been to Tombstone since the fire?"

"Went through there yesterday."

"I heard no one was killed."

"No, but the business district is gone. They're rebuilding fast, though. You oughta go in and take a look."

Jake glanced at the bronc. "I'm too busy here."

After Dobbs was gone, Jake worked with the bronc some more, but he couldn't keep his mind on his business. He knew that Emma, Maria, and Charlotte were all right, because the day after the fire a traveling salesman had stopped by his place and told him all the news. The Silver Dollar was intact, and the man didn't think the fire had gone as far west as the Mexican section. Jake had work to do; he'd spent too much time in Tombstone already.

Charlotte was a survivor. She would be all right.

Chapter Eighteen

Charlotte dragged the high-backed chair over to the window and huddled into it, staring at the patch of sky above the courtyard. She drew the bedspread off the bed and held it around her, too listless to put on the crisp white nightgown Lila had brought her an hour ago, shortly after Aaron Fielding had departed.

She had been a fool. A naive, childish fool to think that

140

any woman could control her own destiny. But she wasn't naive now.

The slashing pain that had ripped into her core and shocked her beyond struggling had subsided to a dull ache, and most of the ache was on the outside of her body, where Fielding's thick fingers had bruised her. She had been able to shut most of what Fielding had done out of her mind, and could not at this moment remember too much. But the thing that stayed with her was the feeling of vulnerability. She had been completely ignorant of the mechanics of rape, even though she'd attained some surface sophistication over the last year, rubbing elbows with prostitutes and macs. She had bandied about words like *soiled dove* and *frail sister* as if she knew what they actually meant. She and Maria had secretly devoured forbidden stories about White Slavery and procurers and ravished beauties, but hadn't really believed that such things happened. Charlotte had even fantasized about that moment when Morgan Earp would take her for his wife . . . but she had not remotely imagined the painful collision of flesh and muscle, nor the overwhelming helplessness that had gripped and paralyzed her, leaving her hopelessly empty.

A part of her brain knew she must overcome her apathy and gather her strength to escape, for as Aaron Fielding had raped her he had told her things.

She would be his wife. He would take her to San Francisco and shower her with lovely things, and every night he would visit this abomination upon her body the same way he had this afternoon—and she would be helpless to stop him. There would be no hope, for once a woman was taken in matrimony, she was property, and no one would help her.

Helplessness caught at her throat, cold and keening like the desert wind in the eaves of a deserted shack.

Distantly, Charlotte heard the clink of glasses and muted conversation. Lila had asked her if she would eat with the gentlemen tonight, but she had refused. The sympathetic expression on the woman's face made Charlotte want to scream: Why did you lock me in here? How could you do this to a person of your own sex? You knew what was coming. You *saw* him. But in the end she didn't have the energy, and knew she wouldn't receive a satisfactory answer.

And so she sat in the chair, one ear tuned to the lock.

Aaron Fielding had promised to sleep with her tonight. She had to put her apathy aside and gather her strength and wits and find a way to escape.

Try as she would, she couldn't keep her mind on escape. She felt it straying off into places she couldn't reach. And then her thoughts would come back with a sharp jerk, and she would try to grasp them and hold them before they could disappear again. She had no idea how many hours she sat in the chair. The square of sky outside turned black.

Presently, Charlotte become aware of a change in the conversation drifting in from the parlor. It was louder, and more boisterous. She recognized the pattern, for she had catered to enough inebriated patrons in her days at the theater.

Her mind seized on this knowledge. This drunken man could be fooled. His coordination would be off, his reflexes slow. With effort, she dressed in the midnight-blue dress. It was torn and sweat-stained, but she was used to that.

A key clattered in the lock. Clanged to the floor. There was a muffled oath. The key slid into the lock this time, and the knob jiggled. Aaron Fielding entered, looking lost and slightly addled. His eyes were red-rimmed and puffy.

"My bride," Fielding muttered thickly. "Ellen Ellen Ellen Ellen." He stopped, trying to focus on Charlotte. His lower eye seemed to be aimed at her shoes. "Charlotte. I'll have to get used to that. There is no more Ellen." He sat down heavily on the bed, and pulled off one shoe. Charlotte had gone over to the window, her back against it. Her heart hammered painfully in her chest. "Charlotte Charlotte . . ." he paused, and a slyness crept into his expression. "I almost forgot to lock the door. That wouldn't do, would it?" He lurched toward it.

Steeling herself, Charlotte hurried over to him and reached up to clasp her arms around his neck. She choked on her revulsion. Using her best cajoling manner, honed from countless nights at the Westphalia, she asked, "Couldn't you leave it open a crack? It's been so hot and stuffy in here, I thought I'd lose my mind."

"You've changed your tune. I told you you would, didn't I?" Then a drunken cunning returned to his eyes. "Or is this a trick?"

Charlotte ran one finger down his lapel. "I don't blame you for thinking that, especially after I was so beastly to you—"

"You called me hideous."

"Yes, but that was before . . ." Charlotte lowered her gaze demurely. "Well, you know. I was frightened, and well, I didn't *know* you very well . . ." He wanted to believe her. She knew it. "But now," she added, "After . . . our . . . the consummation, things are different."

"You liked it, then?" The hope in his voice was tangible.

Charlotte knew what she had to do. She lifted her chin and placed her lips on his. His arm came around her and his fingers tightened against her back. He pushed the door closed with his foot.

Charlotte drew back. "Please, leave the door open just a little. It's so hot."

"I'll open the window."

"It's painted shut."

His expression was knowing. "Oh, yes. This is Pike's prison."

"I don't consider myself a prisoner."

He stared at her skeptically. She prayed her expression was convincing. At last he said, "All right, then. It is a little stuffy at that." He opened the door.

"Pike won't . . ."

"Pike's passed out on the sofa, drunk as a lord. He won't hear anything until morning." With bearlike strength, Fielding propelled Charlotte to the bed, his hands already fumbling with the buttons on her bodice. "So you've come around, have you? I told Pike you would." He shoved his fingers between buttons and massaged a breast above the thick scallop of her corset. "He's afraid of you, you know."

"Of me?"

"Dam' right. Don't know why. I told him you'd come around. You're like Ellen. Sweet and gentle and kind." He dropped one hand and Charlotte heard him unbutton his trousers. Fortunately it was too dark to see him. He had not made much progress with her buttons, and said: "Damn these things. They're too small. You unbutton them."

Charlotte drew away. "I will in a minute." She glanced at the oriental screen near the door, where she had put the chamber pot earlier.

Aaron Fielding smiled indulgently. "I can wait."

Charlotte ducked behind the screen and watched as Aaron Fielding shucked his clothes. Fortunately, she could see little; just enough to satisfy her that he was buck-naked.

"What's keeping you?"

"I'll be there in just a moment." She swallowed, her hands shaking as she lifted the chamber pot with both hands. It had not been emptied since the night before. Stiffening her spine, she started toward the doorway, four feet away.

"What are you doing?"

Charlotte knew he would be quick, even drunk. In two bounds he could reach her.

He jerked back the sheets and got out of bed. Taking a deep breath, Charlotte stepped from behind the screen and dashed the contents of the chamber pot into his face, then threw the pot at his head. The ceramic bowl glanced off his temple and hit the floor, shattering into a dozen pieces.

Fielding howled, hands shooting up to his face. He stepped forward and screamed again as his bare foot sliced open on one of the broken shards. Charlotte darted out the door and ran down the hallway.

Fielding shouted behind her, roaring like a wounded bull. She shut her ears to the man behind her and concentrated on running.

She gained the parlor, her sights on the door Pike had brought her through last night. Every sound, every color, every movement of her body seemed intensified. Her senses shrieked like a mad violin playing at the top of its range, snarling her thoughts. Fielding's shouts pummeled her like physical blows. Through the corner of her eye she saw Pike sit up from where he had been lying on the couch, saw the exaggerated surprise on his face—it would have been comic under other circumstances. He stood up and reached toward her, looming like a black crow in a surrealistic dream, and she brushed past him as if he were a cobweb.

She hit the door with her hands, reached down and fumbled for the knob, felt her sweat-slicked fingers slide off. Grabbed again, expecting it to be locked. It wasn't. A hand wrenched at her arm just as the door flew open, but she twisted and miraculously the hand fell aside. The door banged open, there was a jarring thump and then the scrape of footsteps on the brick behind her. By then she was running, running, into the moonlit courtyard.

Ahead loomed a gate in the wall. Charlotte made for it, feeling the ragged gasps behind her.

Someone grabbed at her hair and yanked. The pain tore through her scalp, tears filling her eyes. She hunched her shoulders and shot forward, felt hair leave her scalp like ripped stitches.

She kept running. Only a few yards from the gate. It was probably locked but she prayed that it wouldn't be. Please God, please God please God—

She heard someone stumbling behind her, the rush of breath as whoever it was fell on the paving stones.

Charlotte darted a glance behind her and saw Pike sprawled on the ground. Fielding, stark naked and still shouting, burst from the little house. His foot was bloody. Charlotte reached the gate and her hands found the bolt just as she caught a sliver of movement off to her right.

"Lila! Get her!" shouted Pike.

Lila had come from the the back of the theater, and she was closest.

The bolt wouldn't budge. Lila was almost on top of her. Then Charlotte realized that she'd been trying to push the bolt the wrong way.

She jammed her hands against the bolt with all her might. It slid with agonizing stiffness, then hit the ground with a ping! She crashed through the gate and into the street just as Lila's fingers curled around her dress.

The dress ripped but Charlotte ignored it, and then she was running down the middle of the street, and the lock on her throat had finally given way and she was screaming, screaming, screaming.

A large cart rumbled toward her. Charlotte ran into its path. "Help me!"

The driver raised his whip. Charlotte reached for the near horse's head and grabbed the bit. The animal jerked backward, almost pulling her off her feet.

"What's the matter with you? You crazy whore!" The driver brandished his whip.

Charlotte held on to the horse's head. The whip caught her across the chin. She barely felt its sting. "Help me! They're after me! Help—"

The whip came down again across her head and she felt blood course down her cheek. Stunned, she fell to the ground as the cart lurched away.

For a moment Charlotte lay there, the wind knocked out of her. But she had to keep going. The sight of Fielding's ruined face swam before her eyes. She stood up, nearly fell again, and stared around her.

The gate to the theater was closed. No one had followed her.

Relief made her legs weak. They must have heard the ruckus she caused and decided not to pursue her. She started running up Sixth Street toward the corner, blood running down her face and into her eyes.

At the corner of Allen and Sixth she stopped. The town was alive with open fires and darting figures were silhouetted against the glowing orange. Piano music came from one of the new structures.

Safe now, Charlotte started to walk up the street, aware of the looks she received. She didn't get far. Now that she didn't need them for running, her legs had started to shake uncontrollably. She made it to a hitching post and had to lean against it.

I'm free! She pulled the night air into her lungs and wiped at the blood on her face with the palm of one hand.

The elation was short-lived. On its heels came the other realization, that Fielding had used her in the most terrible fashion, and she would never be the same again. She was marked now, as a prostitute was marked.

A sick feeling rose in her throat, cold and murky. She couldn't go home. Not like this. What would she tell Maria? How would Roberto—or anyone, for that matter—look at her now? She would have to keep this a secret, and for that she'd need her wits about her.

Charlotte sank to the ground beside the hitching post, unable to face the enormity of this thing that had happened to her. She would have to do something, yes, but later . . . much later. Right now she needed to rest. Completely drained of energy, unaware of the stares she attracted, Charlotte clasped the post in her arms like a shipwrecked survivor clutching a ship spar. She couldn't face her friends now. That was all she knew. But she couldn't go any further in her thinking, either. And so Charlotte sat on the ground and stared straight ahead, her mind at turns muzzy and roiling with ugly, disconnected scenes.

As Charlotte felt her mind slipping away again, she did not try to retrieve her thoughts. She found that if she built up a wall in her mind—just didn't let the memory of this horrible night in—she could have peace. Eventually, she was able to hide all of herself behind that wall, while the physical part of her remained pressed against the hitching post. With her bedraggled dark hair and flat expression, she blended into the scenery. When Jerome Pike and Aaron Fielding rode past later that night, they didn't even notice her. They were used to the Papago women who sat outside the saloons begging for food.

Morgan Earp had a good night at the Oriental, but a bad night at home. He'd been batching it at Fred Dodge's more and more lately, but tonight, flush with his winnings, he had gone back to the house he and Lou shared with Virgil and his wife, Allie. It had been a mistake. Lou wasn't the kind of woman who made a man feel big. All she talked about was her vegetable garden and her aches and pains. She was no longer the carefree Harvey Girl he had married, but a remote, ill woman with no place in her life for him.

It was getting so that he felt oppressed when he spent time at home. And so, after only an hour of her company, he'd taken off for town again. Breathing the heady air of freedom, Morgan forgot about Lou and concentrated on the night's pleasures. Every sense seemed to sing, and he was full of the joy of living. Tombstone was a great town.

Thinking he might join another game, Morgan glanced toward the Jezebel Saloon. He shortened his stride when he saw the woman huddled on the boardwalk. A good officer of the law took nothing for granted, and Morgan was a special deputy now. If this woman was a beggar, he'd have to roust her, so decent ladies wouldn't have to step over her to get to where they were going.

Morgan paused before the woman, about to touch her with the toe of his boot. A couple of things stopped him. One, she was coated with blood. The other was that what little he could see of the dress through the crusted blood stains looked expensive.

He spoke hesitantly. "Miss. Uh, Ma'am . . ."

The woman looked straight ahead, her brown eyes blank. She was dark-skinned but her hair looked red. She had a bruise the size of an egg on her chin, and blood lacquered her face near her ear.

Then he recognized her. "Well, I'll be. It's Charlotte something." Squatting on his heels, he gently tipped her chin up. "What happened?"

She didn't answer.

"Somebody sure beat you up good." He took out a bandanna and dabbed at the blood on her face. "I'd best get you out of here." He tried to uncurl her fingers from around the hitching post, but she held it in a death grip.

He broke her grip finger by finger and scooped her up into his arms. She was light but stiff against his arm, unresponsive.

When Fred opened the door to their bungalow, his surprise was almost comic. "What's this? One of the whores from Baby's?"

Morgan shouldered past. "One of the singers used to work at the Westphalia. Somebody beat the living daylights out of her." He set her down on his bed in the corner of the room.

"What you going to do?"

Morgan stood beside the bed, looking down at the girl. She lay the way he'd set her down, staring beyond him. "I guess we get her cleaned up." He took a dishrag from the kitchen, dipped it in the washstand, and dabbed gingerly at the blood, wrung out the cloth and applied it again. She

149

continued to stare beyond him as if he didn't exist. It spooked him.

Fred hovered nearby. "Aren't you going to undress her?"

"I guess that's the best thing to do." Morgan reached for the top button of her collar, then hesitated.

"What's the matter?" Fred's shadow fell across the girl's face.

"It doesn't seem right."

"What do you mean? You know every whore in this town. What's so different about her?"

"She's not a whore."

Fred snorted. "So? You going to let her stay in those rags?"

"No. But I don't even think she knows where she is. I never took clothes off a girl didn't know I was doing it."

"Morg, you are one funny *hombre*. You never were so particular before."

Morgan pulled back. "You know where Kate is?"

"Probably with Doc. They made up again."

"Would you go get her?"

Fred laughed, but took his hat from the rack and ducked out the door.

Morgan drew up a chair and sat down next to the bed. He didn't know where to rest his arms, but he guessed it didn't matter because she wasn't looking at him anyway. "You just sit tight," he said. "Kate'll be here soon. She'll take care of you."

Kate Fisher shucked off her gloves and swept toward the bed, all business. "Morgan, you idiot, why didn't you undress her?"

"I thought I should wait on you."

"So you let her lie here like this." She bent over Charlotte, her quick, sure fingers unfastening the buttons of the girl's bodice.

Morgan began to pace the room. "Why does she stare into space like that?"

150

"Just be quiet and bring that lamp over here."

Morgan did as he was told. Charlotte Tate's skin glowed as the light played over her face. Kate pushed back the open bodice, preparatory to getting the sleeve over one of the girl's arms.

The shriek almost split Morgan's eardrums. Suddenly the girl was a thrashing dervish, spitting and kicking and screaming all at once. Brown hands flew up and gripped Kate's arms, nails digging in and drawing blood. Kate yelled, "Morgan!"

Morgan nearly knocked the side table over as he lunged forward and grabbed the girl's hands, restraining her. She continued to thrash.

Kate hauled back and slapped the girl as hard as she could. Stunned, the girl stared at her, and for the first time that night she seemed to recognize another human being. Morgan felt her body go slack against him. "You're . . . Big Nose Kate," she said.

Kate laughed. "Not many people have the courage to say that to my face." At the sight of the bruise on Charlotte's chin, she scowled. "Whatever's happened to you, you're with friends now. We're trying to get you changed, so you can stop fighting."

Charlotte shrank back, her eyes wild. Morgan could feel her heart beating against his arm.

Kate's voice was as hard as iron. "Look at yourself. Do you want to wear this all night?"

The girl's gaze fluttered down over her ruined dress and then up again. She looked at Morgan, recognition vying with fear.

"You go outside for a minute," Kate said to Morgan, tipping her head to the door. "If Fred comes back, don't let him in."

Morgan did as he was told, feeling useless. He leaned against the porch post and stared out at the street. There was still plenty of action. He entertained the idea of going out for a game, but he couldn't get his mind off the frightened girl inside. At last Kate opened the door.

"She's asleep now."

Morgan walked into the house and shot a glance at the girl, lying like a statue under a blanket. "What's the matter with her?"

"She had some trouble with Jerome Pike. Seems he had a husband lined up for her she didn't cotton to, and the man didn't have the manners to court her proper."

Heat suffused his face. "She was forced?"

"Looks like it." Kate put her gloves back on. "I'm going home to get some sleep. We had a good long talk, and she'll be no worse for wear in the morning. She's got a couple of bruises and some surface cuts, but nothing my paint pot won't fix. I'll be by tomorrow."

"You aren't going to leave her here?"

"She's asleep, now. Why move her?"

"Kate—"

"Don't worry. I gave her some laudanum. She'll sleep straight through. Thing I want to know, is how Virge can let that weasel Pike live in this town, the things he does?"

"Pike's a friend of Behan's. Besides, if the law rousts Pike, they'll be after all the honest girls who want to make a decent living. You, for one."

"There's a big difference between Pike and the rest of us." Kate pushed past him angrily. "I know Johnny's a sporting man, and Pike lines his pocket better than anyone else, but there's just some things decent people can't stand."

"I'll talk to Virge."

"You do that."

After Kate left, Morgan sat down in the chair and watched Charlotte Tate sleep.

She was uncommonly beautiful. And fragile, somehow, like a doe. He remembered how shy she'd been when he'd flirted with her at the race. She had seemed so innocent then.

And now that innocence was gone, replaced by a fear that chilled him with its intensity. Fear of *him*.

Involuntarily, he reached out and ran a finger down her cheek. "You don't have to be afraid of me," Morgan said softly. "You don't ever have to be afraid of me."

She stirred slightly at his voice, but didn't wake up.

He stayed with her all night.

Chapter Nineteen

Charlotte awoke, disoriented. Morgan Earp was asleep in the chair next to her, and for a moment she wondered how he had come to be here in the house she shared with Maria, until she realized that their house was gone in the fire. Then the knowledge came crashing down on her. She remembered it all: Fielding, her prison, her escape.

Doc's woman, Big Nose Kate, had put her to bed. Kate had listened to her story and given her some laudanum to help her sleep. The elder woman had told her that being ravished wasn't the end of the world, but Kate was a soiled dove herself, so it wouldn't seem so important to her.

Charlotte sat up stiffly. Morgan Earp didn't wake. Charlotte didn't want him to. She supposed Kate had told him what had happened to her, and she couldn't stand to face him now.

She slid out of bed, wincing at the knot in her back. Her bare feet touched the floor. Morgan stirred. Charlotte paused, holding her breath. When she was sure that he was still asleep, she crept to the screen where her dress hung.

One look at the dress told her she could not seriously consider wearing it. The back panel had been torn when Lila pulled at it during her escape, and it was stiff with blood. Charlotte stood there a moment in her chemise and drawers, feeling naked. What would she do now?

"You okay?"

Charlotte spun around. Morgan ran a hand through his red-gold thatch of hair. He looked sleepy.

Charlotte blushed. She pulled the dress down from the screen and covered herself.

Morgan averted his eyes. He seemed as embarrassed as she was. "Kate's bringing you somethin' to wear," he muttered, his voice hoarse from lack of sleep. "I'll go get her."

He circled the room, keeping near the wall, and ducked out the door.

Charlotte stared at the closed door. Morgan Earp acted as if she were still a lady, and actually seemed shy in her presence! Could it be he didn't know what happened to her?

Feeling suddenly weak, she let the dress fall to the floor, walked over to the bed, got in, and pulled the coverlet up to her chin. She didn't have long to wait. Kate bustled in, carrying a purple dress and a valise. Morgan hovered at the door uncertainly. "I'll wait outside."

"How's our patient today?" Kate asked briskly, setting the valise on the chair.

The woman's demeanor instantly put Charlotte at ease. There were no secrets between them. "My back's sore."

"You must have put up quite a fight. I brought you my paint pot to cover those scrapes." Kate tipped up Charlotte's chin and scrutinized her face. "You're lucky Morgan came by when he did. This end of Tombstone's no place to be out by yourself. Someone else could have come along and made it worse. Bunch of coyotes in this town."

Charlotte suddenly felt sick. Kate understood, and held the pot for her to vomit in.

"Get it all out," Kate said, holding Charlotte's head. "I don't blame you, girl."

After she was done, Charlotte sat back shakily. Kate looked out the window at Morgan, who was pacing in front of the house. "Look at that oaf. He really is worried about you."

"Does . . ."

"Yes, lamb, he knows. Don't worry, he won't tell anyone. You can count on Morg to keep your secret."

"He must think—"

"I know what you're going to say. Now you just stop that kind of thinking right now. It wasn't your fault. Morg knows that. Why, you should be proud of yourself you managed to escape. Most girls don't."

"He was very kind to take me in," Charlotte said.

"From the looks of him, he stayed up all night with you. You couldn't have been in better hands." Kate walked to the door and leaned out. "Morgan! You heat some water for this young lady's bath!" She turned back to Charlotte. "I'm assuming you want one."

Charlotte nodded, grateful.

Kate handed her the dress. "It's kind of old-fashioned, but it'll probably fit you. Sorry about the color."

"No, the color's fine." The satin was cheap and garish, but Charlotte wasn't in any position to decline Kate's help.

Fred Dodge came back just as Charlotte was finished with her bath. Morgan intercepted him in front of the house, and Charlotte heard Kate tell the two of them to go out and get themselves some breakfast, they weren't needed around here.

When Charlotte was dressed and her face made up to cover the scrapes and bruises, Kate sat her down on the bed. "You all right, now?"

"I guess so."

"I'll get Morgan to drive you home."

Home. Charlotte swallowed, but still felt sick. Her heart began to pound.

"What's the matter?"

"If I go home I'll have to talk about it again."

Kate sat down beside her and smoothed Charlotte's hair. "You gotta talk it out, honey. Your friend, Maria's her name? She'll understand. Women always stick together on things like this."

Charlotte said nothing.

Kate clasped her hand in her own. "You got to talk about it, have a good cry. Why, she'll be so glad to see you the whole story'll come pouring out, the minute you see her. It ain't good to keep secrets from friends, cause your friends are the ones to help you when everyone else turns their backs on you."

"She warned me about Pike."

"That doesn't make any difference."

Charlotte stood up and straightened her spine. "I'd better go now."

"That's the attitude. I'll go find Morg."

Jake couldn't seem to shake the uneasiness that dogged him. He had no idea what caused the bad feeling, just that it seemed to hang over him like a cloud. The next morning he gave in to his instincts and saddled his horse for the ride into town.

He stopped at Emma's for breakfast. When he heard that Charlotte had left Roberto and Maria to stay at Jerome Pike's, something cold slithered through him.

Emma saw his concern. "You'll go and check on her? I'm sure she's all right, but—"

"I'll go right now."

"She's probably fine," Emma said as Jake mounted his big chestnut sorrel. "In hog heaven, now she don't have to slog in the mud no more." But her voice betrayed her own worry.

As Jake turned his horse up Toughnut Street, his heart pounded. The foreboding he'd felt all morning intensified.

The El Dorado stood at the corner of Sixth and Toughnut, bounded by an adobe wall on the street side. Jake reined his horse up at the entrance. A flash of color down the street caught his eye. A woman stepped out of Fred Dodge's house. Her purple dress shimmered in the sunlight, so bright it hurt the eye. Jake was about to dismiss her as an exceptionally pretty prostitute out for an airing, when she turned her head slightly and he saw the rich dark braid of hair. The slender figure, straight back, and tilt of her head came together like the pieces of a puzzle. It was Charlotte.

His first reaction was relief. It poured through him like a cold stream, numbing in its intensity. But why in God's name was she dressed like that?

Morgan Earp drove up to the door in a buckboard and jumped down. He took Charlotte's arm and helped her up onto the seat. The gaudy purple dress fanned out around her.

Morgan got up beside Charlotte. His attitude was deferential as he spoke some words into her ear. She had been looking away from him, her face averted and slightly downcast, but at his words she seemed to grow like a flower petal opening to the sun. She turned to look at Morgan, and Jake saw her face light up in a smile. Her face was painted.

Jake felt as if a lightning bolt had struck him full force. What was Charlotte doing in a whore's dress and a whore's makeup?

The sorrel fidgeted. Its teeth ground against the bit, showering the ground with green and white flecks of foam. For an instant, blind anger careened through the hallways of Jake's mind, resounded in his blood. Then he realized the horse was backing up in its attempt to get away from the pressure on the bit, and with an act of will he loosened his grip. He forced himself to stare into the glaring morning as the buckboard rumbled down Sixth to Fremont.

Jake had seen enough to satisfy him that Charlotte was safe. More than safe. She had most likely spent the night with Morgan Earp.

"Did you see her?" Emma asked, when Jake returned.

"Yes," he said shortly. "She's all right."

"What's wrong?"

"Nothing's wrong," Jake snapped. "She's fine. I've got to get back to the ranch. I've spent too much time on this wild-goose chase already." He wheeled his horse and rode down the street, feeling strangely light-headed. But try as he might, he couldn't get the image of Charlotte Tate and Morgan Earp out of his head.

Chapter Twenty

Charlotte walked up the street, feeling like a marked woman in Big Nose Kate's dress. She knew that men had paused in their work to look at her; their eyes bored into her back as if they could see Fielding's handprints all over her. As she did whenever she felt threatened, Charlotte straightened her spine and lifted her chin. Every muscle in her body ached. The walk seemed to go on forever. She regretted asking Morgan to drop her off at the corner. He would have taken her all the way home, but she was worried about what Maria would think—as if appearances mattered now. But Morgan's presence would puzzle Maria, and Charlotte knew that the urge would be too great to blurt out the whole sordid story at once. She didn't want to explain about her night at Morgan Earp's. Not until she had told Maria about Fielding.

The structure going up next door blocked their lot from

view momentarily, but now Charlotte could see the adobe bricks, stacked diagonally against one another like a pack of dominoes. She saw neither Roberto nor Maria.

Her stomach tightened. Everywhere else people were working with almost manic ferocity, except for their lot, an island of calm in the baking heat.

Perhaps Maria and Roberto had retreated into the tent for a siesta. She doubted that; the tent was hotter than Hades. Her uneasiness quickened with her pace.

"Maria! Berto!"

Ruff hurtled out from behind a stack of bricks like a brown-and-white bullet, yapping as he reached the end of his tether.

Charlotte breathed a sigh of relief. "Ruff."

Then she saw the tent lying flat in the dust. Her eyes caught a scrap of color near the old wall: Maria's faded blue calico.

"Mari—" Charlotte's voice hitched in her throat as she saw that Maria was propped up against the wall like a rag-doll, her eyes dull. She cradled something gray and red in her arms.

Shock knifed through Charlotte as she realized the thing Maria was holding was a man: Roberto.

Blood drenched his shirt and blotted the front of Maria's dress. No one could have lost so much blood and live. His temple was crushed like a broken melon. Blood plastered his hair to his head.

"Maria! What happened?" Charlotte rushed across the lot, tripping and almost falling over the adobe forms.

Maria looked up. Her eyes were flat and black. Roberto stared sightlessly at the sky.

Charlotte's heart hammered painfully in her chest. "What happened?"

With exaggerated care, Maria transferred her burden to the ground and pushed herself up on her palms, then stood unsteadily. Blood formed a map of rust-colored countries across her stomach and breasts. "My brother is dead, thanks to you."

Roaring filled Charlotte's ears. Thanks to her?

She could see Maria's lips moving but she couldn't hear her, saw Maria's face contort into a fierce mask of hatred.

The buzzing grew louder. "Maria." Charlotte swallowed, nearly choking on her tongue, which felt thick and fuzzy in her mouth.

"Look at you! You painted, disgusting *puta!*" Maria's voice cut across her brain like the scream of a catamount. "Whore!" She stepped forward and spat. Saliva caught Charlotte on the chin. She wiped at it, feeling sick.

This was a nightmare. It had to be. It couldn't be happening to her! Roberto—dear, kind Berto—couldn't be dead; Maria couldn't hate her. She couldn't have been raped and humiliated and be standing here in this heat in a whore's dress with paint on her face. Roberto couldn't be lying in the dust, his head blown away and his chest slick with blood, horseflies buzzing around his open mouth.

"Murderer!" Maria lunged for her, grabbed the purple ruffled collar and jerked hard, rending the material. "Because of you, Roberto is dead!" She dug her hands into Charlotte's scalp and twisted her hair like a rag, pulling. "Killer! Killer!"

Pain clouded Charlotte's eyes with tears. She wrenched away, but Maria caught another handhold of her hair and held on like a terrier. The unfairness of Maria's accusation stung more than the physical pain. "I wasn't even here!" she shouted, trying to restrain the much smaller Maria. "I don't understand—"

Maria wheeled and ran back to Roberto's body and knelt beside him. "Get out of here," she sobbed. "Just get out of here and leave us alone! *Mi hermano es muerto!*" She lapsed into hysterical Spanish, crying and talking at the same time, pressing her cheek against Roberto's and rocking back and forth.

The enormity of it finally crashed home. Roberto was

dead. Maria hated her. Everything that had happened in the last few hours had changed her life irrevocably. Maria needed help, comfort, and Charlotte knew that she must give it whether it was wanted or not. But something seemed to shrivel inside her as she reached out to her friend, who had turned into a mindless, wounded animal. "I want to help you, Maria," she said softly. "I didn't kill Roberto. I was nowhere near here."

"Liar! You killed him as surely as if you pulled the trigger. They came looking for you!"

Suddenly, Charlotte knew what Maria said was true. Nausea assailed her. "Pike," she whispered.

"Yes, Pike! He came for you and killed Roberto. They roped the tent pole and pulled it down around us, and when one man put me over his horse Roberto tried to stop him. They shot him!" Maria paused for breath, her eyes wild. Her breath came in ragged gasps. "They shot my brother! Like a dog!"

Charlotte felt bewildered, lost. It had all been her fault. She stared at Maria, unable to deny her friend's accusation.

"Pike said I was nothing but a stupid Mex slut and didn't they have eyes? And the man threw me on the ground next to my brother, who was bleeding to death! And they asked me where you were, and I would have—" She coughed. "I would have told them, if I knew! You're not worth my brother's life! I told them I didn't know where you were, and they shot him in the head." She shook her fist at Charlotte. "Look at you! Not a hair on your head is touched, and my brother bled to death in my arms! Get out of here! Go back to Sixth Street where you belong!"

Charlotte backed up.

Maria picked up a fragment of adobe brick and hurled it. The brick went wild, crashing into the neighboring wall.

Charlotte turned and ran, hearing Maria's strangled screams and Ruff's barking behind her. She did not stop running until she'd left the town far behind.

* * *

Charlotte didn't know how long she walked, but eventually the furnace heat penetrated her misery and she realized she could not stay out much longer. As if awakening from a dream, she suddenly became aware of her surroundings.

Desert stretched on all sides. She had walked blindly up one scrub-covered hill and down the other, through white sand arroyos and over piles of rocks. Like ocean swells, the hills blocked her view of town.

Charlotte knew that many a person had wandered out into the desert alone and never come back out. Apaches had been raiding again. If the Apaches didn't kill her, heat exhaustion and thirst soon would. Scrubbing her eyes with the heel of her palm, Charlotte turned and started walking up the hill she'd just come down. As she walked, Maria's words pounded in her head. *Puta!* Whore. You killed him!

She could not go back there. She could not face Maria again.

Helplessness overwhelmed her. The lot, with its bricks and tent and Maria and Roberto had been her home. Now she had nothing. She doubted even Emma would help her this time. Yet self-preservation kept her walking. Not knowing what to do next, Charlotte turned back toward Tombstone.

She could not get the image of Roberto's body out of her mind. It burned before her eyes. She remembered the pride he took in escorting her to the theater. His shyness, his silent admiration. The way they had worked together these past couple of weeks, knowing each other better than ever before. She remembered Maria hugging her and saying how she valued their friendship. Her eyes sparkling as she came up with one scheme or other, the way they used to laugh at the people they observed on the street.

All gone. There was no going back now. Charlotte knew it was unfair of Maria to blame her, but she couldn't help but feel she had contributed to Roberto's death. If she hadn't gone over to the El Dorado, Fielding would never have seen her. If she hadn't been so proud, so stubborn, so *sure* of herself, she never would have been raped, never would have caused this tragedy. Maria, Emma, and Jake had warned her. But she knew too much. She had done what she wanted and Roberto had paid for her folly with his life.

The image burned behind her eyes. Roberto, staring blindly at the sky. "Stop it!" She clapped her fingers to her head, but there was no relief.

At last she reached the outskirts of town—the Mexican quarter not far from where she and Maria had lived. Again, people paused in their work to stare at her. Charlotte knew she looked a sight in her dress and makeup, but the censure seemed to go deeper than that. Did they know about Pike's ambush?

Thirst drove her to ask for water from a Mexican who was firing bricks. A stout woman almost concealed by a black *rebozo* handed her the dipper to the *olla,* her face sullen.

Her husband paused in his work and spoke in rapid Spanish. Charlotte heard the anger in his tone, although she did not understand what he said.

The woman shouted back, crossed herself, and stared at Charlotte. Her eyes were brittle with hatred. Still, she let Charlotte drink.

"Muchas gracias," Charlotte said, handing back the dipper.

"You've had your water, now get out of here. I know who you are."

Charlotte turned and walked away, feeling the hostile stares. She wandered through town, trying to decide what to do. Twice, she started for Emma's, but turned back both times. How could she go to Emma now?

Who was left? Only Morgan. Morgan would care . . . and Big Nose Kate. The thought of facing Morgan with Maria's words still ringing in her ears disturbed her. She didn't want her guilt to show on her face. No, she would go see Kate.

She went to Fly's Boardinghouse where Doc and Kate lived, but they weren't there. Kate had her own place in the tenderloin district. Charlotte would have to go to Sixth Street again.

Despite her misery, hunger began to gnaw at her. She had not eaten since breakfast at Pike's yesterday morning. Opening her reticule, Charlotte found fifty cents, enough for lunch at the Russ House. She walked to the restaurant and was led to a table near the kitchen.

Charlotte ignored the shocked looks she received, too hungry to care. When she reached into her reticule to pay for the meal, her fingers brushed up against a slip of paper that must have worked into a seam. She pulled out a yellowed piece of paper with an address scrawled on it.

It was the address Dulcinata had given her. It was the name and address of a woman who ran a variety theater. The theater had long since closed, but Charlotte had heard rumors that this Lottie Hutchinson and her husband, Bill, were planning to build another.

Charlotte asked Nellie Cashman if she could use a mirror to straighten up. After rinsing her face and hands, she coiled her hair up and tore the rest of the ruffled collar off her dress. Then she walked up the street toward the house Lottie Hutchinson shared with her husband, Bill.

Lottie Hutchinson had a well-deserved reputation for kindheartedness. One look at the slender young girl in the purple dress was enough to bring out the maternal instincts in her.

Lottie didn't ask why Charlotte was dressed the way she was, or why a large bruise showed faintly under her makeup. In her business, it didn't do to pry. She sensed the girl wasn't a prostitute—or if she was, she hadn't been in the business long enough for it to harden her. Lottie liked the innate sense of pride that seemed to cling to Charlotte Tate like an aura, although it was obvious she had been through some tragedy. She had to help this child, but she and Bill were still trying to find the money to build their theater. The Bird Cage might be finished by late fall if they started building soon, but that would be too late to help this girl. Lottie put her plump hand over Charlotte's slender one. "Tell you what. I've got a friend who runs a traveling troupe out of Bisbee. I know he could use a pretty girl like you in some of his skits." Uncertainty crossed Charlotte's features. Lottie added quickly, "He's a kind man and he'll take care of you."

"I . . . don't know, I—"

"He's the father of seven girls. I've known him for twenty years and he is as noble a human being as you'll ever meet in this world."

Charlotte frowned for a moment, seemed to come to a decision, then smiled, looking straight into Lottie's eyes. The smile seemed to go to Lottie's soul. "I think I will go see him."

Lottie couldn't keep her eyes off this young woman. Goose bumps ran up her arms. Charlotte had something special, something that, if tended, just might make her a star. "Don't thank me, my dear. You'll be doing me a favor, and DeWitt, too. I'm hoping he'll bring you to the Bird Cage when it's built. Now," she added briskly, taking a piece of stationery and a quill pen from the desk and scribbling a quick note. "This is your reference, so hold on to it. And be sure to remind DeWitt he owes me a favor. You come by tomorrow and we'll get you a proper dress, and I'll book you on the stage for Bisbee. Or better yet, I'll come by your place. Where do you live?"

The girl lifted her head and stared at Lottie. "I haven't anyplace to live."

The next morning, Charlotte, dressed in a new traveling suit, boarded the stage for Bisbee after spending the night with the Hutchinsons. Their kindness had almost reduced her to tears several times. She hugged her newfound friend fiercely, trying not to think of her other friend, the one left behind on Fremont Street, cradling her dead brother in her arms.

As the coach lurched away, Charlotte saw Virgil Earp walking along Allen Street. Her mind turned to Morgan. Perhaps she should have gone to see him. But Charlotte sensed that the time wasn't right, not after everything that had happened. She was numb with shock, unable to think of anything but Maria's screams and Roberto . . . Not even Morgan could fill the void inside her. She needed time to heal. Lottie Hutchinson had offered her an opportunity to better herself, and she would take it.

She'd come back to Tombstone one day soon, and Morgan would still be here. By then she would be stronger, happier; a woman to be loved, not a pathetic creature who needed pity.

If Charlotte had any inkling of what Morgan and his brothers planned for Jerome Pike, she would have had another reason to thank him. But she had already lived in Bisbee a week when several horsemen descended on the El Dorado and burned it to the ground, chasing Aaron Fielding into the desert and shooting him twice in the back of the head.

Jerome Pike's remains were discovered two days later by a traveling drummer. He, too, had run into the desert, but in the confusion and darkness the Earps missed him. He had headed in the direction of Charleston, but lost the trail and became disoriented. It hadn't been long before he'd succumbed to the broiling midday heat.

Part Two

1881

Chapter Twenty-one

Destined to become the largest city in Arizona by the turn of the century, Bisbee started out as a sprinkling of frame houses at the confluence of two canyons. By 1881 it had already started to climb the steep, oak-forested hillsides. When Charlotte's stagecoach arrived late in the afternoon on the first day of July, the sun's last rays sparkled like mica off the window panes of the miners' cabins high up on Chihuahua Hill, a striking contrast to the rest of the town, engulfed in deep mountain shadows. A sulphurous haze from the smelter imbued the canyon with a dreamlike quality, like a fairy-tale land shrouded in mist. The effect was stunning, and would have delighted Charlotte if she had been in any other state of mind. As it was, the fledgling copper camp made almost no impression on her at all.

Her mind kept replaying the scene at Maria's with brutal attention to detail. If only she could go back to those few moments before she saw Roberto . . . if only the outcome had been different.

She saw again the dusty lot, felt again that prickly sensation in her scalp. The adobes were unattended, but that could mean that María and Roberto had gone into town. Everything was still all right. Then Ruff would come running out to bark at her, as he always did. And there was still a chance that the nightmare would not repeat itself.

But always her mind pushed inexorably to the hideous conclusion; she would spy the patch of gray near the wall . . . and everything would come apart. Roberto lay

169

dead and Maria's face contorted as her accusation rang on the air: "You killed him!"

The coach lurched to a stop at the station. A rotund white-haired man in a brown suit and plaid vest stepped forward to greet her. "Charlotte Tate? DeWitt McMann, at your service. I am the proprietor of the Athena Traveling Theatrical and Variety Troupe." Wearily, Charlotte handed him her bag and followed him up the dusty road to a frame house that looked like a little barn. There she met Mrs. McMann and the four youngest daughters still living with them, and after a glimpse of the homey parlor and kitchen, allowed herself to be ushered to the room she would share with the two oldest girls, Viola and Kitty. Without bothering to sponge the dust of the trip off her face, she stripped down to her chemise and drawers, crawled into the bed they had given her, and slept.

She awoke early after having slept fitfully, catching occasional snatches of conversation between Viola and Kitty. Their giggling and whispers reminded her of happier times with Maria. She had tried to keep these memories at bay, but they roiled in her mind all night, sometimes during moments of wakefulness; more often in dreams.

Charlotte dressed silently and tiptoed out past the sleeping girls to the back porch. Although tired from her trip, she felt tense and agitated, and needed to get out of the house. The mountain air was invigorating; the smelter on the hill hadn't started belching its sulphur smoke yet.

Nearby, a mockingbird sang, its sharp voice slicing the air. The town was still in shadow, but as Charlotte walked, the sun peeked over the great rust-red bulk of Chihuahua Hill and flooded everything with golden light. Bisbee was so small after Tombstone; just a few false-fronted wooden stores on either side of a riverbed jumbled with rocks and paved smooth by sand from the summer floods. But the canyon was pretty and far greener than Tombstone. For the first time in days, Charlotte felt a brief lift in her spirits. She was in a new place, among kind people. She would never have to go back to that dusty lot, never again have to face Maria's wrath or the pain it caused. And so she did what she had always done, and pushed those dark memories into the deepest crevice in her mind, refusing to think about them.

Charlotte Tate knew how to deal with tragedy. She had lost her mother and dad, her brother-in-law, and Mary. Shutting the pain away had become second nature to her, and she relied heavily upon that practice now. She would think ahead, for she could not undo the past.

Charlotte's thoughts turned to Morgan Earp. As she walked, her mind lingered on those few hours at his house. She heard his voice again, saw the concern in his blue eyes, the controlled anger in the line of his jaw as he talked about Pike—the dangerous flare of anger on her behalf. There was no doubt in her mind that he cared for her deeply.

Maybe she should have gone to see him before making the decision to move to Bisbee. They might even be married by now. But Charlotte knew that she had to get away from Tombstone, if only for awhile. She felt hollow inside, unable to concentrate on any one thing for too long a time. This was not how she wanted to start her life with Morgan. It was best to stay here awhile, lick her wounds in private, and gather strength to return to Tombstone.

There was no doubt in her mind that she would be going back someday. And Morgan would be waiting for her.

Charlotte hugged herself against the dawn chill. She followed the creek bed behind the McMann house to a clearing among the oak, just below a jagged outcropping of rock. A covered wagon was parked in its shadow, emblazoned with the words the Athena Traveling Theatrical and Variety Troupe. The canvas sides were painted with a number of scenes; a portrait of DeWitt McMann himself, a woman in a dancing costume roman-riding two bay horses, their legs splayed out in a plunging run. One panel showed a young man with black shoulder-length hair and blazing blue eyes who stared out as if he could really see her. In his hand he held a blue pendant on a chain. "Featuring the Amazing Lucifer! Illusionist, Prestidigitator and Mesmerist Extroordinaire! Startling Illusions! Marvelous Mysteries!"

At one end of the clearing was a large tent. Inside were rows of wooden benches. Charlotte sat on one of the benches, pondering how she had come to this place, in a traveling show's tent in a backwater called Bisbee, miles away from her original dream.

"Ah, there you are," said a voice. Charlotte looked up. DeWitt McMann entered the tent. "Come in here," he shouted behind him. "Meet the young lady I brought from Tombstone."

The rest of the troupe entered, their expressions curious and friendly.

"I believe introductions are in order," McMann said. "And then, my dear, prepare to be dazzled. We'll rehearse the whole act for an audience of one."

Charlotte recognized one of the men immediately. His likeness had been painted on the covered wagon. L. J. Bailey, The Amazing Lucifer. Despite the intensity of his ice-blue eyes, he spoke softly and treated Charlotte with a gentle respect. He was assisted in his act by Mollie, a young blond woman billed as Psyche, Maid of Mystery. L. J. Bailey's act consisted of several magic tricks, but he was best known for hypnotizing members of the audience.

The most thrilling part of the rehearsal was indeed Lucifer's act, set against a black velvet backdrop. Charlotte was horrified by the appearance of Mollie on a red velvet swing, her entire lower torso and legs gone. Lucifer swept a sword under the swing to prove that she was indeed only half there.

When DeWitt saw Charlotte's white face, he patted her

shoulder. "It's only an illusion, my dear. Lucifer!" he called out. "Show our fledgling star here how you do that trick."

Obligingly, Lucifer led Charlotte up to the stage and asked her to touch Mollie's stomach. One hand shielding her eyes from the blinding oil lamps suspended in a circle around the swing, Charlotte reached out hesitantly and brushed the crimson material of Mollie's bodice.

"Tap her," Lucifer urged. He demonstrated by rapping his knuckles on Mollie's bosom. Mollie's strained smile abruptly turned to a glower. "Watch that, you lecher," she muttered.

"Go ahead," Lucifer said.

Charlotte knocked on Mollie's stomach. It was wood.

"Hurry up and show her, will you?" Mollie said. "My neck is killing me!"

Lucifer led Charlotte around the side of the swing, where Mollie's body was suspended in a black hammock. She wore the same black velvet material as the curtain behind her.

"You see? It's nothing more than a dressmaker's dummy, cut in half. Get down now, Mol."

With a grunt, Mollie removed her head from the neck of the torso.

Charlotte stared at Lucifer. "Are they all tricks?" she asked. "Cutting off Mollie's head? Making her vanish?"

"Some of them are tricks," Lucifer replied, his eyes twinkling. "And some of them are mysteries of the ages, of which only I am cognizant."

Straightening out her back, Mollie said, "Don't you believe him. The only magic that one's got is with the ladies. Not that he cares."

DeWitt McMann decided that they had enough of a cast to do most of "the Pirates of Penzance," if he himself performed and a couple of the cast members took more than one part. Charlotte was assigned to sing Mabel's role. She spent hours going over her lines and practicing Mabel's arias. In this way she avoided spending too much time with the cast other than rehearsals, which suited her well. Charlotte noticed that the troupe was a family, intimately involved in one another's lives. She wanted none of this. She was pleasant to everyone, but decided it would be better not to get too involved with any one person. It was far better to remain detached, yet friendly. The Athena Traveling Theatrical and Variety Troupe was merely a place to rest and gather her strength for awhile. She would never again allow herself the luxury of close friendships. Not after Maria.

It was the first time Charlotte had been part of a real show, but Delia had taught her well. Often, she stopped the show with her coloratura cadenzas. She always negotiated the difficult hills and valleys successfully, but there were times when she felt her voice soar like a freed bird. The cast members would applaud her vociferously when she was through, and at these times Charlotte felt closer to being fully alive than ever before. DeWitt told her often that she had a very fine voice.

In late July, he took her aside and told her they would be leaving for Willcox in two weeks. "We need to find a stage name for you. What kind of monicker is Charlotte Tate for a performer?" He stood back, his kindly face beaming. "That English skin of yours reminds me of a blushing rose. How about the Bisbee Rose?" His hand ran the words across the air in front of him, as if they could both see them on a marquee.

Charlotte remembered Doc Holliday's name for her. "I like The Tombstone Rose," she said.

The following day Charlotte saw that someone had painted a likeness of her on the canvas side of the wagon. Above her picture was the legend, "Featuring the Fairest Songbird in the West: THE TOMBSTONE ROSE."

Mary would have been proud.

The Tombstone Rose

* * *

The Athena Traveling Theatrical and Variety Troupe played Willcox for one week. Charlotte was very nervous during her first song, but after that, she relaxed. It was easier to perform in an operetta; there were people all around her, so she wasn't the sole object of the audience's scrutiny. The costumes also put her at ease, making her feel it wasn't her standing up there, but a real character. She nailed the coloratura passages perfectly, and received a standing ovation at the end of the first act. But every day before she went on, she would walk some distance from the theater and lose her dinner in the bushes.

The paying customers never saw her distress. They saw only an exquisitely beautiful young woman with a voice like an angel's.

Word got around. The women came to see The Amazing Lucifer, and the men came to see The Tombstone Rose. When DeWitt McMann counted his receipts at the end of the week, he praised all of them for a job well done, but his beaming smile was for Charlotte.

Her weekly stipend—a small share of the profits, was not nearly as much as she could make in one night at the Westphalia. But all her other expenses were paid for, so she spent very little. She'd lost interest in buying new clothes and expensive bric-a-brac—there was little enough room in the wagon she shared with Mollie, and fashionable clothes wouldn't wear well on the road. So she saved her money. Someday, she would have an even more beautiful wardrobe than she'd had in Tombstone—the finest of everything. She was willing to wait.

From Willcox, they traveled to Mesilla, New Mexico, and then to the large metropolis of El Paso. Swinging north through New Mexico again, the Athena Traveling Theatrical and Variety Troupe spent a couple of weeks in Santa Fe before returning to Arizona in early autumn. They roamed from Safford to Globe, then to Prescott,

Phoenix, Maricopa Wells, and on to a long engagement in Tucson.

Charlotte made no effort to renew her acquaintance with her family.

Their second week in Tucson, L. J. Bailey had a visitor. He looked like any other down-on-his-luck miner, with his pinched felt hat, rough clothing and down-at-heel brogans. L. J. introduced the man as Patrick Grady. He joined them at Delmonico's Restaurant and talked about his mining claim in Bisbee. The talk wasn't about silver, but copper, which Pat thought would soon be much more valuable. Charlotte was rarely impressed by people, but this man seemed to know what he was talking about, and she liked his quiet self-assurance. Here was a man who believed in himself. Charlotte recognized this quality because she had it herself.

"I've staked the claim, but I'm going to need help."

"You know I'm no miner," L. J. said.

"I don't need that kind of help. I need money."

"I'll talk it up to my friends, but I don't know how much good it will do. None of us has much cash."

"One hundred dollars from three people. That's all I need to start. Timber, dynamite . . ." he recited a list of things he needed. "It won't be enough to work it like the big boys do, but there's enough ore near the surface that can finance me as I go along."

L. J. shook his head.

Pat Grady leaned forward. "I came to you first, L. J., because you're my friend. I'm doing you a favor." He said it with such authority that Charlotte felt the skin prickle along her arms. She believed him.

After he left, Charlotte asked L. J. about him.

"Pat? He and I have been friends for several years. We went to school together at Columbia University. I dropped out after one year. Decided I liked performing magic better."

"What did he study?"

"Mining engineering."

The next day Charlotte sought out DeWitt McMann. She asked him to advance her twenty dollars.

"I don't see why not. You'll make it up in a week. You got a gander at the fashions in Zeckendorf's store, didn't you?" He patted her head. "You're a pretty thing and a damn hard worker. Go buy some frippery if you want to. You deserve it." He gave her five dollars extra. Charlotte spent ten dollars on a good walking dress, but saved the rest.

That afternoon, Charlotte and L. J. went to the boardinghouse where Pat Grady was staying. Charlotte put in one hundred and fifty-five dollars, L. J., one hundred and forty-five.

"I guess we're partners," Pat said. His steady blue eyes held Charlotte's own. "You won't regret this."

They shook on it. L. J. raised his glass of whiskey in a toast. "To Charlotte, who wouldn't let me pass up a good deal."

"You have controlling interest," Pat said to Charlotte after the toast. "It's only fitting you name the mine."

Charlotte thought of DeWitt McMann's unwitting aid. "Let's call it the Athena Mine."

"The Athena it is."

A week later they left for Tombstone. It was late October.

Word spread quickly that the new singer with the Athena Traveling Troupe had a face and a voice like an angel. No one seemed to remember that the Tombstone Rose was formerly the pretty waiter many a man had pawed at the Westphalia. "Into our midst comes a fresh English beauty, the likes of which we have never seen before. Fair of face and exquisite of voice, the lovely songstress graces our stage and inspires tenderness in the breast of the basest ne'er-do-well. How does such a delicate rose grow in the desert, even a Tombstone Rose? What a joy to worship her, if only from afar." So gushed Harry Woods in the *Nugget*. He had conveniently forgotten the many times she had waited on him at the Westphalia, where his worship had been of a more personal nature.

Every night Charlotte scanned the audience, hoping Morgan Earp would appear, and every night she was disappointed. The time passed quickly, and before she knew it, it was almost time to leave.

Two days before the troupe was to return to Bisbee, Charlotte walked back to the the Fly Boardinghouse. Maybe Doc and Kate were back, and could tell her where Morgan might be.

"Morg's been back and gone out again, so Doc told me this morning. He went to Charleston for the day. Should be back tomorrow," Mrs. Camilus Fly said. "Do you want to leave a message with Doc?"

"No. No, thank you."

Charlotte stepped out into the street. The weather had taken a cold turn. She started walking toward Schieffelin Hall. As always, she scrupulously avoided looking toward Maria's lot farther down Fremont Street. A knife-cold wind howled in the eaves of C. S. Fly's frame house, scooting under the heavy material of Charlotte's traveling suit and chilling her legs above her button boots. The sky was sullen and mottled with ominously dark clouds, and Charlotte shivered involuntarily. The wind was so noisy that at first she didn't hear someone calling her name.

Emma Lake was walking her way. "Charlotte!" she commanded, her arms pumping as she picked up her pace. "Cold for October, ain't it? Where have you been?"

Charlotte told her about the variety troupe.

"The Tombstone Rose, eh? I've heard the name. Didn't know it was you, though. Why didn't you tell me you were leaving Tombstone?" She didn't wait for an answer. "Looks like you landed on your feet all right. I can see I worried over nothing. Jake said you were all right."

"Jake?"

"He went looking for you at Pike's."

Charlotte absorbed this. Jake had come looking for her. He might have been standing right outside the El Dorado while she was being held prisoner. He might have prevented everything. Why hadn't he demanded to see her? How could he have left her in Pike's hands?

"I know what you're thinking. I shouldn't meddle, but when I heard you moved in with Pike, I thought the worst. You are a lucky one, I'll give you that, getting out unscathed from that fire and missing Roberto's murder in the bargain—and here you are, untouched by the tragedy that dogs us lesser mortals. I swear, you walk through life like Moses crossing the Red Sea."

Charlotte stiffened. Did Emma know that Roberto had been killed because of her? She searched Emma's expression for censure, but found only sadness.

If Maria hadn't said anything to Emma, perhaps she didn't blame Charlotte anymore. "Is Maria all right?" she asked quickly.

"Haven't seen her. As a matter of fact, I didn't hear about the shooting till a week later. You know how those Mexicans stick together. By the time I got down to pay my respects, Maria had taken off."

"Taken off?" Charlotte asked blankly.

"Married that Marquart fella and left town. Think they bought a little ranch on the border. Near Hereford." Emma scrutinized Charlotte carefully. "Where did you go, anyway? When I heard about the fire, the first place I thought to look was Maria's, but she was gone."

"I just . . . left town."

"A lot of Pike's girls did. Like rats off a sinking ship." Emma shook her head. "Your cousin would have my head if she knew the bad company you've taken up with."

Charlotte barely heard her. So Maria had married Thaddeus Marquart. Charlotte felt a load lift from her shoulders as her gaze wandered down the street to the lot. A white frame house stood where their adobe had been.

Emma followed her gaze. "Some eastern folks bought the property." She spat. "Greenhorns. Won't last long."

"Have you seen Morgan Earp?" Charlotte asked.

"You aren't still mooning over him, are you?"

"What I do is my business."

Emma snorted. "You haven't changed. Stubborn as ever. Didn't anyone ever tell you Morgan was married?"

Charlotte stepped back involuntarily. She might as well have been kicked in the stomach. She tried to speak but her lips were numb.

"I finally saw her the other day," Emma added. "Louisa, that's her name. So you'd be wise to set your sights on someone else, Missy." She saw Charlotte's stricken expression and her face softened. "Don't take it too hard. He's not for you. He ain't smart enough for a fast number like you."

Charlotte could barely hear her for the rushing in her ears. "Excuse me, I've got to go."

"Well, honey, even if you're stubborn as a Cornishman's jackass, I'd still like to know how you're farin' from time to time. You come visit, you hear me?"

"I will," Charlotte mumbled, and headed toward home.

The wagon was deserted, for which she was grateful. She didn't want anyone to see her cry.

Chapter Twenty-two

In the October 26 issue of *The Tombstone Epitaph*, John Clum wrote: "Be sure to catch the last performance of the Athena Traveling Theatrical and Variety Troupe at Schieffelin Hall, if you haven't already. It's well worth the price of admission, and is less punishing on the constitution and pocketbook than entertainments across town."

Charlotte had overslept. Today would be the Athena Traveling Troupe's last performance in Tombstone, her last chance to see Morgan.

The wind howled around the canvas of the wagon, swatting at the heavy material like a playful cat. Outside, the dark sky looked bruised and swollen above a thin thread of dull pink near the eastern horizon. She dressed hurriedly in the sage-green walking dress, her mouth dry.

Emma's words kept running through her head. "Morgan's married."

Well, she would just have to see for herself. Charlotte coiled her hair and tried to put it up. It took a couple of times for her shaking fingers to push the pins in properly, she was so nervous.

The streets were teeming with merchants, miners and townspeople, all shivering and miserable against the damp chill. Wind licked at Charlotte's legs, bitingly cold. The surrounding mountains were shrouded in opaque whiteness, a harbinger of snow.

Charlotte walked up Fourth to Allen Street and turned toward the heart of town. She had no idea if Morgan would be up already, or if he were in town. But she had to do something. Sitting around waiting for things to happen was not her way.

She walked slowly down the boardwalk, pretending to window-shop at each store. Her heart drummed against her breastbone. Every nerve was alive. She paused near the Oriental Saloon, pretending to shake something out of her shoe. Morgan would most likely be working the faro table there if he were in town. If only she could go inside! But Charlotte was a lady and ladies did not walk into saloons, unless of course they were performing. She tried to see over the batwing doors, but they were too tall.

Across the street was the Crystal Palace Saloon, and above it were offices, including that of the city marshal. Maybe Morgan was with Virgil. At any rate, if he were anywhere, it would probably be in one of these two buildings. Charlotte decided to continue up Allen, and then stroll back, so that she would not appear conspicuous. She walked slowly up the boardwalk, lingering at every entrance, aware that most of the buildings on this block were saloons. She didn't care what other people thought. Why should she? If Morgan were married, she'd be leaving town with the troupe tomorrow, and if he were not—

The door to the Grand Hotel banged open and a man stormed out, nearly knocking her over. He scowled as if *she* had caused the collision, then shouldered past her into the street, brandishing a six-shooter in one hand and a rifle in the other.

Of all the bald-faced gall! Charlotte recognized him as one of the men Maria had pointed out to her on the street, one of the rogue's gallery of rustlers: Ike Clanton, a scruffy-looking specimen with a beard like a goat.

Soon after running into Ike, Charlotte saw Morgan emerge from the marshal's office. He looked incredibly handsome, his broad shoulders filling his checked mackinaw, his russet mustaches sweeping down over his jaw and brushing the collar of his snow-white shirt. His face was rough-hewn by the cold. The wind flapped the lapel of his coat and Charlotte glimpsed the shining Special Police badge pinned there.

Flexing his fingers, Morgan scanned the street, then crossed after a wagon rumbled past. He strode down Allen. His hand hovered near the pocket of his mackinaw, as if he were thinking of grabbing the gun butt protruding from it. Charlotte debated whether to call to him. It wasn't good manners to hail someone from across the street, but if she didn't act soon he would be gone. The devil take manners! This was her chance to get him alone, and she would darn well use it!

But when she tried to speak, her throat seized up on her. What if he was married? What if Emma was right?

Don't be ridiculous! You have to know, don't you? Isn't it better than wondering? "Morgan!" The moment the word was free of her throat she regretted it. What would she say now?

Morgan stopped and looked in her direction.

Charlotte had gone over this moment in her mind a thousand times, so often that she was prepared for a certain reaction. When it didn't come, coldness permeated her entire core.

Where was that slow light of recognition? The smile that was to light up his face, the ardor in his eyes, the quick, ground-eating strides as he covered the distance between them? The crushing embrace that she had pictured—yes, and *felt*—so often? All Charlotte saw in Morgan's face was annoyance, as if he had been in the middle of doing something very important and someone of no consequence had distracted him. His eyes stared out of his ruddy face, two pinpoints of hard blue light. Didn't he recognize her?

Charlotte had to say something. Anything to remind him of that special night they had shared together, his tenderness, his love . . . but she could barely unstitch her tongue from the roof of her mouth. "You will come tonight, won't you?" she asked at last, gulping for breath before adding, "It is the last night."

"What?"

"To the theater. To Schieffelin Hall. I'm performing there . . ."

She stopped as he flicked a glance to the other side of the street. A thin, gaunt-faced woman stood uncertainly on the corner below Marshal Earp's office.

Charlotte rushed on. "I've been gone, that's why you haven't seen me. But I'll never forget the way you—after the night you took care of me . . . after you and Kate Fisher . . ." As she floundered for words he stepped off the boardwalk and strode across the street without a backward look.

With a sinking feeling Charlotte saw him catch up with the woman and grab her by the arm. "What are you doing out here?" he shouted, holding on to the woman's elbow.

"Allie wanted me to fetch Virgil. She's feeling poorly."

In the depths of her despair, Charlotte felt the beginning of anger. How dare he treat her like that! She stared at the woman, who was as plain as a sparrow and sickly besides. She wanted to turn away, but couldn't, held in thrall by some morbid fascination. Morgan spoke again. "Lou, I told you to stay home today. There's going to be trouble, and I don't want you hurt."

What Emma had told her was true! Shame and anger burned Charlotte's cheeks, shame at throwing herself at a man who didn't want her. She felt anger at herself, at Morgan Earp, and most of all at that pale shadow of a woman who stood across the street.

Charlotte glanced away and saw Emma standing outside the Wells Fargo office. Her eyes met Charlotte's, and there was grim satisfaction in them.

Charlotte couldn't stand it. The humiliation was too

much. She wanted to be anywhere but here. Blinded by her tears, she started walking.

He hadn't even recognized her! Here she had bared her soul by speaking plainly, practically *begging* him to remember her—and he didn't even seem to care! Her cheeks grew hot again. How many people had seen her throw herself at him? How many people were laughing behind her back?

A man brushed past. She hunched her shoulders, withdrawing from the contact like a tortoise pulling its head into its shell. The man ran up the street. Something urgent in the way he ran made her look back in Morgan's direction. Virgil had joined Morgan on the corner, and Louisa Earp had disappeared. The man who had run past her reached the Earps and leaned against a hitching post, trying to catch his breath. It was too far away to hear what he was saying, but she caught the word *Ike* several times.

Ike Clanton. She remembered the gun and rifle in his hands.

Morgan was pacing around in a circle, stopping to gesture down the street, his finger jabbing the air. "I'll kill that son of a bitch!" he shouted. Virgil spoke more quietly, his voice fraught with authority. Charlotte heard the words *disarm* and *cowboys*.

And then the messenger was running again, shouting behind him, "I'll get Wyatt!"

So this was what was so important to Morgan Earp that he couldn't even talk to her! The stupid vendetta with the cowboys. Anger was quickly replaced by humiliation, as she again remembered the spectacle she had made of herself. Suddenly she wanted to run away, out into the desert where no one would see her tears of anguish and hurt pride. She didn't care if she ever saw this godforsaken little mining camp again as long as she lived.

Abruptly, Charlotte realized that she was standing in front of the Dexter Livery Stable. They rented horses.

A ride. That's what she needed. To get away from here, from prying eyes and smug, knowing looks. She would gallop over the hills and let the wind take her tears.

Charlotte walked into the stable and asked the proprietor if he had a spirited horse. He glanced at her clothing skeptically, but accepted her money quickly enough. He led out a scrawny brown brute and helped her into the saddle. She touched the animal with the crop he gave her. The beast lurched into a startled lope, nearly running down a lady walking across the entrance. The woman shouted and shook her fist, but Charlotte didn't care. She cared about nothing but the power under her as the horse reached forward with ever-increasing strides, leaving Tombstone and its inhabitants far behind.

Chapter Twenty-three

Emma Lake saw Charlotte go tearing out of the stable on the brown horse. She felt sorry for the girl, but she couldn't help feeling a certain satisfaction, too. Charlotte had things too much her own way. Not that Emma wished her any unhappiness, but sometimes a few hard knocks stiffened the spine. Charlotte was willful and naive, and those traits were dangerous in this country.

The girl would get over it. Morgan Earp wasn't right for her, even if he weren't married. He was impulsive and hot-headed—and for all his golden good looks, Emma thought he wasn't too bright, either. Charlotte needed a steadying influence.

Emma forgot Charlotte's problems as she saw Harry Jones, puffed up with his own importance, leave Virgil and

Morgan Earp at a run as if he were trying to keep two jumps ahead of hellfire. As he passed Mayor Clum, Harry put on an extra burst of speed and announced loudly that he would "go find Wyatt."

All up and down the street people had come out and gathered in excited little knots. There was a circus atmosphere in the air. Every few minutes or so, some darn fool would come running up to the Earps all out of breath with some vital piece of information that only made Virgil look sterner and Morgan angrier. These self-appointed relays reported back and forth between the two Earps and Wyatt and Doc, who must be coming this way with all the fanfare of visiting dignitaries.

Virgil and Morgan started walking toward the telegraph office. Emma had noticed Ike there earlier, still drunk and spouting off about Doc Holliday, waving a gun and a rifle.

It was Emma's considered opinion that Ike Clanton better watch himself, if he wanted to see another sunrise.

Charlotte had difficulty keeping the iron-mouthed stable nag running straight. It resented being ridden and tried to dodge in and out in its efforts to go back to the stable. She slapped the reins back and forth across the brute's flanks, keeping it at a run. The horse scrambled over rocks and through clawing stands of tar bush, up thorny hills, and across sandy arroyos, stumbling often—once to its knees, sending Charlotte's heart into her throat.

At last she hit a flat stretch of grass and gave the horse its head. The sensation of speed was a salve to her hurt feelings. Biting wind whipped color into her cheeks and chapped lips, and her hair came loose and tumbled down her back in a dark red skein. As the tears coursed down her face, Charlotte reached up a numb fist to swipe at them. At last she pulled up on a ridge, letting her heart calm and the horse rest. She felt better, as long as she didn't think about the stinging humiliation she'd suffered.

Annie McKnight

Snow filled the air. She had ridden out in the direction of the Whetstones, unmindful that she had been following the path she and Jake had ridden in happier times.

The hill before her was sheathed in white mist, and as Charlotte let the horse catch its breath, she scanned the hackberry bushes that seemed to poke out, disembodied, from the wraithlike tendrils of fog. As she watched, a horse and rider materialized out of the whiteness.

Her horse spooked, but she held him fast, staring with an open mouth as Jake Cottrell approached. For a moment, she wondered if Emma had sent him after her, but discarded that theory immediately. He had come from the direction of his ranch.

Still sniffling, she wished she were anyplace but here. But she couldn't very well turn around and gallop away. Jake had seen her. She wondered if he noticed her red-rimmed eyes, but it was too late now. Charlotte lifted her chin and tried to smile.

Jake stopped his horse a few feet away. "I heard you were back in town," he said.

Something hard in his expression made her reply haughtily, "I'm leaving tomorrow."

"Then I'm in time to see you perform."

Curiosity overcame her wariness. "You're coming especially to see me?"

Jake grinned, but the good humor did not reach his eyes. "I thought I could combine business with pleasure." He leaned forward in the saddle and scrutinized her. "You've been crying."

"It's the wind. It's made my eyes water."

"I could hear you crying three hills away."

Charlotte tried to look as if she were above that kind of thing, but suddenly needed to blow her nose. Averting her face, she sniffed, but it didn't do any good.

Jake rode up and handed her a handkerchief from the breast pocket of his mackinaw.

188

Charlotte turned away and blew her nose as delicately as she could. "Thank you," she muttered in a choked voice. "I will have this washed and returned to you. Now if you'll excuse me I'll—"

Jake's horse blocked her path. "What's wrong?"

"Nothing."

Jake was about to say something else, but stopped abruptly.

"Would you please move out of my way—"

"Quiet!" Jake whispered, holding up his hand. He sat still in the saddle, his head tilted to the side as he listened.

Involuntarily, Charlotte drew in a quick breath. She heard it, too. The clicking sound of hooves on rock. "I don't see—"

"Shut up!" came the savage whisper. "Apaches."

Charlotte's stomach lurched at the dreaded word. The air seemed colder on her skin. She held her breath, too scared to exhale.

Blood pounded in her ears, almost drowning out her thoughts, but she could still see the woman in Tucson that her cousin had pointed out to her one day long ago, a woman who had been held captive by the Apaches. She saw in her mind's eye the tattoos around the woman's mouth, like drops of blood, and the way the woman's eyes had darted in fear at any sound, the broken line of her shoulders. She had been one of the lucky ones.

Charlotte knew the stories. Most women who met with Apaches were tortured in horrible ways and then killed, or worse—were captured, made to be slaves, and raped repeatedly.

At this thought her mind seized up. Panic—blind, crushing panic—started in her solar plexus and radiated outward. It seemed as if some large animal sat on her chest, depriving her of breath. She wanted to scream, wanted to spur her horse toward Tombstone, wanted to die before she'd be raped again. Charlotte trembled so badly that she dropped the reins.

In an instant Jake was off his horse. He pulled her down into his arms and clamped his hand over her mouth. He stared into her eyes, demanding silence. For what seemed like an eternity they remained balanced on that thread of tension, until the scream in her throat dissipated and she returned his gaze, nodding briefly. He pulled her to him and she burrowed her head into the heavy plaid wool of his mackinaw, feeling the blood pump up through her neck, feeling his arm like a bar of iron across her shoulder blades. Over and over prayers filled her head: *Hail Mary, full of grace, the Lord is with thee.* The solid bulk of Jake's body and her prayer were the only things between her and insanity.

Jake had never seen such naked fear on Charlotte's face before, and in an instant he realized that this was no general fear of Indians, but a specific one. He knew that something terrible had happened to Charlotte, knew it in every fiber of his being. As he held her, he strained his eyes to see through the mist but saw nothing. Jake judged the riders to be a couple of hills over, and the hoofbeats seemed to be retreating. He knew they were Apaches because of the sound of unshod hooves and the few guttural words that drifted through the mist, but they could just as easily be Apache scouts as renegades. Still, he wasn't willing to take any chances.

Jake loosened his grip on Charlotte. The mist was clearing a little, and he knew the Indians would be able to see them soon if they could not find a hiding place. He glanced around and saw an abandoned mine adit dug into a hill not fifty yards away.

"I'm going to let you go now," Jake whispered in Charlotte's ear. "There's a cave in that hill, just over there. I want you to walk toward it as quietly as you can. Do you understand me?"

She nodded.

Charlotte crept toward the mine, mortally sure that every step would be her last. Surely, the thinning patches of mist couldn't obscure her from the sharp eyes of the Apaches.

She knew, however, that she had to trust Jake. She stepped as quietly as she could through the quivering stands of brush, careful not to dislodge even one stone.

At last she reached the mine and shrank back against the craggy wall, grateful for its darkness. She strained her eyes in the mist, but could barely see Jake. He stood with his back to her, every line of his body stiff with tension, his hand clamped over the brown horse's muzzle. Then he was covered by the mist.

She did hear one of the horses nicker, and that struck fear into her heart. The Apaches would hear and would be down on them like a bird on a bug. She would be at their mercy . . . unless Jake could hold them off. But if he didn't—

She shivered. She would kill herself before . . . well, she would. Her hands curled around the hat pin that remained in her hair. It was four inches long and sharp, and if she stuck it in her heart it would kill her.

Charlotte clamped her shaking fingers down on the hat pin and started praying again, holding on to the tiny pearl handle as if it were a rosary bead. She had said enough Hail Marys and Our Fathers to go all the way through the rosary and still Jake did not come back. But at least she wasn't as frightened. There was no way she could maintain the heart-thumping fear of those first few minutes. Pretty soon other sensations came to her: the jagged rock face digging into her shoulder blade, the musty smell of the mine, the pinching of her shoes, and most of all, impatience. Where was he? How could he leave her here all alone, defenseless? Had he been captured, or maybe killed? How would she ever be able to get back to Tombstone on her own? Her mind roiled with unlikely visions. Jake riding off and leaving her. Jake staked to an anthill, being tortured to reveal her whereabouts. The horses getting loose. Could Jake have forgotten where she was?

Time stretched into an hour or more. Where *was* he?

At last, when she thought she would go out of her mind

if any more time went by, she heard a footfall, and the clink of horses' shoes on rock. Terrified that the Apaches had found her, Charlotte felt her way back farther into the dank blackness of the mine.

"Charlotte." Jake's voice.

Her relief was so great that she ran toward the sound of his voice, tripping over a stone and falling headlong into him.

His arm came up around her and he hugged her to him. She hugged back. "Jake! I thought you were killed—"

"It's all right," he soothed, his voice gentle in her ear. "They were scouts from Fort Huachuca."

The adrenaline suddenly left her, making her legs weak. She shook uncontrollably, and to her dismay, started to cry. She didn't know why she was weeping, unless it was from relief of Jake's return. They were not like the tears she'd shed on her ride through the desert, the tears for Morgan Earp. The thought of Morgan now elicited no pain, just a hollowness, as if she hadn't eaten for awhile. But the tears dredged up from her very soul were real, and although she had no idea where they had come from or why she suddenly had to cry, she abandoned herself to it. In the half light of the cave Jake's expression swam through the blur of her tears. She saw sympathy, understanding. She knew instinctively she did not have to be proud around Jake. And so she cried.

Once started, the flood was unstoppable. Her body seized with wrenching sobs, she felt the comforting warmth of Jake's arm pressing her into the hollow of his shoulder, the other hand gently stroking her hair.

"It's all right," he soothed, his voice soft and deep and comforting, his touch like a balm. She only cried more, unashamedly, wetting his collar and the heavy plaid coat. She cried out her pain, which had been in her heart for so long and never been aired. She cried for Tom, and Mary, and her lost innocence. She cried for Roberto's death and the loss of her only friend, Maria, she cried because she had survived a close call and her life had been given back to her when she'd been certain they would both be killed.

Jake's fingers tangled in her hair and drew gentle circles in her back. He didn't know what caused Charlotte's bottomless lake of tears, but again, he sensed that something catastrophic had changed her. He felt like a helpless outsider, unable to divine the reason for such deep unhappiness, yet the fact that she had turned to him for comfort left him absurdly honored. Feelings he'd thought long dead surfaced—a desire to comfort, a desire to hold this slender, lovely creature in his arms and keep her safe, a need to banish her pain and have her happy again.

His hand slid down her back and tightened around her waist as he rubbed his cheek against hers. "Cry it all out," he muttered, and Charlotte drew comfort from the sound of his voice and the feel of his body. He pressed closer to her, his chest flush against the basque of her green dress, and even in the depths of her despair she could feel how good his solid body felt against her. At last the tears abated, and she choked down the last of her sobs. Jake took the handkerchief from her and gently wiped her face, staring down at her as if searching her expression for something he had lost and expected to find in her.

His silver eyes were kind and deep, and she thought how handsome he was—really, better-looking even than Morgan Earp, and this was a complete revelation to her. She found herself staring at his mouth, the strong yet sensual line, and felt the sudden and completely unexpected urge to kiss him. Surely, he could not think her attractive, not after this. *I must look a sight! My eyes must be as bloodshot as a drunken cowboy's, and my nose—*

His lips came down on hers and obliterated any logical thoughts, and she abandoned herself completely to his touch. At the same moment his lips pressed against hers, his fingers tightened on her back and pulled her to him, and she felt with pleasure the sensation of his rough coat and the hardness of his chest against the mounds of her breasts. His

193

lips were warm, with an underlying strength that sapped her of energy and made her feel he had assimilated her into himself. Drained of emotion by her tears, Charlotte had room for other sensations. She felt as if something warm had melted inside her, unusually sweet, like a strawberry ice on a hot day. It was almost a taste, only the taste was deep inside her, making her feel pleasantly drowsy and yet yearning for something more—something she could not name.

Had Charlotte any inkling of just what exactly she desired, she would have been shocked. Certainly, this lovely, tingling feeling would have nothing to do with the brutality she had suffered at Aaron Fielding's hands. But the seeds that had been sown so bitterly now bloomed under Jake's touch.

Jake ground his mouth gently into hers, and she returned his embrace, clinging to him, enjoying the slow, gentle movement of his hands over her body. His lips had left her mouth and chased into the hollow of her neck, one moment voracious, the next soft and gentle, tingling like raindrops along her skin. She felt his hand come up and cup one of her breasts, lazily circling the full mound encased in tight material until she thought she would go mad. His fingers fumbled with the buttons on her basque. Her back hollowed as she leaned against him, her breasts craving the solid caress of his hand, although a part of her knew it was wrong.

It was that part that spoke up, louder and louder, until she heard it dimly through the mist of pleasure. As if slapped hard across the face, Charlotte suddenly realized what all this kissing and hugging led to.

She shrank back against the wall of the cave, shocked. Jake looked at her, his face flushed, and there was something hard and bright and dangerous in his eyes. Why, he was no better than Aaron Fielding! "Don't you touch me!"

Jake stared at her for a long moment, then smiled wickedly. "I see you're back to your old self." He stepped back. "I was going to tell you, when I was so rudely interrupted by your . . . enthusiasm in seeing me still alive, that we can go now. I'll get the horses." He turned and walked away.

Trembling, Charlotte buttoned her basque and tried to pin up her hair. How could Jake try to take advantage of her in such a way? How could he be so vile? As she tugged to straighten her bodice, her comparison of Morgan Earp and Jake reasserted itself.

Maybe Morgan had thrust her away from him, but it was because he was an honorable man. He had a wife. He wouldn't dream of trying to seduce her, no matter how much he might be attracted to her. He had risen above his baser instincts, for her sake as well as his own. But Jake . . . Jake was a disappointment. No, far worse than that. He had taken advantage of her fear and uncertainty and pain.

Forgotten was the slow, sensuous pleasure that had enveloped her like a warm cocoon. Charlotte thought only of Jake's fingers unbuttoning her bodice, and the crudeness of his hand cupping her breast. That she had enjoyed it immensely did not register. She knew what happened down the line, and a more distasteful, vulgar, and out-and-out painful conclusion she could not imagine.

She would never let that happen to her again.

Chapter Twenty-four

How they had ended up outside Camilus Fly's boarding-house, Tom McLaury would not have been able to say. He guessed they were leaving town, which was fine with him.

Since earlier that morning, when he'd gone looking for

Ike Clanton to calm him down, things had gone from bad to worse. He'd encountered Wyatt Earp in front of the Recorder's office, and Earp had baited him into a yelling match, which had ended with Earp hitting him over the head with his gun. He would have fought back, but his ears were ringing and he was still hungover from last night. And so he had gone in search of the rest of his party and found them at Spangenberg's gun shop. His brother Frank was there along with Ike and Billy Clanton, looking at guns.

Tom almost bought a gun, but decided against it at the last minute. While they were at Spangenberg's, Frank's horse had gotten loose and stuck his head in the doorway. Before he knew it, Wyatt Earp was there, threatening Frank to tie his horse up, or there would be hell to pay. He was throwing his weight around, trying to start a fight.

And all the time it seemed as if Tom were hardly there at all, but walking through a dream.

Now they were outside Camilus Fly's house, next to the O.K. Corral. Frank and Billy already had their horses, and he had thought they would head over to the west-end corral to pick up the wagon. But instead, they had gone from the Dexter Corral through to Allen Street, then on through the O.K. Corral alley to Fremont. Tom wondered why their progress was so slow. They should have been out of town by now. He wanted to get out of here. But just then Billy the Kid Claiborne and Wes Fuller joined them, and so Ike had to tell them the whole story—how they were all being persecuted by the Earps.

Still feeling as if he were caught in a dream, Tom ducked into Kehoe's butcher store to complete the business he had been aiming to since yesterday. When he came out, Frank, Ike and Billy stood in the weedy lot outside Doc Holliday's window.

"If that tin horn son of a bitch Holliday shows his face, I will fight him!" Ike shouted.

"He's not home," Claiborne said.

"He's a damned coward," muttered Ike.

Why did time seem to move so slowly? Tom leaned against the rough wooden clapboards of the Harwood house. Wind kicked up divots of dust from the horse's hoofs, blasting the side of the building with fine sand.

Johnny Behan came running up. "Frank, I want you to give up your arms," he said.

"Johnny, as long as the people of Tombstone act so, I will not give up my arms."

Tom started at the steely quality of his brother's voice.

People had come out on the street by now. The air shivered with tension. Frank was too smart to force a confrontation with the Earps . . . wasn't he? His mouth suddenly dry, Tom could feel the cold wind burrowing under his blouse. He wished he had bought a gun when he'd had the chance.

"Let's go home," he said to no one in particular. They would be arrested, now, if Johnny had the guts to do it. He just hoped his brother wouldn't fight, because Tom was willing to bet that if Wyatt Earp commenced to fighting, he would kill them all.

"Give me your firearms or leave town immediately," Behan said.

Tom opened his vest to show Johnny he wasn't armed.

"What about the goddamned Earps?" Frank demanded.

"Wait here," said Johnny. "I see them coming down. I'll go and stop them."

Tom heard his own voice, loud in the stillness. "You don't need to be afraid, Johnny. We aren't going to have any trouble." He scanned his own party, hoping they agreed with him. Ike was muttering darkly, and Billy's eyes were bright as he fingered the butt of the gun stuck into the waistband of his pants. But Frank bothered Tom the most. He looked choleric. Tom knew that Frank was not just a blowhard like Ike. When riled, he went after an enemy like a hornet, and he was riled now.

197

Tom saw Billy Clanton blanch, and followed his gaze. The Earps were walking up the street toward them, ignoring Johnny Behan, who capered at their heels like the anxious puppy he was. Tom swallowed. The air was so thick it was hard to breathe. Despair flooded him, nearly causing his knees to buckle, and his heart hammered painfully against his chest. He felt naked without a gun.

Virgil and Wyatt were in front, striding with purpose. Wyatt's right hand rested in the pocket of his mackinaw, his eyes shining with that fanatic light. Virgil looked grim, resolute. As the Earps clumped down from the boardwalk into the lot, Morgan and Doc fanned out so that they were four abreast. They were close enough to touch him with a rifle.

Tom's eyes registered the long gray coat Doc Holliday wore, a shotgun protruding from the shaggy hem. He'd heard Doc didn't care how or when he would die; he was dying from consumption, anyway.

Tom thought there must be some way out of this confrontation, something he could say to defuse the situation. But no words came to him, and seconds dragged like minutes. He smelled fresh manure; it mingled with the odor of garlic coming from the Can Can Restaurant.

Morgan shouted, "You sons of bitches. You've been looking for a fight and you can have it." His face was flushed with fury.

Virgil Earp's voice: "Throw up your hands!"

Tom's head pounded. As if he were submerged in water, he heard Billy Clanton's cry, muffled, beside him, "Don't shoot me! I don't want to fight!" Tom swallowed, his tongue dry and furry and his heart going like a drum. His bowels churned. This was real.

A voice of reason poked into his consciousness. *Show them you're not armed.*

He reached down to open his vest.

Chapter Twenty-five

Jake and Charlotte rode back to Tombstone, wrapped in their own thoughts. Jake couldn't help wondering what had happened to Charlotte to make her so fearful of Indians. "When you were a child—traveling around as you did—did you have a brush with the Apaches?" he asked.

Charlotte looked puzzled. "No. Why?"

"You seemed so frightened back there."

She looked away. "Wouldn't you be frightened? If you were a woman, I mean?"

It was Jake's turn to be puzzled. "Why?"

"Surely you've heard the stories. About how they . . ." Charlotte colored. "How they treat women. I don't think I could abide it if—I wouldn't want to live if one of them touched me."

"Touched . . . ?" Jake grinned as he realized what she meant. "You wouldn't have to worry about that. Apaches don't rape their captives. It's bad luck on a raiding party. They'd most likely just kill you outright."

Charlotte's face remained averted, but he could tell she was crying again.

"What's wrong?"

"Nothing," she replied, her voice tremulous. "It was just such a close call."

What was the matter with her? He reached out and grabbed her horse's bridle. "Something's bothering you. Don't you think you should talk about it?"

"Leave me alone!"

"The way you were crying back there. What's going on?"

She refused to answer him, which made him even more suspicious. It was almost as if she'd been—

A terrible revelation burst upon him. Charlotte had left town right after the fire at the El Dorado. What had happened to make her turn away from her friends Maria and Emma? He remembered how she had looked the last time he saw her, the purple dress and heavy makeup. Rage, hot and thick, filled his throat, and he had to clench his jaw to keep from shouting. "Did something happen at the El Dorado? Pike didn't make you work the cribs, did he?"

Charlotte turned white with shock. She raised her quirt to strike him but he caught her wrist. She struggled but his grip was too strong. "How dare you talk to me like that!"

"What happened?"

"It doesn't concern you."

"We're friends, aren't we? What happened with Pike?"

"He wanted me for a—a friend of his," she said. "But I got away. I *did!*" she added defiantly as she saw the doubt on his face. "Morgan rescued me."

"Rescued you?" Jake couldn't believe what he was hearing. "Were you hurt?" By *hurt* he meant *raped,* a word he had used casually only a few moments ago. Now the thought of saying it was unbearable.

"No. Morgan saved me." She glared at him, a challenge in her dark eyes. "And a good thing he did, too. You certainly weren't around to help me. Morgan was there and everything turned out just fi-fine. He took me to his house and spent the whole night watching over me, because he cared, because he loves me. He didn't touch me at all. He was completely chivalrous." She started to cry again.

Jake felt sick with guilt, sick at the thought of what could have happened to her. He closed his eyes, grateful that Morgan had been there to save her.

His anger turned inward. Morgan Earp had rescued her from Jerome Pike. All Jake had ever done was manhandle

her as if she really were one of Pike's whores. That day at
the river, he'd told himself that he was showing her what
she could expect from men like Jerome Pike. But the simple truth was, he had wanted her.

No wonder Charlotte had been frightened when he'd
kissed her in the cave. She had every right to be frightened,
repulsed. She loved another man. Morgan Earp, who had
been there when she really needed him.

"I'm sorry," he said at last. "It was none of my business."

"Just leave me alone," she said stiffly.

Jake respected her wishes. They didn't speak the rest of
the way back to Tombstone.

As they reached the outskirts of town, he saw the crowd
down near Fremont and Third. There was a tragic quality
to the milling people—several women were crying and
wandering aimlessly around the street, and the men were
grim-faced and quiet. Jake kicked his horse into a trot.

"What happened?" he called to Johnny Behan, who was
darting helplessly around the edge of the crowd, trying
ineffectually to break it up.

"It's terrible!" muttered Johnny. "I told them not to go
down. I warned them!" He wrung his hands and Jake
thought—not for the first time—what an old woman
Johnny was.

"Coming through!" announced a voice, and several people stepped back. Thomas O'Keefe emerged from the
press, helping to carry an inert body. "In there," he said,
motioning with his chin toward the Harwood house. Billy
Allen came behind him, supporting the shoulders and
lolling head. Blood spattered the dirt like red rain. As they
came even with Jake, the shock of recognition took his
breath away. It was Tom McLaury's body.

Jake dismounted and pushed through the crowd, following O'Keefe and Allen toward the house. "How bad is he
hurt?"

201

"He might already be dead," said Allen.

Out of the corner of his eye, Jake saw Charlotte ride up to the hitching rail and jump down from her horse, her face pinched white with fear. She gathered her skirts and ran through the crowd. He heard her voice, and even as he feared for Tom's life, there was room in Jake for another kind of despair.

"Is he all right? Is Morgan all right?" Charlotte was saying.

Jake saw the crowd part as someone drove a wagon through, and in it he saw Morgan and Virgil Earp, grim-faced and bloody, hunched over their wounds. He saw also that Charlotte was watching them go, her face hauntingly bleak.

"He's not long for this world." Billy Allen's voice broke into Jake's consciousness, and in two strides Jake was near Tom's side.

He tried to ignore the blood soaking his friend's midsection, but he could not miss the murkiness clouding the surface of his eyes. "Tom," Jake said gently, taking his friend's hand in his own.

But Tom was already gone.

The gunfight was the talk of the town. Jake heard several different stories. No one who had witnessed the fight agreed on the particulars. Some claimed the dead cowboys were innocent victims of Wyatt's lust for power and intimidation; others asserted the Earps and Doc Holliday had only been doing their job. But in those few seconds in the empty lot near Fly's Boardinghouse, Virgil and Morgan Earp were wounded, Frank McLaury, Tom McLaury, and Billy Clanton were killed, and not one soul really knew why. In hindsight, it seemed there had been many opportunities for one party or the other to defuse the situation.

Sentiment was rising against the Earps, and both Wyatt

and Doc had been taken in for questioning. Wyatt Earp's Special Police badge helped him very little now. Virgil and Morgan were recuperating from their wounds at Virgil's under house arrest. Doc, too, had sustained a minor flesh wound to his thigh. Of the lawmen, Wyatt, alone, had been untouched by the bullets. Ironically, the one member of the cowboy gang to escape unharmed was Ike Clanton.

Jake accompanied Tom's body to Ritter and Ream, the city undertakers, where the three dead men were dressed in suits and laid in ebony coffins decorated with silver leaves. Their coffins were put on display in the funeral parlor window, with a sign declaring that they had been murdered on the streets of Tombstone.

For his part, Jake surprised himself by realizing he felt little anger toward the Earps. Wyatt Earp liked to intimidate his enemies, whipping the fight out of them *before* it came to gunplay, and Jake doubted that Wyatt had wanted this fight. He also knew that Virgil did not take his position of city marshal lightly. Several people thought that Virgil had meant to disarm the cowboys peacefully. Still, once the firing began, there had been no going back. Bill Allen had seen Tom reach to open his vest at about the time the firing started; that move could have been misinterpreted by the two hotheads of the Earp party, Morgan and Doc, who were believed by most to have fired first.

Jake felt only world-weary and empty, and guilty that he had not been there. While his friend was dying in an alley in Tombstone, Jake had been trying to make love to Charlotte Tate.

I should have done something, he told himself now, as he walked back along Fremont Street in the gathering dusk. He should have known that things could only get worse.

He paused outside Schieffelin Hall and heard a chorus singing within. A playbill fluttered against the wall.

LAST APPEARANCE: THE PIRATES OF PEN-ZANCE, STARRING MISS CHARLOTTE TATE, THE TOMBSTONE ROSE, AS MABEL!

Below was a lithograph of Charlotte, her sweet face tilted alluringly to the side.

She was the most beautiful woman he had ever seen in his life. But he could barely stand to look at her.

Guilt and anger seethed like a nest of snakes in his belly. If it weren't for the time they had spent in the mine, he would have been in Tombstone when he was needed.

Logically, Jake realized he could not have known what would happen today. More than likely, he couldn't have affected the outcome even if he had known. But guilt ate at him anyway.

Jake remembered Charlotte's stricken face as she watched Morgan being driven away in the wagon; he would be all right. For Charlotte's sake, Jake was grateful. The best thing he could do was leave her to her happiness.

A soprano voice soared above the others, drifting out into the frigid air. Charlotte's.

Jamming his hands in his pockets, Jake turned and walked away.

Part Three

1884–1886

Chapter Twenty-six

When Jake rode into Tombstone on a fine spring morning in 1884, he found the town little changed since the day Tom McLaury died. The skyline was almost the same, even though another fire had swept through Tombstone two years before. There were a few new buildings. The mansard roof of the red brick County Courthouse reared against the sky in a half-hearted nod to permanence.

According to Emma, who had visited Jake at the *Rio Plata* last year, the gunfight had marked the beginning of the end for the Earps and Doc Holliday in Tombstone. Although they were acquitted in the ensuing trial, sentiment had turned against them. They decided to move on, but not before losing one of their own to an assassin's bullet. Morgan Earp was shot to death while playing billiards at Hatch's saloon in March 1882.

When Jake learned of Morgan's death, his first thought was for Charlotte. How had she taken it? But he did not ask, and Emma made no mention of her. Jake had also been surprised to learn that Morgan had a wife. Louisa Houston Earp had accompanied her husband's body back to California.

So Charlotte had not been with him, then.

Jake thought back to the day of the gunfight, and remembered his intention to stay away from Charlotte for good. Yet the following day had found him walking toward Fremont Street in the early-morning chill, his heart pounding in his chest.

But when he'd arrived, the wagons were gone. The

troupe had left before dawn. Jake had debated going after her, but what would he say?

It was there that Sixto had found him, still standing in the clearing where the wagons had been, and gave him a message. Alejandro Valdez was ill, possibly dying. Jake rode back to his father-in-law's ranch that day. He took charge of the *Rio Plata* and spent as much time as he could with Alejandro.

The months had stretched into years and still Jake stayed on, loath to leave the only true family he had. He ran the ranch and looked around for someone in the family to take over, but most of Alejandro's relatives had homes of their own in Mexico, and were not interested in a cattle ranch in this hot part of the country. So Jake stayed, bringing up the best of his broodmares from Seep Springs and continuing his breeding program, until at last he'd located a distant cousin in Guadalajara whose youngest son was a good hand and equal to running the concern. Finally, when Alejandro had died last month, Jake had decided to return to the Seep Springs Ranch.

Riding through town, Jake reflected how quickly things could change. When he'd left Arizona, the Earps had a stranglehold on this town. Now they were gone. Virgil Earp's ambitions to serve another term as marshal were shattered, along with his gun arm, during an ambush on Allen Street. Morgan had been killed soon after. Before the remaining Earps left the territory, they avenged Morgan's death by killing his alleged assassin, Frank Stilwell. Wyatt also boasted of killing John Ringo and Curly Bill Brocious in separate shootings outside of Tombstone, but of these two killings no one could be certain. Some—Emma Lake among them—had thought Curly Bill to be alive but in hiding.

At the thought of Emma, Jake felt a familiar ache, not yet deadened by time and memory. The Silver Dollar Boardinghouse looked the same, although someone else owned it now. Emma Lake had been dead six months, killed in a fall from a rogue horse.

As Jake rode through Tombstone, he could feel the ghosts of the past pressing against his heart. He tried to concentrate on the work ahead of him. During his absence, a rancher had bought up the rights to Babocomari Creek, where Jake watered his horses—now he'd have to prove his prior claim.

And so Jake had come back to Tombstone, half expecting to see Emma bustling along the boardwalk on Allen, or Wyatt Earp striding toward the marshal's office. He dismounted and tied the liver chestnut gelding, Aguila, outside the records office. Aguila had replaced the Grulla, who had been gored by a bull on the *Rio Plata*. Still pondering the ghosts of Tombstone's past, Jake gazed at the broad dirt avenue leading toward the desert and the Dragoon Mountains. But of all the ghosts he'd expected, there was one ghost he did not expect to see.

At the end of Fifth Street, where the avenue dwindled to a dirt track, an elegant figure stood against the glare, talking to a man in black broadcloth and a top hat. Shading her face with one hand, the lady pointed to a tract of cleared land.

It was Charlotte Tate. She wore a dress of creamy white, the spring breeze ruffling the frothy skirts, reminding Jake of the gardenia petals of his southern birthplace. Even from where he stood, he could tell the dress was expensive. As he watched, the man unrolled a large sheaf of paper and held it open. Charlotte bent slightly at the waist, the fine strong line of her body inclining as gracefully as a willow as she scanned what must be a set of plans.

Suddenly, the wind gusted, flipping the top sheet into the air. The page cartwheeled through the sky toward him. Jake retrieved it as it flattened itself against a bush.

It was an architect's rendering of a theater on a grander scale than anything he had seen in Tombstone—or anywhere in the west outside of Denver or San Francisco, for that matter.

The man came running up. He was handsome in a girlish way, with searing blue eyes. Long black hair rose and fell with his running steps, reminding Jake of an Apache who had stolen a gentleman's hat.

"Thank you!" he said, as Jake handed him the plans. "I am in your debt."

Jake looked beyond him to the slender figure near the clearing. She waved, then lifted her skirts and walked toward them.

The man followed his gaze. "She knows you," he said, obviously surprised.

"We're old friends. I'm Jake Cottrell."

"L. J. Bailey. Perhaps you heard of my stage name. The Amazing Lucifer." He doffed his hat and made an exaggerated bow. "Formerly of the Athena Traveling Theatrical and Variety Troupe."

Charlotte joined them. "Why, Jake, it's so good to see you." She spoke as if she had forgotten everything that had happened between them in the mine and the tragedy that had followed on its heels. Jake tried to divine the emotion behind the unaffected pleasure in her eyes. His own smile felt pasted on.

Charlotte laid a hand on his arm and turned to address Bailey. At her light touch Jake felt a pleasurable tugging in his groin, and had the grace to feel guilty about it.

"L. J., it's so hot out here. Why don't we go to the Fountain for lunch? Jake, would you care to join us?"

"I'd like that." Jake wasn't so certain how he really would like it, for Charlotte's modulated voice now had a steely quality underneath, as if she were used to getting what she wanted. As they walked into town, Charlotte and L. J. Bailey talked about their project, shutting Jake out. Other than resting her hand lightly on his wrist, Charlotte seemed unaffected by Jake's presence. He didn't really mind, because it gave him a chance to figure out what had changed about the girl who had cried in his arms so long ago.

Charlotte's regal carriage and slimness had always made the most of any garment she wore, and outwardly—except for the fine clothing—she looked the same. But the defiant arrogance was gone, smoothed under a more poised, sophisticated manner. This was a self-assured woman, wearing her authority like a mantle. Whatever battles Charlotte had fought since that day in October, she had won. As they walked through the spring sunshine toward the Fountain, Jake felt a small loss. He doubted she would ever turn to him to dry her tears again. And until he saw her just a few minutes ago, he hadn't known it still mattered.

Laughing, L. J. Bailey wadded up his linen napkin and leaned back in his chair. "So when Copper Queen Consolidated made us an offer to . . . how did that lawyer put it? Avoid trespass litigation? We accepted with alacrity."

Charlotte smiled at Bailey with genuine affection. Jake wondered if there were something between them.

"Otherwise, they'd have had to put the Apex Rule to the test," Charlotte said.

"Apex Rule?"

"When two mines are next to each other," L. J. explained, "the first mine to tap the ore can follow the copper vein, even onto the other fellow's property."

"The Copper Queen had the mineral rights," Charlotte added. "We could have ended up with nothing, but they agreed to buy their competitors out at a fair price."

"More than fair," Bailey agreed. "And to think I balked at putting up one hundred and fifty dollars." He squeezed Charlotte's hand. "How different my life would have been if I had never met you."

Jake wondered if Charlotte and this man were married.

"Charlotte convinced me to throw in with this miner friend of mine. She has a sixth sense about people. I still

211

remember the day Pat found the ore. He came running to us before he went to the assayer. All I saw was a rusty rock. Then he starts talking about mineral content and showing us figures for projected price per ton and asking for more money to drill a shaft."

"We didn't have any money, so our hands were tied," Charlotte added.

"The mine stayed idle for two years. Pat tried to find more partners, but it's a gamble when you're working on a shoestring. Then, six months ago, along comes Copper Queen Consolidated and buys the whole shooting match. For a fortune. In one fell swoop, the Athena Traveling Troupe lost one of the most celebrated beauties of the Arizona Territory, and—if I may be less than humble—a passable magician."

So Charlotte was independently wealthy now. Jake's gaze roved over the fine silk dress tatted with lace, and the pearl ear bobs gleaming in the dim light. He tried not to think of L. J.'s pretty lips on hers. "And the plans?" he asked, tapping the scrolled paper at her elbow.

"The Lancastrian Opera House," announced the magician in a theatrical voice.

Jake looked at Charlotte. "Lancaster's in England, isn't it?"

"It's where Miss Tate was born," Bailey replied. "It has another significance, too. But I don't imagine you know much English history."

Jake returned Bailey's gaze without flinching. "I guess not."

"The royal house of Lancaster fought for the throne of England in the fifteenth century. You might have heard of the struggle. It was called the War of the Roses. Amusing, isn't it? The rose of Lancaster? A play on words." Bailey squeezed Charlotte's hand again. "Have you ever heard Charlotte sing?"

"I haven't had the pleasure."

"You must come to St. Paul's Episcopal Church this Saturday. She will be giving a recital."

"L. J., I'm sure Jake doesn't want to hear about that."

"On the contrary, I'm very interested."

Bailey stood up abruptly. "Ah, there's Lovell. Oh, fair Aphrodite, I bid you adieu." He leaned down and swept his lips lightly over Charlotte's hand, then bowed to Jake. "So good to meet you, ah—"

"Jake."

"Jake." He picked up the check. "I'll take care of this."

"No, I insist."

Bailey's light eyes glittered, and Jake knew the man had seen right through him. "All right then. Well, Jake, I hope to see you again." And he was gone.

"Jake, L. J. would have paid," Charlotte said. "You're our guest."

"I pay my own way." He sounded stubborn even to his own ears.

"Suit yourself." Charlotte sipped delicately from the crystal water glass. "What did you think of the plans?"

"They look expensive. Where are you going to get stone like that?"

"There's a quarry north of Prescott. We'll have to ship it."

"That will take some time."

Charlotte nodded. "We think we'll be able to open the theater around June of next year, if all goes well."

"You think Tombstone will last that long?"

For the first time, Charlotte's poise broke slightly. "What do you mean?"

"Tombstone would need an endless supply of silver to survive."

"But there's plenty of silver."

"I hear the mines are flooding."

She waved a hand dismissively. "They've got pumps to take care of that. The economy is as strong as ever."

Jake glanced at the plans again. "You don't think it's

213

impractical to build a palace like this in the middle of the desert?"

"Tombstone will be more important than San Francisco in a few years. Everyone's predicting it."

"You mean the speculators and boosters are predicting it. They want to milk this godforsaken piece of ground for everything it's worth, but someday they'll pull out, and all you'll have to show for it is an empty building."

"Honestly, Jake, don't you ever get tired of seeing the bad side of everything?"

"I'm just being realistic, Charlotte. Tombstone is a boomtown. Like Virginia City. When the silver's played out, there won't *be* a city."

"I don't believe you."

"I thought you were going to San Francisco if you had the chance. From what I can see, you have money now. What's to stop you?"

"You haven't changed a bit, Jake. Always sticking your nose in other people's business, just like Emma—" Her hand flew to her lips. She had the grace to look horrified. "You know, don't you? About Emma?"

"Yes."

"I know you were good friends. I miss her terribly, too." She paused. "Where have you been, anyway?"

"Over the border. At my father-in-law's ranch." He tried to relax. "Wealth becomes you, Charlotte."

"That's a silly thing to say. Of course it does! Who looks good when they're poor?"

"You always find the grain of truth in every statement."

"It's the only sensible way to be."

He tried to stop himself, but the words left his lips in a tumble. "Do you and L. J. Bailey have a sensible arrangement?"

"What do you mean?" Then her eyes darkened and her smile turned knowing. "You are such an old lady, Jake. Is that your way of asking if L. J. and I are lovers? Of course

we aren't. Can't you tell? He's in the Oscar Wilde mold."
Charlotte smiled gently. "You're very easy to read, Jake.
You should try to hide your feelings more."

"I remember a time when you couldn't hide yours."

"That day in the mine." Charlotte sighed. "I have always
wanted to thank you for that."

"I thought you hated me."

"For saving me from the Apaches? Or for kissing me?
I've kissed many more men since then."

That remark hit home. He wondered if one of the men
she'd kissed was Morgan Earp, and what had happened
between them. How had the wife fit in? But it was none of
his business, so he only said, "Whatever was troubling
you, you seem to have gotten over it."

Charlotte's voice was hard. "Money is a great leveler."

"Money isn't the answer to everything."

"What else is there?"

Jake remembered the joy he had known with Ana.
"There's love."

"Love?" Charlotte smiled bleakly. "What has love ever
done for me? Everyone I ever loved either died or turned
their back on me. No, I prefer money."

"Money can't keep you warm at night."

"What do you know about it? I'm tired of expecting
things from people and being let down. In case you didn't
know, there are no guarantees in this life, and I'm not letting myself in for any more trouble by putting faith in anyone but me. I've already lost everyone I ever cared
about—my sister, Morgan—" She stopped.

So she still loved him. He'd been dead for two years,
and Charlotte still carried a torch for a man who had
belonged to someone else. Jake couldn't help asking,
"Were you in town when it happened?"

"No."

"I'm sorry."

She averted her face, but not before Jake caught the

shine of tears in her eyes. "It doesn't matter," she replied, a note of finality in her voice. Then she smiled, her gaze lingering on his face with a frank pleasure that made his heart lift. Her charm was almost palpable, and Jake could see how she had captivated audiences all over the West. "I'd much rather we talk about you, Jake. You seem to get more handsome every time I see you." She smiled prettily.

The compliment—so obviously an attempt to flatter him—broke the mood. Jake gave her an abbreviated version of the last couple of years, suddenly uncomfortable in her presence. Although she made interested noises, Jake could tell she wasn't really listening. It was just like Charlotte, he thought, only to be interested in those things that directly concerned herself. At last he'd had enough. He stood up. "I have to be going," he said stiffly, picking up the check.

Charlotte looked at him imploringly. "Oh, Jake, you will come see me Saturday night? Please?"

"I've got a lot to do at the ranch."

"Please, Jake. I haven't seen you in so long."

Inwardly, he bristled. He had the feeling she was playing with him, like a cat with a mouse.

As he walked back to the Records office, Jake tried to sort out his feelings. He couldn't forget how Charlotte had cried brokenly in his arms, or the passionate kiss that had followed. Now, she seemed untouchable.

He would finish his business here, and go home. There was nothing for him in Tombstone.

As Charlotte climbed the steps to her suite in the Cosmopolitan Hotel, her thoughts kept returning to Jake. She had the feeling that although he was outwardly polite, he disapproved of her. Well, that was nothing new. Charlotte was quickly finding—now that her plans for the theater had been made public—that many of her Tombstone acquaintances didn't seek her company anymore. The very same people who had made a point of stopping to talk to her when she was an actress and singer now ignored her, sometimes crossing to the other side of the street when they saw her coming. *They liked me better when I was a pretty waiter at the Westphalia!* she thought sourly as her key turned in the lock and the door to her room swung open.

L. J. had warned her that it wouldn't be easy. There was a great deal of prejudice against women in business. "Even the girls in the cribs will have a better reputation than you," he'd warned her when they had first discussed building the theater.

"That's ridiculous, L. J."

"You might as well face facts. Prostitutes serve a valuable purpose in Tombstone. They aren't competing with men for business. What you're doing is seen as unnatural."

"They like Nellie Cashman well enough."

"That may be true, but even if they didn't, she wouldn't give a fig. She faces life on her own terms. You care a lot more about what people think of you."

"Well, I'm certainly not going to don dungarees and go out chasing after fool's gold on the back of a mule," Charlotte had snapped irritably. "People can just mind their own business and I'll mind mine."

But as she slipped off her gloves and stored them neatly in the top drawer of the marble-topped dresser, Charlotte wished for some of Nellie Cashman's aplomb. Or even Emma's . . .

A warm breeze fluttered the hem of the lace curtains at the window, bringing with it the smell of cooking from the Maison Doree next door. Charlotte sat down on the bed to remove her kid shoes. She might as well undress. There was time for a short nap before meeting Dick Nuttall. The private investigator probably wouldn't have anything new on Chesser anyway—he never did.

As Charlotte bathed her face at the washstand, letting

the cool water trickle down her flushed neck, her mind returned to Jake. When she first saw him, her stomach had given a little lurch, and she'd felt as if an unseen string had pulled gently at some pleasurable part of her deep inside. In the space of a few moments she was back in the cave with him two years ago, and he was kissing her.

Blushing, Charlotte remembered Jake this morning, the plans loosely gathered in one hand, his pewter eyes speculative. Perhaps her feelings had shown on her face. But she had quickly gotten control of herself, smoothing her features into an expression of casual interest. She didn't like the fact that he had once seen her at her most vulnerable. And how had he responded to her tears? By taking advantage of the situation, forcing his amorous attentions on her. His actions pretty much proved her theory that all men were snakes—all of them except L. J. Bailey and Morgan Earp.

Charlotte pulled the heavy velvet curtains closed, immersing the room in darkness. She had to admit that she had, to some degree, shared some part of Jake's lust, and that sickened her. She had been unfaithful to the true, pure love meant solely for Morgan Earp.

Charlotte unhooked her dress, letting it slip to the floor, and stepped daintily out of the silky white circle, her motions automatic. At the thought of Morgan, the familiar ache returned. He had died without ever knowing how much she respected him, how well she understood his noble sacrifice. Of course he'd remained loyal to his wife! It was the only course an honorable man could take. But Charlotte knew the real truth. She had seen it that night when he had taken care of her, the glimmer of regret in his eyes that had puzzled her then but which she understood completely, now. He loved her.

Shrugging out of her corset, Charlotte donned a light silk wrapper that had been draped over the foot of the bed. There could be no other explanation. If she accepted this theory, all the pieces fell into place. Even Morgan's seeming rejection of her the day of the gunfight made sense. He was brusque with her because he had to be. It was the only way he could deny the passion he felt for her. In the last two years, the certainty had grown inside Charlotte that Morgan had loved her, not poor, sickly Louisa Earp.

He was dead now, and Charlotte would be true to his memory. Real love often involved the cruelest sacrifice. Real love was the meeting of two souls, even beyond death.

As Charlotte crossed to the mirror above the dresser and picked up the heavy silver-backed hairbrush, she thought of Jake again. Initially, she'd been glad to see him, but he always managed to spoil her pleasure by bringing up unhappy subjects, like the mines flooding. Why did he have to be so contrary? And why did he, of all people, know so much about her?

As Charlotte took the pins out of her hair and shook loose her rippling tresses, she tried to analyze her relationship with Jake. He always seemed one step ahead of her, as if he knew something she didn't know, and was waiting patiently for her to catch up.

Well, she certainly had surprised him today. He had turned quite pale when she told him she had been kissed by many men.

Why had she told him that lie? Perhaps it was because she wanted to wipe that knowing look off his face, the one that puzzled, intrigued and angered her at turns. As if he knew her deepest feelings. She had the feeling he thought she was . . . well, a fake.

That's ridiculous! Charlotte thought. *What's fake about me? I knew what I wanted and I worked for it. And I'm rich!*

But the respect she had expected to come with her wealth still eluded her.

Sour grapes, that's the problem with the people in this

town, she thought sleepily, as she stretched out on the bed. *I'll show them all.* But as she started to drift off, Charlotte realized the person who needed the most showing was Jake Cottrell. And she didn't think her success would make the slightest bit of difference in his opinion of her.

Chapter Twenty-seven

A week later, Charlotte had just come out of the Papago Cash Store when she ran into Jake.

"You're just the person I was looking for," he said with a lazy smile.

"Oh?"

"I have a sorrel mare I think you'd like. Would you like to come out and look at her?"

Charlotte was surprised by his offer. Maybe he wasn't immune to her charms after all. As a matter of fact, she *did* want a suitable mount, and she trusted Jake when it came to horses. "I have to go to the telegraph office," she said. "But I could go with you later this morning."

"Good. I've got some business to do myself. Why don't I meet you at the Cosmopolitan in an hour?" When she agreed, he touched his forelock and walked away.

Charlotte found herself smiling as she walked to the telegraph office.

On the way back to the Cosmopolitan for her appointment with Jake, Charlotte ran smack into the middle of a funeral procession and its attendant crowd. It was nigh on impossible to push through the press; people were lined up along the boardwalk five deep.

"You'd think they'd had enough of funerals," Charlotte muttered as she tried to elbow her way through. But a funeral always drew a crowd, no matter how unimportant the deceased. Judging by the cheap wooden coffin, rib-sprung mule, and dilapidated crepe-hung wagon, this procession was not for a visiting dignitary.

The man beside her asked of his companion, "Who is it?"

"Rancher named Graves," came the reply. "Died of the typhoid, I heard."

Charlotte consulted the watch pinned to her lapel. She didn't want to miss Jake. Perspiration trickled down her brow as she tried to nudge her way past the man who had spoken. His girth was unrelenting.

"That's three in the past week. Whole family wiped out near Hereford."

"Hereford? Wasn't that where that rancher went crazy and shot at Billy Breakenridge? What was his name? Marquart?"

Charlotte had been trying to squeeze past a lady with a large parasol when she heard the name. Marquart. How many men in the territory had that name? It had to be Maria's husband! She sidled closer to the two men, trying to hear their conversation above the crowd.

"—Don't know him."

"Yes, you do. Used to have a general store on Fremont. Married some Mex girl. Got himself a half-breed."

"Them the folks with that little piece of land near Geidritus' spread? He told me about them. Said the man had no idea how to raise cattle. Piss-poor land he picked, too, and all around him is some of the best grass in the county. Why'd he shoot at Billy?"

What had Emma said all those years ago? Thaddeus and Maria had bought some land. It had to be them!

"Well, to hear Billy tell it, he was out tracking the Hover boys and rode in asking for water, and out comes Marquart, screaming like a madman and shoots off Billy's hat.

221

Annie McKnight

Right in front of his wife and kid. Billy could see right off the man was sicker'n a dog. Said it looked like typhoid, but he didn't stick around to make sure. When Billy came back through a few days later he helped bury him."

Thaddeus Marquart was dead! What would happen to Maria and her child now?

Heart thumping, Charlotte elbowed her way through the crowd. She had to talk to Jake. Jake was a rancher; he'd know if Maria would be all right. And then she saw Maria's face in her mind's eye, features twisted with animal hatred. Her stomach contracted, squeezed like a rag, leaving her limp and slightly ill.

By all rights, Charlotte shouldn't give a fig about Maria. After all, Maria had been completely unfair in blaming her for Roberto's death. She hadn't even bothered to hear Charlotte's side of things, condemning her out of hand. *Why should I go out of my way to help her?* Charlotte thought. *She didn't even ask what happened to me, didn't even care that I might have suffered, too. What should I care if she married some fool who didn't know a heifer from a hole in the ground?* Was it her fault Maria's husband went berserk and died? It certainly was not!

After all, she'd offered Maria help before, and she'd been turned down flat.

Charlotte paused inside the doorway of the Cosmopolitan, adjusting her eyes to the gloom. Her nostrils filled with the smell of cigars, leather, and dust. Jake rose from a sofa in the lobby, hat in hand. "What took you so long?" he asked.

Charlotte debated telling him her news, and decided against it. What did she care what happened to Maria? "There was a funeral."

"I saw it. You could have missed the crowd if you walked down Fremont."

"I didn't mind." Charlotte's gaze was on Jake, but she saw only Maria and her child—a little girl, maybe, with the same coffee-brown eyes, now wide with fear. To see her father go

222

crazy and shoot at a man, then succumb to such a horrible illness!

"Is something wrong?"

"No, nothing. I'll be down in a minute."

But as Charlotte's fingers found the banister, her guilt grew to such a proportion that she could feel it like a heavy blanket inside her, smothering her vitals. Maria and the unknown child tugged at her mind. She couldn't help but see them peering out the window of some poor adobe shack, watching as Maria's husband went crazy and shot at the deputy sheriff.

As Jake drove Charlotte out to his ranch, he sensed Charlotte's preoccupation. She sat still on the wagon seat, her back rigid, staring blindly at the scenery.

At last Jake said, "For someone who's about to buy a new horse, you don't look too happy."

Charlotte shielded her eyes from the harsh sun and glanced at Jake. "Maria's husband died."

"Marquart? The store clerk?"

"He had typhoid."

Jake asked sharply, "When was this?"

"I-I don't know. I just heard it today."

Impatient, Jake demanded, "Didn't you ask?"

"I overheard it."

"I see." Jake willed himself not to think of Ana, but the pain assailed him anyway. Typhoid was a terrible way to die.

"Jake," Charlotte began uncertainly, as if she thought her question might be a silly one, "You think Maria will be all right, don't you? When I stayed with the Connors in Tucson, they were . . . well, they didn't have to go into town and buy food to survive. They had chickens and a cow for milk and a vegetable garden—"

"Good God! She's still there?"

"I suppose so. She and her child."

"She has a child? They're on a ranch somewhere, alone?

Charlotte, typhoid is an infectious disease. They could be dead already—or near death."

Charlotte's eyes widened. Their velvet-brown color deepened, reminding Jake of a frightened doe's eyes. "Dead? She couldn't be! Not Maria?" Her hand touched his arm, feather light, and she looked to him for an answer.

Jake cursed himself for being impolitic. "I'm sure they're all right, but they shouldn't stay there. Typhoid is spread by unclean conditions—flies, bad water, bad milk. Even if they haven't caught it from Marquart, whatever caused his death could still be there."

"We've got to bring them back."

Jake felt his stomach lurch, and fear tasted like metal in his mouth. He couldn't tell her he was scared more of typhoid than any marauding Apache or mad gunman. The disease attacked the soul of a man as it attacked his body, turning him into a weak, mewling creature unable to do the slightest thing for himself, unable even to control his most basic functions. Typhoid had taken a vibrant, beautiful woman like Ana and wrung all the humanity from her, leaving her helpless and delirious, so that by the time he got to her she did not know him. And now Charlotte was asking him to bring Maria and her child back to Seep Springs. Asking him to expose all of them to typhoid.

"Where is she?" he asked.

"I think—that is, they said—near Hereford."

"There's a typhoid outbreak there," he said grimly.

Charlotte touched his arm again. He could feel the cool fingers against his shirtsleeve, even as a wall of nausea mounted inside him and made his own skin feverish. "Jake, I'd go by myself, but she wouldn't come with me."

"Why?"

Charlotte was silent. He stared at her then, and thought how beautiful she was, her fine pale skin shaded by the small brim of her hat, a few escaped coils of hair couched by the collar of her gray riding habit. She looked impossibly young and guileless, and Jake wondered if he had only imagined that the intervening years had made a woman out of her. But as he watched, he saw her chin lift and her expression turn determined, and he knew that there was steel beneath the velvet. "If you must know," she said at last, "she thinks I caused Roberto's death."

Jake had not expected this. A falling out between friends, yes. Jealousy over a man, or a petty argument blown out of proportion, but not this. "Go on."

Charlotte's fingers twisted in her lap, and again she looked like a chastened schoolgirl. "You remember I told you about Jerome Pike?" At Jake's nod, she rushed on, obviously trying to get through what she had to tell him as quickly as possible. "He wanted me for a patron of his—I was to be the man's wife." She looked out at the desert, her voice flat. "I esc—Morgan rescued me, but Pike went looking for me. He went to our little house, and shot Roberto. Maria . . . blamed me."

Shock coursed through him. That was what had changed her! No wonder she had cried in his arms the day of the gunfight. Her pain had still been fresh. She had carried the guilt of a man's death on those slender shoulders.

Charlotte's words rushed into the void, as if she were afraid of the silence. "I haven't seen Maria since that summer. But I know she wouldn't come with me."

"Why? Her feelings might have changed."

Charlotte shook her head. "No. Six months ago, after we sold the mine, I sent some money to her relatives in Mexico for her. I thought it might make amends in some way," she paused and avoided his gaze.

Anger surged through Jake, anger at Charlotte's insensitivity, her foolish belief that she could make it up to Maria with money. He said brusquely, "Money can't fix something like that."

"I know that now. Anyway, they sent it back, with a letter—in Spanish. I had it translated. It said, 'Our sister does

225

not need your money.' Please, Jake, if you come with me, I know you can talk her into coming back with us." Her voice was urgent.

Jake guided the horses down through an arroyo. What was it about Charlotte that made him want to help her? He realized that she had always come to him when she needed help, as if some sixth sense told her he could not refuse any request she made. Only once had he let her down—the night Morgan saved her from Pike. But if he'd known . . .

Jake looked at Charlotte again. She made a charming picture staring up at him, her eyes imploring. He doubted that she even gave a thought to the way she treated him, and yet she expected his aid as if he were family. Surprisingly, he didn't mind. Despite her haughtiness, her shallow vanity, Jake realized he liked her. He had always been attracted to her, but this feeling went beyond that. He liked her spirit, her unquenchable desire to make something of herself, no matter how misguided. He liked the strength underneath that calm exterior, the way she never complained about her lot, but always made the best of every situation.

He knew that she had glossed over the story of her attempted abduction by Pike, that it must have been a terrifying experience. Never had she spoken of her rift with Maria, or the knowledge that she had inadvertently caused Roberto's death. She had carried these burdens without complaint, without any overtures for sympathy. Perhaps her solutions were simplistic—offering Maria money to alleviate her own guilt—but there was something unflinchingly honest about Charlotte Tate. She met every calamity head on.

And now she had a plan to save Maria and her child—if indeed they could be saved.

"I could ask the doctor—he could come with us . . . just in case. Please Jake."

Despite the fear that gnawed like rats at the knots in his stomach, Jake squeezed Charlotte's hand. "We'll leave tomorrow," he said.

Chapter Twenty-eight

Thaddeus Marquart's adobe ranch house looked deserted. It sat among gray rocky hills just north of the Mexican border, a barren patch of ground not ten miles from the lush valley where the Clantons and other rustlers had run their stolen cattle up from Mexico years ago. In recent years, cattle had been left on this parcel, overgrazing it before moving on. They left eroded washes and scarred earth. Tar bush splayed in the short yellow grass like open fists, curled leaves gleamed silver in the sun's glare.

Nothing stirred in the dusty yard; stillness hung over the small shack and wooden outbuildings like an invisible ax suspended on a wire of tension. Someone had made a half-hearted attempt at a garden, but all that remained were a few withered stalks poking up like straw. Over to the right a log smokehouse hunkered under a mature cottonwood tree—the only real shade in miles. Just beyond it, in a cleared dirt area, lay two dirt mounds covered with stones, one of them large, and one of them painfully small.

The larger grave must belong to Thaddeus Marquart, Jake thought. But the other . . . they had come too late to save the child. He glanced at Charlotte, who had pulled her horse up beside him. She paled as she saw the little grave.

Jake was aware that he was holding his breath, as if he feared the deathly taint of disease might be borne on the air. He knew that wasn't true, yet he removed the bandana from around his neck and pressed it against his mouth, motioning Charlotte to do the same with handkerchief in her sleeve. There was no sound, except for a white-winged

Annie McKnight

dove's melancholy cry. A breeze tossed the cottonwood leaves.

Doc Whelan dismounted, his face grim. How Charlotte had managed to persuade the doctor into coming with them, he didn't know. There had been a typhoid outbreak at Watervale, and when they'd approached him yesterday evening, he'd been adamant in his refusal, saying that the needs of the many outweighed the needs of the few. What he'd really been saying was that he would not ride all the way out to Hereford to attend the sickbed of a Mexican woman and her half-breed child. Yet here he was. How much had Charlotte paid him?

They left their horses under the cottonwood tree. Jake knocked on the door, and when there was no answer, pushed it open.

The smell hit him immediately. He could never forget it; the cloying sweetness of body organs failing. Charlotte had come up behind him, trying to peer into the darkness. Without thinking, Jake thrust his arm across the doorway, barring her entry. "Stay outside."

"But, Jake—"

"I said stay outside! Do you want to catch typhoid?" The past rose up to meet him, that nightmarish span of time when he had watched Ana die. He was there again in that close adobe shack in Nogales, the years stripped away and the fear breaking over him in numbing waves, and he wanted to turn and walk away—

"Jake!" Doc Whelan's voice broke into his consciousness. "Will you let me through?"

Stunned, Jake stepped aside. Doc Whelan set down his bag and examined Maria. Jake was aware that Charlotte had come into the room, her lilac-scented handkerchief pressed to her nose and mouth.

"She must have been sick for a week."

Maria had been quiet up until now, but suddenly her head lolled sideways and she began to talk, a stream of

228

nonsensical Spanish. Jake remembered that Ana had done the same thing.

As if from a cave, he heard Whelan issue instructions to Charlotte. "Get me some water—no, not from the barrel, from my canteen. That water might be contaminated. We've got to get this fever down."

Charlotte's skirts rustled and for a moment the scent of lilacs overpowered the smell of sickness.

"How is she?" Jake asked.

"She's dying," Whelan said bluntly.

Charlotte had never smelled anything half as bad as this stench. Her stomach revolted, but she swallowed hard on her gorge and held the pan of water for Doc Whelan. He dipped a rag into the water now and wrung it out, placing it across Maria's eyes.

"Jake," Doc Whelan said. "I saw a buckboard over by the smokehouse—could you harness up the horses and go to the river? We're going to need water—untainted water, and lots of it."

Jake agreed to go, feeling relieved. He felt like a coward as he walked out into the fresh air and golden sunshine, free of the sick room and its fulsome odor. But he knew that he was the only one with the physical strength to get the water. That was his excuse.

Charlotte felt like weeping. They must have been here for hours, in this still, hot room. In that time she had helped Doc Whelan bathe Maria's bloated body and change the soiled linen. When he handed her the bedclothes, she recoiled, but the look on his face goaded her into taking them. After boiling up a tub of lye soap, she took a stick and, keeping the linen at arm's length, gingerly swirled it around in the water. She was almost finished when Doc called her back to the sickroom. Jake volunteered to hang them out to dry before taking the spring wagon out to the river to bring back more water.

The late afternoon sun shimmered through the screen of flour sacks Jake had put up to block the open window from flies. Mercifully, the shadows were lengthening and in a few hours the day's heat would end. Charlotte wiped the sweat from her eyes and stared at Maria, who was curled up in a fetal position, shivering and mumbling. She called out for someone named Augustin several times. The name could only belong to the child buried beneath the pile of rocks outside. Her skin had turned sallow, her eyes squeezed shut against what little light remained in the room.

Hours. Hours of watching the woman who had been her girlhood friend die in the most painful manner. The once carefree Maria, wracked with spasms, fever, chills, alternately praying in Spanish and crying out in a hoarse, ugly voice—it was all too much.

I can't stand it anymore. I won't stay here another minute! Charlotte set the pan of water down on the bedside table.

"Where are you going?" Doc Whelan said.

"I'm going outside for some air. Jake should be back in a minute. He'll help you."

"Come back here! I need you!"

"I'm sorry, but I can't." Charlotte fairly bolted out into the yard. She leaned against the crumbling adobe wall, drinking the fresh air into her lungs with great gasps. Her back ached abominably, and the smell still lingered in her nostrils.

Why didn't Maria just go ahead and die? As soon as the thought materialized in her mind, she wanted to obliterate it. What a terrible thing to wish for! But Charlotte's practical side quashed her Catholic-bred horror. It was obvious that Maria was dying. The doctor had said as much. Animals were put out of their misery all the time, yet Maria had to suffer?

A dust devil whirled through the yard. Charlotte's

mouth was dry, but she would not dip the water from the barrel nearby. It might well be tainted.

She trembled as she remembered the moment Maria opened her eyes. Did Maria hate her even now?

Anger, slow and hot, bloomed inside her. *Why should I feel guilty? I couldn't control what Pike did. And even though it wasn't my fault, I tried to make it up to her.*

Maria should have written for help when Thaddeus died. She knew where Charlotte was; she could have moved back to Tombstone. Charlotte had a large suite—she would have shared it gladly. The boy—had he lived—would have been taught English, and been brought up in a proper home. Charlotte would have even paid for him to go to college someday. Instead, Maria had chosen to raise him on this godforsaken ranch, and now he lay under a pile of rocks.

Abruptly, Charlotte's anger abated, replaced by despair. What had she expected? For Maria to run into her arms and tell her that all was forgiven? Had she ridden all this way just to assuage her own guilt?

If only Maria would give her some sign. But throughout the day, Charlotte's hope had turned to bitter anger. Maria didn't know her at all.

Soon after, Jake drove the wagon into the yard. The wind had come up, and the dark clouds that had been hovered over Mexico were moving this way at a tremendous pace. As Jake jumped down from the wagon, a gust of wind caught his hat and sent it spinning through the dust.

"Jake!" Charlotte ran toward him. She couldn't explain the relief she felt at the sight of him.

"How's Maria?" he asked, as he unloaded the barrels of water.

"Oh, Jake, she's so sick. Doc Whelan doesn't think she'll last another day."

Jake nodded. "I thought that when I saw her."

"It's like it was with Ana, isn't it?" Charlotte's hand flew to her mouth at the sight of Jake's expression. "I'm sorry."

Jake was silent for a moment, then said quietly, "Your problem, Charlotte, is you don't think before you speak." He jumped down from the wagon and disappeared into the house without a backward look.

After Jake left, Charlotte stood in the yard for a long time. He was right. She was thoughtless. Selfish. They were not the attributes of the great lady she wanted to be.

Tears pricked the corners of her eyes. Nothing had turned out as she had planned. She had money, she had beauty, she had been adored throughout the territory as a performer, and she still wasn't happy. Everyone who mattered had turned from her in disgust—or died. Mary's dreams had come true, but they had proved to be empty.

She allowed the tears to come. It felt good to cry, good to rail against the gods, who had stacked the deck so successfully against her. No one liked her. Not Maria, not Jake, not even L. J. Eyes blurring, she swiped at her nose and felt a sob catch in her throat.

"Charlotte." Jake's voice, firm and quiet, came from the direction of the shack. "You'd better come in here."

Hastily rubbing the last tear away, Charlotte spun and followed, heart thumping. There was a grim gentleness in the way Jake had called to her.

"Is she—"

"Just come in." Jake held the door open for her.

Darkness enveloped her, and the sick-sweet odor swelled against her nostrils like a noxious balloon. Her eyes adjusted to the gloom and she saw that Maria was very still, her face like yellow wax. She had stopped twisting.

"Maria," ventured Charlotte, her throat almost closing on the word.

"She can't hear you," Doc Whelan said.

Charlotte gasped. "She's dead?"

"No," Jake said, "but Doc doesn't think she'll wake up again."

"She didn't have the resistance most people have," Doc Whelan said. "That's why it's happened so quickly."

Charlotte moved slowly toward the bed. Maria looked like a withered doll, her hands at her sides, body straight. After all the contortions she had gone through, she looked peaceful at last.

"Maria," she whispered, and reached down to take one of her old friend's hands in her own.

Charlotte had not expected to feel so wretched. She had known Maria would die; known it throughout this terrible day. But suddenly she felt as if she were being left behind, as if there would be no salvation for her now. Maria had to forgive her, or she was lost. *Please wake up, just for a moment. Please forgive me!*

"Maria, I'm so sorry. I was foolish, I didn't think— please forgive me, please, please—"

Jake's hands curled around her shoulders.

"Please, Maria, I'm sorry, I never wanted us to fight, if only you'd just say one thing to make it all right, I promise, I promise . . ." she faltered. What good were promises now? Jake's fingers pressed deeper into her shoulders and at the same time she thought she felt a squeeze—an almost imperceptible movement in the fingers enfolded in her own, and immediately after that, Jake's voice broke through, chilling in its finality: "She's gone, Charlotte."

He had somehow turned her around in the circle of his arms and clasped her to him. She felt his firmness against her heaving chest, and she hiccuped twice but did not cry, did not cry because there were no tears left, only a void that seemed to open up at her feet and threatened to swallow her. But even at the chasm yawning beneath her, even with the ache in her very soul, a small, hopeful voice spoke up. *She squeezed my hand. She forgave me!*

Charlotte was barely aware that Jake was leading her

outside, unaware of everything but the idea that she had been forgiven.

Jake sat her down on an overturned feed tub and squatted on his heels, his hands still on her shoulders, bridging them together.

"She forgave me, Jake. She squeezed my hand. I felt it."

Jake said nothing, but stared into her eyes. There was sorrow and something else—pity?—in his expression.

"You don't believe me, do you?"

"She was asleep, Charlotte. She couldn't hear you."

"I know what I felt!"

Jake held her gaze a moment longer, then his glance veered away. "Perhaps you're right."

Doc Whelan left soon after, insisting he needed to get to Watervale, where he could "make a real difference."

Charlotte and Jake stayed behind to bury Maria next to her husband and child. It was the least they could do for the woman who had been Charlotte's closest girlhood friend.

The storm that had been threatening broke with a vengeance, just as Jake finished digging Maria's grave. Wind whipped up and lightning forked through the sky, coming close. Rain emptied from the heavens like God's anger, a hard, pelting rain.

"Go inside!" Jake yelled. "I'll finish up here!"

"But Jake—"

"You don't want to get sick, too, do you?"

Charlotte did as she was told.

She was soaked. Shivering, she realized she must find something dry to wear, or she would follow Maria to an early grave. She could not afford to lower her body's defenses and let typhoid get a toehold, and so she did the only thing that made sense: she looked through Maria's closet and found a dress that might fit her.

She had been amazed at how tiny Maria had become, like a shrunken doll. Nothing of her beautiful, vivacious young friend had remained. The tarletan dress' waist came up to just beneath her breasts, and on the other end, barely reached her ankles. As Charlotte started the stove to warm the room, it came back all over again. Her best friend was dead. She felt the tears come, and gave herself to them, comforted by the fact that before she had gone, Maria had forgiven her.

The door banged open and Jake came in just as lightning flashed again, illuminating the room briefly. Charlotte noticed that Jake's clothes were soaked through. Water channeled along the twin ridges of his hat and crested the brim to spatter the floor.

"You'd better change," she said. "You'll catch your death."

"I don't have anything else."

"I think Maria's husband had some clothes that'll fit you." She motioned to a battered armoire.

He glanced around the one-room shack. "What will you do while I change?"

She met his eyes directly. It was plain she wasn't the same Victorian miss he had met in 1881. "I'll turn my back."

Jake grinned wearily. "How do I know I can trust you?"

"You'll just have to." She turned away.

As Jake removed his boots, his eyes strayed to her again. She was stately and slender in Maria's gray tarletan dress, the dark red fall of hair rippling down her back. He had only seen it loose a few times, and the sight of it stirred him, as did the glimpse of slender white ankle under the too-short hem. He knew that in other times Charlotte would have been mortified at the thought of a man shucking his clothes in the same room, but things were different now. She had gone through hell today; circumstances that left no room for propriety.

She was a woman now. He tried to stifle the excitement

that eeled through his lower body, brushing with a tantalizing sensuality along the hair-trigger nerves in his groin. Even now, after this horrible day and its aftermath, his body still clung to its need for pleasure with a tenacity that amazed and embarrassed him. What was wrong with him? Maria was barely cold in her grave, and yet he wanted Charlotte at this moment more than he'd ever wanted anything in his life. He wanted to cross the room right now and pull her to the ground as he had seen a mountain lion do to a running deer, to rut with her mindlessly on the dirt floor. He didn't care that she might protest. The want was so great that he had to clench his fists and grit his teeth and look away. His lust was an agony; his thirst for her enormous, outsized.

Her head was tilted to the side, as if she were listening to him undressing. Or did he only imagine it? Was she completely immune to him?

He sat on the bed, felt it list, heard the creak of the rawhide straps that supported the straw mattress. He saw the jerky movement of her shoulders at the sound of his weight on the bed—an involuntary start.

He reached down to peel off his pants, feeling like a wound exposed to the air. Scraping across his thighs, the heavy gabardine trousers sounded unbearably loud even under the incessant hissing of the rain. The hairs stood up on his body. His pants hit the floor with a wet slap. Charlotte made no sign that she heard it.

Next came the gauzy web of his shirt. He stood to dry himself. He was stark naked now, his body slick from the rain. He had to swallow a couple of times to keep a moan from passing his lips as he toweled himself dry with the sheet from the bed.

If she looked now, she'd know him for what he was. He pulled Marquart's trousers on hastily, almost hurting himself. The air quivered with tension.

He donned the shirt and pulled on one of his wet boots,

the leather pliant and dark in his hands. He shoved his foot down, then stomped it a couple of times to drive his heel home. His dry socks turned sodden instantly, squishing at the toes.

"You can turn around now," he said, when he could talk.

Her shoulders loosened as if she had been holding her breath and she turned slightly, her hands too busy with the folds of her skirt. She was blushing.

He was glad, and he was ashamed.

Charlotte lay awake in her bedroll, which she had laid side by side with Jake's in the kitchen. She couldn't sleep. Maria's last few hours haunted her. No one should suffer the way Maria had. As the wind howled outside, Charlotte imagined it was the ghost of Maria crying, reaching out to her from the darkness, the wind, and the rain. She saw in her mind's eye the grave Jake had dug, the deep, gaping hole. She thought of the dirt falling down on the upturned face of the girl she had once laughed with, confided in. She thought of the rocks piled on top, the rocks put there to keep the coyotes away.

Somehow it got in her mind that there weren't enough rocks. That even now, in this savage downpour, animals—predators—were rooting among the stones and—

She could not bear it. She glanced over at Jake. He was a still, black shape lying in the dark. How could he sleep in this? The rain banged on the corrugated tin roof, an angry assault. Maybe it was Maria, her spirit lost, pounding her fists on the roof.

It suddenly occurred to her: No one had said the last rites for Maria. There had been no priest. No one to help her get through the darkness and toward the light.

No one to save her soul.

Charlotte closed her eyes, suddenly very frightened. She had been raised a Catholic and had practiced her religion when she felt like it, but this was different. She closed her eyes, trying to block out the animals snarling and fighting over Maria's grave, trying not to think of them as fiends from hell, fighting over Maria's immortal soul.

She felt something break loose in her, something that had tethered her to clear thought. She wanted to scream, as loudly and as long as she could. Her nerves bristled in her body, raw and painful. She had to see the grave for herself. She had to.

Jake awoke to a deafening crash of thunder. Still muzzy from sleep, he wondered at the queer empty feeling in the pit of his stomach, until he realized where he was and that Maria was dead. Something else was wrong, but it took another moment for the realization to hit home.

Charlotte was gone.

Thunder wracked the adobe again, followed by a bolt of lightning that made the cottage as bright as day. She couldn't be out in this storm.

He wrenched open the door and stared into the onslaught. The yard was a sea of mud, but in the next lightning bolt, Jake saw footprints headed toward the corrals.

He ran out into the storm, the rain stabbing his face and eyes like needles. The corral loomed before him in the scrim of rain. Charlotte had somehow managed to get a saddle on her mare and was trying to mount, the sodden welter of her skirts whirling about her legs. The mare would have none of it and wheeled in a circle, her hindquarters bunching as she scrambled to gain purchase in the mud.

Lightning stabbed the hill just south of them, the sizzling smell of ozone bitter in Jake's nostrils. Anger surged through him. How could she endanger them both this way? He wrenched her around by the shoulders. "What the hell do you think you're doing?" he shouted.

Charlotte stared up at him defiantly. "I'm going to get a priest."

Had he heard correctly? A *priest*? She would ride out in the worst storm of the year to get a priest? "Are you crazy?"

She jerked away from him and gathered the reins on the mare's neck. As she stuck her foot in the stirrup the mare sidled away again. There was only one thing to do. Jake hauled Charlotte away from the mare and dragged her struggling toward the nearest shelter, the smokehouse.

Like a twisted wire, a lightning bolt shivered in the air just twenty yards away, splitting a cottonwood down the middle with a crackling hiss. Jake stared at the smoking black wound where a living tree had stood moments ago.

Jake shoved Charlotte into the smokehouse, his own body shielding her as another bolt ripped the sky.

"Let me go!"

"Lightning just hit that tree out there! Do you want to be next?"

"I've got to get the priest."

"Why?"

"Last rites," Charlotte gasped. "He's got to give Maria the last rites."

"Maria's gone. It's too late!"

She looked at him, her eyes wild. "I have to get the priest! She has to have the last rites!"

Jake stared at her. How had she gotten this bee in her bonnet? He had never thought her particularly religious before, although she attended church regularly.

His throat closed and he felt as if he had been kicked in the stomach. Maria's death had been too much for her. Charlotte had lost her hold on reality. Her mind had finally broken under the strain.

He didn't think he could stand it if she had broken. His fear translated to violence. He shook her, hard. "Charlotte, listen to me! You can't go out in this storm!"

In answer, she kicked him and tried to slither out of his grasp. He held her, but it wasn't easy. Charlotte fought him with desperate strength. Her nails raised welts on his arms, her fists were hard and not ineffective as he had assumed a woman's would be—she connected with his stomach, causing a wave of nausea that made him loosen his grip. She struggled to her feet but he caught her and pulled her down again, pinning her with his body to the dirt floor. Hands clamped on both her wrists, he held her there with his weight, dismayed as he saw her eyes go wide with terror.

Her struggling increased and she bucked wildly, trying to bite him. She was shaking and terrified.

My God, he thought, *what is she afraid of?* He had seen her like this only once before, when they'd hid from the Apaches long ago. Then, it had been her fear of rape—

Was that what she was afraid of? How could she know about such a thing, except what she might have heard from other women? This fear was genuine. Visceral. Almost as if . . .

She'd once told him how she had escaped from Jerome Pike. Had she told him everything? His mind rebelled at such an idea. He could not imagine that happening to her. Sick at heart, he put it firmly from his mind.

"Charlotte, listen to me! I'm not going to hurt you. You can't go out there. The road's washed out and the lightning—" He broke off, withered by the look in her eyes. She stared at him like an animal from a trap.

Feeling helpless, he could only hold her to the earth with his body. She struggled beneath him, her sinuous strength everywhere at once, like a sackful of snakes. Shifting slightly, he pushed her arms above her head and, imprisoning both of her wrists in one hand, stroked her face with the other. "I won't hurt you," he repeated gently, his voice soft and as calm as he could make it. "I would never hurt you."

He saw the comprehension in her eyes, saw the fear lessen. But he held her still, afraid that if he let her go she would bolt for the door. He could feel her heart beat against his chest like that of a frightened animal, could feel the tiny bones of her wrists trapped like a bird in his fist. Gently cupping her face in his palm, he let his hand glide over her skin from cheek to jawline, a repetitive motion that he hoped would soothe her. He didn't know he was still talking, didn't know that he was saying "I love you" over and over.

He didn't know when she quieted under him. He let her wrists go, rolling off her so that he was on his side, pulling her to him and cupping her face with both hands as he kissed her. It was a simple kiss, a gentle one, not meant to kindle desire. He stared into her eyes for a long moment, trying to discern her emotion, but could not. Tears shone like diamonds on her lashes, and he kissed them, tracing the wet-shimmering curve of her cheek. Overwhelmed by the tenderness he felt for her, he let himself be drawn toward her lips again, feeling absurdly reverent, shy. But when his mouth brushed hers she responded, first tentatively, and then with an intensity that astonished him. Soon his whole world centered around her lips, her mouth. They worked into each other like two colored threads, two patterns on a loom, forming a tapestry of incredible beauty.

He molded his body to hers, exulting in the feel of her skin through the thin, wet material of Maria's dress. Her hands came around his neck and clasped him closer, and their kiss became a wild thing, savage and exultant. Aching, he fumbled with the buttons of her basque, impatient with the soggy material, and then pushed away her corset cover so that he laid her bare to the waist. Horrified, Charlotte's hand flew up to her chest. "No, Charlotte. I want to look at you." Gently, Jake removed her hand and stared at her, filling his vision with her.

Her breasts were substantial; firm, curved globes that filled and satisfied the eye. Jake felt the exquisite weight of them beneath his fingers, and the sweetness of the moment permeated his body and soul. Like honey, desire ran through him, slow and sweet and thick and hot. He knew that some elemental part of him had always longed for this moment. The rightness of it surprised him. He saw his own desire mirrored in her eyes.

He pulled her skirts aside and wedged his body into the cleft of her, and she felt to him like a strong but supple sapling, filled with life. She met and returned his strength, so that despite the awkwardness of their clothing, Jake felt they might be two sinewy animals at the dawn of time, whose long lean muscles lay against one another out of instinct. Momentarily, he wondered how she could know what was coming, but dismissed the thought as petty, unworthy of them both.

He could barely stand the few seconds it took to tear away the barriers between them, but at last they were both free of encumbrance, and he rolled onto her again. He placed a hand on either side of her and raised up, taking the weight on his stiffened arms. He gazed at her flushed face. Her skin was lucent in the half-darkness, her lips shone a well-kissed pink. She held his gaze, unflinching.

"I may hurt you," he muttered, his throat thick.

For answer she pulled him down to her, and with little difficulty they merged, so that he was immersed in a joy so utterly savage he thought he might not survive it.

Chapter Twenty-nine

Charlotte awoke to rain tapping on the smokehouse roof. An unfamiliar weight rested across her chest; a man's out-flung arm.

The memory of Aaron Fielding's attack burst upon her

consciousness with shocking clarity. The feel of a man's arm against her naked body triggered such disgust and horror that she physically cringed.

But this was Jake, not Aaron Fielding.

Jake. The memory of his touch quelled the beating of her heart. She had been as much a part of last night's lovemaking as Jake had been.

Her face flamed as she remembered how her body had responded to him, welcoming his embrace. She had acted the wanton. Even now, she could feel the slow sweetness pervading her body, and stifled the urge to hold him in her arms again.

So this was the other part of love, the part she had foolishly thought she could ignore. Suddenly her fantasies of Morgan Earp and the nobility of unrequited love seemed shallow, even ridiculous.

How could I ever think I loved Morgan Earp, when I didn't even know him? In the dim light of dawn, with Jake breathing easily in sleep beside her, Charlotte knew she had followed an empty, foolish dream. Morgan was her fantasy. Jake was her reality.

She was all through with that kind of foolishness, now. She had changed, magically, overnight; had gone from child to woman. Jake loved her, and she loved him.

She hugged her joy to her, unable to keep still. Her discovery had enormous implications, and she wished desperately to share it with Jake. But he was sleeping so peacefully that she knew it would be cruel to wake him. For some reason she wanted to let him sleep, because . . . because there was something else, something lurking at the edge of her mind, some intrusive memory she wanted to spare him just a little bit longer. And then a fresh wave of pain hit her as she realized what it was: Maria was dead.

She'd known Maria would die, had prepared herself for it, but nothing had prepared her for the terrible guilt that lay just underneath her newfound joy. She realized that her guilt was *because* of her happiness. She was still alive and in love, while Maria lay across the dirt clearing beneath a pile of rocks in this godforsaken place where nothing grew, having seen first her husband and then her child die before her.

She closed her eyes and remembered Maria in happier times—the wonderful moments they'd shared together, the laughter, the excitement of being young women at the height of their innocence and beauty. Foolish children, really, but they had been so happy. Now a piece of her life was gone forever. Now, just when she had discovered what had been in front of her nose all along. *I've always loved Jake. I just didn't know it!*

Gently, Charlotte slipped out from under Jake's arm, stood up and struggled into her clothes. Outside, the rain pattered on the roof, a softer, steady rain, healing rather than hurtful. Her thoughts seesawed between the sight of Maria's grave and the memory of Jake's love. Elation vied with grief. There was not enough room in her for both emotions, so Charlotte resolved to put Maria from her mind for a little while. She knew she was being selfish, but for a short time she wanted to savor the sweetness of this new discovery.

She walked out into the rain, carefully sidestepping puddles. Mud sucked at her hobnail boots, but she ignored that, too. Nothing could intrude into her new world, not this morning. For an hour she walked in the rain, and returned feeling cleansed and fresh and good. But when the house came into sight, she allowed herself to think of Maria again.

Jake was rolling up his bedroll when she came in. He stopped, his hands on the rolled blankets. "Charlotte, we need to talk," he said.

Her heart lurched. He was going to tell her they had

made a terrible mistake. That he didn't want her, didn't love her.

"I think we should stay here at least a week, to make sure we're free of the disease."

Fear struck her like a fist, and she stepped back. "The typhoid?"

"I don't think we have it, but we owe it to the people in Tombstone—we can't take the chance of exposing them. There could be an epidemic."

Charlotte sat down, her heart pounding, terror muffling whatever happiness she had felt.

Jake sat on his heels before her, held her hand in his. "We'll be all right, Charlotte. It's just a precaution."

She stared at him, her lips numb. Her mind numb. "Jake, I . . . if we do have the typhoid, if we're going to die—"

He shushed her, taking her in his arms and stroking her back.

She pulled away. "What I want to say, Jake, is . . . I'm glad for what happened last night."

He searched her eyes. "You mean that?"

"Yes. With all my heart!"

"What about Morgan?"

"Morgan is dead. I never really loved him. I didn't . . . I didn't know what love was until now."

He smiled, brushed a curl from her brow. Then he leaned forward to kiss her.

Now, at last, they were free to love each other. For Charlotte, every sense was heightened. The painful memories they'd shared only increased their urgency for each other, as if by physical love they could stave off the specter of death. Both understood that life in the desert was tenous and uncertain, both were well aware that one or both of them could contract the typhoid at any time.

Their lovemaking took on a manic quality. Jake and

Charlotte abandoned themselves to long hours of love and afterward lay tangled together in sated sleep. Forgotten was Charlotte's theater, her singing career, her life back in Tombstone. They had retreated to a sheltered island, safe from the battering storms of everyday life.

They did what they wanted, when they wanted. Charlotte decided that since they were there anyway, they should round up Marquart's cattle and sell them, and send the proceeds to Maria's family.

"They won't appreciate it," Jake said.

"I don't care if they do. These cattle belong to Maria's family and they should be reimbursed for them. You can send them the money—they won't even know I had anything to do with it."

Neither one of them could stand to be apart from the other for long, and so Charlotte accompanied Jake on his search for the last of Marquart's cattle. Charlotte rode her new mare, Diamant, astride, wearing Marquart's shirt and pants because her skirts spooked the longhorns. She liked riding astride much better than riding sidesaddle. She knew she made a charming picture in her blousy shirt and her wide sombrero, which also belonged to Thaddeus Marquart. It protected her face much better than the hat that matched her riding habit. "Emma was right," she said one day as they rode down a steep cutbank. "Pants are better for riding. I never realized how unnatural it is to sit sideways on a horse. You know Jake, in some ways, women aren't very bright."

Jake laughed out loud.

She wasn't amused by his laughter. "I'm serious. Why should women truss themselves up like Thanksgiving turkeys so they can't breathe and have fainting spells all the time?"

"You've never complained before. As a matter of fact, you were the epitome of feminine sensibility before you came out here."

"I suppose when we go back to Tombstone, I'll have to wear a corset again," Charlotte mused. "I wish we didn't have to go back."

"But we do."

"Why do we, Jake? We could stay here, fatten up the cattle, and —"

"Have you forgotten I have a ranch of my own? God knows, Sixto is a good foreman, but it's time I tended to business. Besides, you've got a theater to build." There was a questioning note in his voice that Charlotte didn't understand.

"The theater," she said. "I suppose I should get back there soon. No doubt L. J.'s making a mess of it." But try as she might, Charlotte couldn't raise any enthusiasm at the prospect. She wondered if the whole thing wasn't a ridiculous folly. The people of Tombstone resented her, and the Lancastrian Opera House would cost an awful lot of money. Maybe she should sell out her half to L. J. and move to the ranch with Jake. After all, they would be getting married, and she doubted she could persuade Jake to live in town.

But if I sell out, then everyone will think I bowed to the pressure and couldn't stand up to those nasty old blue noses who think a woman can't do anything but have babies and keep house. I won't let them think they've won. We'll work it out somehow.

She put that unpleasant train of thought far from her mind. Jake loved her and she loved him. She was confident their love would overcome any problems the theater would cause them.

Charlotte had no way of knowing that as soon as they were out of sight of the Marquart house, life would become complicated again. She couldn't help wondering how L. J. was faring with the architect, stone masons, and workers in her absence. He could be a bit softhearted, and she knew that one needed a firm hand with those people.

247

She began to worry in earnest. They had been at the Marquart ranch for one week. One week she'd left the building of the theater under L. J.'s supervision.

They rode toward Seep Springs, where they would keep the cattle temporarily until Jake and his hands could get away to drive them to the San Carlos Apache reservation. Charlotte became impatient with the pace, anxious to see what had happened during her absence. They had a difficult time trying to keep the herd together in the sweltering July heat. The longhorns had minds of their own, and it took Jake and Charlotte twice as long to traverse the intervening miles as it would have had they not been shorthanded.

Her anticipation grew with each mile they rode until it jigged and pranced in her skull like Diamant under a tight rein. The last idyllic days lay behind her like an island, receding into the mists as if it only existed in dreams.

As they neared Seep Springs, Charlotte saw Tombstone to the east, sprinkled like tarnished silver across mountains blued by distance. She could barely control her excitement. She stared ahead across the bony backs of the cattle to Jake at the head of the herd, almost obscured by dust.

Of course they would get married. They loved each other. But that didn't mean she could drop everything, did it? She had responsibilities, didn't she?

If the truth were told, Jake annoyed her sometimes. In a moment of weakness, she had mentioned selling her half of the theater to L. J. and Jake had pounced on it, taking it as gospel. He acted as if there were no question about what she would do when they returned. He talked a great deal about how they would build the ranch together, raising the finest bloodstock in Arizona.

She had no doubt they would straighten things out when they reached Tombstone, and though she chafed under Jake's assumptions, Charlotte said nothing.

Chapter Thirty

Jake Cottrell emerged from Koenig's Tonsorial Parlor on Fifth Street and paused on the boardwalk, his gaze straying to the sandstone and brick building going up at the edge of town. Charlotte's carriage was parked before the hitching block in front, but she was nowhere in sight.

Angry, Jake started down the boardwalk. Charlotte would be late again. Obsessed as she was with finishing the Lancastrian Opera House in time for the grand opening at the end of June, it was a wonder she remembered anything else. Jake didn't relish replaying a scene that had become all too common: sitting by himself at the Can Can, looking up every time the door opened, until she came rushing in out of breath and apologizing—and always fifteen or twenty minutes late.

"I lost all track of time. I've got a hundred things on my mind, and you know L. J.'s useless when it comes to dealing with people. I have to watch him every minute or he'll give my money away."

He knew all the excuses. Her morning belonged to John Singer Sargent, whom she had commissioned to paint her portrait, her afternoons she spent overseeing the construction of the theater, and in the evenings she looked over the books. She had not been out to his ranch since Christmas. Whenever Jake suggested marriage, she put him off: "As soon as the theater is finished, we'll have the most beautiful wedding you ever saw. We can have it at the theater." And then she would reel off the names of important people they would invite.

He didn't doubt she loved him. And he had to admit that the times they did spend together were unequaled by anything past or present, even his life with Ana. She had become an expert lover, throwing herself into their love-making with an abandon that bordered on savage. He gloried in her passion, the feel of her willowy, firm body against his own. His problem—if one could call it a problem—was that he wanted to possess her utterly, body and soul, and by her very nature he knew that to be impossible.

Jake knew the kind of person Charlotte was. It had been wishful thinking for him to expect her to give up her theater and live with him on the ranch, raising children and horses far from the limelight.

Jake walked toward the Can Can. He would have lunch whether she showed up or not. The sun was bright and hard as crystal, glinting off harnesses and almost blinding him. The January wind raked down the street, kicking up streamers of dust and blasting him in earnest as he walked out of the sheltering porch at the corner of Allen and Fourth.

Shading her eyes, Charlotte filled her vision with the imposing structure that had taken up so much of her time these past seven months. Despite setbacks when construction had slowed to a crawl, at last it looked like a theater.

The first story, fashioned of battered sandstone, might have been hewn from the earth itself. Horseshoe-shaped lintels of the same rough stone topped each of six tall windows lining the west and south sides of the theater. Charlotte loved the way the salmon pink sandstone complemented the color and texture of the red-brick second story.

The entrance opened onto the corner, giving the building a curious wedge shape—not because there wasn't enough room for an entrance in front, but because Charlotte had seen a picture of a San Francisco theater like it, and thought it the height of fashion. Jake told her the design was ludicrous, as the theater was situated at least a block away from any other building, but the architect —not surprisingly—agreed with her. After all, she was paying him.

A cast-iron facade ran all the way around the roof. It was the facade that concerned Charlotte now. "I explicitly asked for the facade to be painted copper," she told the foreman. "You'll have to take that row down, or have the men go up and paint it."

The foreman, Fred Reeves, was a short barrel-shaped man with arms like two slabs of meat. "As you say, ma'am," he said, and stalked away. She looked down at the plans again. The exterior was almost finished, but work had barely begun inside. Nevertheless, Charlotte could picture what the bare interior would look like. The sixty-foot mahogany bar would be assembled along the south wall, the back bar framing diamond-dust backed mirrors. Her portrait would hang on the wall opposite. Red-flocked wallpaper, burgundy velvet drapes, and lush carpets would add texture and richness to the room.

At the rear of the salon, a staircase swept up to the next story, separating at the top and curving gracefully to either end—the balconies. Inside the theater there would be two hanging boxes balustraded with mahogany. A large cut-glass chandelier would hang suspended from the stamped tin ceiling. The white plaster molding along the ceiling and around the doors would be fashioned into roses—Tombstone roses.

Charlotte was most excited about the stage. Spacious and well-lighted, with a painted drop-curtain, the stage was an accoustical wonder. She would sing on that stage for the first and last time in July. After that, she would never have to bother about performing again.

The wind clawed at her fine midnight-blue satin walking dress. She consulted the watch pinned to her lapel. Twelve-thirty. With horror, Charlotte realized she had forgotten that Jake had left word to meet him for lunch. "Gemmie!" she called to the boy sitting on the hitching block. "Take me to the Can Can."

As the carriage negotiated the corner of Allen and Fifth, a man disembarking from the Wells Fargo stage glanced her way. Charlotte, preoccupied with her meeting with Jake, did not notice him, but he noticed her.

"Who is that?" he asked the stage driver.

The stage driver spat. "See that building going up over there?"

The newcomer followed the man's gaze down the broad dirt avenue of Fifth Street. The imposing structure loomed against the far mountains. "I see it."

"She's building a theater. A woman!" And he spat again before jumping down to unhitch the team.

Woman was an inadequate term for such an exquisitely fine specimen. Just a glimpse of her slender carriage and fine features stimulated the senses. The tilt of her profile, the soft alabaster skin, the glitter of embers in her hair . . . yes, he would have to engineer a meeting.

After checking into the Cosmopolitan Hotel, Dr. Edward Chesser went for a stroll. He followed Fifth Street out to see the Lancastrian Opera House. He wanted to know more about this mysterious beauty who had taken it upon herself to build a theater in the middle of a desert.

Charlotte speared a truffle delicately with her fork, but did not eat it. Instead, she gazed at Jake, her expression pleading. "Just five more months. That's not so long to wait, is it?"

"And then what? Will you be content to let L. J. run the theater when you come to the ranch to live?"

"I'm sure we can work it out satisfactorily," Charlotte replied, but she sounded unsure.

Jake leaned forward. "Do you know what marriage means?"

Charlotte blushed. "Of course I know what marriage means."

"Sexual congress is the least of it," Jake said roughly.

"Jake! Would you lower your voice?" Charlotte whispered, glancing around the restaurant to see if anyone had heard him.

"You are a child, Charlotte. Do you know what you'd be doing if you married me? What you'd have to give up?"

"I don't see that I have to give up anything. Of course, I'll spend most of the time on the ranch, but surely we could come into town on the weekends at least, and see that everything's running smoothly—"

"Ranching is a full-time business. I've been spending too much time in Tombstone as it is, lately. No, you'd have to come out here by yourself."

"I'm sure we'll manage."

Jake wadded up his linen napkin and threw it on his plate. "I'm thinking of you. I've seen the way you've worked on this project for the past seven months, and it won't end once the theater is built. You'll be pulled apart like a wishbone."

"Then what are you saying?"

Jake sighed. He had looked at the problem from every angle, and still couldn't find an answer that would please both of them. He wished he were more like Charlotte, able to pass off their uncertain future with an it-will-all-work-out attitude. Whereas Charlotte glossed over those things that she deemed unpalatable, Jake felt a need to plunge right into the heart of the matter and wrestle every demon into submission. "I'm saying that we should talk about this more. Marriage is a big step."

"We are talking."

"Would you give up the Lancastrian entirely if I asked you to?"

She stared at him openmouthed, and he could tell from the pinched whiteness around her nostrils that she was angry. "How could you ask that of me? Would you give up the Seep Springs Ranch for me?"

Jake felt the familiar heaviness in his chest at the prospect. He had thought of it. And the truth was, he didn't know. He loved his ranch, but he loved Charlotte, too. When he was away from her, his days and nights were filled with longing, and he had no doubt he would give up everything just to hold her in his arms. It was an agony for him; he spent so much of his energy just waiting to see her, the anticipation building inside him like a volcano. Yet lately, when he was with her, small problems seemed enormous. They argued about petty things, avoiding the bigger questions looming on the horizon. This was the first time he had voiced his disenchantment, and Charlotte looked at him as if he were a criminal bent on blowing their planned idyllic world to smithereens.

"Jake?" Her voice was tentative.

"I don't know."

Charlotte placed her hand on his, and his whole arm tingled. "Don't worry. We'll cross that bridge when we come to it." Her fingers traced his palm, featherlight. "I was silly to ask that of you, but you deserved it. You never look on the bright side. You had me all upset for a minute, and *I* know we'll be happy together."

"Why don't you come out to the ranch for a week? You've been working too hard. I'm sure they can get along without you for a few days."

Charlotte considered it, then shook her head. "L. J. has ordered the wrong size pipes. And now the company that sent them won't make an exchange. They're in New York, and everything's so hopelessly tangled." Before he could stop her, she launched into a diatribe about the workers and how if she turned her back for one moment they would rob her blind. Jake listened with resignation.

"Will you come by the Cosmopolitan tonight?" she asked as they were leaving.

"I'm tired of sneaking in through back doors."

"Don't be so awkward. Maurice won't tell anyone, and what's so bad about going through the kitchen? When I was a performer, we always went through the kitchen."

Despite himself, Jake laughed out loud. Charlotte's perversely practical bent intrigued him. It was not in her to understand why he recoiled at their duplicity. "You're a hypocrite, do you know that?"

"What do you mean?"

"Every Sunday you go to that church of yours, showing the world what a pious little Catholic you are—and often enough after a Saturday night with me. Don't you ever feel a twinge of conscience?"

"Why should I? We love each other, don't we? We're going to get married as soon as it's convenient, so I don't see why—"

"Do you go to confession?"

"Of course I do."

"Father MacDonnel's ears must be burning."

"If you must know, I haven't confessed that."

" 'That,' I take it, is your term for our own peculiar sin. It is a sin, isn't it?"

"I . . . guess. But I can't think the Father would be so upset, considering we are going to get married."

"But you haven't tried him, have you?"

"What is the point of all this?" Charlotte asked briskly. "Sometimes, Jake, I swear you say things just to hear yourself talk." Her lips formed a moue, and she tilted her accusing eyes up at him under the sweep of her lashes. "You will come by, won't you? Around eight o'clock?"

"Yes, Charlotte, I'll be there at eight."

As Jake walked back to his hotel, he couldn't stifle a grin. Whenever Charlotte was uncomfortable about a subject, she went on the attack. He would have liked to pursue the conversation further, especially because there was something he had been wondering about for some time.

In the past year, he and Charlotte had spent a great deal of their time together in bed, but she had not become pregnant. Surely by now, she would have, unless . . .

Well, he supposed it was her business. He couldn't help but wonder, though, who was giving her advice. Only one kind of woman was knowledgeable about preventing babies, and most likely she could be found on the wrong side of Sixth Street.

Charlotte was very different from anyone he had ever known—a mass of contradictions. Adhering to some Victorian standards and completely ignoring others, she chose her own path and stubbornly refused to see the holes in such logic. The woman who had harbored in her heart a pure, spiritual love for Morgan Earp for years could not understand why Jake talked about honor when it came to their assignations. She clung to her church tenaciously, unable to understand that the Catholic religion was one of absolutes. She wanted to pick and choose which tenets she would follow.

Jake could laugh at the peculiarities of her personality, but he was not immune to them, or her.

He loved her precisely because she was Charlotte, and no one else. She was the woman who had nursed Maria through her last moments, the woman who called the fashions of the day ridiculous, yet on returning to Tombstone traded pants for whalebone without a word, because it was required of her. She was a survivor. He guessed that she shut the past out of her mind as an act of survival, and he could not fault that logic.

Perhaps he would be happier if he could do the same.

The lobby of the Cosmopolitan was crowded with men. Here and there, cigar smoke uncoiled into the air like the Indian rope trick, stinging Charlotte's eyes. She glanced at the pigeonholes above the hotel desk and saw a slip of paper in her box.

Charlotte looked at the note as she started up the stairs.

"Meet me in the lobby at eight o'clock.

—Dick Nuttall"

It was from the private detective she'd hired more than a year ago to entice Edward Chesser to Tombstone. Although Chesser had owned shares in two mines near Tubac, he had so far shown little interest in Tombstone, despite Nuttall's efforts.

A man coming down the stairs jostled her, causing her to drop her reticule.

"Sorry." He bent down to pick it up. As he straightened, Charlotte bit back the sharp retort that came to her lips.

It was him.

For a moment, she thought she had to be mistaken. But no, it was the same man, only older. She would never forget his face.

"You look as if you've seen a ghost. Is something wrong?" Edward Chesser asked.

He didn't recognize her! Recovering quickly, Charlotte turned the full force of her smile on him. "It's just so close in here, stuffy—"

"Perhaps you need some air. Would you allow me to escort you outside?"

Charlotte's wits raced. She had planned his downfall for so long, she could not make a mistake now. "It might clear my head."

He took her small hand and tucked it over his arm, leading her through the throng and out into the evening air. She willed herself not to recoil at his proximity. Glancing at him furtively, she cataloged his receding hair, the heaviness of his jowls under the beard, how his abdomen protruded against the material of his trousers. His breath came in wheezes as he walked. The years had not been good to him.

"You must be Charlotte Tate," he said pleasantly, as they paused on the boardwalk outside.

So he *had* recognized her! Well, let him be the one to squirm. After all, he had been the one to withhold any help from Mary. The pain hit her afresh, but she refused to give in to it. Instead, she murmured, "You know me?"

"I have to confess that since I saw you this afternoon I have thought of little else. What a remarkable coincidence that we're staying at the same hotel."

Did this monster think she would welcome a casual conversation with the man who let her sister die? Anger surged through her, and her fingers involuntarily clutched at his arm.

"When I saw you today, I had to know who you were." He stared at her, his eyes bright and shiny like beetle carapaces. "So you are the famous Tombstone Rose. I have heard so much about your accomplished singing, your beauty. And now here I am, standing here talking to you."

Could it be that he truly didn't recognize her?

"Would you care to join me for dinner?" he asked.

Charlotte swallowed, her thoughts racing ahead. There was Jake, who would be joining her at eight, and Dick Nuttall. Surely she must talk to Nuttall before spending any more time in Chesser's company. "I'm afraid I have a prior engagement. Perhaps tomorrow."

"Tomorrow it is, then." He lifted her hand and kissed it with a courtly flourish.

As he walked away, she noticed his jaunty step.

He's taken with me, she thought with surprise. The idea filled her with a mixture of revulsion and excitement. Perhaps she might be able to influence him into taking the bait.

Charlotte walked back into the Cosmopolitan, summoned the bellboy, and scribbled a hasty note. She asked the boy to deliver it to Jake Cottrell at the American Hotel. He would just have to cool his heels if he wanted to see her. There would be plenty of time later tonight.

She had an appointment with Dick Nuttall.

Chapter Thirty-one

The private investigator spat into the brass receptacle at his feet. "For a man who'd gamble on two stink bugs crossing the road, Chesser sure has been a cagey bastard." He colored and added, "Excuse my choice of words, ma'am."

"Never mind that," Charlotte said impatiently. "Go on." They were seated in the lobby of the Cosmopolitan. The throng had lessened; most of the hotel guests had departed for dinner or a night of gambling and revelry.

Nuttall shook his head. "I guess the disaster of the Tubac mine cooled his ardor for treasure hunting. It was like pulling teeth to get him to agree to look at the Necropolis claim. Wouldn't be here now if it weren't for the surgeons' meeting." Surgeons from all over the territory had converged on Tombstone in the last two days to discuss medicine and politics.

"You were supposed to be his confidant. God knows I've paid you enough."

"He thinks of me as a brother. Told me only yesterday he would trust me with his life."

"Then why won't he believe you about the Necropolis?"

"Chesser's the kind of man who likes to know what he's getting into. He knows nothing about mining and doesn't have the patience to learn. Why should he meddle in some-

259

thing he doesn't understand, particularly since he was burned once? He won't want to take a chance like this, not and risk getting dunned. You can lead a horse to water but you can't make him drink."

"He's in town now," Charlotte said briskly, "no matter how it happened. You said yourself he'll look at the claim tomorrow."

Nuttall sighed, "He will, but I can't promise anything."

"Then I shall have to go with you."

Nuttall's startled expression amused her. "You? I thought you wanted to keep a low profile. The game's up if he recognizes you."

"I've already met him. He doesn't remember me."

"I still don't think it's a good idea—"

"Well, I do. Women have powers of persuasion that men don't."

Nuttall snorted. "You think you can get around that old roué? He goes through women like cigars. A pretty face won't turn his head."

"We'll see about that. I want to be there."

"And how do you expect me to arrange that?"

"That won't concern you." She paused, catching the eye of a handsome young man coming in the door, aware of the charming picture she made in the rosy lamplight in her bottle-green evening outfit. "Does Chesser have enough money to invest in a mine?"

"He's always cash poor. Spends lavishly, as you ought to know if you've read my reports. But I've made some good investments for him, that's one reason he trusts me. He can lay his hands on the money."

"What about your man, Mister . . . Jaffee, is it?"

"He'll be there."

"I hope he knows which side his bread is buttered on."

"Don't worry about Jaffee. Man's a born salesman. It was Jaffee's suggestion that the miners be given the day off. He doesn't want them messing things up."

Charlotte sniffed. "I shouldn't think they'd be interested. They're just miners."

Nuttall met her gaze, his faded rabbity eyes seeming to weigh and measure her. "You're English, aren't you? Probably know a few Cornishmen from the old country? They're a proud bunch. Don't like to be taken, any more than the next man. If one of them overhears and thinks we're misrepresenting that mine, he's likely to say something, just to be perverse about it." He explained this with exaggerated patience, as if she were a child, and she thought suddenly: He doesn't like me. He probably didn't like working for a woman, although he had never indicated as much in the time he'd been in her employ. It was obvious now that he harbored distaste for this plan or herself, or both.

For a fleeting instant Charlotte wondered if she had taken leave of her senses. It was such a convoluted scheme, and all to destroy one man.

She had no doubts where Jake would stand on this matter. So far, she'd kept him in the dark about the elaborate lengths she would go to to ruin Chesser. Charlotte wondered uncomfortably if what she was doing was a sin, and if it would imperil her immortal soul. She ran through a mental list of the commandments, and could only come up with "love your neighbor as yourself." A mild admonition. Dishing out justice—even harsh justice—wasn't like murder or adultery, was it? It would be a minor sin, if any. She pushed it from her mind.

Charlotte opened a satin-bound ledger, wrote out a check and handed it to Nuttall. He took it as if it were tainted.

"That is the amount agreed on, isn't it?" she asked.

"It's handsome," Nuttall replied. "Judas only got thirty pieces of silver."

"From what I've heard, you've never entertained such scruples before," Charlotte said sharply. "You didn't even know Chesser before I put you on his trail."

"True."

Charlotte felt another twinge of guilt. What she was doing was almost certainly illegal. But it was for a good cause, wasn't it? She had to avenge Mary's death. No one else would. "Tell me about the owners."

"You don't have to worry about them," Nuttall said shortly. "I've got dirt on them both. Besides, you've paid them handsomely, much more than either claim is worth. Both mines are in the area closest to the underground springs. If they dig much deeper they'll be up to their necks in water." He handed her a slip of paper with their names. "Jobe owns the Necropolis and Trevieghan, the Watervale."

Charlotte smiled. "I know Trevieghan."

"Oh?"

"If he gives you any trouble, leave him to me." She changed the subject, deciding to play devil's advocate. "Why should Jobe want to sell out now, just when the Necropolis is showing signs of producing high-grade? He stands to make millions."

"Family tragedy." Nuttall explained the story that he and Jaffee had concocted: Jobe's son was killed in a cave-in in another mine down in Mexico and Jobe wanted nothing more to do with mining. He was liquidating all his holdings and leaving Tombstone for good.

"But couldn't he just as easily sell the mine for a lot more money? It's got all the marks of a top producer."

Nuttall sighed. "We've given it out that Jobe just wants to get out from under. His son died in a mine. To some people," he added pointedly, "money isn't always the first consideration."

"I suppose you're right," Charlotte said, but she didn't understand it. Even in tragic circumstances, she doubted she would let a working mine go for less than it could get. But it was all fabrication anyway. If Nuttall thought it believable, she'd trust him. Besides, the price was steep enough for the type of mine the Necropolis was—it had tremendous potential but that potential was still untapped. Mining was always a gamble. Still, she couldn't help asking, "You think it will work?"

The detective nodded.

"Make sure the Necropolis pays off. We're only throwing a sprat to catch the mackerel."

"What?"

"It's an English expression. Throwing a small fish to catch a larger one."

"Oh. By the way, my name's not Nuttall. Chesser knows me as Joe Perry."

"I shall remember that." Charlotte snapped the ledger shut, but not before the figures on the page made their impression. She had her own financial problems; her partnership in the theater was beginning to take its toll. The Lancastrian wasn't a white elephant, but it certainly ate up her investments like one. And now she had put out another goodly sum of money, with uncertain results. Was revenge worth risking poverty? She stared at the private detective and let the full force of her determination be heard in her voice. "You'd better make this horse drink, Mr. Nuttall."

Jake pulled on his boots. Staring at him, Charlotte again marveled at how handsome he was—perhaps the best-looking man she had ever seen. How had she ever fallen for Morgan Earp? Compared to Jake he was nothing but a pale shadow, and she thought now his looks had been quite ordinary compared to the dark masculinity of her lover. Lover. The thought sent a delicious, naughty thrill through her. She had the grace to feel shamed. *Soon I'll be his wife*, she amended mentally.

As she watched him, Charlotte felt tenderness blossom in her heart. Perhaps there was no one else in Tombstone who liked her—how could they when all of them were green with envy?—but Jake knew her best and loved her. "I wish you didn't have to go," she said softly.

Pulling her down on his lap, he said, "I wish I didn't have to go, either. This time's been too short."

"But the ranch needs you," Charlotte said, trying to keep the bitterness out of her voice. Jake nuzzled her neck, sweeping a hand through her rippling tresses.

"We could have spent more time together last night," Jake said into her hair. "Did you really have to see that business associate?"

"Of course I did," Charlotte replied crossly. "I wouldn't have gone if I didn't, would I?"

"I suppose it was something to do with the theater." His lips trailed down her neck, causing a delicious shiver.

"Mmmmm," she murmured, and surrendered to his kisses. Let him think what he liked; she knew he would disapprove of her plan.

"We still have some time," Jake said, and pulled her down to lie facing him on the bed.

"Your boots," Charlotte protested, but her words were lost as he kissed her again.

Chapter Thirty-two

"Look at this," Dick Nuttall said, picking up a piece of black rock from the detritus on the stope floor of the Necropolis mine. "Did you ever see anything so pretty? High-grade silver ore."

Charlotte Tate, Edward Chesser, Dick Nuttall, and the head of mining operations, John Jaffee, stood at the foot of a jumbled shelf of rocks that had been blasted the previous day. Charlotte lifted her skirts higher, almost to the top of her hobnail boots. She was sorry now she had worn her lilac foulard dress; even in the candlelight she could see the front panel was grimed black from the rocks at her feet, and she had brushed up against the bars of the cage when they were lowered into the mine. No doubt the dress was unsalvageable. But what was one ruined dress when she had a closetful? She had bigger fish to fry.

The damp, musty odor of exploded rock and silica was thick in her nostrils, settling like a membrane in the back of her throat. Ammonia fumes seeped into her skull and gave her a throbbing headache. John Jaffee had warned her that because the ventilation was poor, she might suffer a headache from residue of yesterday's blast. It was plain he didn't want her in the mine, but Edward Chesser did.

Now Chesser stood beside Charlotte, his enormous shoulders dwarfing her. He peered over Nuttall's shoulder at the irregular rock. "It's high grade, all right."

Charlotte disguised her contempt. Any fool would know that you couldn't tell silver just by looking at it—especially in this dark mine. Certainly, the rock looked promising, but Chesser didn't pocket any of the samples to scrape them for color. He had settled for a glance at the books, Nuttall's examination of the assayer's rock up at the hoist shack, and this cursory inspection of the mine. Already he was showing signs of impatience.

He deserves to be cheated. As a partner in the Athena mine, she had read everything she could get her hands on about copper mines. She'd even gone down to inspect her holdings, much to the dismay of the shift boss, who had definite ideas against the idea.

John Jaffee removed his felt hat and wiped his brow. It was like a furnace down here. "You know your ore, Doctor. I thought you said you didn't know nothing about mines."

"I've invested in the mining business before."

Jaffee shook his head. "If I was Elwyn Jobe, I wouldn't let this mine go so cheap. Course, I didn't lose my only boy."

"Yes, it was a terrible tragedy," Chesser murmured. "But about this mine. How do we know this ah . . . strike will last?"

"You mean how far does this vein go? I couldn't tell you for sure, but probably a long way. See this Naco Limestone face?" He motioned to one wall, where the rock appeared to be steel blue in the wavering light of their candles. Large gray veins ran along the face at intervals; Charlotte recognized them as dikes, thin wedges of intrusive rock running against the grain of the mother rock. "These dikes have pried the rock apart. Where the rock's split open water seeped in, leaving deposits that solidified into silver ore and other minerals. It took thousands of years. This ore—" he kicked at the rubble at his feet—"will get you around eight hundred and fifty dollars a ton. We're just one of eight stopes on this level. The Necropolis has five levels. We blast around the clock. You do the arithmetic." He grinned and swiped his arm across his forehead again. "Besides, you know what they say. The deeper it goes, the richer it gets."

"I've heard that saying before," Charlotte said. "In the case of the Athena, it was true."

Jaffee shot an impatient glance at Charlotte. It was obvious he resented her presence. He turned to Chesser. "Sure, it's a gamble. No man will tell you otherwise. But it's as close to a sure thing as you'll find on this earth."

"How exciting!" Charlotte said. Ignoring Jaffee's withering look, she prattled on. "You know, Dr. Chesser, I don't think there's anything quite as exhilarating as striking high-grade." She dimpled prettily. "Of course, *I* didn't find it myself, but I'll never forget that day as long as I live."

Nuttall shook his head. "If I could get my hands on that kind of money, Edward, I'd give you a run for your money."

"As Jaffee said, it's still a gamble," Chesser muttered.

"More like a calculated risk," Nuttall said.

"Perhaps it is too steep a price for you," Jaffee said. "I'm only letting you in today because Joe's helped me out a few times. Tomorrow, the Necropolis will be overrun. I know of three or four companies right now who would jump at the chance." He snorted. "As if they need more millions."

"Millions!" declared Charlotte. "Do you really think so?"

Jaffee shrugged. "Could be. If the vein keeps yielding this kind of ore, there could be millions. We're sitting on pure silver, a bigger lode than the Toughnut."

"If it doesn't peter out," Chesser said.

"I told you before, mining is for a gambling man. But if you don't have the money or the stomach for it—"

"It *is* a lot of money," Charlotte said. "I wouldn't blame Dr. Chesser if he wanted to make sure. That's good business sense."

Jaffee scowled, but Chesser smiled at her. "What do you think, my dear?"

"I wouldn't presume—"

"Please. You have already made your fortune in mining. It's only fair you give me benefit of your expertise." She noted the patronizing tone in his voice.

"Well." Charlotte swallowed, tried to look ingenuous. "I suppose it is a lot of money. But if what Mr. Jaffee says is true . . ." she rubbed her arms and shivered. "Imagine. Bigger then the Toughnut. You'd be famous."

Chesser laughed and chucked her on the chin. "Would that make a difference to you?"

"Oh, no!" Charlotte gasped. "I like you anyway."

Edward Chesser's laughter rang through the mine. "You say what you think. I like that."

Jaffee broke in, "I don't want to press you, but Mr. Jobe wants this settled as soon as possible. He wants to put this all behind him. If you can't raise the money, there are plenty of people out there who can."

"Shut up, man, I can raise the money!" Chesser said impatiently. He rubbed his forehead. "I'm trying to think. Damn hard, with this headache."

"Let's go up to the surface," suggested Nuttall, "where we can discuss this like gentleman."

After two hours of deliberation, Chesser succumbed to his own pride and Charlotte's flattery. He agreed to buy the Necropolis for twenty thousand dollars.

"You won't be disappointed," John Jaffee said as they shook hands. "You'll make the purchase price up in a month. And that's a conservative estimate."

Charlotte gazed at Chesser—Edward, as he'd admonished her repeatedly to call him—over the rim of her fluted champagne glass and listened to him talk about himself. What a monumental fool! Her days of flattering customers at the Westphalia came in handy now as she pretended to hang on his every word.

Her champagne glass was more than half full, but Chesser had already drunk one glass and was almost finished with his second. The more he drank, the more he preened. "I stole that mine," he said, "right from under Jobe's nose. It's going to make me a fortune, and I have you to thank." He covered her hand with his own, and Charlotte repressed a shudder. "You're my good-luck charm."

She smiled, trying to ignore the way his hand rubbed hers, trying to concentrate on what he was saying. But the unnatural coolness of his fingers sliding over hers put her in mind of a gliding snake. If she had to abide his touch one more moment, she would surely jump up and run from the room, and all the progress that had been made today would be ruined.

Charlotte withdrew her hand and picked up her silver escargot fork. Delicately probing the snail shell, she said, "I'm glad you think highly of my company, however insignificant my own part was in your transaction. But I have no illusions. It was your decision. If you should make a fortune, you can be very proud that you were a smart enough businessman to see what others have missed."

Chesser shoveled a snail into his mouth and spoke with his mouth full. "Have to pull my horns in now, though. This mine is costing me a pretty penny." Dark eyes narrowing with speculation, he watched a waitress walk by. His expression was so carnally predatory that Charlotte lost her train of thought for a moment. She wondered if he had looked at Mary like that, then pushed the unpleasant image out of her mind.

"You're not . . ." she paused delicately, "getting in over your head, are you?"

"You look concerned."

"I admit to being softhearted. Especially toward the gentleman who has invited me to such a lovely dinner."

He laughed. "You are an honest one. As I told you before, I like a woman who says what she thinks."

"From what I can see, you like women in general," Charlotte said pointedly as the waitress passed by again.

"I admire pretty women."

"I imagine your admiration is usually reciprocated."

"You flatter me." He ate another snail, the garlic butter thickly oiling his lips and glistening on his beard.

How could any woman want this repulsive creature? But according to Dick Nuttall, Chesser had his pick of women.

Chesser dabbed at his lips with his napkin. "You disapprove of the way I looked at that waitress?"

"It is none of my business how you conduct your private affairs."

"I'd like it to be."

Charlotte looked down, as if the flattery were too much to bear. "You embarrass me," she said softly.

"But I'm serious. You must know you are a very attractive woman. I am quite taken with you."

Charlotte smiled, but underneath she was raging. *He* was taken with *her!* As if she had passed some sort of test! If this bloated swine thought she would fall for him, he had another think coming. She had talked him into buying the mine; her job was finished.

Still, she mustn't reject him overtly. "Mr. Perry said you have owned a mine before?" she said to change the subject.

For an instant Charlotte saw disappointment in his eyes, and more—a naked desire that chilled her to the bone—before his expression turned neutral.

"Yes, I invested in a mine near Tubac." He told her about his interest in the mine Cerro Colorado, and the deaths that had abruptly ended the venture. Charlotte barely listened.

Her anger faded, replaced by an odd excitement. Chesser wasn't a man to wear his heart on his sleeve, and yet the way he looked at her just now betrayed his feelings. There had been—just for a second—something almost desperate about his expression, as if he knew he would never have her.

He wants me badly. Much more than I thought.

Perhaps there was a way to use that knowledge. Certainly, it was another way to break down his defenses, manipulate him to do her bidding. She sensed that in Chesser's mind, the stakes had been raised. He didn't just want the mine, he wanted her along with it.

Charlotte remembered something Delia Delight had told her a long time ago. People always wanted something they couldn't have. She knew it was true. Hadn't she herself wanted Morgan Earp? Morgan hadn't given her any real encouragement, yet she had pursued him beyond death.

"I'll have to sell off a few properties, but it's worth it," Chesser was saying.

Charlotte chided herself for not listening. One of the reasons she had agreed to dine with him was to learn more about his financial condition. "Are you having second thoughts?"

"No, what's done is done. I've got plenty of money on paper, but it's tied up in investments. No doubt I'll have to pay some steep penalties, but I can get the money. And with a mine as good as the Necropolis, I can put back whatever money I've lost."

"So you will lose some money."

"Some. I'll have to mortgage my properties in Tucson, all except my practice, but it will be worth it. You heard Jaffee. He said it is as sure a thing as we'll get on this earth."

Charlotte had difficulty concealing her triumph.

Dinner passed quickly, Charlotte and the surgeon indulging in pleasant conversation and light banter. He approved of her quick wit, and complimented her on many things: her looks, her intelligence, her fine taste in clothing. As he drank more, his compliments became more effusive. Often she caught his gaze on her, but he was still crafty enough to hide the intensity of his feelings. After dessert, Charlotte feigned tiredness and asked Chesser to escort her home.

"I was hoping you'd join me at the Crystal Palace," he told her. "I could use your presence at the faro table. You've been good luck for me so far."

People always want what they can't have. "I'm sorry, but traipsing around that mine has left me exhausted."

"Some other time, perhaps?" There was a strained note to his voice.

"Some other time."

As he escorted her back to the Cosmopolitan, he took her hand and placed it on his arm. They walked in this fashion for a few minutes, then Charlotte removed her hand and moved away from him, so they were walking slightly apart.

271

He glanced at her, puzzled, but she ignored him.

They stopped at the door of the Cosmopolitan. "Would you come to dinner with me tomorrow night?"

"I am afraid I have other plans."

"The following night, then."

"I'm sorry." She could see the impatience in him, the doubts he entertained.

"Well, then, perhaps some other evening."

Charlotte pulled back, allowed herself to appear to consider his proposition in a detached manner. "By all means. Thank you for an enjoyable evening."

"I'll leave you here, then." He fumbled for her hand and kissed it, looking suddenly clumsy and vulnerable.

Smiling, she watched him walk up the street.

A couple of days later, four dozen roses were delivered to Charlotte's suite. In Tombstone, far from the railroad and refrigerated boxcars, the expense in buying and shipping them must have been enormous. Attached to the largest bouquet was a card, requesting her to let him know when they could have dinner together.

Charlotte ignored his message. She managed to avoid him at the hotel, spending most of the next few days at the theater.

Chesser contrived to meet her on Friday afternoon, nearly running her over at the door to the hotel. "Did you receive my message?" he asked hopefully.

"The roses were lovely, thank you."

"When can we have dinner?"

"I haven't a calendar with me."

"What about this weekend?"

"I'm sorry, but I'm busy."

"You are always busy."

"I am building a theater. If you wish to dine with a woman who sits about all day playing cribbage, you are perfectly free to look elsewhere." She left him before he had a chance to reply.

The next morning, Charlotte awoke early. Jake was coming to town today, and anticipation had kept her awake most of the night.

Scanning the room, she noted the wine-dark roses were beginning to wilt, but she loved to look at them anyway. They were a symbol of Chesser's desire for her. Still, it might not be a good idea to have them around when Jake arrived. Men could be foolish about such things.

Charlotte never grew tired of this room. She had chosen the wallpaper herself—light pink, embossed with gold and brown floral stripes. The furnishings were elegant in their simplicity: the rosewood four-poster, marble-topped dresser and matching cherrywood armoire, the Irish linen coverlet embroidered with lilies of the valley. Charlotte glanced at the open window, where lace curtains flirted in the breeze. It would be a beautiful springlike day. The sky was deep blue—the color of the morning glories that would soon be growing along the roadsides. Slipping into her wrapper, her unbound hair tumbling richly down her back, Charlotte walked to the window and looked out at the street.

Edward Chesser stood across the way, staring directly at her window. When he saw her, he quickly averted his head.

Shaken, Charlotte stepped back out of view. How long had he been looking at her window, waiting for her to appear?

She sat down on the bed. Could he be dangerous? It was obvious that he was infatuated with her, obsessed.

Obsessed. The realization scared her, but it was also exhilarating, to think that she could have such an effect on a man. Triumph filled her, heady as wine.

I can control him. She felt like a vessel, filled with the blinding power of vengeance. Hugging herself joyfully, Charlotte realized that she must plan her moves very carefully from now on. She mustn't only keep the man's interest, but must fan the flames to a raging inferno.

Edward Chesser's ruin was in her hands.

Chapter Thirty-three

Edward Chesser dined alone at the Maison Doree that Saturday night. He would be going back to Tucson on Monday. His practice would suffer soon if he stayed away much longer. The Necropolis was in good hands with John Jaffee. He had only stayed this long because of Charlotte Tate.

Damn her, how had she gotten under his skin so quickly? The girl confounded and attracted him at the same time. Perhaps it was her self-assurance, so rare in the kind of woman he usually liked. Perhaps it was the sense that, for the first time in his life, he might not be able to make a woman fall in love with him. She kept him at arm's length, flirting with him one minute, then pushing him away so subtly that it was hard to know if she really were rejecting him. Sometimes she sounded utterly guileless, but underneath he sensed a steel core. A woman who defied propriety to build a theater in a man's world, a woman who had already made a fortune at the age of twenty-three, had to be strong. She never showed that toughness, though. She kept him off balance. This was a new experience for him.

He had been devilishly handsome in his youth, never

lacking for feminine companionship. In the last few years, he knew he had lost that edge. But what he had lost in looks, he had gained in maturity, charm, and wealth. When he wanted a woman, he got her.

Not that there weren't plenty of women who refused him at first; their protestations could usually be laid at the door of feminine modesty. It was easy to overcome that kind of rejection, for it had no deep roots. As a matter of fact, a small challenge added spice to the relationship; he had always relished the pursuit. But Charlotte Tate was different.

She put him in mind of a thoroughbred he'd once owned—a beautiful powerhouse of nervous energy. In the three years he owned that horse, he had felt as if he were sitting on a stick of dynamite. That black devil would throw him the moment he let his guard down. He had never known such exhilaration before or since— until now. Now he was faced with a new challenge: He had to make Charlotte love him.

Just then the door to the Maison Doree opened, and Charlotte Tate entered the restaurant.

The steak in his mouth suddenly tasted like twine. His heart pounded against his ribs.

She was a vision. Her forest-green satin dress glimmered in the dim light, setting off a glowing magnolia complexion. How could he have ever looked at that exquisite face—the even dark brows, straight nose, high cheekbones, full lips, and pointed chin—and thought a plump girl pretty? She was magnificent. Her hair had been pulled into a simple chignon tied at the back of her neck, and a few stray tendrils framed her face. The dress, too, was simple, the mild scooped neckline unadorned. Perhaps it was the simplicity that gave her an elegance that other, more lavishly dressed women in the room lacked.

At that moment, Edward Chesser realized that Charlotte Tate was more than just a conquest. He was in love with her.

The maître d' led Charlotte to a table near one of two tall windows near the front of the restaurant. She accepted the menu with a dignified nod and laid it down on her plate.

Heart hammering, Chesser chewed the ball of steak in his mouth, hating its cold, greasy taste. He swallowed hastily, almost choking, and stood up. He would go over and speak to her. Perhaps she would ask him to join her.

The door opened again and a cowboy walked in, looked around, then made a beeline for Charlotte.

So that was why she was busy tonight! Aware that people were beginning to stare, Chesser sat down abruptly and took a large drink of the cabernet sauvignon at his elbow. It was an expensive wine but he hardly tasted it.

What was she doing with a cowboy? The man was clean enough—he wore a boiled white shirt and gray corduroy trousers—but Chesser had seen enough cowboys in his time to know one when he saw him. He knew from the way the fellow walked, loose-limbed and catlike, the way his eyes scanned the room as if he were used to looking out at great distances.

Aching, Chesser watched the two of them, jealousy uncoiling in his body like a hungry worm. Charlotte and the cowboy seemed suspended in their own world, looking at each other as if no one else mattered. He had waited five days for her to look at him that way, and now he knew why she had not.

So the famous Tombstone Rose loved a cowboy, when she could have anyone! Suddenly he wanted to get out of here, go anywhere, just so he didn't have to see the two of them together. He shook with rage and an entirely new emotion to him—helplessness.

He called for his check and walked to the back door of the restaurant, hoping she did not see his humiliation and his pain.

* * *

Charlotte was in the habit of riding every morning, following a loop trail down toward the San Pedro River and returning by way of the Charleston Road.

After a nice gallop, she turned Diamant toward home, still excited by the run. She was not surprised when Edward Chesser appeared in the road ahead of her and swung his horse alongside hers.

"May I ride with you for awhile?" he asked.

"I thought you were in Tucson."

"I've been there and back," he said.

"Won't your practice suffer?"

"I have arranged to move my practice to Tombstone."

She digested this, trying to keep the flood of triumph from claiming her features. "Isn't that a bit precipitous?" she asked carefully.

"Precipitous? How so? I've just made a very expensive investment. I want to be nearby to keep my eye on things."

Charlotte realized that Chesser's move might have other implications. He would be easier to cheat if he were seventy miles away in Tucson. "Is that the only reason?" she asked.

"I like being near you."

"You flatter me."

"Come now, Charlotte. You must know what effect you have on men. Even that cowboy."

"Cowboy?" Charlotte stared at him.

"I saw you at dinner last Friday, at the Maison Doree."

"You're given to spying on me, then?"

"Do you really think that?"

"No. You are far too worldly for that sort of thing."

"I'm glad you think so. I am curious, however. It's hard to imagine the famous beauty Charlotte Tate in the company of a common cowpuncher."

"What makes you think he's a common anything?" she said coolly, and was rewarded by the sight of Chesser's fist tightening on his horse's reins. The horse pinned its ears back and lashed out with a hind leg. "You must be gentler with your animal," she added.

"This beast is a livery nag and barn sour."

"I detest cruelty."

"I apologize." They rode in silence for awhile. Charlotte sensed that Chesser wanted to ask her more about Jake, but didn't want to appear overeager.

At last he blurted it out. "Who was that cowboy?"

"He is a friend of mine."

"If you will forgive the observation, you looked like more than friends to me."

"Would you be shocked if I told you he was my lover?"

His face turned brick red. He refused to look at her, and when he spoke, his voice was tight. "Disappointed, perhaps."

"You wonder how a woman of my financial and social standing could love a man who raises horses for a living? My God, Edward, you're such a snob."

"You could do better."

"Do you mean by that I could have *you*?" she asked, a trace of scorn in her voice.

His eyes looked tortured. He seemed thinner, too, and the arrogance she'd come to know seemed to have flown from him completely. "I would be a far more suitable match."

"True. You're a surgeon, and that is a very respectable profession." She regarded him coolly. "But I don't want you." She spurred Diamant into a gallop, leaving him in her dust.

Chesser asked around about the cowboy. Jake and Charlotte's relationship was no secret, but for a town that thrived on gossip, people were surprisingly reluctant to talk about it. Chesser was also surprised at the respect with which the townspeople regarded Cottrell. No one would say a bad word about him.

Chesser could also tell that Charlotte was not liked in

Tombstone. Although the townspeople's disapproval was evident, hardly a one criticized her openly. It annoyed Chesser further to know the reason for this: Charlotte Tate was Jake Cottrell's woman, and while she was, they would not say a word against her.

What kind of cowboy garnered respect like that? It galled him no end.

Well, they couldn't be too serious about each other. Jake lived on his ranch and Charlotte lived in town. If just the right pressure were applied, Chesser might be able to thrust a wedge between them. After all, Jake Cottrell was in no position to defend himself. He was too far away for that.

So Chesser decided to apply his own brand of pressure. It had always worked before. He would wear down Charlotte's resistance, make her see that he cared far more for her than the cowboy did. Jake Cottrell didn't love her enough to give up his ranch, whereas he had already proven the seriousness of his intentions. He had moved his practice to Tombstone.

Every morning he met her on the Charleston Road. She didn't seem to mind, greeting him with a maddening indifference. The milder her responses, the more he showed of his feelings. Chesser knew he was acting like a lovesick boy, but couldn't help it. Charlotte's very presence demolished him. He began to wonder how he had ever thought he could get the upper hand. Their conversations were like tennis matches; she met his every volley with a swift, killing return.

He admired her enormously.

He loved her.

Chesser found he could not keep his mind on his work. His heart pounded all the time, and he had energy only for thinking about her. He became lax in his dealings, disinterested in the few patients who came to him. He spent a lot of time at the faro tables or playing keno, and drank more than usual.

Everywhere he went, he looked for Charlotte Tate. He passed her theater likely a dozen times a day, and his whole world revolved around the mornings when he would intercept her on the Charleston Road.

He sent her roses. He sent her other gifts; a massive crystal chandelier for the Lancastrian Opera House, a black carriage with red wheels and trim, and two white horses to pull it. She accepted all of his gifts as her due, like a queen accepting tributes.

He gambled, his losses often in the thousands. At least the mine was making money—lots of it. It was the best purchase he had ever made.

A month passed, but there was no sign of Cottrell. Chesser supposed he was busy at the ranch. Well, the cowboy couldn't be too smart. The man was pushing Charlotte away with both hands—pushing her into another man's arms.

Charlotte agreed to have dinner with him. He dressed for the occasion three times. Black tie? White tie? Perhaps the black tails, a white blouse, and striped ascot.

She wore black, a color that would make any other woman look dowdy, but looked elegant on her. The slight scooped neck, unadorned, had become her trademark, and he could barely keep his gaze from her snowy, swan-like neck, the shadowed hollows of her collarbone and the graceful slope of her shoulder.

"You know, I don't think you really love that cowboy," Edward said bravely.

Her eyes sparkled with amusement. "Why do you say that?"

"I think you're beginning to like me, that's why."

"Of course I like you. I always have."

Edward leaned forward. "Why don't you marry that cowboy if you love him so much?"

"It isn't practical."

"Practicality and love are strange bedfellows. I know what I would do if I was your cowboy."

"Oh?" Her eyebrows raised; she looked amused.

"I would tie you over my saddle and take you away by force."

"Fortunately for me, you aren't Jake."

"He can't love you that much if he's content to leave you here." He swept his hand around the room. "Where is he now?"

Charlotte shrugged.

"You know what I think? I think you have never really cared sufficiently about anyone to know what real love is."

"And you do?"

"Yes," he said, and was alarmed at the passion in his voice. He took her hand in his. "Charlotte, you must know how I feel about you. I—"

Gently, she put her finger to his lips. "Please," she said kindly, "don't embarrass yourself."

"Then you don't care for me at all?"

Charlotte bit her lip and looked down. For the first time, Chesser began to feel he had a chance with her.

"Think what I have to offer you. Money—oh, I know you've got plenty of your own, but that theater is an ambitious project. And position. No one would dare shun you or the Lancastrian if you were married to me. I'm a well-respected member of this community. My name would add legitimacy to your dealings. I could act as a buffer between you and the builders. I could help you, Charlotte."

He glimpsed vulnerability in her eyes. Vulnerability and doubt. And then she seemed to shake herself mentally, and her eyes were cool and indifferent again. "Edward, must you be so tiresome? I was so enjoying this evening until now."

"I hate to see you treated this way."

"Please, I think I'd like to leave now." She rose and started for the door, her skirts sweeping around her, swishing softly along the carpet.

He paid the check and went out after her. She was leaning against one of the porch posts, obviously dejected. When she heard his step, she straightened and smiled into his eyes, but he knew she was hiding her true feelings.

He felt triumph.

Chapter Thirty-four

Spring warmed into a mild March. Edward Chesser and Charlotte were regular companions now. He rode out with her every morning, and in the afternoon accompanied her to the theater to supervise construction. They dined together in the evenings. People were beginning to talk.

With the mine producing so well, Edward abandoned all pretense of running a doctor's office. Why in God's name should he spend his days in the stuffy little office when he could be out wooing Charlotte?

Her resolve was weakening. He could see tiny cracks in her resistance. Cottrell played right into his hands by not coming to see her.

One evening Chesser surprised himself by blurting out, "Marry me, Charlotte."

"Marry you? You must be out of your mind."

"Why not? You know I love you. You said yourself that we're good for each other."

She seemed to consider his proposal for a moment, then

turned her serious gaze to his. "But I don't love you," she said reasonably.

Of course he knew that. But hearing the words spoken was shocking, a fresh pain so acute he had to turn away. Still, he managed to come up with a weak rejoinder. "Love is not the only reason for marriage."

She stared at him bleakly and said nothing.

But later, as he left her in the lobby of the Cosmopolitan, she put her hand on his arm and her touch sent a jolt like lightning through his limbs. "If I married you, it would be with the understanding that I don't love you. Could you live with that?"

He gulped a deep breath, wondering how he could be so joyful and miserable at the same time. "What about Cottrell?"

Her voice hardened. "You are right about Jake."

"Then you don't love him anymore?"

"Of course I love him."

"But you would marry me?"

"I simply asked you a question."

And then she left him.

Yes, things were certainly looking up. Charlotte was thawing toward him, and the Necropolis was everything he could hope for. As the money piled up, he fairly burst with pride. Of course Jaffee put a lot of money back into the mine; there was always some minor problem that could only be solved by spending more money. This time water had seeped into the five-hundred-foot level.

"It's nothing serious," he told Charlotte as they rode together to the river the day after his proposal. She looked lovely as usual in a hunter-green habit and a hat trimmed with ostrich feathers. The land stretched out before them, tan and gray. Ahead of them the cottonwood trees along the river were leafing out in their spring raiment, a filigree of apple-green against the blue mountains beyond. Edward decided not to push her for an answer to his proposal; he would talk of other things. "The water's a nuisance, nothing more. A small pump should do it. But the operating costs can mount up quickly."

For her part, Charlotte was delighted. No doubt Jaffee was keeping Chesser's profit to a minimum, even for a glory hole like the Necropolis.

Still, the surgeon was making a healthy profit, and that was good. In a sting, the victim should always feel he was ahead at the beginning.

Let him enjoy it while he could.

Edward Chesser enjoyed his good fortune for another two weeks.

One afternoon, as he sat in his office going over the profit ledger for the Necropolis, someone knocked timidly on his door.

"Come in," he bellowed. If it was that fool Vogal asking for the rent again, he would throw the man out bodily.

It wasn't Vogal. A short man with narrow shoulders and a head too large for his body entered, carrying a small valise. He wore an expensive suit.

"I'm not seeing any patients today."

"I'm not a patient." The little man cleared his throat. "I'm here on business of a legal nature. I represent Johnny Trevieghan."

"And who's Johnny Trevieghan?"

"Mr. Trevieghan owns the Watervale mine, adjacent to yours. May I sit down?"

"Certainly," Chesser said expansively. "The Watervale, eh? How may I help you, Mr. uh—"

"Marino. Anthony Marino, attorney at law." The man rummaged through the valise and withdrew a clutch of papers. "Perhaps you should read this before we talk further." He selected one sheet of paper and handed it across the desk.

Chesser stared at the paper, then at the lawyer. "What is this?"

"You have heard of the Apex Law?"

Chesser stared senselessly at the paper again, unable to speak. A creeping dread permeated his soul.

"In the Mining Act of 1872, the Apex Law specifically states that 'the locators of all mining locations shall have the exclusive right of possession and enjoyment of all the surface included within the lines of their locations, and of all veins, lodes, and ledges throughout their entire depth, the top or apex of which lies inside of such surface lines extended downward vertically.' " Marino looked up. "In other words, Dr. Chesser, you are pursuing a vein of silver that started on Mr. Trevieghan's property. He discovered and worked the vein a year ago, and that vein extended beyond his property line and into your claim. According to the law, he has the legal right to follow that vein into your property, and to confiscate all profits made by you in your retrieval of ore that is rightfully his."

Chesser tried to absorb what Marino was telling him. He stared at the lawyer, then stared out the window at the blue sky, where puffy clouds grazed along the mountains like sheep. What he was hearing spelled his utter ruin. He licked his lips. "Are you telling me the Watervale has the prior claim?"

"That is correct."

"But that mine isn't being worked," Chesser sputtered.

"It doesn't matter. Mr. Trevieghan doesn't have to pay assessment on patented land. He owns that property."

The buzzing in Chesser's ears grew louder. "I don't understand. Why are they interested now?"

"I should think that would be obvious."

285

"Why should he spend money to retrieve the ore when others will do it for him!" Chesser said bitterly.

"Precisely."

"That's fraud!" Chesser shouted. "They must know I'd find their vein on my claim!"

"I would advise you—in a purely friendly capacity, of course—to keep your libelous rantings to yourself."

"They won't get away with this! You tell your man Trevieghan he can take me to court!"

"I'll pass on the message," the lawyer replied equably, and rose to his feet.

After Marino left, the full impact of the situation hit Edward. Trevieghan was entitled to all monies the Necropolis had earned in the past two months.

I've been spending all this money and working that claim for nothing! For less than nothing! He'd paid twenty thousand dollars for the Necropolis. And that was only the beginning. There was the expensive mining machinery, the miners' wages, the water pump—all to retrieve someone else's ore!

Sick at heart, he stumbled to the window and stared bleakly at the sky. A warm breeze ruffled the damp hairs on his forehead, but he did not feel it.

Another thought entered his mind. A lot of the money earned by the Necropolis—most of it, in fact—had already been spent! Some went on improvements for the mine, but a lot of the money had been gambled away as if there were no tomorrow, because he had believed—sincerely believed— that the mine was worth a fortune, and would keep making him money hand over fist.

He thought of the extravagances he'd lavished on Charlotte Tate—the hothouse roses, the chandelier, the matched pair of horses, the carriage—

Panic ran through him like quicksilver, followed by a desperate mad hope. Charlotte. Perhaps Charlotte would help him.

Chapter Thirty-five

The attorney's office was located in the lawyer's section of
Tombstone, known by the suitable appellation Rotten Row.
It was a weathered frame building set back from the broad
dirt street in a weedy lot.

Inside, the office was bare except for a scarred desk,
desk chair, and two worn-looking cane chairs. Lester Craymore was young, blond, and capable-looking. After hearing what Edward Chesser had to say, he sat back in his
chair and looked at Chesser and Charlotte.

"I'm afraid it's cut-and-dried. Trevieghan has every
right to recover the cost of the ore you have removed from
the Necropolis. If he takes you to court, you'll lose. In
addition to paying Trevieghan, you'll have court costs, not
to mention my fee. As Miss Tate's attorney and friend, I
suggest you give in gracefully."

"Excuse me, Mr. Craymore," Charlotte said softly. "Are
you sure there isn't some other way?"

Craymore shrugged. "The only alternative I can see is if
Dr. Chesser buys the Watervale from Trevieghan."

"Why should I buy the Watervale?" Chesser shrieked.
"It would be like paying for my own damn mine!"

But Charlotte remained silent, her face thoughtful.

On the way back to the Cosmopolitan, after listening to
Chesser rant and rave for two blocks, Charlotte put her
hand on his arm. "I think we may find a way out of this,"
she said.

"I can't see any."

"I know Mr. Trevieghan. I kept a secret for him, a long time ago. When I was a pretty waiter at the Westphalia."

"So?"

"If his, er . . . situation were ever exposed to the light of day, he would stand to lose a great deal."

"What does that have to do with me?" Chesser shouted.

"I am only trying to help you," Charlotte said quietly.

"I'm sorry. I am distraught."

"You could buy the mine, Edward. I'm sure he will sell it to you, once he sees the way things are."

"Why, when he stands to make a fortune?"

"The Watervale hasn't really been worked for years. He'd have to purchase all the machinery, hire miners, retimber. You said yourself that that pump costs a pretty penny to run—"

"Precisely why we should forget the whole thing. Besides, I don't *have* any more money."

"Oh, surely you do. What about all the gifts you gave me? You must be a wealthy man."

"I have some holdings left, yes, but why throw good money after bad? Craymore's right. I should cut my losses and get out."

"Will you be able to pay Trevieghan everything you owe?"

"If I liquidate some more assets."

"But Edward, don't you see? If you owned the mine, the profits would remain yours. If you quit now, two months' work and your whole investment will be lost. You said yourself that the Necropolis is a great producer."

"It is, but I can't afford it."

"You'll have to liquidate anyway. Why not take a gamble, Edward? Why not salvage everything with one bold stroke?"

"I could never get my hands on enough money to buy another mine!" Chesser said savagely.

"I know Mr. Trevieghan. I know we can get the price down. Please. Let me try."

"Why are you doing this for me?"

"Because I care about you."

He stared at her, and despite his misery, felt a certain warmth steal into his heart. She met his gaze, and there was a challenge there. Her luminous eyes, so fine and large, almost hypnotized him. He wanted to take her in his arms and hold her, have her soothe and comfort him with her cool, loving hands. If she believed in him, how could he fail to believe in himself?

"You go talk to him," he said, his voice rough with desire. "If you care for me, I will take a chance if I can."

She smiled, and for a moment the smile seemed to him fake, almost predatory. But that was impossible. "You won't regret this, Edward. You will save everything by acting boldly. And—" she reached up and ran a finger down his cheek—"I admire a man who is not afraid to take a chance."

Chapter Thirty-six

Bernard Waldbaum, the manager at Olin and Wasser Territorial Bank, glanced one more time at the promissory note before rising from behind his desk and shaking Edward Chesser's hand. "That will conclude our business," he said. "I hope this venture will prove very lucrative. Miss Tate." He nodded to Charlotte, who stood behind Chesser. She wore a hat with a stippled lace veil, so it was impossible to judge her expression, but he guessed she was pleased.

Annie McKnight

Bernard had always thought her a most interesting woman, and he often paused to watch her walk through town, admiring her beauty and poise. Still, he wouldn't want to know her better—she had always given him the feeling that she could read a man's mind, and he wanted nothing to do with a woman like that.

Right now, Charlotte didn't have to read Chesser's thoughts; they were plain on his face. He was simultaneously worried and pleased with himself, remarkably happy for a man who had spent more than sixty thousand dollars in the past two months when his mine had produced only a little more than half that amount in silver.

He had exhausted every avenue to raise the thirty-eight thousand dollars needed to buy the Watervale Mine. He'd mortgaged or sold outright his last property holdings in Tucson. Even so, he'd had to borrow more than ten thousand dollars from the bank. It was indeed a bold stroke.

As they walked out into the late May sunshine, Chesser reached out to steady Charlotte against the crowd, cupping her elbow gently. "Well, my dear, it's done."

"But Edward, did you have to sell off everything? That doesn't leave you with any sort of cushion. What if the mine stops producing?"

"There's no reason to think it will. Jaffee assures me the Necropolis will produce for years. And I have you to thank for Trevieghan's cooperation."

Charlotte dipped her head modestly. "It was nothing."

"Nothing? Trevieghan could have sold the Watervale for twice the amount. Just what did you have on him, anyway?"

"That wouldn't be fair of me to tell you, would it? Then it wouldn't be a secret anymore."

"Well, I suggest we go to lunch and celebrate."

At lunch, Chesser ordered a bottle of champagne. Charlotte accepted one glass and sipped it; she had never really cared for the stuff and she liked a clear head. Chesser finished the bottle.

290

"Let me propose a toast, my dear." He held up his glass, eyes sparkling. "To the most beautiful woman in the world."

"I cannot drink to that. How about to the Watervale? And to you, Edward, the newest independent mine owner in Tombstone."

"All right. A toast to my mine. But I'm changing the name." He paused, a crafty glint in his eye. "From now on both the Watervale and the Necropolis will be known by only one name, after the woman who made it all possible. The Tombstone Rose."

Charlotte raised her glass in response, but didn't drink. Fleetingly, a shiver ran up her back like a breeze ruffling the calm waters of a lake. For some reason she could not fully understand, she didn't like the idea of her name being lent to the doomed venture.

Jake Cottrell wondered why Mack Harvey, proprietor of the City Lunch Room, didn't seem all that glad to see him.

Well, nothing could spoil Jake's fine mood today. During the busy spring at the ranch, he'd had a lot of time to think. He and Charlotte needed to face their problems now, before their love for each other withered and died from lack of tending. By the end of this weekend, he wanted the wedding date set, and some kind of consensus on their living arrangements.

"Hey, Mack, where's that coffee?"

The brawny man in the long white apron came over and poured the coffee, avoiding Jake's eyes.

"What's the matter? Aren't you happy with that colt I sold you?"

"He's fine." Mack Harvey glanced nervously at the white-painted tin ceiling, trying to avoid Jake's eyes.

"It's not Charlotte, is it? She's all right?"

Mack snorted. "Looks all right to me. Jake, I hope you don't remember I'm the one who told you this and hold it against me—"

"Just tell me!"

"Miss Tate, she, uh . . ." He blurted it out. "She's been going around with someone. I'm sorry, Jake. I didn't want to be the one to tell you."

Jake's stomach constricted. "What do you mean, someone?"

"A man—a doctor, name of Chesser. He's new here, just bought the Necropolis Mine. I'm sure it's nothing serious, probably just old friends, but you ought to know . . ."

Chesser. Jake let this piece of information sink in, ignoring Mack's rambling explanation. So Charlotte had drawn him to Tombstone at last.

Jake caught the look in Mack's eyes, and was surprised to see pity there. He wondered briefly if other friends would look at him that way. He wouldn't be able to stand it if they did. When your friends began to pity you, you lost something that could never be replaced. In Jake's world, respect was more valuable than money.

Jake stood just inside the doorway of Charlotte's suite at the Cosmopolitan. The expression on his face made her cringe. "Congratulations," he said. "You've finally lured him into your web."

"What do you mean? Who?" At the look in his eyes, Charlotte realized immediately that bluffing wouldn't work. "You mean Chesser? Isn't it marvelous? After all this time trying to get him to Tombstone, he came for a doctor's convention! I never expected it to work out this way, just as I planned it—"

"You're babbling, Charlotte."

"I'm sorry. It's just that I've waited so long. You are happy for me, Jake, aren't you?" She looked up at him, a charming appeal in her eyes.

"Don't try that weaker-sex routine with me," Jake said shortly. "You forget I know you too well."

He could be infuriating. She pouted, tilting her eyes up

under her dark lashes, and knew she made an irresistible picture of offended feminine sensibility. "Oh, you don't have one romantic bone in your body!"

"Because I don't fall at your feet every time you make that simpering face?"

"I don't like the way you're talking to me. There are other men who—"

Jake grabbed her wrist, and she could feel the raging power in his grip. "People are feeling sorry for me, Charlotte. Do they have any reason to?"

"I don't know what you're talking about."

"No, I don't suppose you do." Jake let go of her wrist and walked to the window. "You see nothing wrong in letting Edward Chesser squire you around town, when everyone knows that you and I are getting married."

"Jake, you know how I hate Chesser. I've waited five years for this moment. Don't you see? I have to make friends with him, I have to, because—"

"I don't want to hear the sordid details."

"But you have to understand!"

Jake turned around to face her. "Oh, I understand. Did you really think I was jealous of the man who let your sister die? Give me credit for some intelligence. No, I believe you when you say that you're only buttering him up for some crazy scheme of yours."

Relieved, Charlotte asked, "Then you're not angry?"

"You haven't listened to a word I've said, have you? Whether or not you're true to me in your heart, you're still making us both look like fools."

"I don't care what other people think."

"No, Charlotte. You don't care how I feel."

Puzzled, Charlotte stared at him. "You're not making any sense."

Jake shook his head sadly. "I guess it's too abstract a concept for you to grasp."

"You're insulting."

Jake sighed, and Charlotte thought: *He looks so sad, so weary.*

"You're using me, Charlotte, and I won't stand for it."

Charlotte felt her anger rise. He wouldn't stand for it? He'd sooner see her lose forever her chance at destroying Chesser, rather than suffer a little bit of gossip! She had gone to a great deal of trouble planning the surgeon's ruin, had invested money—lots of it—and now Jake felt he could come along at the last minute and tell her he wouldn't stand for it? "Don't you tell me what to do! You don't own me." She flung the words at his head as he strode past her back toward the door. His face was white.

"You're right. I don't own you," he said quietly.

Shaking with rage, Charlotte faced him. "I will not stop now. I've almost got him, and I won't let him get away without making him pay for what he did to my sister!"

Jake stood near the door, his hand on the doorknob. "You'd give anything to ruin this man, wouldn't you?"

What did he mean? Dread gripped her. Suddenly, this grim-faced man looked like a complete stranger, not the warm, loving Jake she knew. Frightened now, but unwilling to give in, she raised her chin and glared at him.

"You can't have it both ways, Charlotte."

"What are you saying?"

"You've made your choice." Jake opened the door. "Good-bye, Charlotte."

Panicked now, she hurtled toward him. "Jake, you can't mean this! I love you—you know I do—and you love me!"

But even as she spoke these words, she saw that his eyes were hard, and there was no evidence of love in the grim line of his mouth or the stern set of his jaw.

"Jake," she said, despising the pleading note in her voice. "It's only for a little while. I just want to get into his confidence, make him depend on me . . ." she trailed off. He didn't seem to be listening. Didn't he care at all? "Afterward, we can go on just as we've always done. I *love* you, Jake. You know that. We'll get married. We'll get married at the theater and everyone will be there, just as soon as I take care of Chesser. But you must know I can't let him get away now. Not when I'm so close."

"As soon as Chesser's out of the way, we can pick up where we left off, is that it?" Jake asked, and Charlotte felt weak with relief.

"Yes, yes! I promise you! It will be exactly the same. No. *Better*. Because we'll be married then and everyone will know how happy we are, because we can tell the whole world—"

"I'm sorry, Charlotte, but I'm just not made that way."

"You can't mean you're really leaving me?" Her voice was choked by her horror.

"I guess you don't know me as well as you think. Yes, I'm really leaving you." Before she could reply, he pulled the door shut. She heard his feet on the carpeted stairs.

She ran to the door and flung it open. "Jake!"

But he was gone.

That afternoon, Charlotte sent a note to Jaffee, pleading illness and postponing their meeting. Then, careful to avoid anyone who might want to see her—particularly Edward Chesser—she took Diamant out for a ride. She had to be alone for a while.

Charlotte remembered another time she had ridden out of Tombstone at a gallop, the pins coming out of her hair and the tears scouring her face. It was the day of the OK Corral gunfight, the day she had met up with Jake and he had held her to him while she cried out her pain and frustration. If only she could turn the time back. If only he were here now, beside her, soothing her with his kisses.

I was a fool then. A simple-minded little fool who wouldn't know love if I fell over it!

But she knew it now. And despite herself, she might have lost it forever.

The grassland stretched out before the sorrel mare's thrashing forelegs, heaving shoulders, and billowing blond mane. The sky stretched over her, brilliantly burnished a deep blue, and if Jake were here she would be rejoicing in the feel of the wind on her face and the pounding of the hooves beneath her. But now she felt only desolation . . . and a heart-wrenching fear.

If Jake didn't love her, than she was truly not worth loving. It was quite possible she would spend the rest of her life alone, an aging spinster.

She spurred her mare on harder over the rough terrain, the tar brush whacking and clawing at her skirt. She remembered how she'd ridden in pants, rounding up the Marquart longhorns with Jake. So many images filled her vision, all of the man she loved more than anything in the world.

But perhaps not more than anything. She wanted to destroy Chesser more. As Jake said, she had made her choice. Charlotte leaned closer over Diamant's mane and cried shamelessly, her tears soaking the front of her blouse.

For a long time she was lost. Lost to her tears, lost to the wind that rippled the hair across her face, to the rhythm of the mare's pounding hooves. Lost to grief.

Much later, she drew rein and rode back toward town. The tears had cleansed her, letting the grief flow out so that at last she could think clearly.

Jake couldn't mean what he said; he was simply angry. She had done a host of foolish things, and he had always stood by her. *He loves me. He couldn't just turn his back on me. He's angry now, but he'll get over his hurt pride. After all, he knows how much I love him.*

It wasn't as if she had been unfaithful to him. He knew she loved him. How could he possibly reject her love, when he felt the same way?

*As soon as I've dealt with Chesser, he'll come back.
He'll mope for a while—I can hardly begrudge him that—
but in the end he'll come around. He loves me.*

Cheered by this logic, she rode back to Tombstone.

Chapter Thirty-seven

Might as well be hanged for a sheep as a lamb, Charlotte
thought bitterly as Edward Chesser proposed marriage
again. The Lancashire idiom reminded her freshly of Mary,
making her more determined than ever to avenge her sister's death. The expression had its roots in the dark days of
English history when a man could be put to death for steal-
ing a lamb to feed his starving family. If you were going to
be punished anyway, the offense might as well be worthy
of the crime. Jake already blamed her; he might as well
have something to blame her for.

The proposal came as they were having a late dinner at
the Russ House, after attending a theatrical production at
Schieffelin Hall. Chesser had been working up to this all
evening long; Charlotte was expecting it, and was ready
with her answer.

It was Jake's fault. She never would have considered
such a drastic measure if he hadn't walked out on her. But
in the past week she had come to the conclusion that to
truly ruin Chesser, she must destroy him emotionally as
well as financially. It was no more than he'd done to Mary.

"Then you will marry me?" Chesser asked, sensing that
Charlotte was seriously considering his proposal.

Charlotte could not bear to look at him. She cast her

297

gaze downward in what she hoped would be taken as lady-like modesty. "Yes," she said softly, feeling as if a stone were lodged where her heart should be.

"I cannot believe it!" His voice was thick with emotion. He squeezed her hand until she cried out in pain. Releasing her as if bitten, he babbled, "I'm so sorry. It's just that I never dreamed . . . I'm overcome . . ."

"If you don't mind, I'm very tired," Charlotte said. "The play was so long, and the excitement—"

"I understand completely." Chesser called for the check, paid it, and ushered her to the door with fawning attentiveness. It was so completely unlike the world-weary Chesser Charlotte knew, that she had to smile despite herself.

Then the realization of what she'd done struck her. Her ears rang and the room swam before her. The whalebone corset pressed against her rib cage like a vice, making it impossible to breathe. For the first time in years she felt as if she might faint.

Chesser was saying, "You won't regret it, my dear. I will make you an excellent husband, and with time . . ."

With time? Charlotte thought distantly that there would be very little time for Chesser to enjoy his newfound happiness. But, oddly, this knowledge did not exhilarate her as she had expected it would. Instead, she felt dirty, used. She saw Jake in her mind's eye, his voice remote and cold as he told her he was leaving her.

Could it be he really meant it? Cold emanated from her core, causing her to shiver. Chesser lent her his coat.

The walk to the hotel seemed to go on forever. She could not get a deep breath. Chesser was talking, his voice rushing into and over her like a raging river, bruising in its force, pummeling her like water against stones. She ignored him, feeling beaten, detached and apathetic, as if her body were not her own but some sort of machine that walked, talked, and responded on its own.

"Perhaps we can sit in the lobby and discuss our wedding plans," Chesser said as they gained the Cosmopolitan's entrance.

"No, Edward. I am so tired I can barely keep my eyes open," Charlotte replied. It was true. She was bone-tired. "I will see you tomorrow."

In the safe haven of her room, she undressed automatically.

Well, she had done it. She had set the trap with the bait Edward Chesser most prized—herself. Yet she felt no elation, no triumph.

Somewhere deep in the tiniest corner of her brain, a voice warned: No good will come of this.

She ignored it.

They would announce their engagement in late June, a week before the grand opening of the Lancastrian Opera House. Although the theater wouldn't be completed by then, they could hold the party in the salon.

Charlotte threw herself into planning the evening, concerning herself with little else. She wanted everything to be perfect, but that wasn't the only reason for her obsession. Something had changed in her since the night she accepted Edward Chesser's proposal. She felt detached, disconnected from the events in her life, viewing even the opening of the Lancastrian with little enthusiasm. By spending her energy choosing announcements, hors d'oeuvres, linens, and flowers, Charlotte avoided thinking about an uncomfortable present and an unbearable future. Not that she would marry Edward Chesser; that was impossible. She told herself over and over that she was only throwing a sprat to catch a mackerel—and tried not to be alarmed that this time, she was the sprat. But the fact that she had accepted his proposal—and his proprietary attitude toward her—made her feel that all this was somehow real. To set her mind on that path would lead to madness; she forced herself to think of nothing more taxing than who would sit where.

Charlotte tried not to think about Jake, but sometimes he intruded upon her mind, bringing fresh grief. It happened when she took the announcements to the engraver. If the world were truly right, the announcements would be for her and Jake—not this unspeakably hideous sham.

She wondered if Jake had heard about their plans. The engagement party was no secret. Earlier this week *The Tombstone Epitaph* had run a short column:

"We have it on good authority that there will be a truly stellar occasion at the Lancastrian Opera House on the twenty-third of June. It will be marked by an announcement that will come as no surprise to anybody with eyes in his head. Our felicitations to the happy couple."

It was too late to go back now; the machinery had been set in motion. Besides, she still had faith that Jake would come back to her when it was over; life would be unbearable if he did not.

Although Edward Chesser was happier than he had ever been in his life, he actually saw less of his beloved than he had before she'd agreed to marry him. She always had an excuse to put him off—she was either making arrangements for the party, directing construction on the theater, or pleading exhaustion from all the work.

Well, it would all be over soon. He would push to have the wedding as soon as possible. On their wedding night he would have her all to himself.

His only real worry was the Tombstone Rose Mine.

Keeping the pumps running ate into his profits. The flooding seemed to be increasing. There was ore down there, all right, but retrieving it was becoming increasingly difficult.

Already deeply in debt, Chesser wondered how he

would make his next payment to the bank. He had made it—just barely—staving the wolf from his door for another month. But Chesser's lack of ready cash had left him with fewer options and no cushion to protect him if something went wrong. In mining, there were always setbacks—often annoying nickel-and-dime expenses that would not hurt a solvent company, but could destroy a weak one. He fell further behind.

The price of silver dropped. Not that much, but enough to make a difference to a marginal company. More water flooded the Necropolis shaft, surging through the network of underground connecting tunnels. They had to abandon the lowest level, where the ore was richest. Edward Chesser was learning the hard way that mineral wealth was not enough to make a successful mine. There had to be a relatively inexpensive way to get at the ore, and with the water level rising daily, they were unable to make the progress Jaffee had forseen.

He had to borrow more money from the bank to keep the pumps running, rather than risk closing down the next level as well.

But at the end of May, he knew he would not be able to make the next payment. When, during one of the few times Charlotte joined him for dinner, he told her about his problem, she wrote a check for the whole amount without a word.

"I can't expect you to bail me out."

"Nonsense, Edward. You would do the same for me. If we are to be married, we must put aside useless pride and help each other."

He accepted the check, feeling small.

After that, things looked up for a while. Another vein was discovered above the water level, and although it was not nearly as rich as the ore they had lost, it did allow Chesser to break even for the month of June.

* * *

On a hot, sunny morning toward the end of the month, Edward walked to the bank. His heart was light. Last night he and Charlotte had gone to see a play at the Bird Cage Theater. For the first time in ages he truly believed in his heart that their upcoming marriage would become a reality.

Inside the Olin and Wasser Co. Bank, light filtered through the open windows near the ceiling, casting lozenges of topaz-hued sunlight across the hardwood floor. Cigar smoke imbued the interior with a golden haze. Chesser stood in line for the bank teller. It was a simple transaction and he didn't need to bother the loan officer. He would simply make his payment and leave.

When he reached the cashier's cage, he wrote out a check and handed it to the teller. "If you'll excuse me, sir, I'll see if everything is in order." The tall red-haired young man wore a green eyeshade and an easy smile.

Chesser hummed under his breath as he waited. The teller seemed to be gone a long time. When he returned, his easy smile was gone. Bernard Waldbaum was with him.

Edward Chesser felt the first prickle of nervousness at the base of his skull. "Is there something wrong with my check?"

"No, your check is good. Since it's drawn on your account here, we know you have the money to cover it."

Chesser licked his lips. "Then what is the trouble?"

"I thought you had been informed."

"Informed? About what?"

"This is highly irregular. They must have notified you."

"Out with it, man!"

"Calm down, Dr. Chesser," Waldbaum said stiffly. "You are making a scene. We cannot accept payment on your bank loan, because we no longer hold your note."

Chesser felt the floor drop out beneath him. His bowels turned to ice. "What are you talking about?"

Waldbaum scribbled a hasty note on a slip of paper and handed it under the cage. "This is the name of the company that holds your note. I believe this concludes our business."

Edward Chesser stared at the slip of paper, feeling ill. His bank loan had been transferred to Dick Nuttall, Inc., a private detective agency in Tucson. What would a private detective in Tucson want with a note on a mine?

Whatever it was, it did not bode well.

Edward pounded on the door of Charlotte's suite. He hoped she would answer; she only answered the door when it suited her. His head ached and his hands shook, and he longed for some opium. But Charlotte Tate was stronger than any drug. Strong and levelheaded. She would know what to do.

He had spent a discouraging three days in Tucson trying to find Dick Nuttall. The detective agency was a dingy office manned by a shifty-eyed man who claimed to be Nuttall's personal secretary. Despite reasoning, cajoling and even threats, Chesser could get no satisfactory answer from him. Nuttall was out of the office. He kept his records on his investments at his home. Chesser went to Nuttall's home, but Nuttall was away and the place locked up tight.

He knocked on Charlotte's door again. "Charlotte! Please let me in!" At last he heard the rattle of a lock and she opened the door.

How beautiful she was! She wore an amethyst-colored morning gown, a froth of gray lace at each sleeve. The gown flattered her coloring. Her hair fell in rippling waves around her shoulders. It was the color of garnet. For a fleeting moment, his fear was replaced by desire. This perfect creature had agreed to marry *him*!

Her delicate brows knitted into a frown. "Don't stand there gawking, for Heaven's sake," she said impatiently.

"Come in, Edward. I don't want everyone to see me like this."

He entered, feeling foolish. Next to this fragile, willowy woman he always felt like a large draft horse—a large, stupid draft horse. She motioned to a chair with her lace fan, and then sat down opposite him on the love seat, arranging the folds of her dress around her. "What is it, Edward? I was just going to take a nap when you interrupted me."

At first he floundered for the words, but eventually poured out the whole sordid story.

She did not seem impressed by the gravity of the situation. "So someone else holds your note. Is that so bad?"

"Bad? Don't you understand? I don't know this Dick Nuttall from Adam. What if he decides to call in the note? I couldn't pay him that kind of money. I'd be ruined!"

If he was expecting sympathy, he didn't get it. "Surely you're exaggerating the danger."

"What am I going to do if he calls in the note?" Edward wailed.

"It may never happen," Charlotte replied calmly.

Edward sank into himself, head bracketed by his hands. "I don't know if I can survive this. I tried to find him, but I got such a runaround . . . I'll have to go back up there and talk to him."

"You're really worried about this, aren't you, Edward?"

"I'm scared to death."

Charlotte's voice was hard. "You should have thought of this eventuality before."

"How could I know this would happen?"

Her next words floored him. "I might as well tell you, although it was supposed to be a surprise." The corners of her lips came up in a tiny smile. "I bought your note from the bank."

Edward stared at her, fear crawling into his heart. At that moment she reminded him of someone, someone he couldn't quite remember. He knew only that the relationship had ended disastrously. Something about her face . . . the shape . . . only different. . . . No, it wouldn't come to him. His memory was obliterated by fear, bright and sharp as a knife, twisting inside him. He could barely think at all. "*You* bought my note?"

"Yes, darling. I bought it for you." She rose gracefully and came around behind his chair, entwining her arms around his neck. It was the first time she had ever initiated physical intimacy between them, and the scent of verbena and the petal-soft touch of her cheek against his drove all thought from his mind.

Maddening desire flooded through him as she feathered a light kiss across his lips. But he was in danger, and he knew it. He felt like a fly struggling in a web, becoming weaker and weaker. What did she mean, she had bought the note? Why had she looked so hard just a moment ago, like a perfect stranger? "For me?" he asked weakly. "I don't see . . ."

"Oh, men can be so obtuse sometimes. I bought the note as a surprise. It's a wedding present, for both of us. I've always wanted a share in your life, Edward."

Relief flooded him, making his limbs weak. He couldn't believe his ears. He was all right. Everything would be all right. She had come through for him after all. He had imagined the hardness in her voice, her eyes. Perhaps she had been teasing him. Women were like that.

"The Tombstone Rose will be ours, my darling, free and clear. As soon as we're married, we'll make a bonfire and burn the note together." Charlotte nuzzled his neck, her dark red tresses sliding over him in a silken net.

Like a condemned man reprieved, he started to shake uncontrollably.

Chapter Thirty-eight

Jake awoke the day of the engagement party with a hangover. It was the first time in years he had spent the night trying to get drunk, and he had succeeded beyond his greatest expectations.

Although his head throbbed abominably, he rose before dawn. He always awoke early, and didn't see any reason to change his habits now.

He tried not to think about Charlotte and the celebration at the Lancastrian. Fortunately for him, he wasn't invited. Charlotte's callousness hadn't extended that far. Or perhaps she knew he would refuse. Whatever the reason, he was grateful. He didn't want to be a party to the horrific spectacle that would surely take place tonight.

Jake ate with the ranch hands and walked to the house. In the west, against a backdrop of glowing apricot, threads of radiant white light stitched scraps of blue-gray clouds together in a patchwork quilt. It would be a beautiful night.

The house was gloomy. Jake didn't bother to put on a light. His head felt better now, but his stomach still felt a little queasy. He sat on the bed and took off his boots.

His mind kept wandering to the engagement party. He couldn't help wondering what Charlotte was planning. She might think she could lead the surgeon by the nose, but Jake doubted she knew what she was up against. It was common knowledge that Chesser frequented the opium dens in Hoptown, the Chinese section of Tombstone. Such

306

a man could be unpredictable, dangerous. This scheme of hers could backfire. Well, she had made her bed. Let her lie in it.

He stared at the boots he had just removed. Then, with a sigh, he reached down and put them on again. Putting on a clean shirt, he walked out to the corral, caught up his best saddlehorse and rode for Tombstone.

Charlotte's heart wouldn't slow down. She could feel it pounding against her rib cage. Hands shaking, she buttoned the basque of her creamy white dress, staring at herself in the mirror. The basque was covered with hundreds of seed pearls, catching the light and throwing it back like a handful of tiny arrows. She had dressed her hair simply, her trademark chignon secured low on her neck. Charlotte had never fancied the current fashion for evenings, in which women dressed their curls high on the head. She thought simplicity set off her features better.

Her stomach twisted; she could almost taste the anticipation.

Here, at last, was the exhilaration that had eluded her for the past several months. Tonight she would be nervous, yes, but it was worth it. And when the night was over, she need never humor Edward Chesser again.

It was dark by the time Jake reached Tombstone. Ahead of him, at the edge of town, the Lancastrian was lit up like a Christmas tree. Carriages lined the block. The theater proper was not finished yet, but Charlotte had rushed to complete the salon for the occasion. Strains of the "Blue Danube" drifted out into the night. A man stood at the door, taking invitations.

Jake felt foolish. Why had he ridden all this way? If he tried to get past the man at the door without an invitation, it would cause a scene. Charlotte would hate him for it, and rightly so. As twisted as her motives were, she had every right to them. He had given up any claim to her when he'd walked out on her.

The orchestra swung into another Viennese waltz. Jake recognized some of the people walking into the theater. Most of them didn't even know Charlotte. They were here for the free food and drink, and to see the interior of the Lancastrian. Even her enemies wouldn't turn down a first glimpse of the most lavish theater in Arizona. Jake knew they would be waiting to see Charlotte make a fool of herself, and he feared they would not be disappointed.

Perhaps he should leave now, before anyone noticed him.

Just then, L. J. Bailey drove up in his carriage. Jake left the shadows and met him as he was getting down.

"Jake. What are you doing here?"

"I need to get in."

"I don't think Charlotte wants you here," L. J. said stiffly.

"Don't you know what she's planning?" Jake noted Bailey's puzzled expression and knew he'd guessed right. "Do you really think she's going to announce her engagement to Chesser tonight?"

"Whyever wouldn't she?"

"She never told you about her sister."

"Her sister?"

"Charlotte thinks that Chesser was responsible for her sister's death." Jake paused as L. J. digested this information. "I think she's going to do something tonight, something rash."

"And you're her guardian angel?" the magician asked sarcastically. "Charlotte can take care of herself. You're the last person she'd turn to for help."

Jake said nothing, but let his words sink in. If there was danger, he knew Bailey didn't want any part of it. He could almost see the man's mind working.

At last, Bailey said, "Come around to the stage entrance

and I'll let you in. But I hope you don't spoil this evening for her. She's worked very hard."

"I won't spoil it," Jake replied. That honor belonged to Charlotte.

Charlotte stood in the circle of her admirers, the same men who had opposed her entry into the business world. They were drawn to her as moths to flame, drawn by her beauty and wit, the freshness of her personality. Their wives were grouped near the door, as if to venture in further would taint them forever. They talked among themselves, open in their disapproval of Charlotte and her lavishly furnished salon. Several of them had snubbed her outright. Yet they stayed, unable to keep from showing their awe.

Their eyes are popping out of their heads! Charlotte thought with nasty satisfaction. She knew what they thought of her, but she didn't care. She'd waited a long time for this night. She felt giddy. Perhaps it was the glass of champagne, but more likely it was the nervousness in the pit of her stomach, rising like the champagne bubbles to her head. Her pulse raced, her heart fluttering in her chest as it tried to fly into her throat. She saw Edward talking to Bob Hatch near the bar.

"Fine piece of workmanship, eh? It's a Brunswick-Balke-Callander bar, made of Circassian walnut," she heard him say. "Imported from Belgium." The way he said it reinforced her hatred for him. He was talking as if he already owned the Lancastrian.

If only L. J. were here for moral support. Where was he?

Suddenly she recognized a familiar face at the edge of the crowd. Jake.

Charlotte had to steady herself by putting out a hand against the wall. Blood pounded in her ears. What was he doing here?

Edward appeared at her elbow. "What's that damn cowboy doing here?"

Charlotte shrugged and tried to sound disinterested. "Who knows?"

"He doesn't have an invitation, does he?"

"No, but he might as well stay. He could make a scene if we ask him to leave." Why would she want him to leave? The only man she had ever loved.

"I hope he won't take our announcement personally," Chesser said, his gleeful expression belying his words. The pompous ass. He'd soon find out where her real affection lay.

He kissed her on the cheek. "Well, my dear, I'm going to talk to John Jaffee about our mine. When will we make the announcement?"

"In another hour," Charlotte said absently.

Many people made demands on her, trapping her into uninteresting conversations. She listened with half an ear, her gaze following Jake. For his part, he seemed immersed in a conversation with Mayor Clum.

She was getting increasingly nervous. The fact that Jake was here made it worse. What would he think of her when she made the announcement? Would he hate her all the more?

I can stop this. Just let the evening go on and let it die a natural death. Tell Chesser quietly tomorrow. I don't have to humiliate him in front of everybody.

And then Edward Chesser took the decision out of her hands. He appeared suddenly at her side, holding a parfait glass aloft. To Charlotte's horror, he banged a spoon against it and called out, "May I have your attention, ladies and gentlemen!" He paused, scanning the crowd, which had formed a horseshoe around them. "The Lancastrian won't officially open until next week, but Miss Tate has graciously allowed us to see the salon for this very special occasion."

There were a few nervous giggles from the crowd.

Charlotte could barely hear him. She concentrated on

her breathing, which had become shallow, like a bent blade of grass in her chest. Feeling slightly faint, she closed her eyes. Pinpricks of yellow light danced under her eyelids. No, she thought. She could not do it. Jake would hate her.

"I'm sure that Charlotte would like to make this announcement herself," Chesser was saying. "After all, this is her theater." He took her hand in his, and stood beside her, beaming.

Revulsion swept through her. How dare this man think he was good enough for her! His hand fastened tighter around hers, his thumb burrowing suggestively into her palm.

"Thank you, Edward, for your kind words." She glanced up at him, saw the greedy light in his eyes. The sight of him made her stomach turn. All those times she had let him touch her, as if he had any right! And now he expected her to marry him, to bear his weight in bed as if he had the same rights as Jake.

She cleared her throat. "Edward Chesser, as I am sure you all know, is a new member of our community, but already well-known." She caught Jake's eye and faltered. He looked away, and it occurred to her that he had known all along what she would do.

The room seemed to close in around her. She felt as if she were breathing molasses. Fighting her claustrophobia, Charlotte did what she always did when she was frightened. She straightened her posture and lifted her chin imperiously, and in that simple movement the strength flowed back into her. She was aware that Jake was looking at her again, and this time their eyes met and held. It was as if they were holding a conversation no one else could hear, a conversation transcending space and time and sound.

Her eyes asked him a question. He sent the question back to her, unanswered.

All right then, if he would not help her, she would follow the script. She took a deep breath. "As you also know,

311

Dr. Chesser recently bought a mine." Raising her voice, she spoke clearly. "Dr. Chesser bought the mine, but I hold the note on it." She turned to the man beside her, slipping her hand out of his, and met his eyes. "I am calling that note in now."

Time slowed; seconds stretched into minutes. Charlotte saw Edward Chesser's beaming smile turn to disbelief, and then to horror. His mouth worked almost comically before the words sputtered out. "You can't—Charlotte." He swallowed, smiled weakly at their stunned audience. "It's just a little joke. As you know, we are going to be engaged and—"

"It's no joke," Charlotte said. Her voice could cut a diamond.

"Charlotte, you can't mean . . . you know I can't pay—" And then he understood. Her hatred for him rushed across the small space that separated them like a conduit, and she saw that he recognized that hatred.

"You still don't know who I am, do you?" she asked. Everyone else in the room disappeared; there were only the two of them here now.

"Mary Connor," he whispered. "You—you were there."

"So you remember." Charlotte's voice dripped with such sarcasm that she herself was shocked by the sound of it. A corner of her mind cried: What will Jake think?

"You were the girl. Her sister."

"Your memory is excellent."

"The sister," Chesser whispered. He added urgently, "There was nothing I could do, nothing! Don't you understand? It was impossible. She had angina—"

"I'll give you until tomorrow noon to pay off your note, or I will take possession of every piece of property you own."

Chesser was incredulous. "I'll be ruined!"

The crowd started to murmur. All eyes were on Edward Chesser. His face had gone from dead white to an unhealthy brick red. "You can't do this to me, Charlotte! What about our engagement?"

Charlotte laughed. Her laugh sounded bitter to her own ears—and again she thought of Jake. She turned to look for him, but he must have moved. The room seemed to spin. She felt as if she were on a carousel, a mad, wild ride. "Are you mad? Any fool could see there never was any engagement!"

"You planned all this," Chesser said, his voice soft and seething with hatred.

"You stood by and watched my sister die; you didn't lift a finger to help her. And now you're paying for it."

"You bitch!"

"Don't waste time with recriminations. I imagine you'll have some fancy footwork ahead of you if you want to pay off the note." She nodded to Bernard Waldbaum. "There's a banker. Perhaps you should start now."

Chesser loomed over her, violence in his eyes. "I should kill you!" he shouted, and one hand came up to swipe at her.

Another hand caught his wrist and yanked him backward. "Don't do anything you'll regret." It was Jake. He let go of Chesser's arm, thrusting him away and blocked the surgeon from Charlotte with his body.

Edward Chesser stared at him for a moment, as if measuring his opposition. Apparently, he thought better of taking Jake on, but straightened his coat and shot his cuffs with an angry jerk. "You're in on this, too, aren't you?"

"Get out."

Chesser turned to Charlotte. "You haven't seen the last of me." He shouldered past Jake and stalked from the room. Charlotte closed her eyes, suddenly weak. Jake had come because he knew something like this would happen. He had come despite everything, because he still cared.

"Thank you, Jake—" She opened her eyes in time to see the back of him as he followed Chesser out the door.

Defiant, Charlotte stared at the crowd. Stunned and

embarrassed, the men refused to look at her. The women were already muttering, and she heard the words "breach of promise" and "dirty laundry" before she turned away. L. J. Bailey announced rather self-consciously that there was plenty of food and drink.

The old cats left first, huffing and puffing in displeasure. Strained and uncomfortable, the husbands milled for a few minutes before making their apologies and taking their leave. Within ten minutes Charlotte was alone with L. J. He asked her if she wanted him to lock up.

"No, I'll stay here for a while," she replied. "You go on home." She could barely stand to see the relief in his eyes.

Charlotte walked through the lavishly decorated salon. She had expected the victory to vitalize her, make her bigger than she was, but surprisingly, she felt small. She wandered along the tables dressed with snowy tablecloths and heaped with the finest foods. Two large salmon on platters, barely touched. Game hens, ham, fruit, paté, imported biscuits, beluga caviar. After that spectacle, it was little wonder that no one was hungry. She had planned to make her announcement later, after everyone had eaten, but Chesser had taken that decision from her.

She felt utterly, completely alone. Walking among the expensive furnishings, Charlotte realized that she would always be an outsider. Surprisingly, the knowledge gave her little sorrow. A lot of things that had mattered a great deal now made no impression on her at all. She didn't care about Chesser anymore; she was weary of the whole sordid mess. And this theater . . .

She didn't care much for it, either. The hideous scene tonight took away its beauty, tarnishing it in the eyes of the people of Tombstone—and her own. Charlotte realized now that she had called this curse willingly upon herself.

For revenge. Her vengeance tasted like dust in her mouth, hollow in her heart. Jake was the only thing that mattered to her now.

And she had lost him forever.

Chapter Thirty-nine

The day after Charlotte called in his note, Edward Chesser approached three banks. None would advance him the money to pay off his debt, despite his vociferous assertion that the Tombstone Rose Mine would yield a fortune. He was considered a bad risk.

Money was tight. Banks refused to make loans even to solvent mining companies. The underground springs beneath Tombstone spread through the mining district by way of the interconnecting tunnels. Only the big companies could afford to keep the pumps running.

Very likely, Chesser would have been ruined anyway. But Charlotte Tate's hand in his undoing was visible for all to see.

He had heard of such elaborate stings before, but to be the target of one was unthinkable. Charlotte had played him like a fish. Now he realized that every step along the way she had set him up, appealing to his greed, his gambler's nature, his vanity.

He hated her.

He loved her. Both emotions clawed at his insides, giving him no relief. He still wanted her, with a violent need that surprised him. He wanted to take her, ravish her, plunder her beauty. Depression vied with fury, obsession with

shame. He was broken. Everything he prized had been
stripped from him; pride, wealth, power, standing in the
community, and worst of all, the foolish fantasy that she
had loved him.

Chesser approached a lawyer, seeking to sue Charlotte
for breach of promise. He was laughed out of the office. In
Tombstone, a man who couldn't control his woman was no
man at all. Worse than losing every penny he owned was
the way people stared at him on the street. Disgust, pity,
ridicule followed him wherever he went, rubbing against
his psyche like air across an open wound. People thought
he was a fool, and he could not blame them for it.

Edward Chesser tried to salve his injured pride in an
opium haze. As he sprawled, drugged, on the settee at
China Mary's house of prostitution in Hop Town, one point
became clear. Charlotte Tate belonged to him. She had
promised to marry him. She was his property, to do with as
he wished. His.

The people of Tombstone might ridicule his suit for
breach of promise, but God's law was greater than man's
own. He memorized those words, chanting them over and
over. God's law was greater than man's law.

The object of his affection fared little better.

Stunned and bruised, Charlotte sleepwalked through the
next week. She had lost interest in the theater, lost interest
in everything. Jake, of course, had gone back to Seep
Springs, probably that very night. He cared enough to protect her when she needed him, but Charlotte wasn't fool
enough to believe that he would come back to her now. Too
late, she finally understood Jake Cottrell.

Charlotte neither knew nor cared where Chesser had
gone. Nuttall would track him down if he tried to leave the
territory without paying what he owed. At one time she had
derived the greatest pleasure from fantasizing about
Chesser's pain and fear, but now she could not think of it at

all. For the first time in years she was content to stay in her rooms, often not bothering to dress for the day. She spent her hours daydreaming of the Marquart ranch. Because Charlotte learned to fantasize at an early age, it was a simple matter to return to that time and place, and spend long, langorous hours in Jake's arms. But she always awoke to reality, its crushing weight bearing her down more with every sunrise. She slept a great deal, yet there were dark circles under her eyes. Food did not interest her, and in one week's time her body lost that pleasing hourglass shape that so enchanted audiences throughout the west. Her collarbone stood out in relief against her fine skin.

The few times Charlotte ventured onto the street, she could feel the animosity of the citizenry. It was palpable, as if her very presence would taint them. Even the prostitutes in their shiny dresses would walk to the other side of the street when they saw her coming. She could see the victory in their eyes; at last there was someone lower than themselves.

She grew more listless. Only L. J. came to see her, reporting on the progress of the theater. "It's finished," he told her three days before the grand opening. "Why don't you come down and see it?"

Charlotte, wearing a silk wrapper, sank down on the love seat and pushed a palm against her aching eyes. Last night she had ordered brandy with room service, although she had no head for drink. It had staved off the emptiness for a time. "I'll see it soon enough at the ceremony."

L. J. leaned forward. "I've never seen ⋅you like this before. You worry me."

She sighed. "I'm just tired."

"Don't listen to what people are saying, Charlotte. You can't let them get to you. You will be at the opening, won't you?"

"I'll be there."

"Don't let them win."

After L. J. was gone, Charlotte bathed for the first time in three days. He was right. If she gave in now, the victory would be theirs. All the people who had tried to pull her down, all the people who thought that a woman wasn't tough enough to survive in a man's world, would win. She could at least summon up enough will to make it to the grand opening. No one need know that inside she felt empty, dead.

And when it was over, she would retreat to lick her wounds in private.

The day of the grand opening was hot and still. At eleven o'clock in the morning, Charlotte Tate stepped daintily onto the bunting-draped platform before the theater. She joined a small group of dignitaries congregated at the rail: the mayor of Tombstone, the editors of both newspapers, the builder, the architect, and several other interested parties. Charlotte was as beautiful as ever, her hollow cheeks adding a haunting quality that accentuated her gracefulness. She wore a plum-colored silk surrah dress. The overskirt stood out from her waist like a puffed pastry, gathered at intervals by jet bows. A white frilled collar buttoned high to her neck. Her hat was tall and trimmed with black velvet, its mesh descending from a short brim to cover the upper half of her face. She stood straight and slim, with that unforgettable carriage that was the envy of every woman in Tombstone.

Despite their blanket disapproval of Charlotte Tate's actions, the citizens of Tombstone were nothing if not curious. Few people would miss an occasion like this in such a small city. Everyone turned out; merchants, miners, prostitutes, ranchers, Mexicans, Chinese. At the edge of the crowd, a newspaper boy sat on his stack of papers to watch the festivities.

At a prearranged signal, the band started up, playing a rousing march. After it had ended, Charlotte stepped up to the rail. Her clear, precise voice floated over them. Her speech touched on Tombstone's great reputation as a city, and how she hoped it would be the cultural center of the west. "Today it gives me great pleasure to—" Her notes slipped from where she had placed them on the railing and fluttered down to the floor. As Charlotte leaned down, twisting, to pick them up, someone said very clearly, "Man's law is not God's law."

A loud report rent the air. Charlotte crumpled, sinking to the dais floor. Someone shouted. A man darted through the crowd, flung himself onto a nearby horse and rode hell-for-leather through the throng.

The newspaper boy stood up as the horse barreled toward him. The horse tried to swerve but the rider spurred it on, and the animal's shoulder caught the boy and knocked him to the ground where he lay limp.

Confused, the crowd milled, but several outraged onlookers ran for their horses. "Get him! He killed that boy!"

"It's Ed Chesser!"

"Goddamn son of a bitch! He killed an innocent boy!"

Charlotte lay stunned on the platform, uncommonly weak. She remembered that she had been collecting her pages when someone had clapped her on the back—hit her a hard thump above the right shoulder blade—knocking her off balance. Embarrassed, she struggled to rise, but suddenly felt dizzy, numb.

And then the most peculiar thing happened. She had the sensation that someone had pulled her up by the shoulders. She floated backward, up into the air, her head and arms and legs weightless. Horrified, she looked down and saw her body lying face down in a jumble of boots and pantlegs. The dignitaries on the platform rippled like a cornfield in the wind; dust and noise shivered in the air. Several men bent down to help her, their faces white with shock. She saw blood—her blood—an ever-widening pool of gore near her outflung arm, leaking from under the armpit of her dress. How oddly unnatural she lay, and so still.

Her senses swam again. With a jolt, she returned to the still form on the platform. It was hard to breathe, as if she were wrapped in a stifling blanket. She smelled people, fear, gunpowder, and dust. A pair of shoes loomed before her eyes and then someone held her under her arms, although she couldn't feel it, and was pulling her up, but not before her ruffled collar dipped into the pool of blood. It spattered her face, smelling coppery and bitter, and her gorge rose almost to her throat but backed down again. Then the pain came.

Mercifully, she lost consciousness.

The act of bending down to retrieve her notes saved Charlotte's life. The bullet had entered high above her right shoulder blade and exited at an angle, shattering her collarbone. If it weren't for the loss of blood, she would not have been in any danger at all. Her recovery, however, would be painful.

Charlotte spent several days at Doc Whelan's, feeling weak as a kitten. The fractured collarbone made it difficult for her to move her head and neck.

Doc Whelan had always been taciturn, but now he regarded her with unalloyed loathing. She asked him what had happened, and he told her as if he were reading a laundry list.

"It was Edward Chesser, then?" she asked.

"Yes."

"Has he been caught?"

"Posse's still out. Your friend Jake's with them."

Jake. Charlotte felt the familiar bleakness at the sound of his name. To her recollection he had not come to visit her. Only L. J. Bailey had bothered to come.

"I hope they catch him," she said.

"I do, too," Doc Whelan said curtly. "But not because he shot you, that would be no loss to this community. He killed that boy in cold blood—aimed his horse right at him. If they catch that son of a bitch, I hope they hang him where he stands."

Charlotte shifted. Her wound itched. "Do you know the boy's name?" Maybe she could set up a trust fund for his family.

"Why do you want to know? To assuage your guilt the way you tried with that Mexican girl? It wouldn't help. Might make you feel better, though, since you're almost as much to blame as Edward Chesser."

Charlotte was stung by Whelan's words. How unfair of him to say that! Tears filled her eyes, but Whelan merely glared at her with disgust and left the room.

How could Whelan say such a thing? She had nothing to do with the boy. It was just a freak accident that the child happened to be sitting in the path of that horse. How could anyone in his right mind blame her?

Suddenly she remembered Roberto's death. She hadn't had anything to do with Roberto's murder, either—not directly. But her actions had led Pike there as surely as if she had pulled the trigger herself. And if she had not shamed Chesser before every prominent citizen in Tombstone, if she'd left him even one shred of self-respect— then maybe he would not have shot her, and in his escape, run the boy down.

How often did she have to make excuses for her actions? How long before she saw that ultimately, she *was* responsible? Her stubborn will to forge ahead despite the consequences had led to two senseless deaths.

Charlotte had a long time to think about Whelan's words. Most of her time was spent lying on her back, staring out the window. She had only the pain in her collarbone and her guilt for company. She was universally hated now. People in Tombstone could forgive her a lot of things, but the boy's death was not one of them. She was a pariah.

L. J. said as much when he visited her for the third time in a week. The grand opening came and went, but hardly anyone attended her theater. The few who did come were an unruly, low-brow crowd who booed and heckled the actors.

"I'm afraid we'll have to close down if people don't start coming," L. J. told her. "The door receipts won't pay for the actors, let alone the cost of keeping the theater running." He enumerated the expenses. She had never seen him so depressed.

After L. J. left, Charlotte thought about it. She didn't care about the theater anymore. It meant nothing to her. Perhaps if she sold her share to L. J.—perhaps if she was not associated with the Lancastrian—maybe people would come.

The Roman Catholic part of her rejoiced at this solution. Wasn't she supposed to do penance when she sinned? That was the only way for her to find favor with God again—and maybe even Jake. Yes. That's what she would do.

Excited now, Charlotte asked Doc Whelan to find L. J. and to send for a priest.

"Why do you need a priest?" he asked brusquely. "You're not dying."

"Just do as I say."

When Father MacDonnel came, he looked at her with disapproval. "Haven't you caused enough trouble already, Charlotte? What do you want from me?"

"I want to say confession."

"It will take a lot of confessing to whiten your soul."

Charlotte ignored the priest's testiness and crossed herself.

"Father, forgive me for I have sinned," she said.

Chapter Forty

The posse rode in two weeks later. They had followed Chesser into Mexico, but luck was on the surgeon's side. Some Federales from Fronteras took exception to the posse, and soon Jake and his companions had enough to do defending themselves. By the time they'd retreated and regrouped, Chesser— a lone man on horseback—had slipped away.

Outside the barber and bath next to the Crystal Palace, Jake swung down from his tired horse and wiped the sweat from his eyes. His gaze automatically strayed to the theater up the street. It stood alone against the backdrop of high desert and the blue distance of the Dragoon Mountains. The sandstone bricks of the lower story gleamed like pink chalk in the sunlight.

Jake knew Charlotte was out of danger. He tried to visit her the day after the shooting, but Doc wouldn't let him see her. "She'll be all right if she doesn't lose any more blood," Doc had told him. "That young woman has a sturdy constitution. It's the Lord's oversight that she doesn't have the brains to go with it. She could have saved us all some grief." Then Doc Whelan told Jake about the boy.

Jake reflected that this wasn't the first time Charlotte was blamed for something beyond her control. Her arrogance, stubborn pride, and condescending attitude toward the people of Tombstone had come home to roost. If the mayor gave a speech and the same tragic chain of events had occurred, no one would blame him. But Charlotte had

never made it easy for herself. She was an easy person to
hate. Jake remembered a different Charlotte; the woman
who had nursed a dying woman with courage and forti-
tude. He owed that Charlotte a visit, if only for old time's
sake.

Hot and exhausted, Jake's first priority was to wash the
dust of the trail off his skin. Afterward, he would go to the
Cosmopolitan, where Charlotte had been removed to complete her recovery.

A young Mexican woman answered his knock. Charlotte lay on the fainting couch near the window, her red
hair spread out on the pillow. Her face was pale and
slightly pinched, but when she saw him her eyes lit up.
"Jake!" She propped herself up higher against the pillows,
modestly tucking the white wrapper around her sling. She
looked thin. Jake was surprised to see how dark the shadows under her eyes were.

"You may go now, Lupe," Charlotte said. The woman
nodded and left. "I heard you were with the posse. Did you
catch him?"

"He got away near Fronteras."

"Oh." Strained silence followed. They were two people
who knew each other well, but who had lost the ability to
communicate.

Then, to his surprise, she started to cry silently. She tried
to cover it up by looking away, but couldn't. He watched as
two tears trembled on her lower lashes and then spilled
over, streaking her cheeks. She wiped them away and
glared at him defiantly. "I knew you'd come. Out of a sense
of duty, if nothing else. Well, Jake, you've been absolved
of your duty. You don't owe me anything. You never did."

He didn't know what to say, so he said nothing.

Charlotte stared out the window. Time stretched, punctuated by the ticking of the grandfather clock near the door.
Jake leaned against the doorjamb, wondering why he
didn't take her at her word and leave. When would he stop

trying to shoulder other people's responsibilities? Charlotte was strong. She could get by without his help. Yet he made no move toward the door.

She glared at him. "Would you stop looking at me like that? I can't stand anyone feeling sorry for me."

Jake turned toward the window. The street was crowded with wagons and horses.

"You were right, of course," she sighed. "I suppose you'd relish saying 'I told you so.' "

Jake said nothing. He felt no moral victory, only emptiness. She had wrung any other emotion from him long ago.

"I loved you. I really did. I don't know why I—" She caught herself and bit her lip. "It's too late now for apologies. They never mean anything, anyway."

"You don't have to explain your actions to me."

"You don't understand," she wailed. "How could you? Everyone always liked you. They hate me, Jake. Everyone—even Doc Whelan. They blame me because that boy got killed—I swear if I had known what Chesser would do I wouldn't have—" She stopped. Jake knew she was thinking that nothing would have kept her from the path she had chosen.

"Charlotte," Jake said gently. "It was in your nature."

"But I *can* be a better person. To say I can't help myself is saying it's hopeless! You remember—you remember how I was with Maria, on the ranch? I was different then. Please don't say it's my nature, because then I might as well be dead and buried and forgotten!" She turned her face into the pillow and he heard her crying, a tortured, lost sound.

Somewhere deep inside him, Jake felt a stirring of the love he had once known. He crossed the space between them, meaning to comfort her. But even as he reached out, his arm faltered and fell back to his side.

Don't be a fool, he told himself roughly. *For all her good intentions, she'll never change. Haven't you learned*

*that in the five years you've known her? To get tangled up
with her again would only destroy us both.*

But Charlotte must have sensed his presence, for she
turned and with difficulty reached out and clasped his arm.
"Please take me with you! I can't stand it here! You have
no idea what it's like having people cut you dead in the
street. I want to go to the Seep Springs, I want to get *clean*
again. It could be just like it was at Maria's ranch, if only
you still loved me, if only you still cared—but even if you
didn't—even if you could never love me again, I'll just be
happy to work for you. I can clean the house, cook—whatever you want! But please, if you ever cared for me at all,
please take me away from here!"

"What about the Lancastrian?"

"Oh, bother the Lancastrian! After . . . what happened
there, I can't stand the sight of it. It's spoilt for me, Jake.
Please," she begged. "Please take me out of here. I want
clean, fresh air and horses and sunshine and—" She broke
off, looking miserable. He knew what she had been about
to say. *I want you.*

His heart felt like a stone. The burgeoning tenderness
he'd experienced a moment ago disappeared, leaving the
same detachment he had felt since the day he walked out
on her. Was she trying to use him again? He knew she
wasn't serious about the theater; it was the most important thing in her life, now that she had ruined Edward
Chesser.

She seemed truly remorseful for her part in that night's
work; perhaps she had learned something after all. He felt
sorry for her. But he had fallen into this kind of trap before.
Love was a long way from pity.

She sensed his ambivalence. "I promise I'll leave you
alone. I can't hope for you to love me again, and I'm not
expecting it. But I can't . . . face this town anymore." She
held his eyes with her own, pleading, and he could see the
desperation in them. He didn't like it. The Charlotte he

knew was foolish but defiant; this woman was a frightened stranger.

Charlotte clutched his hand. He recoiled. Catching his expression, she turned away. "Forget I said anything," she said quietly. "I didn't mean to burden you with my problems."

"I'll come see you tomorrow," Jake said.

"Don't bother." The reply was muffled in her pillow. Feeling ill, Jake opened the door and walked out.

Jake stayed in Tombstone that night. He found himself walking the streets in the purple twilight, seeing Charlotte's face in his mind's eye. At last, she had scraped the bottom of the great reservoir of self-respect she'd always had in abundance. In all his dealings with her over the years, he had never in his life expected to pity her, to think of her as a pathetic figure. It depressed him.

He found himself on the road to the Lancastrian. The theater was dark. A notice on the door read ALL PERFORM-ANCES CANCELLED.

A full moon had risen above the jagged outline of the Dragoons. Gray clouds curved across the sky like the mottled spine of a herring, edged with silver.

A scrape of a shoe alerted Jake to another person's presence. He turned around to see L. J. Bailey.

"Hello, Jake. I hear Chesser got away."

"He won't live long. He's an opium addict."

"A man is always bedeviled by something," Bailey said, his voice thoughtful. "Isn't she beautiful in the moonlight?" he asked, folding his arms and staring up at the Lancastrian. "I wonder if future generations will think she's as beautiful as I do." He paused, and when he spoke again his voice was grave, an orator's voice. " 'Round the decay of that colossal wreck, boundless and bare, the lone and level sands stretch away.' *Ozymandias* by Shelley." He glanced at Jake. "I don't suppose you read poetry."

Annie McKnight

"I've read some."

Bailey sighed. "Ozymandias was an Egyptian king. He was under the mistaken assumption that his legacy would remain intact forever. 'My name is Ozymandias, king of kings: look on my works, ye Mighty, and despair!' "

Jake motioned to the sign. "I thought you just opened three weeks ago."

"Business has not been brisk."

"Will you open again?"

"I don't know." L. J. shook his head sadly. "It isn't just the way the townspeople feel about Charlotte. I think Tombstone is on its last legs and doesn't know it yet. It was a foolish thing to do," he added ruefully. "Building a palace like this in the desert. I was a wealthy man when we started. Now it looks as if I'll have to go on the road again, if Charlotte's solution doesn't work."

"Solution?"

L. J. smiled bleakly. "Next week I am reopening the theater under new ownership."

Jake couldn't believe his ears. "You're selling out?"

"I'm not. Charlotte is."

Jake felt as if someone had struck a blow to his solar plexus. "Charlotte sold her share of the Lancastrian?"

L. J. nodded. "We are hoping that this move will save the theater. It became obvious to both of us that no one would patronize the Lancastrian because of her association with it. The boy's death was the last straw."

So Charlotte had meant it when she told him that it was spoiled for her. He felt a sharp disappointment. Why did she have to take such a drastic measure? Had all the fight gone out of her?

"You look surprised," L. J. said.

"Were things really that bad?"

"I've no doubt people would come around in a while, but by that time the theater would have been doomed. We

328

can't afford to keep a theater open when no one is buying tickets."

"It's not like Charlotte to give up."

L. J. grinned. "I have a theory about that, if you care to hear it." He continued without waiting for an answer. "In all my life, I've never seen someone so determined to get her own way. Yet when she does, she's inevitably disappointed. Turns out, it really wasn't something she wanted after all. I honestly believe she doesn't know what she wants." He paused. "That's probably true of most of us. I, for instance, always wanted to be wealthy. And now I find it a terrible headache. Sometimes I wish I could just go back on the road with the Athena Traveling Troupe, pretending to catch bullets in my teeth." He glanced at Jake. "You've seen her?"

"She's changed," Jake said bitterly.

"No, Jake, she hasn't changed. Charlotte's been sidetracked for a while, but she's made of sterner stuff than you're giving her credit for. She'll survive." He paused, looking forlornly at the theater. "You know, I think I'll polish up my magic act for the opening. Do you think that's a good idea, Jake? It's not unseemly for the proprietor to perform on his own stage, is it?"

Jake said he thought it would be all right, but L. J. Bailey didn't seem to hear him. The magician stared up at the blank windows above the entrance, deep in thought. When Jake left him, he didn't turn to say good-bye.

That night Jake dreamed of Charlotte in the cave, but this time the Apaches found them and Jake tried to reach for his gun but he was paralyzed, rooted to the spot, and could only watch helplessly as one of the braves pulled Charlotte up over his saddle and started to ride away. She called to him, her voice filled with fear, "Save me, Jake, please!" But he could not do anything. The brave and Charlotte struggled on the horse, and Charlotte grabbed the Apache's gun and turned it on herself. He heard the shot, loud, and saw blood flower on her breast, saw her topple to the ground, and then he was at her funeral, her body lying in state in the Lancastrian, and Edward Chesser was there laughing. "You let her die, Jake," he said, tears of mirth streaming down his red face. "You gave up on her and let her die."

He awoke, sweating.

Three hours later he knocked on Charlotte's door. Lupe answered. "Miss Tate is not up yet."

"This will only take a moment." He brushed past her and opened the door to Charlotte's bedroom. Charlotte rose halfway up in her bed, the sheets up around her neck. Her hair was disheveled but she was still beautiful, and for just a moment her face lit up with a joyful glow before her features sank again into neutral lines.

"If you want to go to the Seep Springs, I'll take you."

She stared at him, stunned.

"I'll take you on two conditions."

"What are they?" she asked weakly. She looked as if she might cry—from relief or sadness or happiness, he did not know.

"Don't talk to me about love, because I don't want to hear it."

He saw the hurt in her eyes, but she was stoic. "Go on," she whispered.

"I want you to try to get better. Not for me, but for yourself. I'm giving you what you want—fresh air, a clean life, a chance to get away from Tombstone. I want you to make the most of it, that is, until you're strong enough—ready to move on."

Her pain was evident, but when she spoke, her voice was quiet and firm. "I accept your conditions."

He rented a buggy that afternoon, and Charlotte Tate started her slow, painful journey to the Seep Springs Ranch.

Chapter Forty-one

Charlotte was surprised at the depth of emotion she felt when they topped the hill above the Seep Springs Ranch and she looked down into the valley.

Therc was thc bunkhouse, nestled in the cleft of two hills and shaded by a cottonwood tree that glittered in the sunshine. And there, about a mile beyond, was the house Jake had built for Ana. The hip-roofed adobe was bracketed by a wooden veranda and surrounded by large oak trees. Charlotte glanced at Jake, who sat impassively beside her on the buggy seat. He had not spoken one word to her since they started out. But at least he cared enough to bring her here.

Charlotte and Lupe stayed in Jake's house and Jake moved to the bunkhouse. Lupe admired his high morals. Charlotte reflected that it wasn't so much morality that spurred him to leave his home, but the simple fact that he did not want to be in her proximity. She could hardly blame her for that.

As summer mellowed to fall, Charlotte put her mind to recovering. Before long, she was able to go for short rides. Some sixth sense told her that Jake would not approve of her riding after such a trauma, so she did not tell him. She always went alone, having Sixto saddle Diamant and bring her to the house whenever Jake wasn't around.

These were the best times. For a while she could forget everything horrible that had happened in her life and pretend that Jake still loved her, and as the lady of the ranch she was riding out to survey her domain. Each fall day was like the next, perfect as a jewel. The sky was saturated with a blue so dense it shimmered, colliding with the crowning ridges of the Whetstone Mountains.

Charlotte savored every tactile offering of nature; the sun on her back, the cool breath of autumn against her cheeks. Grassland rose up to her horse's belly, and often the grass tops worked through the laces of her boots and punctured her stockings like tiny spears. She loved the ocean of grass, though; loved to ride through it, turning back to watch the flaxen tops stand up in her wake like feathered arrow tips. The scent of pine needles drifted down from the Huachuca Mountains, tantalizing her and making her feel clean.

She had to keep Diamant to a sedate walk, but just the feeling of being in the saddle again acted like a tonic upon her. To Lupe's dismay, Charlotte wore pants and a shirt and rode astride. "You don't expect me to twist myself into that ridiculous position with a shattered collarbone, do you?" she'd argued when Lupe protested. The woman had crossed herself, muttering, and returned to the house.

Jake avoided Charlotte. She hardly ever saw him, and when their paths did cross, he was polite but detached. Charlotte feared Jake would make good on his promise to send her away as soon as she was healed.

She knew she could not get around him, and didn't even bother to try. He did not love her anymore. But she discovered that even with the loss of hope, there were still good things in life, things worth embracing: Topping a hill and suddenly coming across the mares and their colts grazing in a valley, watching the long-legged youngsters gambol and fight mock battles. The peace and beauty of the ranch, the quiet simple life she had never thought was for her. Little things, like finding eggs, still warm, from the nests in the chicken coop. A barn cat who loved to sit on her lap, soaking up the autumn sun. Talks with Lupe about her family. Charlotte realized that she loved the Seep Springs Ranch, loved it more than she had ever loved the world of the theater. *All this time I thought I wanted the bright lights, when deep inside I wasn't that way at all.*

This revelation heartened her. Charlotte had tried to be one way all her life—because of Mary's expectations and later, because of her own. Being an actress was just another dream that wasn't half as good in reality. She belonged here. Too late, she discovered this truth about herself.

Charlotte was glad she didn't see Jake much, for his presence always aroused a mixture of desire and hopelessness that affected her for hours afterward. She couldn't block him from her mind: the way he walked, his mannerisms, the fine strong lines of his body, the innate honesty that showed itself in the way he dealt with everyone, from cowhand to small child. When he didn't know she was around, there was an easiness about him that reminded her of those long-ago days on the Marquart ranch. Sometimes she'd catch him smiling at Lupe, a genuine, honest smile. If only he would look at her that way!

These times, she sank into despair. She prayed morning and night, accepting her lot as the penance she must pay. Please, Heavenly Father, if I can't have Jake, don't take Seep Springs away from me. I can't bear it if I lose that, too.

She would have to make herself indispensable. When she was almost healed, Charlotte decided to take over as cook for the Seep Springs outfit.

"You're not needed here," Jake said, his voice taut with anger. He had just ridden in from line camp, where he had been for several days. "Besides, you're still recovering."

Charlotte stood before the stove in the bunkhouse, where she was cooking up carrots and onions for a stew. "They think I'm needed." She motioned to the men grouped on chairs or leaning against the wall of the bunkhouse.

"Let her cook for us, if she wants to," said one of the

hands, who particularly liked her biscuits. "Jeeter's meat's so tough I lost a tooth in it."

Jake knew when he was beaten. His face shut down and Charlotte knew he was very angry. "All right, act like a scullery maid if that's what will make you happy." He turned on his heel and walked out.

Winter came. Charlotte became a fixture at the bunkhouse. She was the object of a great deal of puppy love among the younger hands. Respectful and shy, they made her feel better about herself than she had in a long time.

But it was to Sixto Charlotte turned to most often. He would tell her stories about his life with horses, first at the *Rio Plata,* and then on the Seep Springs Ranch. He spoke of the Spanish mustangs of his youth, horses like the Grulla, and lamented that their unique qualities would soon become lost to mankind, due to the breeding policies of modern ranchers who crossed them with other breeds.

"Jake has two Spanish mustang mares," Charlotte said one day. "Why doesn't he find a Spanish stallion for them? He could keep the strain pure."

"There is one mistake common to all men who pride themselves as breeders of horses," Sixto said sadly. "They believe they have been selected by God to improve the animal, even when it doesn't need improvement. It is Jake's one blind spot."

No, Charlotte thought. He has two blind spots. Horse breeding, and me.

Jake stayed away from the main ranch for days at a time. The stallion and mares had been run out until October, and now Jake and his hands went out in search of them. Old Scratch would be turned back out on the flats with a couple of his favorite mares until spring. The rest of the mares would be separated into three groups: those to be culled, those to be trained and sold for whatever reason, the remainder turned out on the winter pasture.

Jake was grateful for the exhausting work; it left him little time to think. Still, there were times when his mind wandered back to the ranch house, and he wondered what Charlotte was doing.

She was so much like the Charlotte he knew at Maria's ranch that he found himself warming to her despite himself. She seemed to blossom under the respectful treatment of the hands. Jake listened with half an ear to her discussions with Sixto, and was surprised at how much she knew. He forgot that he himself had taught her about horse breeding.

He began to think of her as a fixture on the ranch. He never gave a thought to her leaving, so consequently did not notice the trepidation with which she regarded him. Certainly there were times that she looked drawn and unhappy, but it never occurred to him that he might be the cause.

Visitors came often to Seep Springs, and Jake always made room for them. One of the visitors said he had met Wyatt Earp in the Coeur d'Alene district of Idaho a couple of years back when Earp was deputy sheriff there. A few hours after the conversation Jake saw Charlotte standing by the corrals, staring out toward Tombstone, her face a mask of ineffable grief. So, she was still pining for Morgan Earp.

One day, as Jake rode in from checking his mares, he topped a hill and saw Charlotte below him, watching the yearlings run and play. She sat astride her sorrel mare, wearing a plaid shirt and trousers, and for a moment he imagined they were on the Marquart ranch again. The memory ripped through his mind like a flashfire, blinding hot and painful.

She heard his horse and turned her mare to face him. Her

face—so animated a moment ago—lost expression. Hurriedly, she thrust a book into her saddlebag.

"What's that?" he asked.

"It's nothing important."

The sight of her looking so wholesome and beautiful, so much like the girl he had known on the Marquart ranch, made him angry. "There are no secrets on this ranch. I'd like to see it." He held out his hand.

She withdrew a leather-bound ledger from the saddlebag and handed it to him. He opened it, and saw that she had listed the colts and fillies in the yearling band, assigning each of them a name. Notes in the margin described their color, conformation, and disposition. "Jupiter, copper dun with star and snip, white sock off-hind, large, bright eye"; "El Moro . . . tendency to rear, watch him"; "Pretty Polly . . . sickle-hocked"; "Tomcat . . . bay, good depth of shoulder, close-coupled, fast. Stallion prospect?"

Charlotte watched Jake with trepidation. Would he think she had overstepped her bounds as a guest on the ranch? He must see she was almost well now, able to ride all day if she had to. Would he send her away now that she had recovered? She bit her lip and tried to keep from showing her fear.

At the last notation, Jake said curtly, "You're wrong about that colt."

"Wrong?"

"He's a good looker, all right, but he's got a nasty disposition. He won't get a chance to pass on his temper. There's no room here for a horse like that, no matter how pretty he is." He thrust the book into her hands, and without another word, pivoted his horse and rode away.

At Christmas, Jake drove his wagon up into the mountains and cut down a young pine for the bunkhouse. They hung the tree with strings of popcorn and some ornaments that Ana had brought with her from Mexico. One of the ranch hands was married and had three children, so Jake rigged a piñata to the cottonwood tree for them. Blindfolded, the children took turns swiping at the pink and yellow ceramic donkey, until one lucky blow cracked it open and the gifts and candy inside spilled to the ground. Screaming with delight, the children fell on the prizes like a pack of wolves. As she watched them, Charlotte was reminded sharply of the little grave on the Marquart ranch, and tears pricked the corners of her eyes. She felt Jake's gaze on her, and she turned to look at him. He looked away.

For Charlotte, Christmas was a bittersweet time. Jake spent more time at the bunkhouse, but he was unreachable. At least when he was gone, she could pretend he cared for her. But here he was, laughing and talking with the hands and children, even flirting with Lupe, yet when he regarded her his eyes were grave. At various times she could discern a sadness in him when he looked at her, and at others, his expression turned to a thoughtful scowl. He always watched her when he thought she wasn't looking, and hardly ever met her gaze. Charlotte became convinced he had decided she was well enough to leave Seep Springs. That fear pierced her heart deeply, so that despite her happiness, she was always watchful.

Knowing that this might well be her last Christmas with Jake, Charlotte threw herself into finding the perfect gift. Perhaps then he would understand how much she loved him.

On Christmas morning they gathered around the tree. As Jake entered the bunkhouse, Charlotte held her breath and glanced at Sixto, feeling almost sick with anticipation. Sixto had come back from Mexico just this morning, bringing Jake's gift.

It was a cold, gray morning, and the wind howled around the bunkhouse. The potbellied stove warmed the barren-looking room a little, but there were chinks in the adobe, particularly near the rafters, and everyone shivered from the cold. The hands all had simple presents for one another, from chewing tobacco to *reatas* and handwoven hackamores.

It seemed all the presents had been handed out. Charlotte cleared her throat, her heart thudding in her chest. "I have a present for you, Jake. Actually, it's from Sixto and me."

She caught a glimpse of raw pain before Jake's expression turned neutral. "You didn't have to do that, Charlotte."

"I wanted to." She darted a glance at Sixto. He nodded and, walking to the door, motioned everyone to follow.

Outside, still in the single rig saddle and hackamore Sixto had ridden him in, a mustang stallion the color of blue steel tossed its head and trumpeted to the skies: a high, keening sound. The horse's resemblance to the Grulla was remarkable.

"What in God's name—?"

Sixto said, "His name is Lucero, for the star on his forehead. He's a half-brother to the Grulla. His ancestry can be traced to the horses of Cortez."

Jake spun around and stared at Charlotte. "This is your doing?"

She nodded, feeling shy. "I thought you would like to breed—"

"I have a stallion."

Suddenly afraid that she had done something terribly wrong, Charlotte forged on. "I-I thought you could breed him to the mustang mares, and . . . maintain the line."

"Two stallions on one ranch are one too many." Jake's voice was brusque.

"This horse is very fine, Jake," Sixto broke in. "Charlotte bought him from Porfirio Diaz himself."

Jake glared at Charlotte. He was so close to her that she could feel his breath on her cheek, see the brittle ice of his eyes. "You have a habit of trying to buy your way into people's affections. Your grand gesture is wasted on me. I raise quarter horses, not mustangs, and I can't be bought." He turned on his heel and walked away.

Charlotte watched him go, the stunned silence loud in her ears. Lupe touched her arm gently, and the hands looked away, embarrassed by their boss's outburst.

"I'll help Sixto cool Lucero down," she said, almost strangling on her tears.

After everyone was gone, she helped Sixto brush down the little stallion, swiping at her eyes with the back of her hand. She felt foolish to be crying in Sixto's presence, but couldn't help it.

Sixto untied the lead rope from around the fence and led the stallion to the corral. "Don't worry, *querida*. Jake liked your gift. He loves this stallion, I can tell it already. But it's hard for him to admit he's wrong."

"Wrong? About what?"

"About you, *querida*. He'll face it soon enough, that you are not the devil woman he wants you to be."

Christmas passed, and then New Year's Day, 1886, and the little Grulla stallion remained in the corral. When Charlotte asked Jake what he planned to do with him, he replied shortly, "Nothing."

"Couldn't you breed the mustang mares to him, when they come in season?"

"You can have the mares."

"Me?" Charlotte was confused. "What could I do with them?"

"Breed them to your stallion."

"But Lucero is yours. I gave him to you."

Jake spoke with exaggerated patience. "It's too fine a gift, Charlotte. I can't take something as expensive as that stallion from you." His gentle pity was worse than his previous coldness. "All I ask is that you keep Lucero and his mares away from Old Scratch. I don't want any stallion fights. Congratulations," he added. "You and Sixto are in business."

Charlotte choked on the reply that flew to her lips. She didn't want to be in business for herself! She turned and left the room.

Jake's rejection of her gift made her even more certain that he planned to send her packing at the first opportunity. Perhaps Jake would ask her to leave soon, but she would make good use of her time here. Despair turned to determination. She would be whipped if she would stand around and do nothing! She and Sixto would breed Lucero to the two Spanish mares, and search for more mares to build up the herd. And when the stallion's offspring grew to maturity, Charlotte would pit them against Jake's own horses, and then they'd see what was what.

She ordered books from New York on breeding, drew up charts, and studied bloodlines. She had Lucero's pedigree from Mexico, and decided to trace the mares' pedigrees. The mares were true Spanish mustangs; anyone with half an eye could see that. Pony-sized, but deep of heart and girth, both mares had intelligent wide-set eyes and strong, clean legs.

Charlotte had read that a well-conditioned stallion was a more potent sire. As his band of mares grew, great stamina would be required of Lucero. Charlotte eschewed riding her own mare for Lucero—despite warnings by the ranch hands that a woman couldn't manage a stallion. She rode him far afield every day, trotting him for miles, building up his endurance and condition until his coat gleamed from good health. At last, Charlotte had something to think about besides Jake.

But Jake continued to look at her thoughtfully, as if he were weighing her mentally. She didn't like it.

One cold sunny day, Charlotte was hanging out laundry before her ride when something made the hairs on the back of her neck rise. She turned and saw Jake standing in the bunkhouse doorway, staring at her.

"Hello, Jake." Could this be the day he would send her away forever? She clutched the shirt she had been about to hang up, twisting it nervously.

"You're going to wrinkle that shirt," he said.

"I'm sorry." She dropped the shirt back into the laundry tub as if it had bitten her.

Jake continued to look at her, the same thoughtful frown on his face that she had seen many times recently. "You're sorry a lot, lately."

Charlotte's throat closed. He was going to ask her to leave.

"Would you stop looking so cowed?"

The annoyance in Jake's voice broke her fear. What was she thinking of, acting as if she were at the mercy of some petty nobleman? If he wanted to get rid of her, she would take her medicine like the adult she was. She drew herself up and stared him straight in the eye.

"That's better."

"What do you want?"

"I thought we'd do some target practice."

"Target practice?" Relief vied with puzzlement. "Why?"

Jake stepped down out of the bunkhouse and walked toward her, holding a gun in one hand. "You remember that drummer who came through here about a week ago?"

"Yes." Charlotte remembered the drummer as a big, loud man who liked to drink too much for his own good.

"He asked me about the mines in Tombstone, said he'd been talking to a man in Willcox who had a real producer but didn't have the cash to work it. Said this man might sell it to him cheap."

Charlotte went cold.

"The mine was the Tombstone Rose."

"Chesser," she breathed. Her pulse thudded in her ears. "You don't think he'd come here, do you? I mean, to—"

"Kill you? He might not even know you survived. I doubt if he'd come here, but I think it's worth taking a few precautions. You're always riding off by yourself on that stallion of yours. You should know how to shoot."

"Then let's get on with it, shall we?" Charlotte said lightly, but dread gripped her. She had ruined Edward Chesser so completely that he had nothing to lose by killing her. Wordlessly, she followed Jake out to a clearing below the bunkhouse to an empty corral.

Jake placed cans on five of the fenceposts. He pointed his Smith & Wesson American at the first target with casual grace; the air imploded as the can flipped in the air.

He demonstrated how to load the revolver and handed it to Charlotte. She cocked it carefully, holding it in both hands. The gun was very heavy. The index finger of her right hand poked all the way through the trigger guard.

"Use only the tip of your finger," Jake said. "Look down the barrel and aim it just like you're pointing at the target. Squeeze slowly."

The gun kicked; Charlotte's arm flew up and back, almost hitting her in the face. Deafened by the noise, she winced as the aftershock traveled up her forearm. Her hand felt numb.

"Try again."

She shot the rest of the cylinder, and Jake waited patiently as she reloaded and shot again.

Over the next several minutes her aim improved remarkably, but after awhile her arm grew heavy and her concentration fragmented. She began to miss by wider margins.

"That's enough for today," Jake said. She handed him the gun.

She was sorry that the session was over. She had quietly enjoyed his presence: the sound of his voice, the patient way he showed her how to load the gun, his broad shoulders occasionally brushing her own.

Suddenly the realization that she would never hold him

in her arms again was unbearable. "You're not going to send me away, are you?" she blurted out.

He looked surprised. "What makes you think I'd do that?"

"You said—you said that when I got well, you would . . ." She swallowed, unable to continue.

"What kind of man do you think I am, Charlotte?" Jake demanded. "Do you really think I'd desert you now, with Chesser back in the territory?"

No, Charlotte thought. He was too honorable for that. Her temper flared. She was tired of being treated like a poor relation. Tired of Jake's stoic morality, his sense of duty! Tired of him feeling sorry for her, keeping her here even though he couldn't stand the sight of her—all because of some twisted sense of honor and fair play! "It's your duty to protect me, is it? Well, bother your duty! I can take care of myself!" She wheeled away from him.

Jake grabbed her arm. "You're not going anywhere, you little fool. You attract trouble like horses attract flies, and I'm not having your death on my conscience! You'll stay on this ranch until Chesser is caught!"

"Let go of me."

"Not until you listen to reason." He stared at her, breathing hard. She could feel his hand clamped around her wrist, could feel the blood coursing through the hard cables of his veins beneath tanned skin.

"Goddamn you," he said slowly, his eyes hard and dark and seething with hatred. "Goddamn your worthless hide." And then his other hand came up and cupped the base of her skull, tangling in the loose knot of her hair, and without warning he lowered his head and his lips came down on hers, hard, savage. He released her hand and pulled her to him, one arm closing around her waist, almost lifting her off her feet, his punishing tongue invading her mouth, and she could feel his hatred.

She could not help responding, although she knew this

kiss wasn't fashioned of love, but of fury and despair—as if he had resolved that he would never be free of her. Every vein, every corpuscle in her body responded to his kiss, dancing around inside her like whirling flashes of light. He molded her to him, his hands quick and hard, rending the material of her shirt, and pulled her roughly to the ground. Charlotte stared up at his face and saw the same hard-looking stranger who had walked out on her at the Cosmopolitan. He kissed her again, but it was meant to be a punishment, not an expression of love. Part of her rejoiced that at least he wanted her again, but she was frightened—more so than she had ever been in her life, because this was Jake; good, dependable Jake, and never in her wildest dreams would she believe him capable of using a woman this way.

"Please, Jake, please don't," she whispered, shoving at his chest with her hands.

Her words broke the spell. Stunned, he dragged his lips from her neck and stared down at her for a long moment, and she could see the self-hatred in his eyes. He rolled away from her, sat up and ran a hand across his face. He did not look at her. "I'm sorry." His voice was colorless.

"You don't have to be sorry." Charlotte stopped, confused.

Jake was staring at her as if he'd never seen her before. "You thought I wouldn't stop," he said slowly.

She couldn't keep from shaking. "It's been known to happen," she mumbled through chattering teeth.

Jake's eyes were like flint. He grabbed her elbow. "What's been known to happen?"

"Nothing." She jerked her arm from his grasp.

"That story you told me about Pike," he said, his voice grim. "You only told me part of what happened, didn't you?"

"I don't know what you're talking about."

He pulled her around to face him and said through gritted teeth, "You said you escaped from Pike. You didn't tell me he raped you."

"It wasn't Pike," she said automatically.

"Who was it, then?"

Now that Charlotte had started this conversation, she wished she had never brought it up. She couldn't say the man's name, couldn't even bear to think about him. She had put him out of her mind for so long, had pretended that it hadn't happened at all, that now she wondered if it was only a nightmare.

"Why won't you tell me his name? Are you protecting him?"

"No!" Her breath hitched as salty tears filled her throat. "Just leave me alone."

"I'll kill him." Jake's voice was quiet, dangerous.

She put her face in her hands. "If you must know, the Earps killed him."

"Morgan Earp again!" Jake said savagely. He wrenched her around to face him and shook her shoulders. "What can I do to get Morgan Earp out of your head?"

"Morgan?" What did Morgan have to do with it? She had forgotten he had ever meant anything to her at all. It seemed so long ago. Morgan had always been more dream than reality. "Morgan's dead."

"I wish you believed that."

"But I do!" She could not hold it back any longer. She knew she was breaking one of his conditions, but she had to put into words her feelings for him. "I love you, not some silly schoolgirl's dream like Morgan Earp."

No lightning struck her. Jake did not say anything at all.

She said it again, gathering strength from the words. "I love *you*, Jake. I love you."

"You don't know what love is!" His voice was tortured.

"I love you and I know you love me—Jake, look at me—you know it's true." She knew no such thing, but why else had he treated her that way? Certainly he hated her, but wasn't hate akin to love?

Then at last he returned her gaze. There was defeat in his eyes. "God help me," he said softly. "It's true."

Charlotte reached out hesitantly, touching his face with wonder. Roughly, he pulled her to him. He held her in a viselike grip, and she could feel his heart pound against hers. He buried his face in her neck and she felt the wetness of his tears against her skin, although he gave no other sign that he was crying.

She knew he hated himself for loving her. She had to win back his trust somehow, had to make it good between them again. It would be an uphill battle, but Charlotte Tate was never one to take the easy path. She held him to her, stroking his hair and reveling in the desperate strength of his embrace.

I'll turn over a new leaf, she thought happily. *He'll never again have reason to doubt me.*

Chapter Forty-two

From the moment Jake made his tortured admission, Charlotte thought everything would be different. Before too long, she came to realize that very little in fact had changed. It was clear Jake regarded his love for her as an affliction.

Her first instinct was to hold on to him tightly, so terrified was she of losing him. But a still voice inside, a voice she didn't recognize or understand, told her she must wait. And so she pulled back. She made herself available to him, but concentrated on getting to know him again. Trying, somehow, to bring back the good times they'd spent together as friends in those early days in Tombstone, before all the terrible events that had destroyed her innocence, before her willfullness and thirst for revenge had come between them.

Three nights after their encounter in the yard, Jake knocked on her door. Charlotte's heart leaped—he wanted her. In that moment, she was overwhelmed by the exquisite memory of their lovemaking, and longed desperately for that feeling again. But on this night she could tell he'd had too much to drink. The time was not right.

She bolted the door and stood just on the other side, trembling. "I think you'd better go, Jake. I don't want you to do anything you'd be sorry for."

He cursed at her, but left. The following morning, by way of apology, he offered to take her out with him to look at the colts.

That day was the turning point; the first step back to the friendship they had lost.

Much in the way Jake trained his broncs, Charlotte found herself standing still, waiting for him to come to her, letting him see for himself that she was not the *bruja*, the witch, he'd thought she was, out to steal his soul.

They spent their days together. She tried cooking new dishes for dinner—some of which worked out and some of which didn't. They laughed at the antics of the new kittens in the barn, spent hours sitting on the porch talking horses and bloodlines. They picnicked down by the creek. She went with him on the spring roundup.

He did not come to her door again.

One day as they walked to the barn, he reached out and took her hand. Her heart beat like a schoolgirl's; she could not imagine anything more exciting than the simple clasp of his hand on hers.

That night, after sipping lemonade on the porch, Charlotte rose to go to bed. Jake stood as well. Charlotte stepped toward the door, too quick for Jake to move out of the way, and for an awkward moment they stood there, almost touching. Then, he bent forward and kissed her on the lips. It was just the brush of his lips against hers, but it carried with it a reverence that thrilled her.

She wanted more, but the little voice inside told her not to push him.

In early April, they went into Tucson on a business trip, and stayed in separate rooms. After Jake's business was completed, they dined out, afterward walking arm in arm under the full moon, inhaling the scent of orange blossoms.

And that night, when he kissed her, neither one of them wanted to stop. Taking leave of each other at Charlotte's door was like rending a bolt of perfect cloth into two useless rags.

Frustrated and lonely, Charlotte lay in her bed, aching for completion. Aching for him to hold her and tell her he loved her, to be safe forever in his arms. And she knew that Jake lay in the other room, wanting her as much as she wanted him. The passion they had unleashed was like a genie let out of a bottle—it could never be put back.

The next morning found him at her door early. They had breakfast and walked up the main street of Tucson. He paused on the boardwalk outside a jeweler's shop. "I have to pick up something," he said.

It was a fresh, sunny morning, and she could still smell orange blossoms. A white-winged dove moaned nearby. "If you don't mind, Jake, I'd like to stay out here."

He rested his hands on her shoulders and looked into her eyes. "I wouldn't mind, usually, but I need your advice."

"My advice? For what?"

"I'm planning on asking a girl to marry me. Don't you think she should pick out the ring?" And as time stood still, he added, "I love you, Charlotte. I want you to be my wife."

Chapter Forty-three

Jake and Charlotte were married on a beautiful late spring day at the Seep Springs Ranch. It was a simple ceremony. Lupe was the maid of honor, and Sixto, the best man. A Catholic priest from Benson—a newcomer who was not acquainted with Charlotte's notoriety—presided over the wedding. L. J. Bailey, proprietor of the rechristened Athena Opera House, was the only guest from Tombstone.

They held the ceremony outdoors. The bunkhouse was decorated with colorful paper flowers, and luminarias, sand-filled bags containing candles, lined the flat roof. In the evening, the candles would be lit and the bags would glow bright orange in the night, and there would be a wild, joyful celebration for the boys of the Seep Springs outfit.

The ceremony itself was dignified, almost solemn. Charlotte wore a simple white satin dress, the bodice woven with lace and pearls. With Lupe's lace mantilla draped over her trademark chignon, Charlotte stood straight and slim beside Jake as the mass was read. She had eyes only for her husband. Her skin glowed as lucent as the pearls she wore, mirroring the happiness that radiated from her soul. The Tombstone Rose did not exist anymore; there was only Charlotte Cottrell, the woman who rode a blue stallion astride and stayed up until dawn, talking bloodlines with the man she loved.

That evening, after a full day of festivities, Jake and Charlotte made their excuses and left the fiesta in full swing. Their house gleamed in the moonlight, welcoming them. The air was redolent of woodsmoke and the odors of Lupe's cooking; chiles, tamales and *carne seca*. Strains of mariachi music drifted through the cool night air, and Charlotte could hear voices raised in boisterous, tipsy banter. L. J. had left to oversee the opening of a new play at the Athena Opera House. Father Ybarra, too, had gone home, leaving only the ranch hands and Lupe, who had put off returning to the house so Jake and Charlotte could enjoy the privacy of their wedding night.

Moonlight spread a pale cloak across the ground. A breeze stirred the branches of the oak tree shading the house, casting wavering shadows on the lime-stuccoed wall. Jake handed Charlotte down from the wagon and led her up the steps to the veranda.

Charlotte was aware that she held her breath. She still couldn't believe that Jake had married her. For the first time in her life she focused solely on the present.

She knew Jake felt the same way. Once he proposed to her on that Tucson street, he had let her back into his heart with surprising swiftness, as if, now the wall between them had fallen, there was no need to examine the pieces. He had insisted, however, that they live apart until the wedding, and Charlotte had agreed. The consumation of their marriage would be a newly minted coin between them, untainted by previous bankruptcies.

They paused on the veranda. Charlotte's hand tingled at Jake's touch, and an invisible thread of delicious tension held them in thrall, growing tauter with every second. They had waited so long for this moment, Charlotte could hardly believe it had finally come.

Jake bracketed her face gently in his hands, his lips only inches from her own. She always marveled at the strength and beauty of his face, the deep almost fathomless depths of his eyes. Gently, he lowered his lips to hers. They stood in a noose of shimmering moonlight, all senses tuned to the exquisite rightness of the moment, oblivious to the world around them. At last he drew away, still bridging the distance between him with his gaze.

"I want this to be our first time," he said.

Charlotte nodded, her heart growing big, too big for her chest. She knew what he meant. Their first lovemaking had been born in the depths of grief, a desperate pairing to chase away the ghosts that bedeviled them both. And although they had come together often after that, each time had been tinged either with the denial of death, or the clashing of two wills on opposing sides. But this time, there would be an unhurried tenderness, and the knowledge that their love was enough, an unbroken thread binding them together. Tonight, no other thoughts would intrude upon them. They would start over.

"The first," she whispered, as he caught her in his embrace.

And so it was.

Chapter Forty-four

Charlotte sat on the veranda of the ranch house, savoring a few moments of quiet before she started her day's work. Lupe had gone down to see her family in Mexico for a few weeks, so Charlotte was all alone. She enjoyed the peaceful beauty of the morning, and for once was glad that even Jake was gone. Sometimes she needed time to herself to think about the enormity of the change in her life.

All those years as a pretty waiter, the miles of performances with the Athena Traveling Theatrical and Variety Troupe; all the money and dresses and jewels and adoration meant so little to her now. Mary's dream had been a fake, pretty bauble; nothing more. At last, Charlotte was living her life as she was meant to, for herself.

She rarely thought of her long journey to this place. It was so painful to remember those who were not so lucky: Mary, Roberto, Emma, Maria . . . so many gone. Yet she, who had hurt them all in one way or another, still lived and thrived. Not only that, but she had Jake's love. Charlotte hardly ever pondered this inequity, the unfairness of life. There were too many other things to think about now, like the new mares Sixto was bringing up from Mexico. And soon, there would be another consideration: Jake's child.

A puff of dust far across the valley caught her eye. Jake said he'd be back by noon; it was late morning now. Smiling, Charlotte waited for him, wondering if he would greet her with the same sweetness with which he had left her at dawn.

Edward Chesser heard about Charlotte's marriage entirely by accident.

In the past year he had wandered from village to village throughout Mexico, patching up the local populace and delivering babies in return for opium, food, and a place to stay. He was insensible most of the time, since when lucid, his thoughts ran like rats before a fire, filling his brain with agonized shrieks and a blinding heat that flared behind his eyeballs and caused a throbbing pain in his skull. Only opium successfully dulled the pain.

He knew he was wanted by the authorities in Arizona. That had not mattered to him on the hot, tumultuous day he had calmly walked into the crowd before the Lancastrian and shot Charlotte Tate. What, after all, did he have to lose? All that morning he had been tormented by the thought of Charlotte going on with her life, serene and happy—married to that Cottrell fellow, no doubt—while he skulked among the lowest populations, begging for scraps and working as a dollar-a-day laborer. He, a medical doctor.

But that wasn't the reason he had sought her out that day.

The fury that had twisted his stomach in knots, the flaming anguish that had driven him in a fever to the crowd, gun in hand, stemmed from love. If he could not have her, no one else would. At the moment he had fired the shot, Edward realized with shock that he had done an unpardonable wrong—not only to Charlotte, but to himself. With an agony subsequently dulled by drink and opium in many filthy little villages and mining camps, he realized that he had destroyed forever any hope that she might come back to him.

In some small quarter of his mind, he believed that she loved him. It was a completely irrational belief, and it hadn't been borne out by her actions, but he clung to it anyway. If he didn't believe she loved him—even a little—he would go mad.

Finally, tired of hiding out in Mexico, Edward hired himself out as a laborer on a reconstruction project for the railroad line near Willcox. One day after work he stopped at a bar on Railroad Avenue. As he ordered his drink, he overheard a cowboy talking to his friend about a woman.

"She the one I hear tell wears pants and rides that stallion like a man?" the cowboy's friend asked.

"That's the one. You remember The Tombstone Rose? Saw her once. She had the sweetest voice I ever heard. Of course, most voices I hear are bovine," he added, and his friend guffawed.

Heart pounding, Edward insinuated himself into the conversation. "What ranch did you say this was?"

"Jake Cottrell's place. The Seep Springs. Worked there all this spring."

The two pieces of information scraped across his mind. Charlotte was alive.

Charlotte and Jake Cottrell were together.

Slowly, a plan formed in his drug-hazed brain. He had to see her. He would rent a horse, ride out to Seep Springs, and see for himself if she were still alive. If it were true— if God had given him a second chance—he would throw himself at her mercy and beg forgiveness, make her see how much he still loved her.

After that, he did not know what would happen.

As the horse and rider approached, Charlotte realized it wasn't Jake. Even from a distance, the rider did not seem at ease with the animal, and the horse had a lunging, awkward gait that Charlotte did not associate with the Seep Springs horses. With a start, she recognized the broad, ugly face, wreathed in a black beard. Edward Chesser.

Charlotte remained on the porch for another second or two, her mind racing. Jake had prepared her for this eventuality. Without further hesitation, she slipped into the house and walked calmly to the table where the Smith & Wesson .44 lay. She lifted the gun, found the bullets, and loaded it. The American New Model 3 still felt alien and heavy in her hand despite hours of practice; Jake had promised to buy her a Derringer. It was too late now. If she held it with both hands and kept a cool head, she could find her mark.

As Charlotte opened the door again, an odd excitement seized her. Anticipation of the next few moments made her mouth dry, but it was a pleasant feeling. She realized that she wanted to face Edward Chesser. She wanted to make him pay for what he had done to her.

Chesser reined his horse to a trot as he saw her standing on the veranda. His eyes widened in surprise.

"Stay where you are!" She leveled the gun at his chest.

His tiny black eyes glittered; with fear or desire, she could not tell. Charlotte licked her lips, felt the surge of adrenaline to her limbs, and the feral, vicious part of her

354

suddenly rose to the surface, triumph blazing in her heart. He would not hurt her again. Not now, not when she had Jake's baby to protect.

"Put down that gun before you kill somebody."

She laughed bitterly. "Such an ironic statement, coming from you."

He put up his hands. "I don't have a gun, I assure you."

"Why did you come here?"

"To apologize."

Charlotte couldn't believe her ears.

"I mean that, Charlotte, with all my heart. Please—just give me a moment, let me explain—" he stopped abruptly, and Charlotte could see he was staring at the muzzle of her gun. How did he manage to look scared to death and sheepish at the same time?

She kept the gun steady. "Go on."

Chesser was sweating now, large beads of perspiration running down his white face. "Could you point that thing away from me?"

"Very well." She realized that she was enjoying this. She lowered the gun but kept both hands on it. "Don't think I can't use it. Jake taught me."

At Jake's name, Chesser's face contorted with anguish. "Do you love him?"

"Of course I love him," she said harshly. "I never stopped loving him."

"Then it's true. You never cared about me." He seemed confused.

"If you remember, I told you I didn't. Several times."

Charlotte wasn't prepared for his reaction. Uttering a shout of rage, he launched himself from his horse and stormed the veranda. Charlotte raised the gun and squeezed off a shot, but her thudding heart and shaking hand spoiled her aim and it went high. He came on regardless, all his fear gone, and before she could aim again he knocked the gun out of her hand and hurtled into her, sending her sprawling.

The breath was knocked out of her for an agonizing moment, and as she lay gasping under his weight she thought that this was it: She would surely die.

Abruptly, she saw her own death, saw herself lying on the veranda, blood pouring from her as it had on the platform outside the Lancastrian, and Jake would find her—

His dead wife, his dead child. The idea was unbearable. To have so much, and lose it all. These thoughts ran through her mind, a separate organism from her body, which screamed for air. At last a rush of air filled her lungs again, sharp and painful.

"You goddamn bitch!" His hands came around her neck and he pulled her to her feet, his face red with fury. She clawed at his hands but he held her in a tight grip, his thumbs pressing into the delicate flesh of her neck. His face swam before her, blurry, and yet still he pressed and pressed, and when she thought she would pass out from lack of breath he suddenly released her. She gasped the air into her lungs, dizzy now from lack of oxygen. One paw swiped at her, knocking her backward, and she heard his voice as if her ears were plugged with cotton batting: "You love him, do you? We'll see if Jake Cottrell will take damaged goods!"

The implication galvanized her. Summoning every bit of energy she had, Charlotte scrabbled sideways, kicking violently as he reached for her. His hands missed her body, but he caught her hair and pulled. Too breathless to scream, Charlotte kicked again, but her skirts bound her legs. He heaved his weight on top of her and buried his face into her neck. She turned her head, avoiding his kiss. The .44 lay two feet away from her.

Chesser didn't notice it. Triumph flooding his face, he rose up on one elbow. "You played me for a fool, Charlotte. I loved you. You never would have wanted for anything, but you had to destroy me." His breath came in ragged gasps. "You are *mine*, can't you get that through your head? As evil as you are, you still belong to me, not Cottrell!"

Her hands were imprisoned by his. Charlotte knew he was much stronger, and she had to buy time. She shrank from him, pretending to be cowed, but all the time measuring the distance between her hand and the gun. "Please," she pleaded, her voice small and frightened, "please don't hurt me. Edward—"

He shifted his position, almost crushing her, and transferred both of her wrists to his left hand. His right hand reached down for her skirts.

There was only a split second when his left hand moved on her wrists, seeking a firmer grip, but it was enough. Her forearm, slick with sweat, thrashed wildly in his grip, and to her surprise, slipped free. Her hand shot out and she touched the gun butt with the tip of her fingers. It skittered from her grasp, but she stretched, every muscle straining until she felt a hundred little pops up and down her arm, and then the gun butt fell into her palm. With a lightning quickness born of anger, Charlotte's arm jackknifed back and she put the muzzle against his head. "Get off me or I'll blow your brains out," she commanded, her voice steady despite her need for breath.

Slowly, he drew himself up and away from her. Charlotte kept the gun pointed at his face. She sat up, keeping the gun steady.

"You really would kill me," he said, his words filled with wonder.

For answer, she cocked the .44.

Abruptly, all the fight left him. She saw the fear wiped from his face, replaced by ineffable grief. His skin looked gray, and he sighed heavily. "I loved you more than I ever loved anything on this earth," he said bleakly. "You might as well shoot me. I'm already dead." His voice seemed to come from a vast, featureless void deep inside him.

Shocked by this turn of events, Charlotte felt the gun

waver in her hands. She heard the approaching hoofbeats, and out of the corner of her eye saw Jake fling himself down from his horse. "Charlotte! What—" She heard his intake of breath, heard him walk toward them, then stop again. "What's going on, Charlotte?"

She steadied the gun. "I'm going to kill him."

"No."

Time stretched. They made a tableau, the three of them, caught in the late-morning stillness.

At last Jake said: "Charlotte, don't do it."

"I have to! He tried to—" She felt the tears start in her eyes. But the gun remained steady in her hands.

Jake said quietly, "If you kill him, things will never be right again."

"He killed Mary! He deserves to die!"

"I don't care about him. You'll destroy everything we have if you shoot him now."

The wisdom of his words got through to her. Her hands began to shake. "All right," she said softly. "You take him in." She lowered the gun as Jake jerked Chesser to his feet and tied his hands.

She saw Chesser's face cave in with hopelessness, and the day lost its warmth. She shivered. He really had wanted to die.

Jake handed Edward Chesser over to the sheriff's deputy in Tombstone, and rode back to Seep Springs.

Much later he learned what happened.

The deputy, an incautious man with little imagination, turned his back for a moment to open the cell door. With a quickness unusual for such a large man, Edward Chesser snatched the gun from the deputy's holster and made his escape.

He ran through town toward the Tombstone Rose Mine, the gun clasped between his bound hands. When a few bystanders tried to approach him, he waved it menacingly.

He reached the mine, deserted now except for the machinery rusting from disuse. Staggering around the hoist, tears running down his face, he waved the gun and cried out, "I am ruined. She has killed me."

A crowd gathered. No one was brave enough to venture within shooting range. The deputy and sheriff came at a trot, but they were too late.

Not a graceful man, Chesser somehow managed to fumble the gun around and point it at his own face. And then he blew his brains out.

Epilogue

They drew rein on the brow of a hill overlooking the
rolling hills that eventually flattened into the tan, blue-
veined alluvial plain of the San Pedro Valley. A file of yel-
low-green cottonwoods marked the river's path, and a few
puffy white clouds shimmered against the late August sky.

Charlotte reveled in the moment. It was another colorful
thread in the tapestry she and Jake had woven of their lives
together. She regretted that soon she would be too heavy to
ride. But that time would come and go, and they would
pick up this thread as they had picked up others.

"Do you remember that day we worked the cattle on the
Marquart ranch?" Jake asked.

"Which day was that?"

He maneuvered his horse close to hers and took the reins
from her hands. "The day we—rested, under the mesquite
tree."

She smiled, her heart lighting up with the memory. "I
remember it vividly."

Without another word, Jake turned his horse toward a
nearby arroyo, pulling Diamant along with him.

"Jake, this is madness. We have a perfectly good bed at
home."

He said nothing, but led her to an oak in the cleft of the
arroyo, and helped her down from her horse. The oak
leaves smelled dry and bitter, mingling with the warm
masculine scent of Jake's skin. As Jake led her to the tree,
Charlotte could barely suppress the tingle of anticipation
that started deep inside her. Clasping both of her hands in

360

his, he looked down at her for a long moment, the strong planes of his face softened by the dappling shadows of the tree. His eyes were dark with desire, and Charlotte could feel the wellspring of emotion that surged from his heart across the space between them. She could almost see it. His love for her shimmered, as golden and generous as a wheatfield touched by the late-afternoon sun.

He sat under the tree, pulling her down with him, then ran his fingers gently over her face, as if he were a blind man memorizing her features. He bent to kiss her, his lips fluttering from her mouth to her eyelids, then trailing warmly along her neck, increasing the delicious pressure against her skin as he deftly unbuttoned her blouse. He pushed down the straps of her chemise with strong, gentle fingers, and buried his face in the cove between her breasts. She arched her back and lifted off the ground so that he could peel away the rest of the dress. He spread it beneath her like a cloak.

A breeze tugged at the branches of the hackberry bush on the bench of land above them, sending a shower of dry ocher leaves across Charlotte's skin. To Charlotte, they could have been rose petals.

Jake was always aware of the changes in Charlotte's body and thought first of her comfort. His tanned skin brushed against hers at a thousand pleasure points, all the more exciting because the touch was so light. He showed infinite care as he raised up on one muscled arm beside her, gently lowering his head to hers and brushing her lips with lazy desire.

For her part, Charlotte felt like a sun-warmed flower, opening up to the sun. At last she couldn't stand it anymore. "Stop teasing me," she mumbled against his mouth, feeling as if she had just awakened from a lovely dream. Jake pulled her into the shelter of his body, and they abandoned themselves to a world where time was suspended, where sensations overwhelmed them. They joined and came apart, their lovemaking gentle, familiar, completely different from the violence of passion that so often marked more stormy times. This was the love of two people who had been through many trials and tragedies, whose bond had strengthened, rather than broken, from the strain. It was the lovemaking of survivors.

They lay entwined in the velvet warmth of the desert listening to a cicada, Charlotte's head in the hollow of Jake's arm. Diamant and Aguila grazed nearby, the sound of their rhythmic munching filling the air. Diamant lifted her head and nickered—a sound of contentment that mirrored Charlotte's own. "I'm so happy, Jake. I don't think I've ever been this happy in my life," she said, rippling her fingertips along Jake's chest.

Jake kissed her on the forehead. "So there are advantages to keeping you out of Tombstone."

"What do you mean?"

"We were together a long time, months after we left the Marquart ranch . . ." He trailed off, looking uncomfortable. "I always wondered."

"Jake!" She tried to act affronted at what he was hinting, but it didn't seem important now. So he'd known all along! Well, Blonde Marie's contraceptive salve had worked well enough when she'd wanted it to, but he needn't worry about that now.

She smiled, thinking that her husband was no fool. It was just like Jake to let her know she hadn't gotten away with anything. She changed the subject. "L. J. came by yesterday."

Jake stroked her face. "I'm sorry I missed him. How's the theater doing?"

"Very well. It's the most popular in the territory."

He rose up on one elbow. "You don't regret giving it up, do you?"

"How could I? No one would patronize the Athena if I had anything to do with it. Besides, I've got my hands full with the horses."

He laughed. "One thing about you will never change. You will be practical until the day you die, which I hope will be a long time from now."

As they rode back toward the ranch, Charlotte thought wistfully of the Lancastrian—the Athena. When L. J. had come by yesterday, she had shamelessly pumped him for information. Who was playing there, who attended the show, what were they wearing? He had to describe the chandeliers, the boxes, the stage all over again. She listened hungrily as he described the performance.

For a short while after L. J. was gone, Charlotte had felt a pang of regret. Then Jake had returned, and she promptly forgot it.

Still, it might be nice to visit the theater again, just to see what changes L. J. had made. And the bustle of Tombstone would make a pleasant diversion. She'd have to do it soon, before her condition made it impossible for her. It was the height of rudeness to walk around town with a belly like a broodmare. Maybe sometime in the next month or so . . . now that Lucero had been turned out with his mares, there wasn't that much to do—not until the foals started coming. Yes, she would ask Jake to take her into town.

Jake put Aguila into a sedate canter. He glanced back at Charlotte, and she knew he was doing it to humor her. Not long ago they used to run their horses, sometimes racing each other when the ground was level. But since she had told him about the child, Jake insisted they ride more carefully. She missed her days of conditioning Lucero, but the stallion had a new job now. He was starting his new life, as she and Jake were starting theirs.

Charlotte leaned forward and clucked to Diamant, feeling the mare respond, enjoying the wind on her face. Jake had gotten quite a head start on her. For just a moment Charlotte succumbed to the excitement of the moment and let Diamant stretch out into a full run. When Jake looked back she had already reined the mare into a hobby horse canter, all innocence.

But soon enough, she caught him.

SUPERSTITIONS

ANNIE McKNIGHT

Beautiful young Billie Bahill is determined. Despite what her father says, she knows her fiancé won't just leave her. So come hell or high water, she is going to go find him. So what if she rides off into the deadly Superstition Mountains? Billie is as good on a horse as any of the men on her father's ranch, and she won't let anybody stop her—especially not the Arizona Ranger with eyes that make her heart skip a beat.

___4405-6 $5.50 US/$6.50 CAN

WANTED. FAMILY MAN. MUST LOVE CHILDREN. PAYMENT NEGOTIABLE.

Rider Magrane knows what "wanted" means; he's spent time running from the law. Those days are over now, and he's come back to Drover to make amends. But the man he's wronged is no longer in town. Instead he finds the most appealing woman he's ever met—Jane Warner—and she thinks that he's come about the ad he now holds in his hand. To be near her is tempting, but what does a cattle rustler know about children—or love? Jane posts the ad to lure a capable male into caring for her nephews—she herself has never been part of the deal. But examining the hunk that appears at her homestead, all she can think of are the good aspects of having a man in her life. The payment is negotiable; she's said so herself. No price is too dear for this handsome stranger's heart.

___4625-3 $4.99 US/$5.99 CAN

PRICKLY PEAR

RONDA THOMPSON

Daddy's little girl is no angel. Heck, she hasn't earned the nickname Prickly Pear by being a wallflower. Everyone on the Circle C knows that Camile Cordell can rope her way out of Hell itself—and most of the town thinks the willful beauty will end up there sooner or later. Now, Cam knows that her father is looking for a new foreman for their ranch—and the blond firebrand is pretty sure she knows where to find one. Wade Langtry has just arrived in Texas, but he seems darn sure of himself in trying to take a job that is hers. Cam has to admit, though, that he has what it takes to break stallions. In her braver moments, she even imagines what it might feel like to have the roughrider break her to the saddle—or she him. And she fears that in the days to follow, it won't much matter if she looses her father's ranch—she's already lost her heart.

___4624-5 $4.99 US/$5.99 CAN

Dorchester Publishing Co., Inc.
P.O. Box 6640
Wayne, PA 19087-8640

Please add $1.75 for shipping and handling for the first book and $.50 for each book thereafter. NY, NYC, and PA residents, please add appropriate sales tax. No cash, stamps, or C.O.D.s. All orders shipped within 6 weeks via postal service book rate. Canadian orders require $2.00 extra postage and must be paid in U.S. dollars through a U.S. banking facility.

Name_____
Address_____
City_____ State_____ Zip_____
I have enclosed $_____ in payment for the checked book(s).
Payment <u>must</u> accompany all orders. ❏ Please send a free catalog.
CHECK OUT OUR WEBSITE! www.dorchesterpub.com

LOVE FOREVERMORE

MADELINE BAKER

The West—it has been Loralee's dream for as long as she could remember, and Indians are the most fascinating part of the wildly beautiful frontier she imagines. But when Loralee arrives at Fort Apache as the new schoolmarm, she has some hard realities to learn...and a harsh taskmaster to teach her. Shad Zuniga is fiercely proud, aloof, a renegade Apache who wants no part of the white man's world, not even its women. Yet Loralee is driven to seek him out, compelled to join him in a forbidden union, forced to become an outcast for one slim chance at love forevermore.

___4267-3 $5.99 US/$6.99 CAN